**Also available from Rhenna Morgan
and Carina Press**

Rough & Tumble
Wild & Sweet
Claim & Protect
Tempted & Taken
Guardian's Bond
Healer's Need

**And watch for a new spin-off series featuring
characters from the Men of Haven universe,
coming soon!**

Also available from Rhenna Morgan

Unexpected Eden
Healing Eden
Waking Eden
Eden's Deliverance

For those of you who hold it all together for the many people in your life. I wish for you a special someone who can take the reins and simply allow you to let go—even if only for a little while.

STAND & DELIVER

RHENNA MORGAN

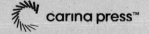
carina press™

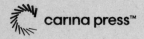

carina press™

Recycling programs
for this product may
not exist in your area.

ISBN-13: 978-1-335-00621-9

Stand & Deliver

Copyright © 2018 by Rhenna Morgan

www.CarinaPress.com

Printed in U.S.A.

STAND & DELIVER

Chapter One

Equal opportunity advocates wouldn't know what *fair* meant if it bit them in the ass. At least not in the world of personal security. It didn't matter how many accolades a person racked up, or how much of a badass they were. If the person in question had curves and boobs you could damned well bet a man would get the job before the woman would.

Not that Gia was bitter or anything.

Pushing open the scarred black door to one of Lower Greenville's most understated yet popular pubs, she let out a heavy exhalation and forced the patent bored-yet-stern expression she used on security details into place. Hanging out at Trident with work associates on a Friday night was the last thing she wanted to endure after her afternoon's turn of events. Yeah, Trident was a cool place. Like a hipster and biker had stacked hands and created the ultimate don't-give-a-damn environment complete with plain concrete floors, black woodwork and brushed chrome everything else. Even the bar was made of concrete. Perfect for withstanding even the nastiest of bar brawls while still coming off über cool. And at 5:30 on a Friday night, the place was packed where the other pubs on Greenville had plenty of parking spaces out front.

Up front by the wide windows, a horde of worker-bees dressed predominately in khakis and polos were elbow-to-elbow around a string of four-tops they'd pushed together. All the other tables and the bar were populated by straight-up bikers who could've cared less about the August heat so long as they got to ride, hang with their friends and knock back a few cold ones.

No signs of agitation or trouble. At least not yet. But in another hour or two, that could turn on a dime.

Clocking every detail as she wound her way through the bar was pure instinct. Habit born from years clawing her way up in a profession that insisted she didn't belong. Right about now, she'd give a lot to forgo it all, pour a glass of chardonnay and take a long hot soak in her tub. But hell would freeze over before she left her best friend high and dry with the lot of testosterone-laden meatheads she often worked with.

Strolling through the arched entrance to the back room, a wave of mostly masculine laughter hit her right about the time her gaze locked onto the sole woman in the room—Darya Volkova. Or Darya Torren, now that she'd married Knox. With winter-white hair and the body of a runway model, most people assumed she was as soft on the inside as she was on the eyes.

Nothing could be further from the truth. From the day Gia met her a little under a year ago, Darya had demonstrated a level of tenacity and bravery some of the most hardened military men couldn't have managed. An angel with a deceptively solid coat of armor beneath her porcelain skin.

"Hey, Gia." The perky brunette who'd served their

table during last Friday night's happy hour popped into Gia's path out of nowhere. The fact that Gia hadn't even seen her coming and couldn't remember her name was a testament to how off her game today had thrown her. "I'm about to make a fresh round for the table. You want the usual?"

Another round of laughter swelled loud enough Gia could barely hear her own answer. "No Scotch tonight." For a second, she paused and considered going with the chardonnay she really wanted, but the last time she'd ordered wine around these goons, they'd mocked her the rest of the night by drinking their beers with their pinkies lifted. "How about a Corona?"

"You got it."

The waitress hustled off just in time for Gia to catch Darya beaming one of those sappy love-story-perfect smiles at her new husband. One that earned her a hungry look back from her man.

Okay, so maybe Knox wasn't a meathead like the other security professionals gathered round the table. A techno junkie maybe, but not a meathead. Come to think of it, none of the men Knox and Beckett called their brothers fell into that category, which made it too damned bad Knox was the only one of the brothers in attendance tonight. They were a whole different brand of males. Confident. Brash when they needed to be, but loyal to a fault.

And those who'd fallen had an insanely huge soft spot for their women.

Now the ones without women? Well, Axel she pegged as a wild man with a dirty streak a mile wide and Danny was too soon to call, but Beckett…he was the one she couldn't figure out. Though God knew, she'd tried. Endlessly. And the bulk of those musings tended to kick in at night when her wishful thoughts and sex-starved body entertained a host of fantasies that could never, *ever* happen.

"Well, helllooo, gorgeous." The scrape of Decker's wooden chair legs against the concrete floor blended with his booming voice, effectively halting conversation and turning all heads her way. Compared to the rest of her business acquaintances, Decker was fairly new to security, scraping and clawing his way into whatever gigs he could find and working on certifications. He was also the muscled teddy-bear type that loved to cuddle any gorgeous and willing woman.

He held out his arms, head cocked to one side to match his goofy grin. "What's got the infamous Gia Sinclair all dolled up today? Had a rough day covering the socialites at the Galleria? Or was it romper room duty at the elementary school?"

The taunt hit a little too close to home considering she'd spent the afternoon dressed like a stylish mom and guarding twin teenage girls hell-bent on finding the limit on their daddy's black AmEx. She rolled her eyes to cover it and pulled out a chair beside Darya, completely bypassing the friendly hug Decker offered. "Can it, big guy. My curled hair and lipstick just earned me an easy paycheck." She dipped her head toward Decker's generic black T-shirt with SECURITY emblazoned along the back. "I see you've spent another day manning the doors for a bunch of roadies again."

It was a low blow. One she hated throwing. Especially with Decker, who was really a nice guy with a lot of muscle and a killer right hook. Still, with these guys there was no such thing as letting down her guard. Ever.

Another of her colleagues, Judd Rainier, grinned and raised his beer bottle in salute from his seat near the end of the table. "You could learn a lot from her, Decker. Perps always underestimate her. Draws 'em in nice and close so she can cut their nuts off before they even know she's drawn a weapon."

Decker grumbled and settled back into his seat. "Shit, Gia. I was only razzin' ya. I kinda like it when you get all gussied up."

Yep. A total teddy bear. All brawn and heart. "It's all good." Eager to redirect everyone's attention back to whatever topics had kept the conversation going before she got there, Gia zeroed in on Knox. "Where's your other half tonight?"

Knox slid the arm resting on the back of Darya's chair up to her shoulders and hugged her tight to his side. "Kind of hard to miss my other half when she looks like this."

"Not that other half," Gia said, "the other, more obnoxious one."

"You get I've got six brothers and that describes the lot of them."

"You know who I mean. Where the hell is Beckett? He's the one that set this shindig up."

With a quick and dirty rock-star smile, Knox chuckled, checked his watch then snagged his beer. "He's on his way. Said he had to pick someone up on the way here. Why? You two planning another verbal sparring match?"

"We don't spar."

"Um, yeah, you do. It's practically an Olympic event."

Darya giggled, but interjected with a playful shoulder nudge to her husband. "Leave her alone, Knox." She poked the lime floating in her vodka with a red cocktail straw and turned her ice-blue eyes on Gia. "And Beckett's not obnoxious. He's cute."

Cute? No. Not even close. Cute was bunnies, balloons and a baby's butt. Beckett Tate was pure predator, all muscle, keen intellect and intoxicating male confidence. At six foot four he had a full foot on her heightwise, but it was the way he carried himself that made him seem like a giant. A mix of feline grace and unrepentant swagger. It'd been bad enough keeping her wits around him when they first met, his dark hair and blue eye combo striking enough she'd stammered with introductions. Then he'd aimed his shit-eating grin at her and struck her stupid. "Are you sure we're talking about the same guy? Bullheaded? Lives for the next debate and has control issues?"

Waggling her eyebrows, Darya sipped on her straw in a flirty way that would have made Knox whisk her out of the bar for a quickie if he'd caught the action. "Hello, pot. Talking about the kettle, I see?"

Gia harrumphed and took the Corona from the waitress. Even with the AC cranked, the bottle was already damp from the humidity, but nothing combatted August in Texas better than a beer. "You know, for a woman who speaks English as a second language, you know a scary number of idioms."

Darya's grin turned devious. "I gained a husband, two mothers, six brothers, three sisters and a best friend in less than six months. To say I've got a lot of teachers to draw from would be an understatement."

She wasn't wrong on that score. Beckett and Knox's family took the word *family* to a whole new level. Gia was only on the outskirts of their tightly knit group, but she'd been close enough a time or two to understand its impact was heady stuff.

Darya set her drink aside, glanced over her shoulder and made sure Knox was deeply engaged in conversation with their new computer tech. "You know, there's nothing wrong with it?"

For a second, Gia thought maybe she'd missed something and scanned the table for some clue as to what it might be. "Wrong with what?"

Lowering her voice to just above a whisper, Darya leaned in closer. "You know—having a thing for Beckett."

Well, hell. Talk about your surprise attacks out of left field. Gia frowned in that overblown way she always used when trying to dodge her mother's attempts to fix her up with a nice Southern boy. "You're out of your mind. I don't have a thing for Beckett."

"Mmm." Darya paired the smug sound with a purse of her lips and crossed her legs as if she'd solidly proven her point. "Okay. Play it that way if you want."

"I'm not playing anything."

"Sure, you are." Darya dipped her head toward the men at the far end of the table and cocked an eyebrow. "But just so we're clear. Just because they don't see it, I do."

"You're seriously overthinking—"

Darya cut her off with a playful wave of her hand. "Nope. Not listening to it. Not that you have to explain it to me, anyway. I love Beckett. A lot. And personally, I think you're exactly the kind of woman he needs."

"I'm exactly the kind of woman he *doesn't* need. For crying out loud, we work together. And you already pointed out how bullheaded we both are. Can you imagine what would happen if the two of us went head-to-head in a relationship?"

Darya plucked the straw out of her nearly empty drink and popped it in her mouth, the sly way she grinned around it promising a whole bundle of trouble. "Oh, yes. A huge explosion. One I'd say is very much overdue."

Now *that* part she agreed with. At least when it came to her being overdue. She couldn't remember the last time she'd even been tempted to take a man home. Those who didn't shy away from her strong personality always ended up showing their ass before dinner or the first round of drinks were over. The nicer guys she'd been fixed up with seemed too hesitant to do so much as move in for a first kiss.

Somehow, she had a feeling Beckett wouldn't hesitate. "First, it's a bad idea to get involved with people you work with. Second, he'd have to actually notice me before anything could happen, and odds are good hell will freeze over first."

As if the mere conversation had conjured him, Beckett picked that exact moment to stroll through the archway. Per usual, he was decked out in a pair of Levi's that looked like they'd served a solid ten years and one of those high-end T-shirts that molded to every defined muscle. This one was just a shade darker than ice-blue and made his killer blue eyes pop from his striking dark face. No doubt the cotton was the finest money could buy, a fact that made her fist clench with the need to sample it for herself and feel the hard warmth beneath it.

Unfortunately, the statuesque blonde at his side with her arm wrapped around his waist doused that idea as soon as it popped up. "And there, my Russian friend, is reason number three. When was the last time you saw him with the same woman twice?"

Darya sighed and aimed a sad look at Beckett. One that spoke of secrets and empathy. "Yes, but have you ever considered why you never see anyone a second time?"

She had. Countless times. But broaching that topic with anyone but Beckett reeked of high school, and she'd be foolish to bring it up with him one-on-one. It was too intimate. A first step toward a conversation that would only breed more intimacy, and God knew she didn't need any more gravitational pull where he was concerned. "Well, the *Smart Girl's Handbook* says men who can't get past date number one aren't typically inclined to settle down. Call me old-fashioned, but I'm not up for being a stop on his never-ending bed hop. Even if I *am* overdue for an enthusiastic hop of my own."

Rather than laugh at the quip like she usually would, Darya turned her soulful blue eyes on Gia and studied her for long, considering seconds. When she spoke, her voice was low and thick with emotion out of place in such a boisterous venue. "I've learned a lot about Knox and his brothers in the past year. About what it means to have a family. One thing you can absolutely be sure of— there's a lot more to them than what's on the surface."

Without considering her actions, Gia's gaze slanted back to Beckett and his date. The woman was truly beautiful. Someone you'd expect to find showcased in a *Town & Country* article right down to the willowy sundress and understated makeup.

She was everything Gia wasn't. The complete opposite. And yet, somehow Darya's statement felt like a key to Pandora's box.

At the far end of the table, Beckett slapped one of the guys on the shoulder, turned and locked eyes with her. "Hey, G. I wondered if you'd make it."

"Well, I wasn't going to leave Darya alone with the lot of you." How her brain managed to wrangle up a response in the middle of its latest puzzle was a mystery. Much as it pained her, she dipped her head toward the woman next to him. "Good to see you brought someone else to even out the balance. On an IQ scale, it would've been close with just two of us against the rest of you, but with three against ten it's a cinch."

His quick smile paired with the way he hugged the woman tighter dug like a dull blade between her ribs, but she kept her smile pasted in place.

An introduction to a woman she wouldn't remember, a whole lot of polite banter and thirty minutes of trying not to look at Beckett later, Gia sat her empty longneck aside and stood. "I'm making a run to the bar. Anyone want anything?"

Beckett stopped in the middle of whatever he was saying to Decker and focused on Gia. "Why? Tiffany's on the way back with another round."

Tiffany. Right. That was the waitress's name. "Because I decided to switch to something stronger and don't want her running two trips when I can get off my ass and handle it myself."

Not exactly the smoothest retort she could have come up with, but admitting how hard it was to watch the affectionate way Beckett kept his date tucked close and teased his thumb along her bare shoulder wouldn't be kosher either.

The wait at the bar was blessedly long, the number of patrons waiting shoulder to shoulder for a chance to order giving her time to relax and even out. Why she tortured herself by being around Beckett was beyond her. Like buying her favorite chocolate, leaving it out on the counter and refusing to eat it in the name of staying healthy for her job.

Well, she was tired of the temptation. At least for tonight. One more drink and she'd be able to call it a night without earning the killjoy label the guys always tagged her with.

The bartender finally made eye contact in that nonverbal way that said she was ready for Gia's order, but Judd's voice sounded before Gia could speak. "So, you didn't bail."

Gia just barely managed not to drop her head in frustration and kept her sights on the bartender. "Shot of tequila."

With a smoothness that surprised her, Judd slid between her and the biker holding down the bar stool next to her. "Decker just tried to bet me twenty bucks you'd beelined it out of here."

Rather than give him her attention, Gia watched the bartender. "You didn't take him up on it?"

"'Course not. I know you better than that." He splayed his hand low on her back, and moved in close enough his lowered voice was like a caress. "Seriously, you okay? You seemed upset."

Fucking Judd. Really, he was a nice guy. Cultured. Good-looking. A walking Ken doll with a voice as smooth as warm molasses. And he was right. They'd known each other a very long time.

She twisted enough he had no choice but to drop his hand on her back and rested her elbow on the bar. "You know, despite what my parents tell you, you don't need to babysit me. I'm a big girl."

His quick smile was full of perfectly straight white teeth, but she still remembered what he'd looked like as a pre-teen sporting braces—one of the benefits of having been neighbors for as long as she could remember. "Who said anything about babysitting? Maybe this is just my way of showing you I'm not giving up."

This time she did hang her head, sighing and scrunching her eyes tight as she did. They'd had this conversation more times than she could count. Not just with Judd, but with her parents, who'd been absolutely certain since she was in high school that she and Judd were a match made in heaven. "Judd, you know how I feel about this."

"Oil and water," he said with the usual unshakable smile in his voice. "An odd couple. Not right to mix work and pleasure. Yeah, I think I've got them all memorized." His warm finger drifted from beneath her ear and along her jawline to her chin then gently nudged her face to his. "I hate seeing you this sad. This alone. Can't you even consider it? We *know* each other. Have the same interests and complement each other better than most couples who've been together for years."

Oh, she'd considered it. Especially early on when both sets of parents had gone above and beyond to arrange every possible scenario where the two of them were accidentally together. A tag-team effort that would have paired the daughter of Atlanta's most successful criminal attorney with the golden son from one of the world's foremost shipping company presidents.

Judd was easy. Comfortable like a lamb's-wool-lined pair of house shoes in the middle of winter. Going with the flow and seeing where things led would have been the simpler course for sure, but she just couldn't shake the idea that something was missing. That some critical piece in their relationship was a tad skewed or out of kilter. In the end, she'd ended up relocating from Atlanta to Dallas just to find a little breathing room.

And then she'd met Beckett.

If there'd been any doubt before about what she wanted as far as a connection between two people, Beckett had shored up her ideals. Sure, he hadn't noticed her, but he'd made it crystal clear what she wanted when she finally settled in with someone. That swirl low in her belly. The snap and crackle of electricity whenever her someone walked into a room. But more than that, she wanted respect. Mutual respect. The kind her parents never had, or had lost well before she could remember it existing.

But maybe she'd been wrong. Maybe that kind of relationship didn't exist. Or maybe it just wasn't meant for her. "Do you remember that field competition in high school?"

"The one where you cut in front of me on the home stretch and nearly made me bust my ass in front of everyone? Yeah, I remember it."

"That's me, Judd. I'm competitive as fuck."

He flinched at the vulgarity. Or what their mothers would consider a vulgarity. For her, it was more of a sentence enhancer. A subtle exclamation point to drive the message home without shouting. "You were pissed at me for weeks, but I'm always going to be that girl."

Judd inched closer and slid his hand along the curve of her hip with the familiarity of longtime lovers. He wasn't quite as tall as Beckett and definitely not as broad, but in that moment, she felt tiny. Feminine. And she hadn't been able to claim that sensation in a very long time. "I was eighteen with a teenage ego. I promise you, the man I am today can take any competition you dish out."

God, it was tempting. To be appreciated. Touched. Even if she knew to the pit of her gut it wouldn't go anywhere. All she had to do was lean in, press her hands against his chest and pray he'd take over.

"Tell me you've got a damned good reason for having your hand on her."

Beckett.

His voice hadn't been loud, but it cracked with the same potency of a violent storm. Enough so the men on either side of her ceased their conversations and leaned a good distance away.

As to her, she couldn't decide whether to thank God for his intervention, or toss the full shot glass the bartender had plunked down at Beckett's head. Damned if she did, and damned if she didn't—just another night at the same old rodeo. If she'd learned nothing else in the time she'd worked with men like Beckett and Judd, it was that the closest thing to a non-response was the best response. Hard for a guy to get their ego stroked or wounded if you gave them no foothold to start with.

She playfully swatted Judd's hand away and turned for her shot, diffusing the situation with a whole lot of *meh*. "Don't worry about Judd. He's just fucking around." She knocked the tequila back, raised the glass toward the bartender for another, then glanced up at Judd. "Isn't that right?"

Like always, Judd kept an even expression, but his tanned skin had a hint of red to it and a burn behind his eyes only mirrored shades could've covered. He held Gia's stare, eyes narrowing just a fraction before he studied Beckett. "Yeah." His gaze slid back to Gia and he huffed. "Just fucking around. Wasting time like always."

With that he turned and lifted his chin toward Beckett. "Have fun with your *date*."

The bartender plunked a fresh shot on the concrete surface just as Beckett moved into the space Judd had vacated.

Gia ignored him and tapped the space beside her glass. "I'm gonna need a few more of those."

"No, she's not." Beckett reached for the shot, but Gia caught his wrist before he could make contact and glared at the bartender.

"He absolutely has no say in what I drink," she managed without growling. "So, when I say I need a few more, I mean I need a *few more*. After that, we'll see." She eyeballed the older biker sitting on her right who was clearly enjoying the show. "Kind of depends on how the next five minutes go."

Chapter Two

Beckett hammered on the women's restroom door hard enough the hinges protested and the beat-up doorknob rattled. Even with the racket he'd created, the sound barely registered against the party now in full swing in the main bar. "Darya, open the goddamn door."

"Man, if you bust that door down over a drunk woman, Jace will give you shit for months." Not the least bit concerned with Beckett's aggression, Knox leaned a shoulder against the wall beside the restroom door and crossed his arms. "Just chill. Darya can handle Gia no problem."

Darya manhandling one seriously shitfaced woman wasn't the problem. It was the guilt presently using his conscience for a punching bag that was causing him issues. Not that he was gonna clue Knox or anyone else into that little tidbit. "Did you see how much fucking tequila she drank? Hell, *I* couldn't drink that much and I've got a solid 120 pounds on her."

"Yeah, that was whacked. Never seen her go for the booze that heavy before. But you gotta admit, she's a friendly drunk."

That was an understatement. She'd forgone their private table in the back of the bar in favor of making a whole new slew of friends up front. Within thirty minutes, every damned biker in the place had not only fallen in love, but was giving her their undivided attention. Hence, the reason he'd flat-out lied to Katy about a security crisis and got her a private car to take her home so he could stay close to Gia. It was either that, or break every man's neck before he left the bar.

The bathroom door swung open with a groan, and Darya propped it with one high-heel-shod foot. The glare she aimed at Beckett might have made him feel bad on any other night, but all he could process at the sight of Gia upright and somewhat healthy was solid relief. Her eyes were glazed over and the arm she had anchored around Darya was the only thing keeping her vertical, but her cheeks were flushed and her goofy smile promised she was feeling zero pain.

"I had enough on my hands without you banging on the door every five seconds," Darya said, her Russian accent a whole lot stronger than normal and weighted with a good amount of frustration.

"I was worried." Beckett moved in to peel Gia off her and take her weight himself.

Darya held up a hand and stopped him before he could manage the task. "What do you think you're doing?"

"I'm getting her home and staying with her until she sleeps this off."

"No, you're not. I promised her I'd take care of her."

"When?"

Knox picked that moment to stop grinning at the two of them and straightened from the wall. "I think it was somewhere between the fifth and sixth shot. There were also muttered vows I couldn't quite make out, but

I thought I heard killing anyone with a set of balls, so I'd tread carefully, brother."

And there it was. Proof he'd seriously fucked up. "She's pissed at me. I caused it, so I need to make it right."

The way Darya pursed her mouth—a mix of anger and pure feminine justification—confirmed his suspicions without a single word spoken.

Knox, on the other hand, was clueless. "Whoa. How the hell'd you cause anything?" His gaze cut to Gia. "What'd I miss?"

Gia picked that moment to surface from her happy daze and frowned at Beckett. "He cock-blocked me." The furrow between her brows deepened as she tried to focus on Knox. "Or is that only when a guy does it to another guy? Oh, wait!" She smiled up at Darya. "It's a clam jam!"

Darya laughed at that and shifted her stance to better juggle Gia's wavering balance. "Bushwhacked!"

"Clitoference!" Gia volleyed back.

"And now we know what was taking so long in the bathroom." Knox waved Darya out of the bathroom. "Come on, angel. We'll split the difference on everyone's sense of fair play. You drive Gia's car home. I'll follow you in my car, and Beckett can haul Gia home in his."

"But I promised her."

"And Gia's already puked once. Where do you want her puke the next time? Her car, or Beckett's?"

"Beckett's," Gia answered with a solemnity only a drunk person could manage. "Definitely Beckett's."

The grin Darya shot Beckett should have terrified him. Hell, just thinking about anyone hurling in his

'Vette would have made him cry like a schoolgirl under normal circumstances, but at least he'd be able to keep Gia in touching distance until he knew she was safe. "See? We've got a plan. Now, come on, gorgeous. Let's get you home."

He moved in to pick her up, but Gia staggered out of reaching distance. "You're not carrying me. I'm not a wimp."

Translation: Even in her drunken state she was still keyed into the fact that a load of their peers were still blowing off steam. Hard to blame her, though. The guys always gave her a hard time. A fact that had pushed him to nearly punching half of them at one time or another. "You're not a wimp. Just gonna move in close to help you keep your balance. That's all. No one's gonna suspect a thing."

She tightened her hand on the vanity and gave him a distrusting look. "You promise?"

"Scout's honor."

Knox chuckled. "Just for the record, Beck was never a Scout. Although, he did booby-trap some tents for a few guys who teased him in sixth grade."

"You're not helping," Darya murmured, but reached out to guide Gia to Beckett. "Come on, girlfriend. Time to get you home."

In the end, getting her to his car was far less of a fire drill than he'd anticipated. Whether it was years of keeping herself on guard within a male-dominated profession or sheer stubbornness that allowed her to mask how blotto she was, he couldn't say. But by the time they hit the first stoplight on Lower Greenville, she was lights-out, her temple resting against the passenger window and her dark hair spilling softly around her pretty face.

God, she was a walking contradiction. Petite, curvy and incredibly soft on the eyes, she was the type of woman a man instinctively wanted to protect. A classic Southern belle. But she could hand most men their ass before they'd had so much as a chance to say, "Excuse me, ma'am." The whole dichotomy turned him the fuck on like no one's business. A fact he'd tried for years to ignore, but kept losing ground.

He never should have interfered between her and Judd. He'd never once seen her hook up with a guy, let alone someone they worked with, but when he'd walked into the main bar and seen Judd's hand on her hip, he'd nearly lost his shit.

With Darya and Knox trailing behind him, he navigated the upscale neighborhood to her town house and parked his 'Vette out front. What the three-story structures lacked in landscaping, they more than made up for in curb appeal, the whole brick-and-stonework combo somehow making the place look like an old English suburb. He'd barely known Gia a few weeks when the one she ended up purchasing had gone on the market, but it had been one of the few times he'd truly seen such openly displayed joy around those she worked with.

He'd barely made it around the back of his car to get Gia out of the front seat before Darya was beside him and handing over Gia's purse and keys. "Are you sure you don't want me to stay? You're not exactly Mr. Observant where she's concerned."

Something about the tone of Darya's voice and word choice pricked his attention enough he paused before picking Gia up. "What's that supposed to mean?"

Too quickly, Darya's gaze sliced to Knox still wait-ing behind the wheel of his Audi in the parking lot.

"Darya?"

She shrugged, but still didn't meet his stare for a few beats. As if she had to take the extra time to either for-mulate her words, or make damned sure she schooled her expression. "I'm just saying…men don't always see the things women do."

"Such as?"

Huffing, she shook her head and dipped her head toward Gia, still out cold. "Just take care of her. And for once, really *pay attention*." With that, she spun and sashayed off back to Knox, the click of her high heels ricocheting off the concrete between the tall buildings.

As light as Gia was, getting her in the house was a breeze, and thanks to Knox, her alarm didn't pose a problem either. Thank God, he'd actually convinced her to let his company be the one to install the system when she'd moved in. Otherwise, he'd have had a whole different set of problems to juggle.

Soft lamplight spilled from the corner of the living room, so Beckett aimed that direction and laid Gia out on the couch. Once settled, he crouched beside her and smoothed her hair away from her face.

The impact hit him instantly, the soft and silky strands jolting his amplified need for touch into high gear and tempting him like a junkie on a four-day dry spell. As out as she was, he could toy with the long strands and sample the skin on her face and neck for hours and she'd likely never remember the thing. The thing was, if he ever got the chance to touch her that way, he'd *want* her to remember. Would want to see the response in her eyes and learn how her body reacted to his touch.

He braced one hand on the couch above her head instead. The fabric was nowhere near as luxurious as her hair, but it was soft like the chairs he kept at his place and kept him from giving into touching where he shouldn't.

That was the thing about people like him. Touch was everything. The thing he needed to stay in balance and keep his head and impulses in check. While his sensory processing disorder—or SPD—wasn't as debilitating as it was for some people, he'd sure as hell learned not to underestimate it.

He leaned in and lowered his voice, knowing full well she probably wouldn't hear or understand a word he said. "How about you chill here for a bit, gorgeous. Let me go get things ready for you upstairs."

Gia moaned and rolled to one side, tucking her hands beneath her cheek.

He couldn't help but chuckle. The pose was cute. Totally innocent and sweet. Which meant she'd be mortified if she had any clue he'd seen it. "I'm gonna take that for a yes."

Forcing himself to stand and move away from her, he made his way to the staircase at the back of the first floor. She'd made a lot of changes to the place since the last time he'd seen it. When they'd first installed her security system, the townhouse had been empty and about as bland as a saltine cracker. Now, it was decked out in comforting grays and a greenish-blue color that reminded him of ocean water over a powder-white beach. The furniture ran more to the contemporary side of things, but without being cold and uptight. Totally classy, just like Gia.

Hustling to the master bedroom on the second floor, he flipped on the light, expecting to find more of the same—and stopped hard in his tracks. To say the décor in her room was a shock was an understatement. Yeah, he knew Gia could put the *girl* in *girly* when she needed to, but he'd never in a million years expected her private space to be anywhere near this feminine.

Where she'd stuck to neutral colors everywhere else, the basics for this room were white and a pink. And not the brash, oh-my-God-my-eyes-are-blinded pink, but a soft ballet color that encouraged you to take a load off and linger awhile. Especially the bedspread. He'd be damned if he had any clue what kind of fabric it was—something silky that could have passed for an exotic animal's coat if it wasn't pink. He combed his fingers through the fluffy surface, all too easily picturing Gia spread out naked on top of it.

He shook his head to clear the image and peeled back the comforter, only to find innocent white sheets that looked as soft as the ones he kept at home. Oh, yeah. Totally an invitation to let his mind go about a hundred different places it had no business going.

Fisting his hand to keep from sampling the surface, he took two unsteady steps backwards.

Focus, dumbass. She needs clothes. Not you perving out in her bedroom.

One glimpse in the top drawer of her dresser was enough to have him slamming it shut as fast as he'd opened it. Unfortunately, his eager brain had clocked the lacy bras and panties neatly tucked inside. Gia might be fond of pale colors in her bedroom, but clearly, she was open to racier, bolder stuff against her skin. "And Darya says I'm not observant. Fuck that."

He yanked open the next drawer. And the next. "Come on. She's gotta have T-shirts somewhere."

On the bottom drawer, he got his answer—but it wasn't T-shirts. Nope. The tiniest badass of the century was a silk-nightie girl. A bit of an addict really, given the number he had to choose from.

For a second, he just stared down at the contents, his fingers and his imagination all too eager to dive in.

He deserved this torture. Truly, he did.

Yeah? And you'd be cool with Judd being the one slipping in between those sheets? Not to mention between Gia's thighs?

Oh, hell no. That motherfucker rubbed Beckett all kinds of wrong. From his Malibu looks, to his suave bullshit routine, Judd was all window dressing and no substance. Or at least that was Beck's take on the man.

He exhaled slowly and ran his fingers along the pristine white nightie on the top of the pile. He could do this. He could absolutely do this. And if he was lucky, his dick might calm the hell down sometime before the next century.

A moan sounded from downstairs followed by unsteady footsteps on the hardwood floors.

"Gia?" He tossed the nightie on the bed and hauled ass downstairs.

Sure enough, his walking, talking fantasy was on her feet and weaving toward the stairs, an almost comical focus marking the features on her face.

"Girl, what are you doing up? I told you to sit tight."

At the sound of his voice, she halted so fast she almost fell over. She caught herself, though, and frowned up at him like she couldn't figure out who he was, or which of the three versions of him she should talk to. "Why are you in my house?"

Guess that answered if she knew who he was. "Because you're hammered and I'm the one that put you on the fast track to getting there, so I'm on puke patrol."

As if the mere mention of the word stirred her stomach, she tucked her chin in a little and swallowed hard. "I don't feel so good."

"Yeah, I don't doubt it." He moved in quick and swept her up in his arms.

She floundered for a minute, but finally settled one arm around his shoulders. "What are you doing?"

"Taking the express," he said, covering the stairs faster than was probably wise with a drunk woman in his arms. "Figured that was better than adding cleanup detail to tonight's agenda."

He was two steps into her room and on track for the master bath when she spoke, the desperation in her voice pushing him to move faster. "Beckett…"

"Yeah, gorgeous. We got this."

He made it with one retch to spare, barely getting her hair pulled out of the way before she let loose. Not that she had much left in her stomach after round one at Trident.

The weird part? It didn't bother him. Not in the slightest. Granted it'd been years since Knox had pulled a bender worthy of talking to Ralphie on the big white telephone, but watching Knox in the same situation had always made Beckett want to hurl himself. With Gia, he was fine. Like taking care of her was a privilege instead of something to endure.

The second the muscles in her shoulders eased and

she sat back on her ass, he let her hair go and nabbed a washcloth out of the cabinet. "Feel better?"

She moaned, pulled her knees up in front of her and crossed her arms on her knees, resting her forehead on top of them.

"Ah, it's not that bad." He crouched beside her and wiped her mouth, grateful the green-around-the-gills tint to her skin had been replaced with a healthy flush. "You think you can stand up long enough to rinse out your mouth?"

"I think so."

Surprisingly, that part went somewhat easy, routine kicking in and taking over when she reached for a toothbrush. At least, things stayed fine so long as he stayed planted behind her and held her steady. Otherwise, she tended to sway like a drunk pirate on the top deck in the middle of a hurricane.

She tapped her toothbrush on the counter, wiped her mouth with a fresh washcloth and met his eyes in the mirror. "I can't believe I just puked in front of you."

"Doesn't matter. You're not gonna remember it in the morning anyway, so I'll swear I never saw a thing."

Her head dropped back against his chest, but her eyes were closed. "Sleepy."

Sleepy.

"Right. Time to get you in bed." Although, how he was gonna get her into that nightie he still hadn't figured out. Opting for the fast route to the bed, he swept her up and got her settled on the edge. "You think you can get yourself changed?"

She clocked the nightie on top of her comforter, paused for at least a seven-second delay, then frowned up at him. "'Course."

There she was. Undoubtedly the most indomitable woman he'd ever met—even three sheets to the wind. Rather than cup the side of her face and sample her skin the way he wanted to, he straightened and forced himself back a step. "Atta girl. I'm gonna wait out in the hall, but if you need me, you just give me a shout."

Clearly, getting into bed was a huge priority, because she was tugging at what had once been a crisp, tailored white button-down before he could turn for the door.

What felt like twenty, but was probably only five minutes later, the shuffles and indelicate grunts coming from the bedroom grew silent. "G?"

No answer. Not so much as a heavy sigh.

"Gorgeous, you done?" When she still didn't answer, he peeked around the door frame, only to grab ahold of the wood just to balance himself from the visual punch that greeted him. "Fuck, baby. You tryin' to kill me?"

Of course, she wouldn't answer. Couldn't since she was out cold and stretched out on the comforter. With her dark hair, white nightie, and creamy skin against the pale pink surface, she was every man's fantasy centerfold come to life. And with the way the silk draped high on her hip, he was pretty damned sure the nightie was the *only* thing she had on.

Don't go there, Beck. She's a friend. Nothing more, nothing less.

He killed all the lights save a small one in the bathroom and tried to blank his thoughts the way he did at the gym. Unfortunately, the image of the blank white wall he relied on to clear the clutter in his head kept shifting to white silk and the possibility of what lay beneath it.

Standing beside the bed, he pumped his fists, the des-

perate need to ground himself through touch burning
his palms. Yeah, the slick fabric would help center him.
Would ease the agitation he'd fought since the second
he'd seen Gia leaning into Judd. But tonight there was
more. Pure primal need. A demand to claim her. Take
her. Mark her so thoroughly and deeply she wouldn't
be able to ignore him ever again.

He leaned over, pried the covers he'd partially peeled
back out from under her dead weight and dragged them
up over her legs. God, she was tiny. Firm, but still giving in all the right places. Even her scent sucked him in,
a mix of crisp ocean air and sultry nights on a beach.

She opened her eyes and her words came thick with
sleep and wonder. "You're in my room."

He liked that look on her. Her full lips relaxed and
slightly parted. Her eyelids heavy over soulful dark
eyes. He'd give a lot to see them that way when she'd
remember it. Preferably after a long night spent doing
everything except sleep. "Better me than Judd."

"No, not Judd." She smiled, a soft, wistful one as her
eyes slipped closed. "Judd's not who I want."

"Yeah? You could have fooled me." He sat next to
her on the bed, careful not to jostle her too much. No
easy task considering his bulk. He gave into temptation and smoothed the backs of his knuckles along her
jawline, the delicate sensation drawing everything inside him to laser focus.

He shouldn't ask. Shouldn't take advantage, but the
question pushed free despite the minute blip from his
conscience. "Who'd you want to go home with?"

Her eyes opened and the raw vulnerability in her soft
gaze nearly cut him in half. "You."

His lungs stopped working.

Hell, he was pretty sure his heart had kicked it, too. Or maybe it was just a case of his ears giving up the ghost after one too many of Axel's concert venues. "You don't mean that."

"Shhh." She scrunched her eyes closed for a second and nearly missed pressing her fingers to his lips. "It's my dream. Don't mess it up."

He caught her wrist before she could pull her hand away and dragged his thumb across her palm. "You think this is a dream?"

She chuckled. A low, dirty and delicious sound best relegated to moments where no clothes were involved. "Oh, I know it is." Mirroring the touch he'd given her, she grazed her fingertips along his jawline and cocked her head on the pillow, a soft sigh slipping past her lips. "You don't look at me like that in real life. Only in my dreams."

He couldn't think.

Couldn't move.

Didn't want to for fear of losing the way she kept touching him. Letting her hand drift down to his shoulder and arm and the covetous way her gaze followed behind it.

"I don't want to wake up." A whispered confession that hit him square in the solar plexus. Truth offered from unknowing lips.

Using what she'd shared was a shit move. An act Gia would not only kick his ass for at some point, but would probably try to cut his nuts off for just for fun.

But fuck if he was going to ignore it. Not when the holy grail of women had just drawn a great big X on the path to every fantasy he'd nursed for three years.

He stretched out beside her and tucked her as close

as the sheets and comforter between them would allow, guiding her head so it rested on his chest. He'd sleep for shit like this, if he even slept at all, but no way was he pausing to shuck his clothes like he normally did. Not if it meant letting her go. Not until he'd had time to formulate what to do with his newfound knowledge.

Men don't always see the things women do.

Darya had all but whacked him over the head with her words. Had told him to pull his head out of his ass and *pay attention*. For the life of him, he couldn't figure out how he'd missed it. Couldn't mesh the way Gia acted around him with her words tonight. But if it was the truth…

He smoothed his hand up and down her spine, thinking. Remembering countless details over the time they'd known each other. She always kept her distance. Kept things polite and professional, yet friendly.

But she watched him. He'd felt it. Caught her on several occasions, but he'd thought it was just her being observant. He waited for her breathing to even out before he trusted himself to speak. "Gia?"

In way of an answer, she snuggled closer and set free a contented "Hmmm?"

"I've always seen you." He speared his fingers through her hair and savored the weight of it. The summery scent and cool slickness against his knuckles. "And I *want* you to wake up. I want your eyes wide-open and your thoughts crystal clear the next time you see me." His grip tightened against her scalp, conviction pushing the words free in an almost violent surge. "Because your days of dreaming are over."

Chapter Three

Bright light danced behind Gia's closed eyelids, prodding her from a deep, comfortable sleep. Her temples ached like they did when she'd gone too long without eating and her mouth could give a cotton ball a run for its money, but her muscles were looser than they'd been in months.

Cocking one eye open, she fumbled for her phone on her nightstand—and found nothing.

Weird. She never went to bed without it close by.

She flopped back onto her pillows and frowned up at the ceiling. What the hell had she—

Oh, right.

Tequila.

Lots of it. Almost every shot matched one-for-one with an ornery-looking biker with shoulder-length gray hair and a wicked grin.

On the heels of that memory came another less pleasant one in the bathroom. Though, she also thought she remembered extracting a pinkie promise from Darya to get her home safe and sound. So, where the heck was she? And more important, what freaking time was it?

She rolled to one side for a better view out the window, squinting at what had to be at least mid-morning sun working its way up the horizon, when a subtle yet out-of-place scent drifted up from her pillow. Definitely not her dryer sheets, but the scent was familiar. Like cedar with a little kick of orange or bergamot thrown in and undeniably masculine.

Beckett.

The thought yanked her upright with a gasp and the throbbing at her temples went from mild nuisance to the mother of all bass drums. She swallowed the best she could and pressed her trembling hand to her stomach.

Oh, shit. She was in a nightie?

One glance at her clothes scattered in an uncharacteristic mess all over the floor and her panic jumped another notch. "Please, God. Say I didn't..."

She pushed back the covers and started to stand, unwilling to even think the possibility to herself, let alone say it out loud. But the second she moved the fact that there was *nothing* under her jammies but the skin God gave her registered crystal clear and she froze.

No. She couldn't have slept with Beckett. Tequila or not, her brain would never let a single detail of such an event slip free. Not after the number of nights he'd starred front and center for her imagination. And wouldn't she be sore? It'd been too long to count since she'd slept with anyone, so she'd have to feel *something* the morning after. If not, she was going to have to seriously rethink his place as her model fantasy man.

From downstairs, a muted click and whoosh sounded. The filtered water dispenser in her fridge if she placed it right.

So...what? He was still here?

She gripped the faux fur comforter in her damp palms, torn between running for the bathroom to hide and stomping downstairs for an explanation. God, what had she been thinking? And what was the protocol for a snafu like this anyway?

Oh, hey. Good morning. Thanks for bringing me home. Did I do anything stupid? Like, you know...puke on you? Jump your bones? Fall asleep at an inopportune time?

Wood creaked on the staircase, followed by the soft pad of feet steadily headed her direction.

Okay, so she'd have to meet things head-on. Beckett was a decent guy. And things couldn't have been too awful if he'd stuck around for face-to-face time the morning after. Right?

Even with the mini impromptu pep talk, her heart punched almost painfully when he sauntered into view. While he still had on the jeans and T-shirt he'd worn the night before, his feet were bare and his usually hard focus seemed softened somehow. As if he'd not yet shaken the dregs of sleep or donned the mask he put on before meeting the rest of the world.

"Ah, good. You're up." His mouth crooked in a sly smile and he lifted the glass of water in one hand. "Hope you don't mind I dug around your bathroom and kitchen, but I figured you'd want something for your head when you woke up."

"Thank you." Nowhere near the *I'm a little fuzzy on anything past the third round of shots. Could you fill in some of the blanks for me?* she'd have rather asked, but at least she'd managed something besides a simple nod.

Thankfully, she managed to take the glass and the Tylenol he offered without dropping either one.

Like he'd been there a thousand times before, he

stretched out on his side beside her, cocked one knee and propped himself up on one elbow. "Sleep good?"

Getting the pills down made for a decent delay tactic. Not that her mind managed to cough up much in the way of sly strategies to ask the obvious. "How bad was I?"

Not a bad approach. Open-ended and formed in a way he could take any number of ways.

"Well, I'll tell you this. You're the only woman I know who can make puking a classy affair."

She kept from hanging her head, but just barely. Her eyes closed of their own accord, though. As if by visually blocking out the room, the humiliation wouldn't sting as bad. Although, on the bright side, if she'd thrown up in front of him, it probably meant she hadn't actually slept with him. It also meant the odds of that fantasy ever happening for real had been firmly cemented in Never Never Land. "I take it you got a ringside seat for my performance?"

"I got round two. Darya got round one while we were still at Trident."

Yeah, that one she remembered. Or at least most of it. And the first chance Gia got she was going to read Darya the riot act for breaking her pinkie promise. Scooting over enough to put some decent room between them, Gia tucked the covers tighter around her waist and twisted enough to make eye contact. "I'm afraid to ask how I got in my pajamas."

Dammit, she shouldn't have looked. In the last three years, she'd built some seriously stout defenses against Beckett's many expressions, but the playful one he aimed at her in that moment was the Trojan guaranteed to slip past her guard. Especially with him splayed out on her bed and comfortably rumpled by sleep. "Well, I'd have been a heartless bastard if I'd left you to sleep in your clothes..."

Her stomach clenched, images of her passed out, drooling and as cooperative as a newborn blasting through her head.

"...but once I asked if you could handle changing alone, you dove right in. So, I waited for you in the hall."

The breath she hadn't been aware she'd been holding rushed out.

Beckett chuckled at the obvious reaction and reached across the distance she'd created. Before her mind could reengage and project his trajectory, he smoothed one finger along the line where her hip disappeared beneath the sheets. "Gotta admit, though. I was a little disappointed you were good for duty. I wouldn't have minded helping. Not one bit."

It was a simple touch. A single point of contact that shouldn't have carried such impact, but every nerve ending in her body stood up and took notice. Begged for more and drew a hundred pathways to other suggested stops needing attention. She couldn't talk, let alone breathe. And apparently, her libido had overwritten any ideas of stopping him.

"You make cute little noises when you sleep."

Her shock at his statement must have telegraphed on her expression because he kept going as if she'd verbally requested a confirmation.

"Not quite a sigh and not a moan either. More somewhere in between."

"I do not."

"You do."

Was it her imagination? Or had he moved closer? "If I did, it was only because I'd had too much to drink."

He traced her hip through the sheet, then down to follow the outline of her thigh. "You're also a cuddler."

Goose bumps lifted along her exposed skin and her breasts grew tight and heavy behind her nightgown. Even without a visual confirmation, she was absolutely certain her nipples were not only hard but embarrassingly obvious.

"What are you doing?" A whisper was the best she could manage, every muscle locked tight and torn between scrambling further away and inching closer to his heat.

He slid the hand he'd teased her with just above her knee and gently squeezed. Just a squeeze. Nothing more. But somehow the simple touch combined with his confidence made the contact feel erotic. A precursor that made her sex weep and ache for more. "Just making sure you're okay." Like he had all the time in the world at his disposal, his gaze dropped to her breasts and his startling blue eyes heated. A shift from midday-sky blue to a snapping indigo flame. "And maybe laying a little groundwork while I'm at it."

The depth of his voice vibrated through her. Coiled the muscles low in her belly tight…right up until his words registered. "What's that supposed to mean?"

His eyes cut back to hers, but the intensity behind them had shifted. The narrowed focus of a predator holding her as firm as a cat pinned by the scruff of her neck. "Nothing you need to worry about this morning. Later, but not right now." In a move that should have been difficult for someone of his height and build, he rolled off the bed and strolled toward the door without so much as a backward glance. "Grab some of the coffee I started downstairs, take a long hot shower and shake the rest of last night off first."

Under normal circumstances, the aggressive routine would've ratcheted her asshole defenses to DEFCON 1, but combined with the sudden shift in topic, she found herself tossing the sheets aside, scrambling off the bed and plunking the glass of water onto the nightstand. "Before what?"

"Before you meet me this afternoon." He paused at the threshold, gripped the door frame and gave her a languid once-over, head to toe.

Through sheer will, she kept her response to merely smoothing her hand down the front of her nightie instead of squirming or crawling back under the comforter. "We don't have anything on the books for this afternoon."

"We didn't. We do now."

"You got a job lined up between last night's pukefest and this morning?"

This time when he smiled, it was pure sin. One-hundred percent wicked promise with a kick of indecency for good measure. "No, we're gonna work out for a bit and then spar."

Oh, no. One of the biggest rules in her book after spying Beckett shirtless in the gym was no more sharing workout space. Keeping her cool in the field was one thing. With that much skin and muscle on display, she'd never be able to focus. "We never spar."

"We never have before. Doesn't mean we can't now. Besides, I got you home safe and sound, and even got you through a night kneeling at the porcelain throne. A good workout will make us both feel better."

Yeah, but it wouldn't be the kind of workout she wanted from him. "I can't. I've got a job in Houston Monday morning. I pack and fly out tomorrow."

"Like you need all weekend to pack for a job." He cocked his head and whipped out the playful grin. "Although, I could see why you'd be hesitant. Me wipin' the floor with you before a gig would probably jack with your confidence. So, yeah, maybe it's a bad idea."

"You won't wipe the floor with me."

"No?"

"No."

"Prove it."

Ugh. Stupid, arrogant, good-for-nothing men. Although, maybe she shouldn't add stupid to the list in this instance. After all, he'd been savvy enough to know which of her buttons to push and she'd jumped right in the middle of his trap. "Fine. Where and when."

"My office. Five o'clock."

Shit. Shit. Shit. She'd forgotten he had his own gym. A very *private* gym with almost no one around to offer distraction or buffers. Especially on a Saturday.

She opened her mouth, praying her brain would either cough up something witty or provide a convenient out.

"Better rest up and nurse that coffee, gorgeous," he said before either happened. He winked and sauntered down the hallway, but not before he tossed a zinger over his shoulder. "Come tonight, all the rules you're used to one-on-one are off the table."

Chapter Four

Beckett fisted his hands on top of his desk and glared at the security monitor with its image of the parking lot empty of all but his 'Vette and Danny's Harley. Twenty after five and no sign of Gia was not a good sign. She was never late. Hell, she was habitually early.

Snatching his phone up off the gleaming mahogany surface, he checked his texts again, only to find the same thing he'd found the last five times he'd looked.

Nothing.

For a solid minute, he stared down at Gia's number on the screen. If she'd waffled and decided not to show, the last thing she'd want would be him badgering her for reasons. But since when had Gia ever been the type to be anything but straight-up about what she did or didn't want? A no-show didn't make sense. He hit the button and paced his office, every ring escalating his agitation. By the time her voicemail picked up, the casing around his phone groaned a desperate protest.

Tossing the phone back to the desk, he stood, rolled his shoulders and paced along the wide windows that fronted his half of the building he and Knox had purchased with the brotherhood's help almost five years ago. Back and forth, he smoothed his hand against his

T-shirt at his stomach. It was the most basic of his coping techniques. A way to feed his need for sensory input and find his balance without drawing too much attention from the people around him. But this time, the simple yet practiced gesture and the exceptionally soft cotton did absolutely nothing to uncoil the ramping itch beneath his skin.

He shouldn't have pushed her. Ever since Beckett had let himself out of Gia's town house this morning, the thought had dogged him nonstop. Which was weird, because his instincts when he'd woken with her tucked tight to him had been crystal clear—push the envelope just enough when she woke up to see if her revelation from the night before was true, or only the tequila talking. Then he'd walked through the door to her room and found her sitting in the middle of her king-sized bed, her soft sheets piled around her, her pretty face framed in her sleep-tousled dark hair and her dark eyes wide with confusion. He could've no more kept away than he could've stopped breathing.

And holy hell, had she responded.

The second her husky whispers had slipped past her lips and her nipples had hardened behind her silk nightie, his dick had not only stood up and saluted, but practically insisted it get in the game pronto. A fact she'd have no doubt seen for herself if she hadn't been so twisted up trying to piece together what had happened the night before.

Then he'd gone and dropped that taunt about sparring.

He paused and checked the parking lot again, craning to check Knox's side of the building. God, that had been a fucked-up move. Yeah, he'd nudged her competitive nature and gotten her agreement, but the second he'd slid into his car to drive away, an almost smothering doubt had assailed him. The last thing he needed was her remembering they worked together. He'd seen her fend off practically all the men they worked with in the time he'd known her, which was one of the primary reasons he'd never tried for something more.

Well, that and the fact that she came from a polar opposite background from him. He might be doing well for himself now, but the piece-of-shit life he and Knox had scraped and clawed their way out of was a whole different reality.

The crawling sensation wriggled stronger beneath his skin and the tension along his neck and shoulders thickened. "Fuck it." He stomped back to the desk and grabbed his phone, thumbing up Danny's number. While he'd never expected things to go too far this afternoon with Gia, he'd at least counted on the hand-to-hand contact to take the edge off. But if that wasn't going to happen, then something else needed to fill the gap or he'd be bat-shit crazy by nightfall.

That was the thing about his disorder—either he kept a tight hold on his psyche via a steady amount of touch, or his brain would overload, grab him by the emotional short-hairs and turn him into Mr. Hyde. Anything from a simple hug to a right hook would do the trick, but without Gia it'd have to be the latter 'cause he damned sure wasn't in the mood for any other woman touching him.

Not after last night.

The feel of her was burned into him. The soft and trusting way she'd snuggled next to him unwinding his inner demons until it was like his SPD didn't even exist. The drugging mix of toned muscles and sexy curves so tempting it had taken ironclad determination not to explore every inch while she slept.

So, yeah. No women. Not until he saw where things went with her, and even then, he'd likely have to line his brothers up and let them use him for a punching bag for a good long while. Long enough for him to forget. Assuming that was even possible.

"Yo." Danny's gruff voice cut through the phone line, the heaviness and preoccupied tone of it slapping Beckett with the reminder of how he'd already pawned off a sizable corporate security system install to his newest brother. "Thought you had a meeting with someone right about now."

"Yeah, it's looking like they're a no-show. How much longer till you're done with setup? I need to blow off a little steam."

The clipped thunks of heavy shoes on metal sounded through the line, ladder work no doubt, given the cameras they'd planned to install for good measure. "Got at least two more hours. You gonna be able to make it that long, or should I put this job on hold?"

Funny. Danny might be the newest man to join the brotherhood, but once he'd learned about Beckett's need for a regular physical outlet, he'd been more than willing to trade punches when needed. Whether it was his desire to learn what Beck could teach him in the way of self-defense, or he had his own demons riding his ass, Beckett wasn't complaining.

Forcing himself to focus, Beckett let out a slow exhalation and rolled his head to relax the muscles in his neck. "Nah, I can make it." At least he thought he could. There was also the option of calling Darya and seeing if he could sweet-talk her into one of those wicked good back rubs. Of course, that would mean a long stretch of Knox scowling at him while she did, because while Knox would give him anything, letting his woman soothe his best friend wasn't something that went down easy.

"You sure?" The sharpness in Danny's voice said he'd stopped whatever part of the install had held his attention and was solely focused on Beckett. "It's a Saturday. Ain't like I've got someone here clocking my time. I can be there in thirty tops and circle back here when we're done. Hell, for that matter, you can throw a hand in and we'll finish up faster."

That was true. Danny had picked up the tools of the trade fast enough, but Beckett had been installing systems for years. He turned toward his desk to power down his computer and opened his mouth to answer, but the words stalled out at the site of the snappy white Lexus convertible whipping into the parking lot.

"You there?"

It took a good four-second delay for his brain to tug his attention away from Gia uncoiling herself from behind the wheel and all but power-strutting toward the building's front door. How any woman could look so full of fire dressed in workout gear and a high ponytail, he'd never know, but she pulled it off.

When he finally managed an answer, he was pretty sure his voice sounded supremely smug. "Yeah, I'm here. Turns out I'm gonna be good after all. She just showed up."

"*She?*"

Well, hell. So much for keepin' a lid on things. Still, every one of his brothers not only knew Gia, but adored her. Especially after all she'd done to help Natalie and Darya. He punched the electronic release that unlocked the front door. "Just meetin' with Gia to do a little work this afternoon. No big deal."

A long pause echoed back at him before Danny finally spoke. "Business."

"Yep." Not a complete lie. He imagined he'd have to talk a little shop before he could move them into the topic he had in mind. Or better yet, the actions.

Danny grunted as if he wasn't buying a lick of it. "Well, if you change your mind let me know. I'm swinging by and switchin' to my bike before I wrap up tonight. Axel said he's got a sweet new band booked at Crossroads tonight and thought I'd check 'em out. You game?"

Man, he hoped not. Walking away from Gia this morning had gone against the grain on a fundamental level. If he had to do it again tonight to gain her trust, then so be it. But he'd much rather finish off the day with her as close to him as she'd been last night. "Let's wait and see how long this thing with G goes. Stop in when you come in to pick up your bike and I'll let you know then."

"You got it." He paused a beat and his gravelly voice lifted in an audible smirk. "Have fun workin'."

This time it was Beckett who grunted, thumbing the end button and cutting off Danny's low chuckle.

The click of the front door's latch sliding back into place echoed down the hall that led to his half of the building. "Beckett?"

He paused just beyond the door that would bring her into view, savoring the sound of her voice. Most of the guys they worked with always called him Beck. Or Tate. But like Jace and Axel's moms, Ninette and Sylvie, Gia always called him by his full name. Hell, now that he thought about it, all the Haven women did that. But with Gia it still sounded special. Like warm Southern honey.

Forcing himself back into motion, he rounded the threshold. "And here I thought I was gonna get to claim an easy victory with a no-show."

"Not on your life." The spunky retort was exactly what he'd expected, but her flushed cheeks and uncertain gaze showed an uncharacteristic hesitancy. She shrugged and wiped her palms on her hips, the perfect curves on prime display in black and tropic green leggings. "I'm sorry I was late. I dug into answering some emails and lost track of time."

Now, that was a bullshit foul if he'd ever heard one. If the way she'd fidgeted when she'd said it hadn't cinched it, the fact that she'd broken eye contact would've. The real question was *why* she'd felt the need to dodge him to begin with, but he'd figure it out. Eventually. "Hey, you're here. A few minutes behind schedule isn't going to put me off." He jerked his head toward the back of the building where his private gym was located. "Let's do this."

For the next thirty minutes, he gave her room to warm up on the treadmill and chase off whatever had her acting jumpy. Jumping into weights without warming up himself wasn't exactly best practice, but the lifting section of his gym gave him a great angle to watch and strategize from, not to mention giving her space to settle in.

Only when she shifted the machine's pace for a cooldown did he restack his weights and meander to the wide blue mat directly behind her. "You sure you're good to do this today? All bullshit aside, I'm not gonna give you grief if you're still hurting from last night."

Giving her the out was a risk he was loath to take, but the last thing he wanted was her here only because she felt backed in a corner. She already got enough of that shit from the other guys. No way was he adding his name to the list.

Her gaze locked with his in the mirror and, for a second, his gut dropped with the certainty she was going to grab the excuse and run with it. Instead, she hit the kill switch, braced her feet on either side of the belt and snatched her towel off the machine. "No, I'm good. Actually, the run helped more than I'd thought it would."

Wiping her face and the back of her neck, she jumped off the machine and strolled toward him. The concentration in her expression and the way she marked him toeing off his shoes and the room she had to work with on the mat further proved she was already in the game. "So, what's the plan?"

Get you as close as possible and hear the truth without tequila's guiding hand.

Not that he'd ever admit that particular motive. He shrugged, turned his back to her and peeled off his shirt, leaving him in just his Haven tags and loose black track pants. "Well, considering hell's gonna freeze over before I'll ever be able to throw a straight punch at you, I thought we'd stick to jiujitsu and whatever self-defense you want to add in. That work for you?"

He tossed his tags on top of his shirt, the muted jingle as they hit the ground the only answer he got. "G?" Twisting enough for eye contact, he found her full attention locked on his bare torso.

Well, now. If that wasn't a fine segue into the evening's agenda. "You good with that plan?" he prodded again. And damned if his body didn't get in on the action, pride and a whole lot of hope pushing his shoulders back as he ambled toward her.

She shook her head and got to work on her own shoes, the way she yanked her laces promising a whole lot of pent-up aggression he was looking forward to having aimed at him in short order. "Rules?"

"Do we need them?"

Her head snapped toward him and she kicked her last shoe aside. "I don't know? Do we?"

Fuck no. In fact, once he confirmed she was really into him, she was in for some serious no-holds-barred attention. "Not on my account."

She jerked a terse nod and proceeded to shuck her tank, leaving her in only a sport bra and her leggings. "Good." She flung the shirt aside with a bravado that made his dick want to get in the action. She braced her hands on her hips and pushed her shoulders back to mimic his, putting her beautiful tits on prime display. "Then let's do this."

Oh, yeah. This was gonna be hell and a dream come true all rolled up into one. He stepped on the mat, blood pumping on a surge that had zero to do with cardio and everything to do with the woman across from him. "Ready when you are, gorgeous."

She rolled her eyes and stomped onto the mat. "Stop calling me that."

"Why? It's true." The banter was the same routine they'd shared since day one, and he'd always been sincere when he'd used the endearment, but he'd never pushed things further. Not like he was going to today.

Circling closer, he bent his knees a fraction, intentionally telegraphing a potential strike. "So, the job in Houston...what's that about?"

"Corporate exec traveling to San Diego and taking the whole family." She mirrored his move and shifted in the opposite direction. Like Beckett, Gia was a private agent and booked her own gigs. But unlike him, she was a one-man—or one-woman—shop and had to contract out with other peers when the jobs she secured called for it.

"Any real threats, or just an ego to protect?"

Gia grinned, but her focus never wavered. "Probably warranted this time. The company just went through some massive layoffs. News they're wining and dining customers at a weeklong out-of-town event isn't making those impacted feel warm and fuzzy."

Before he could volley back another question, she struck, aiming a shoulder low and to one side for a flip.

He dodged it, but just barely. A fact she well knew by her sly grin. "Fast little thing, aren't you?"

"You have no idea."

Ignoring the husky edge to her response was impossible. More like a spur to his flanks urging him to move faster. "You guarding the whole family or partnering with someone?"

The frown that moved across her face was quick, but marked. Enough to draw him off center and put all his senses on high alert. "Had to partner up."

"With who?"

Her gaze lasered in on his rather than watching his overall stance for all of a second. "Judd." Before he could even process the answer, she shot forward and tried to swipe his feet out from under him.

It didn't work. Not even by a long shot. He countered on pure instinct, years of training and the mention of Judd's name pushing him to full offensive mode.

But Gia met him move for move, never giving up until he'd navigated her off the mat. She straightened and braced her hands on her hips. "You know, for a big guy you move quick."

"Only when I'm fighting." He backed up to his side of the mat and motioned her forward, but punctuated the rest of his words with a purposeful head-to-toe appraisal. "The rest of the time, you can bet I'll take my sweet time."

One second. One tiny spark of desire behind her dark eyes and a small softening in her stance was all he got in the way of confirmation he'd hit a mark. Not nearly as much as he wanted, but it was a start.

Back on the mat, she made a show of taking her time to reengage.

Fortunately for him, he'd watched her use that ploy a time or two with other people and anticipated the rapid-fire attack that came at him with little warning.

He fended off each approach, intentionally staying on defense. When she finally stepped back to catch her breath, he dug in deeper. "How'd you end up partnered with Judd? Thought you didn't like working teams with him."

"I didn't have a choice. The family's agenda was too spread out, and I needed a second body for the job."

He straightened just enough to make her think he was disengaging from their bout. "You could've called me."

Surprisingly, she bought the ploy and straightened as well. "You hate family gigs."

The opening was exactly the one he'd waited for, and before she could so much as draw in a shocked breath, he had her pinned on her belly, his body firmly blanketing hers. "Yeah, but I like you."

She dropped her forehead to the mat and grunted,

tapping out with open disgust she'd been sucked into the ploy. "You get that point. Now, get off me, you damned brute."

Logic said he should back the hell off and keep things light a little while longer, but after a night of holding her and a day full of making plans to make it happen again, common sense wasn't in high supply. Not to mention, the lingering thought of Judd spending time with her for a weeklong gig had him itching to leave an indelible mark.

He gave her just a fraction more of his weight, his hips perfectly pressed to her sweet ass. He dipped his head, teased his lips across the bared skin just behind her ear and murmured, "Make me."

She snapped her head around and pressed her arms with all she had against the mat, but the breathiness from this morning was back. So was the wide-eyed hunger in her dark gaze. "Are you fucking kidding me?"

"You said no rules." He grinned even knowing it was going to piss her off more than he already had. "Beautiful woman like you? Just consider it good practice for real life."

She rolled.

He countered.

She bucked, twisted enough to wedge her knees underneath him and put a surprising amount of muscles into dislodging him.

He went with it, using her momentum to drop to his back and pulling her with him. From there, all it took was one quick flip and she was pinned to her back beneath him, his hips perfectly cradled between her thighs. "Much better."

She tried to jerk her wrists free of his hands anchored on either side of her head and scowled up at him. "Okay, you proved your point. You've got size and weight on me. Kind of hard to tap out if you're being a dick about it."

Harsh words, but as sweet as her body felt next to his and her crisp ocean scent filling his lungs, she could have lashed him with the harshest words on the planet and he'd have taken it. Happily.

"Swear to you, gorgeous. I'm not being a dick." Keeping enough pressure she couldn't slip free, he slid his hands up to her palms and laced his fingers with hers. More than anything he wanted to pull back and savor the look of her beneath him. To let his gaze take its fill and imagine them in his bed without anything but skin between them. Instead, he forced his attention from her full, raspberry-colored lips to her soulful dark eyes. "Maybe a conniving and opportunistic ass, but I promise you, I've got a reason."

The anger in her expression shifted, more of a wariness aimed up at him than a furious woman ready to maim if not kill. "What reason?"

He lowered his head, holding her gaze as he did. "I wanted to know the truth." Tempting as it was to take her mouth, he teased his lips along her jawline. "I figured the only way I was gonna get it in less than twelve months was to fight dirty."

She drew in a shaky breath and, thank Jesus, she shifted her head just enough to leave the sweet curve of her neck exposed. Even her grip shifted, the contact more of a desperate hold than an effort to push him away. "What truth?"

He froze, her pulse point pounding beneath his lips and her body pliant. He could kiss her. Claim her mouth and pray it was enough to bridge where he wanted to go. To take her off the inquisitive path long enough for him to build ground to work with.

But this was Gia. A woman he not only appreciated physically, but respected the hell out of professionally and intellectually. She might not have said as much with words, but she'd given him enough clues to solidify last night hadn't been a fluke. Now it was time for him to man up and give them what they both wanted.

He lifted his head, meeting her wide gaze head-on. "Who did you want to go home with last night?"

Shock.

Fear.

Realization.

All three moved across her features as undoubtedly fuzzy pieces from the night before got crystal clear. "What are you talking about?"

"Don't bullshit me, Gia. Give me the truth. If I'd opened the door to something between us last night—or any other night the last three years—would you have walked through it?"

That tough-as-nails defensive mask she always used against the men who gave her shit slammed into place. "I don't know what—"

"I said no bullshit. Not with me. Not between the two of us. Not ever again." Giving her any physical leverage was a hellacious risk with the amount of fire burning behind her eyes, but with the subtle tremors moving through her body he had to give her something. Needed to show her she was safe with him. He released one of her hands and cupped the side of her face. "You told me last night *I* was the one you wanted. Now I want to hear it without the liquid courage."

Sure enough, she gripped his shoulder, but rather than push him away, she squeezed as if she couldn't quite decide what to do. "I was drunk."

"And we're both stone-cold sober now, so remember that when I tell you..." He traced her lower lip with his thumb, her warm breath moving across his skin in short, shallow puffs. "I want the same thing. Always have."

One heartbeat.

Then another.

"No, you don't. You never even—"

"Saw you?" He slid his hand to the back of her head, her ponytail a thick silk rope against his forearm. "Gorgeous, I've watched you from the very first day."

"No, you haven't. Every other woman in the Dallas/Ft. Worth area maybe, but not me."

One twist and he fisted her ponytail, effectively stealing the breath from her last word and angling her head for full access to her neck. If she wanted to argue, he'd meet her verbal attack punch for punch, but he had a hunch he'd finish the match more with actions than anything else. He kissed the spot where her shoulder met her neck. "Saw you long before you saw me." A little higher. "Saw the way you held yourself with all the other guys. Heard you put a few of them in their place." He nipped the pulse point that had tempted him earlier. "But then I met you, learned about you and didn't want to fuck things up."

"Oh my God." Spoken with a mix of a moan and a whisper, she punctuated the statement with a flex of her hips and speared the hand he'd released in his hair. "We can't do this. It's a bad idea."

"It's a fan-fucking-tastic idea." He kissed his way to the hollow of her throat.

"No, it's not. We work together."

Fuck it. Maybe it was time to give her mouth something better to do than argue. "Yeah, we do." He lifted his head and zeroed in on her lips. "And we're gonna take that to a whole new level."

Her breath moved across his face, her eyelids heavy and her mouth parted, ready for his kiss even if her words said otherwise.

Finally.

The heavy clank of metal on metal fired gunshot-potent through the wide room, halting him before he could make contact.

"Yo, Beck!"

In perfect timing, Beckett and Gia both jerked their heads toward Danny standing mid-threshold to the gym with one hand bracing the door open.

"Hey, man," Danny said, clearly not cluing into his shit timing. "We've got a problem."

Gia wiggled beneath him and murmured, "Beckett, let me up."

"Kind of in the middle of something," Beckett said to Danny, not budging an inch from Gia.

Either Beckett's tone, or Gia's position beneath Beckett finally seemed to register with Danny. "Oh. Shit. Yeah." He glanced over his shoulder then jerked his head toward the main office. "Well, we tried to call you, but I'm thinkin' your phone's in your office."

"And?"

"You remember that band Axel's got lined up at Crossroads?"

"Beckett." Gia wriggled again, but this time her voice was nowhere near as quiet.

Beckett scowled down at her and growled low

enough only she could hear it. "You think I'm gonna let you up right now, you're out of your goddamned mind." He twisted to Danny. "Yeah, what about it?"

"Well, the two guys you sent out for security lost their shit with a couple of the roadies and we've got six guys headed to the ER."

Fuck. "Where's Zeke?"

"Waiting for them at Baylor, but the band's manager is saying lawsuit about every other word, so you've got some PR work to do pronto." Done delivering his message, Danny volleyed his attention between Beck and Gia. "Sorry, didn't mean to break up a thing."

"It's not a thing," Gia bit out, shifting just enough to get an opportune knee free.

Beckett rolled just in time to miss his nuts getting shoved up into his guts. "Oh, it's a thing," he snarled back, but held out a hand and hauled her to her feet. "Danny, need you to hang around and make sure Gia gets out all right."

"Sure, man. Whatever you need."

Gia rolled her eyes and stomped over to her discarded tank. "Pretty sure I can manage getting in my car just fine. I can even tie my own shoes and everything."

"Humor me," Beckett said as he snatched his tee, tags and shoes off the ground.

"I already did that."

"Not nearly enough." He paused on the way to the door and moved in close enough to keep his parting shot for her alone. "And don't think for a second the next time I see you, we're not picking up right where we left off."

Chapter Five

It was a damned shame a woman couldn't knock off her problems the way a shooter on a gun range took out their targets. God knew, Gia had racked up plenty of challenges to aim at over the last five days and none of them appeared to be going away anytime soon.

Her phone buzzed in her back pocket, one of those shorter zings that signaled a text message instead of a call. She sighed and tried to focus on the competitor moving quickly through the obstacles and targets set up along the gun range's course. In a timed action event like this one, focus was critical, but all she could do was wonder if the newest message was another clever check-in from Beckett, or a repeat in a long string of apologies from Judd.

If she was smart, she'd turn the damned thing off.

She clearly wasn't, though, as evidenced by the fact that she'd checked every damned one of them since Saturday night. Judd's attempts to mend the latest hole he'd dug in their friendship she could do without, but those texts from Beckett had proven to be addictive. Persistent and creative. And not one apology in the bunch.

Winding through the crowd, she moved to the side of the wide viewing area and pulled her phone from her pocket.

Beckett: You can run, but you can't hide.

Hmm. Not nearly as inventive as the gif he'd sent this morning of Deadpool sensually stroking his costume-covered chest. The odd image had given her a chuckle right out of the gate. Then he'd followed it up with a clip of a steaming cup of coffee and a text that said:

Beckett: Knox hacked your flight schedules, so I know you're home. You can't ignore me forever, gorgeous.

She sighed, tucked her phone back in her pocket and crossed her arms on her chest, braced to wait until her turn to shoot. At least she'd have a chance to burn off some of her frustrations with her bullets and maybe, just maybe, win a little of her confidence back in the form of a competition win.

The shooter finished, unloaded their firearm and made their way back to the range master. With the wall between the spectators and the firing range, ear protection wasn't necessary for those watching, but the conversation around her still seemed to swell a little higher without the rapid fires to gobble up the quiet.

Her senses pricked to someone moving close behind her a second before Beckett's low voice wrapped around her. "Well, at least I know you're reading them."

Just like at her house and the gym on Saturday, goose bumps lifted up and down her arms and her breasts tightened in response. She could listen to him talk for hours. Especially when he hit that low-pitched, rumbling range reserved for one-on-one.

Thankful her crossed arms hid her traitorous nipples behind her fitted tank, she twisted enough to cock an eyebrow and shot him a perturbed scowl. "Do I need to scan my things for GPS now? Or did you really go the extra effort and put a chip under my skin somewhere while I was passed out Friday night?"

He grinned, taking the taunt in stride and shrugging as he anchored his fingertips in the tops of his front jeans pockets. "That's overkill, even for me." He jerked his head toward the firing range on the opposite side of the glass. "You never miss one of these, so I knew where you'd be."

The range master called out, "Load and make ready," giving her a solid reason to give Beckett her back and mask the subtle pleasure moving through her. Why him being so keyed into her hobbies and where she spent her time made her want to preen and giggle like a high school girl, she couldn't say, but there was no denying the sensation was potent. Even nearly enough to make her do something stupid like lean against him and see if he'd wrap those insanely strong arms around her again.

No, no, no, Gia. Don't think about it.

Yeah, like that pep talk had done any good the last five days. Even working, she'd had a heck of a time not revisiting how good he'd felt next to her. How his aggression had flipped every damned button she had and how hard it had been to keep an angry facade. How in that tiny span of time, she'd been able to almost let go. To not portray the strong and unforgiving persona her business required. For her male counterparts it was easy, but for a woman, even the slightest hint of weakness would work against her.

She straightened her stance as if it might better armor her against the memories and zeroed in on the newest competitor, a kid that didn't look like he was even old enough to be out of high school. She'd seen him shoot before, though, and he had an amazing mix of speed and accuracy.

Out of habit, she scanned the waiting crowd, all predominantly men except for a few wives and girlfriends who'd come to watch.

Which meant she was the only female competing. *Again.*

Beckett's big hands settled on her shoulders near her neck and gently squeezed. "Relax, gorgeous. You're an ace at these gigs. Today won't be any different."

To anyone else, the contact probably looked like a friend or a coach mentally prepping a contestant for their turn in the barrel, but damned if the subtle massage he gave her wasn't insanely sensual. "Beckett?"

He moved in closer, his heat blanketing her back even as he dipped his head close to her ear and turned her legs to jelly with a low "Hmmm?"

"You're not helping."

Rather than move away, he chuckled and smoothed his hands out to the ball of her shoulders. "Not thinking about the match anymore, huh?" He inhaled long and slow and glided his hands back in. "I warned you what to expect, G. Don't think it's not going to happen." With one last squeeze, he dropped his hands and gave her a few inches. "But I'll give it until you kick everyone's ass to push the issue if you'll tell me what the hell's got you so uptight."

The loss of contact and the reminder of her Houston debacle tossed her back to reality none too delicately. "I'm not uptight."

"Right. And that scowl you marched in here with an hour ago was all because you couldn't contain your competition glee." He swaggered up so he stood beside her and mirrored her stance with crossed arms. Between his height, his shoulder span and biceps nearly as big as one of her thighs, he pulled off a whole lot of visual intimidation without even trying. "Come on. Tell me what happened."

The offer was tempting. If nothing else it would give her an outlet to clear her head before it was her turn to shoot. "Judd screwed me in Houston."

His head snapped her direction, the once laid-back expression he'd held replaced with a rapidly mounting fury. "He what?"

Well, duh, Gia. You use the word screw *with Beckett and he's going to take it literally.* "I mean he undercut me with my client."

It took a few beats before his tension eased, but he kept his focus trained on her, an entirely different level of calculation moving behind his startling blue eyes. "Undercut you how?"

She shrugged, focused on the range and forced a nonchalance she didn't even remotely feel. "He scheduled an earlier flight than me, showed up at my client's office and introduced himself as his assigned cover."

"He left you with the mom and kids?"

"Pretty much."

"G, that's whacked. You booked the gig, that means you run the gig the way you wanna run it."

"I know that. You know that. Judd knows that. But my client didn't. If I'd walked in and arranged otherwise, I'd have made it look like I didn't have control of my own crew—which apparently I didn't."

"You lay into his ass afterwards?"

Oh, she'd laid into him. Repeatedly and at a level

he'd not forget anytime soon. "Suffice it to say, Judd's persona non grata at present and is the only one giving you a run for a world record on text messages." She smirked up at him. "Though, his aren't anywhere near as fun as yours."

The quip did what she'd intended, shifting Beckett's focus back to more appealing matters. In a business dominated by males, being adept at diversion was a golden asset she'd had loads of opportunities to hone over the years.

He grinned and leaned a little closer. "You think my texting skills are fun, wait till you take a turn with my creativity one-on-one."

Yeah, that was the one thing she didn't need to do. No matter how many fantasies she'd entertained otherwise since Saturday night, common sense insisted crossing the line with Beckett was trouble waiting to happen.

As if he sensed her line of thinking, he straightened and redirected back to her Houston trip. "Thought you and Judd were tight."

Apparently, Judd had thought that, too. Enough so he could waltz in and rearrange her plans to suit his ego. "We go back a long time, but I wouldn't call us tight."

"What would you call it?"

"Neighbors."

The comment earned her a frown from Beckett.

"Our families," she explained before he could start digging in with questions. "Growing up, we were *literally* neighbors. Or as close as two families can be when property lines stretch two or three acres and sport rock privacy walls and motorized gates."

He huffed out an ironic chuckle. "You don't like home much, do you?"

"I like Atlanta just fine. It's Mom and Dad's idea of what a woman should be when they grow up I have a problem with."

"And that is?"

She twisted to meet his steady gaze, and this time she couldn't hold back the bitterness when she spoke. "Married with at least two kids and totally reliant on my husband. You wouldn't believe how many years they tried to hook me up with Judd. Hell, they may still be plotting for all I know."

"You?" The shock behind his response caused more than one person to look their way. "I can picture you tacklin' all kind of jobs, but a stay-at-home housewife isn't one of 'em. And you'd have Judd's nuts severed and stored in the pantry inside two weeks."

Maybe the fact that he was so incredulous to the idea should have rubbed her wrong. Instead, all she could process was a hefty amount of gratitude and relief that someone saw the same picture she did. "Yeah, they don't get it. Plus, everything between me and Judd has been a competition for as long as I can remember."

In the range, the next shooter finished their round and unloaded.

Gia motioned toward the lockers. "I'm up after the next guy. Gotta get my gear ready."

She'd thought the task would make for a clean cut in the conversation and give her some time to clear her head before her round, but Beckett just fell in beside her. "What do you mean everything's a competition?"

"Just what it sounds like. Everything from spelling bees in fourth grade to who got into the best college and had the highest GPA." She rounded into the storage area and the long rows of gun lockers. From here the gunfire was still audible, but far more muted. Unfortunately, it was also a lot less populated. The last thing she needed was alone time with Beckett Tate.

"You think that's why he pulled the stunt in Houston?"

"Maybe." Oh, who the hell was she kidding? That was exactly why Judd had done it. Another ongoing move in a lifelong tit-for-tat. She dialed the combination and jerked the base down hard enough the metal door rattled. "No point in rehashing it though. Lesson learned—moving on."

Beckett leaned one shoulder against the locker next to hers. "And next time you call me."

"Yeah, that's not going to happen."

"Give me one good reason."

She tucked her gun case under one arm, draped her earplugs around her neck and hooked her eye gear on the collar of her tank. "I can give you several, but for starters, how about the shit you pulled on Saturday. Oh, and the fact that you hate family gigs. Especially kids."

He moved closer, the bass of his voice a low, delicious stroke against her skin. "You liked the shit I pulled on Saturday. Tell yourself different all you want, but I was there. We both liked it."

She slammed the locker door closed, clicked the lock back in place and stomped back toward the main viewing area, aiming a scowl at him on the way. "Would you leave it alone?"

"Hell, no I won't leave it alone." He caught her by the shoulder just before they hit the hallway and turned her to face him. Despite the intensity in his expression, he cupped the side of her neck with a lover's touch. Firm and commanding, yet giving, too. "I told you Saturday we were picking up where we left off. You think I'm persistent now, keep trying to put me off and see what it gets you."

A shudder moved through her, the mix of his words and the subtle glide of his thumb along her pulse point a one-two punch that derailed a good chunk of the good intentions she'd stockpiled the last few days. She pasted on what she hoped was a locker-room banter face and shot for a teasing tone, but it came out shakier than she liked. "A stalker?"

He chuckled at that. "Hey, at least I'm honest. Your problem is you don't want to admit you might like it." He released his hold on her neck and stepped back, shifting into casual mode as if he hadn't just sent her stomach on a roller-coaster ride. "I'll get you there though. I just need time and opportunity. And for the record, I'm great with kids. Ask Levi. He thinks Uncle Beck is the shit."

Gia took the space to hightail it back to the main viewing area and the rest of the spectators. "Ha! Indulging kids and guarding them are two different things."

"True," he said from right behind her. "But if you'd called me, I'd have had your back." When she found a decent place close to the front, he leaned down and murmured, "I'll always have your back."

God, that would be nice. And coming from Beckett, she had no doubt he'd back the claim up if she ever took him up on it. If she'd learned nothing else from him and the men he called brothers, it was that they never made a promise they couldn't keep. "I'll think about it."

He paused all of fifteen seconds, moved in next to her and made a show of checking out the newest contestant's performance. "While you're thinking on it, start wrapping your head around the next time we're together, too."

"Let it go, Beckett. Not going to happen."

"Yeah, it is. We'll go slow."

Whether or not he heard her low laugh over the gun-fire she couldn't be sure. "You forget, I've seen you with women. Slow isn't in your repertoire."

"Sure, it is. Go out with me and I'll prove I'm not what you think."

"No."

He cocked his head, gaze still trained on the range. "I'm thinking dinner. Tomorrow night."

"That's your version of slow?"

He shrugged. "It's a Friday night. I'm free. You're free."

She faced him full-on, visions of Knox hacking into her online accounts making her forget all about the fact that it was almost her turn to shoot. "How do you know I'm free?"

He grinned, the dirty edge to it enough to make a nun consider trading in her habit. "I didn't, but I'm pretty sure that reaction means you are."

The shooter finished and the range master's voice rang out through the room. "Gia Sinclair."

"Say yes," Beckett said before she could head to the door separating the two spaces.

"You're a pain in the ass, you know that?"

"So my brothers and their women tell me. Now say yes so you can go kick ass and picture my face on all the targets."

She shouldn't. Giving in was a bad idea on too many fronts to count. But her concentration had been crap since last Saturday. Maybe having dinner and getting him to see reason would at least put things to rest for both of them. "Dinner. And it's only so we can talk."

"Gia Sinclair?" The range master called again.

"Talk. Right." He squeezed her shoulder and gave her a smile she was pretty sure meant she'd just stepped into a tidy trap. "Go get 'em, gorgeous."

She managed a grunt and hustled to report in for her turn. So much for going into the first round fully focused. Although, she had to admit—the banter had helped her shake the anger she'd walked into the building with. Heck, she might actually be able to talk to Judd for a solid minute without killing him right about now.

Checked in with her unloaded gun and clip resting on the table in front of her, she put on her glasses and earplugs and waited for the previous shooter to exit the range.

"Load and make ready." The range master clicked the stopwatch.

Gia grabbed her gun, punched the clip into place and pulled back on the slide.

One second.

One heart-stopping, blurred second with the unexpected blast of gunfire filling the space around her.

The range master's voice rang out right behind it, punctuated by a whole lot of shuffling and shouts behind her. "Disarm."

Flipping the safety back into place the best she could with adrenaline firing out of control through her body, Gia dropped the clip and emptied the chamber.

She'd barely finished the task when the range master firmly pulled her gun from her grip and checked the chamber himself. "What the hell, Gia?"

What the hell, indeed. "I don't know what happened. You saw me, I barely even brushed the guard."

"Son of a bitch," a man bellowed behind her. "She almost took my head off."

Gia turned to see the lumberjack of a man who'd served as one of the contest staff out of his chair and poking his finger in a hole about three inches to the left of where his head had been.

The blood rushed out of her head and the rising voices around her took on a hollow sound. Everything around her got hazy. Everything except the gouge she'd left in the wall.

"Woman, that's a goddamn weapon, not a toy." The man's escalating tone and its growing proximity yanked her out of her stupor just in time to find him bearing down on her fast and furious. "Another inch or two and I'd be dead."

"Ricochet," someone else muttered beside her. "Must've kicked off the concrete just right."

She braced for a whole lot of in-your-face, but a giant hand hit the man square in the sternum and held him at arm's length. "She knows goddamn good and well what could've happened and could shoot your fucking nuts off without nicking your dick if she wanted. Now stand the fuck down."

Beckett.

Thank God.

The next thirty minutes went by in a haze. An accidental discharge disqualification. A ton of grumbling and ass-chewing from the lumberjack she'd nearly killed and more eyeballing and pointing from the viewing area than she'd wish on her worst enemy. Only once the range master had finished writing up the incident was she allowed to pack up her weapon and escape.

Through it all, Beckett stayed rock-solid beside her, a literal defensive wall whenever someone dared to get too close.

At the door to the locker room, he splayed his hand low on her back. "Take a deep breath, gorgeous. We'll get your shit, find someplace you can unwind and figure out what happened."

"What? You don't think I'm just a clumsy woman who wouldn't know a barrel from a stock?" The second the snide quip was out, she stopped in front of her locker, hung her head and pinched the bridge of her nose. "I'm sorry. You didn't deserve that. I just… I can't believe I did that."

Rather than answer right away, he smoothed his hand along the back of her neck, gripped her tight enough to turn her away from the wall of lockers and steered her into his arms. "Told you I'd have your back. If you need to take a few swings at someone—physical or verbal—I can take it."

Wrapping him up at the waist and simply melting into his strength was tempting. Hugely so with the lumberjack's condescending rant still ringing in her head. Instead she straightened and took a step back. "I'm just mad at myself. I should have checked the gun before I went in."

"They don't do warm-ups before a competition. And what's checking your gear got to do with an accidental discharge?" Beckett went scary still. "Something wrong with your gun?"

That was the thing. No matter how many times she replayed the incident in her head, she couldn't shake the idea that she'd accidentally brushed the trigger. She slid her stowed gun in the locker and sighed.

"Spill it, G. No one's more careful with a weapon than you. So, what happened?"

Gripping the locker door with one hand, she faced him. "I practice and do qualifications with this gun all the time."

"Yeah?"

"So, I know how it feels. How tight the trigger is."

His eyes narrowed, but he kept his silence.

With one more beat of hesitation, she shared the suspicion she hadn't been able to shake. "I'll swear when I guided my finger around the guard to ready my aim, I barely skimmed the trigger and it went off."

His gaze cut to the case in her locker then back to her. "You think someone messed with it?"

"Now, how the heck would anyone mess with it? I only use this one for practice and contest, so I keep it locked up here. More importantly, *why* would anyone want to mess it with?" She shook her head and slammed the locker door shut. "Had to be a malfunction. One I should've caught." She lifted the lock to slide it back in place. "I'll take it in and have it looked at."

Beckett caught her wrist before she could shove the lock home. "Give it to me."

"What? Why?"

He nudged her hand away and crowded in so he could grab the case himself. "'Cause I want to check it out."

She tried to wriggle her way back in and grab the case, but he just lifted it up and over her head. "Um, I just said I'd handle it."

"You got someone you trust to look at it?"

"Well, no. Not yet, but I will."

Beckett shrugged, tucked it under his arm and motioned for her to shut the door. "I already do. Trust me. I'll handle it. Besides, you've got more important things to do."

She closed the lock and glared at him. "Like what?"

He grinned, slung his arm around her shoulders and tucked her close to him. "Like gettin' ready for tomorrow night."

Chapter Six

"So, what's everyone's read on Ivan?"

Trevor's shift in topic from the construction of Axel's outdoor concert venue to bringing on a potential brother should have snagged Beckett's attention more than it did. Unless he was working out alone, driving or at home, his thoughts never strayed from the business at hand. Especially not at rally with his brothers. But for the last twenty-four hours, he'd been fixated on picking apart every second of Gia's incident. Well, that and hounding the hell out of the gunsmith he'd taken her piece to early this morning.

"Two years is a long time in the barrel," Zeke said from his place beside Trevor. "I haven't heard him grumble once and he's been rock-solid with what we've shared so far."

Next to Beckett, Knox rocked back on the rear legs of his chair, knees wide as he balanced it on his toes, and crossed his arms. "He's not gonna share further than us with anything. If that was gonna happen, he'd have spilled after Darya's deal."

"Could just be he's got a high respect for the Russian mob's version of containing information, though." Jace shifted his attention to Trevor. "Not knocking Ivan's character. Just sayin', he's smart enough to know that Sergei would plug his ass in a heartbeat if he so much as thought about what went down in the wrong company."

Trevor grinned, not the least bit offended. "Yeah, he knew who we were dealing with, but Knox is right. Ivan's solid. He could have helped the Feds and ratted me out with the thing we did for Nat, too, and he's been silent as the grave. I think it's time."

"Speakin' of silent as the grave," Axel said from his end of the table, "haven't heard a bloody word out of you since you came in."

It took a beat of silence and the weight of all his brothers' stares before Beckett realized the comment was aimed at him. He lifted his gaze from the distracted glare he'd had aimed at the massive conference table's scarred maple surface, sorely tempted to just offer up a bland comment to keep things moving.

But these were his brothers. Men who'd not only helped him make something of his life, but who stood behind him in everything. Hell, if he was honest, he *wanted* to talk about what was eating him. Needed their direction. It wasn't like he hadn't shared personal shit in the past. Yeah, it'd been weird as fuck sharing about his SPD, and he'd felt like a scared little two-year-old boy when his mom's abandonment had come up, but bringing Gia into the mix took things to a different level. One he hadn't entirely figured out how to process himself.

"Something happened yesterday," he said. "It's not sittin' right."

"And?" Axel volleyed back.

Just like that. Two simple sentences and he had every man's undivided attention. "Gia's big into marksmanship competitions. Does field events and timed accuracy gigs at least once a month."

Danny chuckled and grabbed his beer off the table. "Gia's big into anything that's a competition. Half the fun of hanging around her is watchin' the guys she whips up on walk away with their tail between their legs."

Every man around the table chuckled, but it was more about appreciation than the usual emotional bandage other men used to mask their insecurities. Then again, Gia had stepped up for them more than once and they'd seen her throw a man twice her size around. Hard for any of them not to hold her in high regard.

"It's the competition part that's bugging me," he said. At least he was pretty sure that was the crux of his worry. He'd also spent a crazy amount of time imagining what would happen if that bullet had somehow hurt her instead of ricocheting toward someone else. Every time that particular worst-case scenario had bubbled up, he'd had to fight back the urge to plant a fist in someone's head. "She had an accidental discharge when she was loading her gun. Hadn't even lifted it to take aim when it went off. The bullet ricocheted and hit the wall behind her just a few inches away from a scorekeeper's head."

Trevor frowned. "Not sure how that ties to competition being a worry."

"Because Gia's a practiced shooter and that gun is one she uses to compete on a regular basis. She knows the feel of it, and she swears her trigger was off."

"You think someone jacked with it?" Jace said.

"Well, it didn't get that way on its own sitting stored in her range locker." Beckett turned his attention on

Danny. "She was the only female on the lineup Thursday, and you should have heard the jackass she nearly hit. Popped every chauvinistic line you can think of before they let her leave the range." He scanned the rest of the men at the table. "Kind of makes me wonder if someone she's outmatched in the past wanted to dish out some humble pie in a public setting."

"So, get the gun checked," Axel said. "You're tight with Maury. He'd give it a once-over in a heartbeat for any of us."

"Already took it in. He said it'd take him until Monday to get to it."

"Hell, I can get an answer faster than that," Knox said. "All the ranges have security cameras these days. If I can get tapped in, we can tag someone getting in her locker."

Shit, he should have thought of that right off the bat. But then again, his processing had been laggy ever since Gia's drunken confession. "That'd work."

Zeke leaned forward and crossed his arms on the table, the casters on the funky orange, black and ivory kitchen chair he'd brought in from his parents' house in Philly waggling on the basement's unfinished concrete floor. "What's Gia think about all this?"

"You mean aside from kicking her own ass up one side and down the other?" Beckett shook his head. "Hard to call. Aside from admitting the trigger was off, she wouldn't talk about it."

"She's not suspicious?" Jace said. "That doesn't sound like Gia."

"Under normal circumstances, no. But Danny's not wrong. She's competitive as hell, so when something with that much crowd exposure goes south, she's bound to lick her wounds for a while."

"So, there's a bigger question here, no one's asking," Danny said with a sly grin. When everyone just looked at him with a blank stare, his grin turned into a smirk. "No one's askin' what Beckett was doin' at the range with Gia."

Knox chuckled and slouched a little deeper in his chair, the look of a man settling in for his favorite part in a movie. "He was also mighty adamant about being the one on puke patrol last weekend when Gia tied one too many on."

"Give it a fuckin' rest, Knox. I told you why I did that."

"Uh-huh. Something about a cock block. Which begs the question—why'd you interfere in the first place?"

"Come to think of it," Danny cut in before Beckett could answer, "the last time I saw the two of you together, Gia was pinned to the mat in the gym and you didn't look like you were in any hurry to let her tap out."

The quiet laughter from Zeke and Trevor across the table wasn't too bad—more two men commiserating with a man dredging through familiar territory than anything ridiculing. Jace popped a toothpick In his mouth and smiled, but it was Axel who dug to the heart of the matter. "Sounds like things are shiftin' between you and the lass."

The old familiar itch kicked in. A prickling beneath his skin that demanded attention and promised to derail his train of thought sooner rather than later if he didn't do something. He smoothed his hand along his jean-clad thigh, the well-worn surface not nearly enough input to level him out considering the scrutiny aimed his way, but enough to tide him over until their talk was over. Then he'd drag Danny to the gym over the garage and see if he couldn't grapple his way back to normal. "What if they were changing?"

How he admitted that much was a shock. One that was equally shared by everyone else in the room if their expressions were anything to go by.

"You know how this works," Jace said. "Anyone that's yours has every one of us at their back, too."

"Yeah, we're nowhere near that point. Not sure it can ever get to that point."

"Why the fuck not?" This from Axel who frowned liked he'd taken personal offense at the remark.

"Because our backgrounds couldn't be more different. She's educated. Comes from big money and an even bigger name in Atlanta. And, as far as I know, doesn't have any funky quirks that make her reliant on having a half a dozen psychological crutches in reaching distance."

"Backgrounds don't mean a damned thing," Jace said. "If it did, everyone around this table would either be slummin' it, in jail or dead. I may not know Gia like you do, but I can't imagine a woman like her would define a man by who his daddy is or what school he went to."

"And the last time a woman actually scored a trip to your bedroom, she came out grinnin' like she'd won the damned lottery," Knox said. "So, I'm thinking your tactile needs work to a woman's advantage."

"He's right," Axel said. "If you couldn't abide touch, I could see you having a concern, but you're the opposite. Women don't get that kind of physical attention in or out of the bedroom, so when they find it, they're usually all over it."

Yeah, that was the reason he seldom let things go too far with women he dated. Or at least one of the reasons. The last thing he wanted was for any of them to think his need for touch had to be sexual and the misconception was too easy to draw with the way he responded to it. The other reason he'd buried so damned deep he didn't dare try to unearth the skeleton.

The thought jabbed a little too deep. He shook it off and frowned at the lot of them. "Y'all need to let this shit go. We're havin' dinner. Nothin' else."

"So, *that's* why you hit the grocery store this morning." Knox swept the table with a wry smirk. "I can count on one hand the number of times he's been to the grocery store this year, but today I busted him unloading a ton of fancy ingredients before noon."

"Mmm." Zeke nodded and lifted his Bohemia Weiss in mock salute. "The domestic play. Doesn't sound like *nothin'* to me."

"You sure you cooking is a good idea?" Trevor said. "I've never seen you operate anything outside a microwave."

"Believe it or not," Knox said, "he actually can. He's just normally too hungry to spend time doing it."

Beckett grunted and slouched deeper in his chair, dropping his head back to glare up at the ceiling. The gray wool covering the old slip chair was insanely soft and worn, but the chair itself was sturdy as hell, perfect for his big frame. "Yeah, well, it's probably wasted effort. She only agreed so she could talk me out of anything else."

"Then shift the focus and don't take no for an answer," Jace said.

"This is Gia we're talking about. She's got more stubborn in her than the bunch of us rolled together."

"Because she has to be," Axel said. "She's a strong, independent woman fightin' to make her way in an industry with few women. There's no room for her to let her guard down. No safe place for her to be anything other than tough as nails."

Beckett lifted his head and locked gazes with Axel, the insight resonating with a certainty he hadn't felt in days.

"Be her safe place," Jace added as though he'd zeroed in on Beckett's thoughts.

"How?"

Jace shrugged and slowly rotated his Scotch on the table's surface. "Show her you're not going anywhere. Have her back the way you did last night. Might take a while, but slow and steady wins the race."

Axel's chuckle was about as wicked and dirty as they came. "You could do it that way." He sipped his Scotch and eyeballed Beckett over the rim. "If it was me, I'd just tie the lass down and work her until she's too sated to say anything but yes."

Beckett shuttled his attention to Jace. Slow and steady? He'd accomplished a lot in his life, but none of it had happened as a result of patience. Hell, any epitaph carved in his headstone would likely have reference to tanks or pit bulls.

He zeroed in on Axel. "You got any rope stashed in that toy closet of yours?"

Axel's quick smile showed a whole lot of teeth. "Now we're talkin'."

Chapter Seven

It was a night of firsts, and so far, none of them were comfortable. Gia shifted in the bucket seat of Beckett's refurbished 1970 Corvette, tucking the loose sundress she'd foolishly worn closer to her thigh. Not having a clue what Beckett had in mind for tonight, she'd thought going with the snappy black and turquoise dress with its thin straps and flowing hem would make for flexible attire no matter where they went. Then she'd opened the door to Beckett and been on the receiving end of a leisurely once-over that promptly reminded her he'd never seen her in anything but pants.

That had been "first" number one. Or first number two if you counted her breaking her no-fraternization policy to begin with. First number three was the awkward silence filling the car's interior. In all the time she'd known him, she'd never once had to scramble for something to say, but tonight her brain coughed up a big fat conversational zero.

Beckett glanced over his right shoulder and shifted to the exit lane. He drove with the same smooth efficiency as when he fought. No move was wasted, but those he initiated were beautiful to watch.

He downshifted and took the exit.

For some stupid reason, her attention kept shifting back to his big hand on the gearshift. Remembering the feel of them around her wrists was all too easy. As if he had burned the impression onto her skin and no amount of showers or wishful thinking could will the lingering touch away.

"I could be wrong on this," Beckett said, not taking his eyes off the road, "but breathing might go a long way to you unwinding and actually enjoying yourself."

Per usual with Beckett, it was exactly the right thing to say. She huffed out a shaky chuckle and rubbed her palms atop her thighs. "I don't know how to do this."

"Ride in a car? Eat?"

The irritated scowl she shot him was familiar at least. "You know what I mean."

"Dating. Right. That's tricky stuff." He nodded and took a right she hadn't expected.

Come to think of it, she wasn't aware of any restaurants in this part of town. The southwest stretch of Downtown Dallas was more centered toward urban living in repurposed industrial buildings than entertainment. "We're not dating. I only agreed to this to help you see reason."

Right, Gia. That's why you spent two hours standing dumbfounded in your closet and twice the usual time getting ready.

She twisted to study the cross street they'd just passed and the reality of where they were headed finally clicked. "Where are we going?"

Just as she faced forward again, he whipped into a parking garage beneath a redbrick building that spanned the whole block. "Where's it look like we're going?"

"I thought we were going to a restaurant. Not your loft."

He shrugged right before he whipped into his reserved spot. There were other spaces marked Reserved all around it, but every one of them was empty.

She scowled up at him. "Are Knox and Darya here?"

"Absolutely not. They're spending the weekend at Haven and staying the hell out of my hair." He killed the engine and yanked the emergency brake. "Now sit tight and let me get your door."

Alone.

With Beckett.

At his freaking house.

Or loft.

Whatever she called it didn't make a difference. There was only one reason he'd bring her here and it was the exact opposite of what needed to happen.

The sharp chunk of her door handle filled the car's interior a second before the door swung open. She always had to crane her head a decent amount to meet Beckett's eyes when she was standing close to him, but seated in the low-slung seat with him towering uncomfortably close and his hand outstretched, he was a damned giant. "Take me home."

He frowned and planted the hand he'd offered her on the black convertible top, the other braced on the passenger's window. "Now why the hell would I do that? We just got here."

"Because you said dinner. I thought you meant someplace public where we could talk. Where I could be honest with you and help you understand all the reasons why us being anything more than business partners is a bad idea." The fact that she'd entertained a host of other outcomes was beside the point.

For a second, he just stood there, a look she couldn't quite translate moving across his hard features. He crouched beside her and rested his elbows on his knees. "Whatever you've got to say, I'll listen, but I'll tell you up front, I've got my arguments and I plan to share them."

He paused a beat, fisted his hand as if fighting an action he was hesitant to take, then carefully splayed his hand just above her knee. "This is going to happen, Gia. I won't rush it. Won't take you anywhere you're not ready to go, but I'm also not gonna treat you like some stranger I gotta go through some bullshit routine with. Whatever ideas you've got of me when it comes to women, they're pretty damned shallow, and to fight it I'm gonna have to actually talk to you. I'd rather do that in my place where I can actually hear what you're saying, feed you food I made with my own hands and not have strangers interrupting us every five seconds."

So much information. So much sincerity. But the way his thumb shuttled back and forth over the soft fabric along her thigh, her brain was having a hard time properly processing the words or the emotion. All she could focus on was the confident weight of his touch, the warmth soaking through to her skin and the delicious anticipation of feeling more. "You cooked for me?"

His quick smile stirred a host of flutters in her belly. "Homemade gumbo, good old-fashioned Cajun potato salad and French bread."

No way. Picturing Beckett at home in a kitchen wouldn't compute any more than she could picture herself in one. "And you picked it up from somewhere and warmed it up?"

"Nope. Every single bit from scratch." The hand on her thigh moved higher, leaving ripples in its wake until he covered her fisted hand with his and squeezed. "Come inside with me."

She shouldn't. Common sense all but demanded she refuse and keep her butt in the car until he agreed to take her home, but God, his touch felt good. And while she'd gone out with her share of men, not once had a date actually cooked for her. To see Beckett in a kitchen? To have another few hours of him looking at her like he was right now—steady and totally focused like she was the only human in existence? Surely the risk was worth it. "You'll bring me home when I ask you to?"

"*If* you ask me to, sure."

"You're awfully sure of yourself."

He used his grip to turn her hand, ran his thumb along her pulse point and then dragged it lower to her palm. "Cocky. Confident. Determined. Call it whatever you want, but a man like me doesn't get a taste of a woman like you and walk away without exploring more." He laced his fingers with hers, stood and urged her from the car. "Now pry your amazing ass out of my car so I can get you inside and start working on dessert."

The trip inside ran thick with an awkwardness she hadn't felt since her first date as a senior in high school. Sure, she'd been to the home he shared with Knox a few times before, but those trips had been with Darya by her side. This time it was an entirely different experience. An exploration into the private confines of a man she'd thought she'd known pretty well, but was beginning to realize she'd only scratched the surface. The décor was a tasteful mix of raw masculinity and urban style complete with exposed brick walls, a state-of-the-art kitchen, and dark stained wood beams. The concrete floors were plain gray and finished with a high shine, but thick, shaggy rugs in deep gray, cornflower blue and chocolate made them seem more welcoming.

The industrial metal door slammed shut behind them a second before Beckett splayed his hand low on her back. "You hungry?"

Not letting her eyes drift shut or leaning into him for more contact took everything in her. Her stomach answered for her, growling at the scent of spices and simmering sausage that filled the sprawling space. "It smells amazing."

"Don't sound so shocked." He chuckled and guided her toward the massive island, motioning to the concrete surface and the dark wood stools surrounding one side. "Take a load off while I get the stuff out for dessert."

"Hard not to be shocked. You with firearms and throwing someone on the floor, I can picture pretty easy. You in an apron is something else altogether."

"Yeah, no apron. Not for cooking anyway." He jerked open one side of the industrial-sized stainless-steel fridge, pulled out a clear plastic bowl that had something orange inside and stacked what looked like dough wrapped in cellophane on top of it. "Now if you've got some kitchen fantasy you want to share, I might consider it."

Nope. No talk of fantasies. Not now. Not ever. She sidestepped the topic and dipped her head toward the bottles of nutmeg and vanilla he added to the growing ingredients. "So, what's for dessert?"

He pulled two measuring cups out from under one of the cabinets, added them to the pile and turned for the canisters lined up along the back kitchen counter-tops. "Peach pecan cobbler."

Her breath hitched and she swore time did a mini-freeze-frame while her brain scrambled to connect the dots. "I love peach pecan cobbler."

He turned, slid two of the canisters onto the island and met her stare head-on. "I know."

That hole-in-the-wall diner in Richardson. It'd been maybe a month or two at most after they'd met on a job and she couldn't have remembered the name of the place to save her life, but they'd had peach pecan cobbler on the menu. She'd seen it and ordered it for a main course. "You remembered that?"

"I remember just about everything where you're concerned." He placed a big high-end Dutch oven her momma would have salivated over onto the stove then crooked a finger at her. "Now get over here. I'm puttin' you to work."

"Oh, that's a bad idea."

He cocked an eyebrow and pried the lid off the plastic bowl he'd pilfered from the fridge.

"I'm worthless in a kitchen. Always have been. Much to my mom's disappointment."

His easy smile moved over her like warm honey. "Nice try, gorgeous. You're still helpin'." He tipped the bowl and fresh peeled peaches spilled into the pan. Jerking his head toward the wrapped dough, he fired up the gas burner. "If you can take a man down, you can roll dough. Doesn't have to be pretty."

The rolling pin sat beside the dough, the glow from the pendent lights overhead reflected off the shiny surface, taunting her. Surely she could handle rolling dough. And it was cobbler. Not some epicurean entry in a county fair.

Quiet settled as she made her way to his side of the counter and peeled the plastic wrap away with clumsy fingers. "Your mom must be pretty proud of the fact you can cook."

For just a beat, Beckett hesitated in adding sugar to the mix. "My mom didn't teach me." Another pause, this one weighted as though considering his words. "She left when I was two."

It should have been weird. Or at least embarrassing given she'd obviously stumbled on a sore spot. But somehow the information eased her own discomfort. Like he'd shared a piece of his past to level the playing field.

Or to prove he'd meant what he'd said.

Whatever ideas you've got of me when it comes to women, they're pretty damned shallow.

More than anything, she wanted to dive deeper. To open the door a little wider to the past he'd offered and hear more about how he'd grown up. She focused on the chilled dough in front of her instead and put her weight into kneading it. "Then who taught you to cook?"

"A Cajun lady who lived next door to me and my dad." He glanced at her, but never broke from stirring the mix in his pan. "Dad wasn't around much, so Knox and I spent a lot of time at her place. She put us to work."

That's right. She'd known he and Knox had been friends when they were kids. She just didn't realize it had gone so far back. "What did your dad do?"

The scoff that slipped free was pure disgust. "Not much."

She paused mid-squeeze and looked at him. "I'm sorry. I didn't mean to pry."

He stared at the pan's contents. "You interested in getting to know about me?"

She was. More so than she cared to admit. "Yes."

His gaze cut to hers and the intensity behind his blue eyes burned hot as the flame on the stove. "Ever consider *why* you want to get to know more about me?"

Because to her he was larger than life. Because she'd wondered what events had formed the man she'd watched from a distance for years.

Because he was Beckett.

"I'm curious by nature?" she answered instead.

The grin he gave her should have warned her to run, but she stayed rooted in place like one of those idiots in a classic horror flick and watched as he lowered the flame to simmer. "Not buying that one."

Instincts prickling that it was time for a speedy retreat, she centered the now pliant dough in the center of the space she'd cleared, grabbed the rolling pin like it was a weapon and prepared to roll.

She felt more than saw him move closer, the sheer power of his presence moving over her in a commanding claim. His heat and hard body blanketed her back a second before his arms came around either side of her and stilled her hands on the rolling pin. "Wanna know what I think?"

He could think? Because she sure as hell couldn't. Not with his deep voice whipping to life long-ignored needs and desires.

He set the pin aside, picked the dough up with one

hand and sprinkled a healthy amount of flour in the spot
where it had been. Every move was casual and yet thick
with an understated sensuality that had her heart thump-
ing a demanding rhythm. He placed the dough back in
the center, put the pin back in her hands then braced
his own on the counter, caging her. His lips grazed her
cheek when he spoke. "I think you want to know more
about who I am because—deep down where you're too
afraid to look—you want more than just business."

She couldn't move. Didn't want to. Didn't even want
to talk for fear of losing the delicious sensations dancing beneath her skin. "I'm not afraid."

"Yes, you are. Afraid to let that armor of yours down
and just be a woman. But I promise you, Gia. You're
safe with me. Nothing between us goes further than us.
No matter what happens."

Safe.

The simple word resonated deep, shoving reason off
the shelf and jetting dangerous cracks through years
and years of fortified defenses. As temptations went,
it was the one with the most teeth. A man might have
confidence and intelligence in spades, and chemistry
could be through the roof, but without trust none of it
was worth a damn. Her mom and dad were living proof
of what happened without it.

She forced herself into motion and pressed the pin
into the dough. "What do you have to drink?"

The shift in topic was a chicken move, and the way
Beckett hesitated before answering said he knew it, too.
Still, he straightened, gently cupped one shoulder as if
to let her know he understood, then moved toward the
fridge. "I picked up some chardonnay this morning.
That work for you?"

"You're a wine drinker?"

Beckett barked out a sharp laugh, all the intensity of the moment they'd left behind replaced with his normal casualness. "Hell, no." He set the bottle on the counter and dug through a drawer full of all kinds of utensils. "You had a ton of the stuff racked up in your kitchen though, so I grabbed a few while I was getting groceries this morning."

Observant and considerate. Two more ticks in the plus column. She glanced at the bottle. Not surprisingly, it was the brand she kept the most of at home. Her favorite.

He paused and looked at her, wine opener in hand.

She met his gaze and the crack in the wall wound a little deeper. "Thank you."

Chapter Eight

Of all the outcomes for tonight Gia had anticipated, ending it sated on amazing food, barefoot, relaxed and kicked back on an oversized sectional with a glass of wine in hand hadn't been one of them. She rolled to her side for a better view of Beckett finishing cleanup detail and propped her elbow on the back of the couch. "I really wouldn't have minded helping. I'm better with washing dishes than I am cooking."

He tossed his kitchen towel onto the island, snagged her nearly empty bottle of wine and strolled her direction. "You feel good?"

"I feel great." How could she not? For two hours they'd had nothing but easy conversation, peppered with more and more evidence that there was more to Beckett Tate than she'd thought. He'd always listened to her when she'd talked before, but tonight she'd had his full attention. As if the restraints he'd kept bound around their interactions had been obliterated by her drunken admission.

He topped off her wine and set the empty bottle on the sofa table behind them. "Then I'm not going to jack that up by putting you to work." He sat roughly an arm's length away and motioned for her to shift on the couch. "Sit back and put your feet up."

"Why?"

"I fed you. Humor me and don't ask questions."

A cautionary prickle sparked along her neck and shoulders, and her stomach muscles tightened.

You're safe with me.

Was she? Really? Sure, he'd proven he'd support her as a colleague and a friend. If not by his actions getting her home when she was drunk as a skunk, then by standing by her at the range and keeping those determined to ride her ass at bay. But her instincts insisted this was something more. Something with far more potential risk.

He waited and watched, his stare steady and patient.

You want more than just business.

His words hit her as hard the second time as they had when he'd spoken them. And he was right. Would it be so bad to risk just this once? To test the waters and see what happened?

She shifted the way he'd indicated, resting her back against the arm of the couch and stretching her feet out in front of her.

His expression shifted, the warmth behind his eyes and the softening of his features denoting both pleasure and approval. And damned if that didn't suck her in even deeper, lulling her like a tender stroke along her spine.

Holding her gaze, he slid forward, lifting her feet as he went and letting them rest in his lap. "That wasn't so hard, was it?"

Hard? No, that hadn't been hard at all. Not in comparison to holding back the moan that crept up her throat when he cupped the outside of each foot and dragged his thumbs along each arch. God, the heat alone was enough to make her melt. Never mind the perfect pressure he employed along with it.

Her eyes slipped closed of their own accord and she scrunched down further on the couch, resting her head on the thick armrest. "You're really good at that."

He said nothing, but his practiced strokes never faltered.

Now that she thought of it, he'd touched her a lot since that night when he'd taken her home. Never anything inappropriate, but more subtle contact. A reassurance here, or a comforting connection there. "Beckett?"

"Hmmm?"

"You asked me about what my life was like growing up."

"Yeah."

"And I told you." Probably more than she should have really, but the wine and the food had loosened her tongue more than she'd intended. From her family's elite neighborhood and her father's social connections, to how her relationship with her parents had begun to unravel her senior year when she refused to follow the path her parents wanted. The only thing she hadn't delved into was her father's string of indiscretions and her mother's inability or unwillingness to stand up for herself. "Tell me about you."

Silence.

She forced her eyes open.

Attention trained solely on her feet, he seemed totally absorbed in his task, but his features had sharpened. Where he'd seemed calm and unhurried before, now his lips were firmer and the pressure from his fingertips deepened.

"Beckett?"

His gaze lifted to hers. "It wasn't anything like yours."

Between the few snippets she'd garnered over dinner as to how he'd met Knox and the abrupt way he'd stated his mother left when he was two, she'd guessed as much. "It doesn't matter what it was like. It matters that it was yours." She probably shouldn't push. Shouldn't poke in the dark spaces he didn't offer willingly, but the hunger to know more about him—the real him—prodded her to say more. "You want me to trust. It's a two-way street."

He held her stare, a rawness she'd never expected to see on full display behind his beautiful blue eyes. "My mom left me when I was two."

Left *him*. Not that she'd just left, or left his dad. But him. An innocent two-year-old boy. "What happened?"

He lowered his gaze and moved both hands to one foot, giving it his full attention. "I was a tough baby to deal with. At least that's what my dad said. Special needs."

"Special needs, how?"

His touch lightened just a fraction and one hand slid higher, slowly caressing the back of her calf before circling up and back down her shin to the top of her foot. The touch was amazing. Sensual and thick with a connectedness she couldn't figure out. But there was a desperation to it, too. "Needy. Cried a lot. Didn't sleep much either."

"Sounds like half the infant population to me." The words hopped out without censure, fueled by a punch of anger that fired out of nowhere. "Not everyone gets an easy baby to raise. Heck, I'd bet most of the parents you talk to would say their kids were a struggle in the early years. Dealing with it is part of being a parent."

A self-deprecating grin curled his lips and he switched to the other foot. "Yeah, well, she wasn't planning on being a parent to begin with, so..." He shrugged and grew silent. Thoughtful. He pulled in a slow, bracing breath. "I wasn't much better growing up. Fought a lot. Chased girls like crazy once I got older. Pissed a bunch of dads off. Fought a lot more. A school counselor had enough of the fights my sophomore year and threatened me with expulsion if I didn't meet with a therapist."

"What did you do?"

He huffed out a sharp chuckle. "I might have been a bruiser, but I wasn't stupid. My dad never had decent jobs because he was a dropout. So, I met the therapist."

"And?"

His hands stilled, but his fingers tightened. Braced. "He said I've got SPD. Sensory Processing Disorder."

"I don't know what that means."

"Yeah, I'm not sure anyone really does." He pulled his hands away, resting one elbow on the couch back and fisting the other on his thigh. As though the last thing he wanted was to break contact. "You ask me, it's a hodgepodge catchall for anything to do with senses. Some people can't stand strong perfumes or odd smells. Some people can't stand the way certain things feel or being where there's too much noise. Has to do with the way your brain processes input."

It couldn't be sense of smell. She'd seen him in too many environments where that would've put him over

the top. The same for loud places. And from the second she'd woken up after her drunken confession, he'd
been very hands-on. Heck, he was always touchy-feely
with his dates and they were always the same with him.
So much so she'd been tempted to break a few wrists
over the years.

He opened his hand and rubbed it along his jean-
clad leg.

Back and forth. Back and forth.

Her gaze drifted to his T-shirt. Soft. Always soft.
And she'd often seen him rubbing his hand across his
stomach, an act she'd always thought meant he was either terminally hungry, or just had an odd tic for when
he mulled things over in his head. "This processing
thing. Does it work in the opposite?"

Bingo. The answer was right there in his eyes the
second her question met air. "No touch for a long time
makes me bat-shit crazy. Like someone's piping electricity under my skin. Gets worse when I'm agitated
about something. But I've figured out ways to deal.
Soft stuff. Massages. Wrestling."

"Fists," she added, but just barely clamped her mouth
shut before she added, *Touchy-feely women*. She pulled
her feet out of his lap and shifted closer to him. "Beckett, I don't know your mom. I couldn't pick her out of
a lineup if I had to, but I *can* tell you her leaving isn't
on you or the fact that you need touch. It was pure self-
ishness and irresponsibility. Nothing more and nothing less."

His gaze stayed rooted to the ottoman in front of
them.

Instinct more than wisdom lifted her hand to his face.
You couldn't say he had a beard. More like perpetual

morning-after stubble. But on him it was sexy as hell. It tickled her fingertips as she traced his harsh jawline.

He snatched her wrist, stilling her with a firm grip. "I'm not a freak."

Four words, but the pain and humiliation in them sunk jagged claws inside her. Snagged on emotions and struggles she understood all too well. Granted, her demons were completely different and nowhere near as stigmatizing as his would have been growing up, but they were still demons. Ugly, unforgiving monsters that kept her bound into a prison of her own making.

"I don't think you're a freak." She swallowed hard and twisted her wrist until he loosened his hold. Even then, he still hung on. "I think you're just like the rest of us. Doing your best to reach for what you want and shouldering whatever challenges you end up with."

This time when she touched him, her fingers trembled, the enormity of what he'd just shared—of the ridicule it could earn him with the type of people they worked with—forging something she didn't dare study too closely. "Thank you for sharing with me."

His gaze dropped to her mouth.

Her heart lurched, so eager for the heated promise behind his eyes it didn't care if it killed her with its exuberance.

"You wanted my trust. I just gave it to you." He cupped the side of her face, his thumb skimming along her lower lip. "No one knows what I just told you. No one but my family."

And by family, he meant Haven. She'd been around his brothers, their women and Axel's and Jace's mothers enough to know they were everything Beckett's parents hadn't been. Everything she'd wished she'd had in her own family. "And no one will ever hear it from me. Ever."

He lowered his head. His warm breath whispered over her skin and the space between them coiled as tight as a trigger just before release.

A muted chime broke the silence.

Beckett hesitated, his grip tightening a fraction. "Knox has shit timing."

She chuckled, a low but sharp sound that blossomed to full-blown laughter the more her brain reengaged and pointed out the hilarity of the situation. "You know it's Knox by the tone?"

Beckett grunted and lifted his head, but rather than go for his phone like she'd anticipated, he hauled her across the few inches that separated them and firmly planted her sideways on his lap. "Don't knock it. Defined tones tell me who to ignore and who to answer without looking. He'd never mess with me tonight with you here. Not unless it was important."

He shifted and reached for his phone in his back pocket, tucking her tight to him as he did.

She should tease him. Something along the lines of where he drew the line on who to ignore and how many ringtones it took to set up his audible priority system, but her mouth wouldn't work. There was too much closeness. Too much muscle. Too much Beckett.

Wait.

He'd never mess with me tonight with you here.

"Knox knows I'm here?"

He frowned at the screen. "Course, he knows." He paused only long enough to glance at her then went back to scrolling through the text. "All my brothers know."

Part of her wanted to rail at the information. To move

into damage control and insist he put a cap on tonight being shared further than it already had been. But another, far more vulnerable part of her, gloried in it. As if in brushing the edges of his family—even if only in conversation—she'd been included in the tight-knit group.

His frown shifted to barely suppressed fury and the arm he had banded around her waist squeezed tighter.

"Beckett?"

At the bottom of the text was a link. Before she could angle for a decent view of the bolded header, he lowered the phone and studied her. "Gorgeous, we gotta talk."

All the warmth and anticipation he'd built in her through the night fizzled like slow-encroaching waters on smoldering embers. That voice didn't spell anything near the realm of conversation. More a precursor to one of those ugly info bombs that rattled reality. "What's wrong?"

His lips flattened, obviously bitter words squatting on his tongue. "The thing at the range yesterday…someone got a clip of it."

No, not a bomb. More of a shotgun being chambered and aimed directly at her. Being a woman, she already had to fight twice as hard to shore up gigs on her own. Negative social media would kill her. She held out her hand, demanding the phone without saying a word. "Where's it posted?"

He handed it over, but looked like he'd rather take a knife to the gut. "YouTube. It hit about three hours ago. Knox got an alert."

Hitting the play button, she tried to stand.

Beckett clamped down hard and held her in place.

"You're not going anywhere. If you're watchin' it, we're doin' it together."

Distorted crowd noises punched from the speaker followed by the all-too-clear mention of her full name for the spectators.

She wanted to argue. Wanted to take the damned phone and lock herself away someplace private. Someplace where she could pace and fume and maybe hit a few inanimate objects for good measure.

"Load and make ready."

The range master's cue sucked her into the carnage. The discharge. The scrambling crowd. The shouts and subsequent outrage. But worst were the clips of her, stoic to the point she came across uncaring.

"That's not raw footage." Beckett's voice rumbled with an anger that mirrored her own, a threat of barely contained violence. "That's heavily edited."

"I know what it is." The sharp quip was the last thing he deserved, but she could no more contain it than she could calm the adrenaline jetting through her body. She shoved the hand he'd anchored her in place with off her hip and scrambled to her feet, heading toward the kitchen. "It's also going to tank my business."

Beckett followed her. "It's a shooting competition on YouTube, G. Not a reference database. No one out to hire security is going to pay attention to that."

"That's bullshit and you know it." She set his phone aside on the kitchen island, snatched her purse and dug for her own phone. "Our business is all about reputation. Hard to have credibility when there's evidence on the Internet I don't know how to handle a gun."

"What are you doing?"

Too hopped up on outrage, she spoke without thinking. "Calling a cab. I need to get on this."

Two seconds at most and her purse was back on the counter, her phone tossed on top of it and her back firmly pressed against the island. Beckett caged her with arms on either side and leaned in close, a modern-day dragon breathing fire and ready to stake its claim. "You're not going anywhere."

On another day it would have been sexy as hell. Every dominant dream come to life. Tonight, it just pissed her off. "Don't fuck with me, Beckett. If I want to go, I'll go."

"You're not *going* anywhere. You're running."

The barb stung, hitting a little too close to home, but she rolled to her tiptoes and got nose-to-nose as best she could. "I'm taking care of my business. It's called damage control and you'd do the exact same thing."

"Knox already is."

She opened her mouth, waited for a fresh retort to jettison free, then snapped it shut. "What?"

Pure male smugness tilted his lips. "He's already tracking the source and getting it taken down."

"Knox can't hack Google."

"Knox doesn't have to. He's got friends. He'll know the source and have it down before you get your panties unwound."

He could've let the fire die down. Could have used the information to divert the conversation back to steady ground, but noooo. He had to go and play the woman card. She gripped his wrists, making sure he felt her nails as she squeezed. "You really don't have a very strong sense of self-preservation, do you?"

His blue eyes lit with pure anticipation. "Either that,

or I've got a keen sense you want to take a strip out of someone's hide and need an outlet."

"And you're volunteering?"

He grinned, quick and dirty. "Try not to break anything."

Decency and good judgment tried to rein her in, but it was too late. She was already in motion. Punches fueled by anger. Dodges fueled by fear. Grunts and accusations charged with years of frustration and loneliness.

Beckett matched every one of them, blocking and meeting her need for outlet.

But there was no offense. Only careful defense and clever guidance that kept them contained in the loft's most open space. As soon as the two embarrassing facts clicked into place, she disengaged, her breaths coming even more haggard than she probably looked. What the hell had gotten into her? Fighting? In his loft? And she was in a dress for crying out loud. Could she be any more of an idiot?

She shoved her hair out of her face and stomped to her purse, embarrassment lighting a flash fire across her cheeks. "I'm going home."

Beckett's hand clamped around her wrist before she'd made it a third of the way to the island. He spun her, dipped and hauled her over his shoulder like a sack of potatoes.

"Beckett!" She tried to lever herself upright, but with him in control of how she was balanced on his shoulder and using it to his advantage, she couldn't stay upright. "Put me down. I need to go."

"Yeah, that's not going to happen."

Even if she'd been more familiar with the other unexplored parts of the loft, she couldn't have seen where he was headed. Not with her loose hair blinding her to anything but his ass and his bare feet on the concrete floor.

Humiliation, as cold and unforgiving as the blood rushing to her head, slammed into her. She'd never live this down. Not any more than she'd get past the discharge and the fallout from social media.

For a second, she gave up. Simply let the ugly reality of the moment lug her along the way her dead weight hung on Beckett's shoulder.

Then she was up and moving through the air, dimmed lights and neutral earth colors blurring past her swirling perspective. Beckett's hand cupped her head a second before the rest of her *whooshed* into a thick, welcoming mattress.

Beckett loomed over her, one hand holding him propped in place, his wide shoulders blocking out the source of the soft glow behind him and his knees anchored on either side of hers. "You gonna stay put on your own, or do I need rope to make that happen?"

"You wouldn't."

He cocked an eyebrow.

Okay, so he probably would. Who could blame him, though? She'd acted like a complete loon and gone apeshit in his house. She swallowed hard and forced herself to meet his slightly amused gaze. "I'll stay put long enough to apologize. I shouldn't have lost it like that, I just…"

He waited, no judgment whatsoever on his face.

"I'm not like most women."

His lips twitched. "I think I got that a long time ago."

She exhaled hard and shifted her gaze to the ceiling. "No, I mean, when I get mad I need an outlet. Some girls cry. Some girls go shopping."

"You need something physical," Beckett finished for her. He shifted his weight and stretched out beside her, his big body pressed tight to hers and one leg comfortably resting between hers. "Just told you not fifteen minutes ago that I can't go a single day without some kind of touch to ground me. You really think I'm going to judge you because someone posted something you took seriously and you wanted to let off a little steam?"

"I did it in your house."

"This place is huge. Lotsa room where you're safe and with someone who could take it."

There it was again. So tempting to believe. She focused on his sternum and the indistinct outline of the dog tags he always wore beneath his soft cotton tee. "I'm embarrassed." Admitting it out loud was twice as bad as losing control.

"You're missing something here, gorgeous." He slipped his hand out from under her head and cupped the side of her face, forcing her attention to his. "I *like* who you are. You're smart. You're tough. You don't take my shit. I've got height and weight on you and you still aren't afraid of me. I can talk guns, computers or criminal jargon and not lose you in the conversation."

"You can't talk food with me."

He grinned and pressed his thumb to her lips. "Don't need you to talk food with me. Just need you to eat what I cook."

She couldn't help it. Her mouth parted and her tongue slipped out for a quick taste.

His eyes heated, a languid panther who'd just perked to the promise of a tasty treat. "Gia?"

God, she could look at him like this for hours. Days if she could get away with it. "Mmm?"

"You got anything else you need to get off your chest?"

Nothing he hadn't already figured out. Namely that she was terrified of failing in her chosen profession, and that he was right. She *was* afraid. Polarized by how she wanted things to go between them and the risks that came with it. "No."

"Good." His gaze dropped to her mouth and the hand at the side of her face shifted to the back of her head, his fingers spearing through her hair and holding her in place. "Then it's time we both get our fix."

He claimed her mouth. A head-on attack that robbed her breath and left every self-defense stunned and helpless.

And holy hell, could Beckett *kiss*. Deep, long and without mercy. His tongue dueled with hers. Demanded its due even as his slick lips teased and glided against hers. Not a prelude to something bigger and better. Not a requisite step on a predetermined path, but a glorious event all on its own.

She smoothed her hands up along his triceps and over his shoulders, the powerful heat and strength beneath her hands ripping a moan up the back of her throat. So long, she'd wanted to touch him like this. To explore and roam without limit. She stroked higher, dragging her palms along the tightly cropped hair at the base of his skull and further to spear her fingertips through the longer strands on top.

"Damn, baby." Beckett lifted his head, eyes closed, and arched his neck, seeking more of her touch. "You keep petting me like that and I'll be the pushy tomcat who won't leave your front stoop."

Fascinated with his response, she gently raked her

nails along his scalp then trailed a path down the back of his neck. "I thought cats only hung around if you gave them milk."

He opened his eyes, but it wasn't an innocent tomcat staring back at her. It was a predator. One tethered by a strained and threadbare leash. "It's not milk I want."

Her sex clenched. A fluttering fist and release that said her body was on board with anything he wanted so long as it ended with the feel of him inside her.

He lowered his head, holding her gaze as he licked her lower lip.

"Beckett."

His eyes slid closed and he skimmed his mouth up along her jawline. "Mmm?"

"This is dangerous."

He nipped her earlobe hard enough she jolted under him.

"Beckett, be serious."

Chuckling, he nuzzled the sweet spot just behind her ear. "You pack a gun when you go to work and you put yourself between strangers and bullets all the damned time." He kissed a trail down the line of her neck and caressed the curve of her hip. "This isn't dangerous." Further down he worked, skimming his lips along the neckline of her sundress and teasing her pebbled flesh. "This is off the charts fan-fucking-tastic begging to happen." He lifted his head. "Say yes."

God, she wanted to. So bad. She smoothed her hands across his pecs, down and around his lats, then high on his back, the light whisper of her nails against the cotton loud in the otherwise quiet room.

He groaned and rolled his shoulders, stretching back

for more of her touch. "Please, God, say that's your way of giving me the go-ahead."

I like *who you are.*

You're safe with me.

She was. Always had been. In that second, the truth stood spotlighted bold and beautiful in front of her. He'd shown her who he was. Not the facade he kept in place for the people they worked with. Not the player all the other guys thought he was, but the real man. The one he was with his family. Opened up and shared his secrets. "You never were good at subtle."

His blue eyes flashed, aggression and caution warring behind his narrowed gaze. "Yeah?" He shifted higher, giving her more of his weight and pressing his hard cock firm against her clit. "Since when do you like subtle?"

Her breath hitched and her hips flexed against his on instinct. "Outside of talking to my momma, never." She arched her neck to meet his hungry gaze and dug her nails into his shoulders. "So, consider this a definite yes."

One second. One freeze-frame moment packed with explosive tension while her words washed over him. And then he was in motion. Growling as he plundered her mouth. Holding her head steady with one hand at the side of her head and devouring all she offered as though afraid she might take it back.

But that would never happen. She was too lost. Utterly consumed by his kiss and floating on a pliant haze of lust and wonder. His taste. His weight. His heat and raw masculine scent. They all melded together into one powerful weapon that both pinned her in place and left her free to feel.

Releasing his grip, his hand took a long, leisurely exploration. Down her neck. Over the curve of her shoulder. Down her arm then up along the curve of her hip and in to splay low on her belly. Reverent. Or maybe purposeful. A man taking his time and committing every inch to memory. Learning her and taking his sweet damned time doing it.

Nowhere near the greedy exploration her own hands had taken on. With the breadth of his torso, there was too much ground to cover. Too much curiosity and need surging to the surface at once and demanding she take action. Frustrated with the cotton impeding her progress, she slipped her hands beneath his shirt.

His abs flexed beneath her fingertips and he hissed into her mouth, but he lifted his body enough to let her push his tee higher. He nipped her lower lip. "Baby," he panted against her mouth between kisses, "tryin' to go slow."

"No slow," she barely managed beneath his assault, her own breath coming just as fast and heated. She shoved the cotton up as far as his otherwise occupied arms would let her and savored the hot, hard slab of his chest. "Shirt. Off."

The sound that rumbled up his throat was somewhere between a grunt and a grumble, but he grudgingly relinquished her lips and shoved back to his heels. In one smooth move, he reached one arm over his head, yanked the shirt off and tossed it to the floor. "Givin' you this because I want your hands on my skin, but I'm not givin' up slow." He braced both hands on either side of her head, his bulk making the already defined muscles along his shoulders, chest and forearms flex in masculine perfection. Tattoos done only in black ink but with so much shading and detail they may as well have been full color marked his taut, tanned skin, and the dog tags he and his brothers each wore settled against her sternum, their weight a startling connection she felt well beyond skin-deep. "Get those hands on me, gorgeous. I'm damned sure gettin' mine on you."

Like he'd have to ask her twice. Though, when she lifted her hands from his thighs her fingers trembled, the enormity of where they were headed and the raptness in the way he watched her adding an unfamiliar intimacy to the act. She pressed one hand to his abdomen and traced the gothic-styled H above his heart. Unlike the simplistic letter on his tags, this one was worked into an ominous background, surrounded by a pack of feral wolves.

She flattened her hand.

His heart thrummed against her palm. A demanding beat that belied his hunter's demeanor. And yet, he didn't hide it. Didn't try to layer on another wallop of macho. Just lowered himself closer, keeping himself propped up on one arm while the other stroked her from wrist to shoulder. "More."

She could do more. A lot more. For as long as he wanted. She circled her hands around his waist, dipping her fingers beneath the waistband of his jeans. And good Lord, wasn't that a temptation. In faded jeans, Beckett's ass was a thing to behold, but if the curve teasing her fingertips was any indication, seeing it naked would be an eighth wonder.

He inhaled deep and skimmed his lips along her jawline, his hot breath fanning out against her skin. "My turn."

His turn?

Before her mind could summon a theory as to what he meant, Beckett eased back just enough to hook his fingers in the straps of her sundress and started to peel them off her shoulders.

Oh, damn.

Fast and frantic she could do, but him taking his time? To watch him touch her the way she'd touched him? It was too much. Too exposed. A desire too hot to grab onto.

She moved quick, using surprise to her advantage and wrestling him to his back. Legs straddling his hips, she blanketed his chest with hers and kissed him. Devoured his mouth with the same eagerness he'd taken hers.

He groaned into the kiss, clamped one hand on her hip and fisted the other in her hair. But rather than take the cue she'd hoped for, he used his hold in her hair and tugged her mouth away from his. He frowned up at her, eyes narrowed and way too sharp.

Shit. Thoughtful Beckett was bad enough. Shrewd and observant Beckett wasn't anyone she wanted to deal with under present circumstances. She stroked her hands down his chest, her lungs and heart doing overtime. "Beckett—"

"What just happened?"

She tried to lean into him, if for nothing else but to calm the rising storm she sensed building, but with the relentless grip he kept on her hair, she barely budged. "Nothing, I just—"

"Don't bullshit me, G. Not here. Hell, not anywhere. What the fuck just happened?"

Every muscle from her toes to her fingertips quivered, adrenaline from the looming truth poised on her tongue and raw lust from the way he held her immobile whipping through her bloodstream. Admitting her flaws to anyone had never been a strong suit, but lowering her defenses in this particular arena was a completely foreign concept. She sucked in a bracing breath and held his promise of safe close. "You scared me."

Leveraging the same technique she'd used on him against her, he rolled her to her back and pinned her down, her wrists manacled in his hands on either side of her head.

Too overloaded on sensations to hide her response, she sucked in a sharp gasp and arched her back, the sheer rush of him overpowering her, leaving her laid bare. Eyes closed and lost to the moment, it was all too easy to imagine more. Naked and vulnerable to whatever he wanted. However he wanted it.

"Gia, baby. Look at me."

The concern in his low voice broke through the haze and she forced her eyelids open.

He studied her, his gaze roving over her face, her chest, then flicking to where he held her wrists. His attention had barely latched onto the point of contact when it shot back to her. That thoughtful and annoyingly perceptive look she'd grown to know all too well moved across his face. Slowly, he eased his grip on her wrists and guided them to her sides as he sat back on his heels, but did it with eyes locked to her. Watchful. Categorizing every second. "What scared you?"

Everything.

Not that she'd ever admit that to him. At least not yet. But after her yo-yo behavior the last few days, she at least owed him this. "You were watching me."

"You're fucking gorgeous. An amazing woman I've wanted in my bed for years. So, hell yeah, I was watching."

She swallowed huge and splayed her hands atop his

hard thighs. "I felt… I don't know. Exposed. Vulnerable. Like a dumbass who'd dropped their guard with Floyd Mayweather."

She'd hoped that last one would make him laugh. Or at least sideswipe him with a chuckle to break the tension. Instead, he gripped her hips and dragged her so her ass touched his bent knees. "What were you afraid I'd see?"

Yep. That was Beckett. Always cutting to the chase and pinpointing the root of anything. The real question was how well he'd take the answer. She braced and voiced the one truth she'd never thought she'd utter. "That I liked it."

Silence.

No visible physical response to help her gauge his re-action save a slew of what looked like rapid-fire thoughts moving behind his eyes. Releasing her hips, he slid his hands to cover hers, picked them both up and rubbed his thumbs along her pulse in a soothing caress. "Should have taken Axel up on his offer for supplies," he murmured.

"What?"

His lips quirked. "Nothing." He trailed his gaze along her body in a leisurely glide and sucked in a long, slow, sexy breath. "Put your hands by your sides."

Oh, hell.

She was so screwed. As in fifty different ways to Sunday with no way to wrangle herself free. Even bolting for the front door was a crapshoot with the glint in his eyes. Not that her body would cooperate with an es-cape. Between the goo her muscles had turned into at the deep rumble in his command and the building pulse between her legs she doubted she'd make it two steps past the bed without stumbling. "Beckett—"

He stopped her with a look.

A fucking *look*.

And her sex practically rejoiced. A damned halle-lujah shiver that made her wonder if he'd even have to touch her to make her come at this point.

"Now, Gia. Hands to your sides and eyes on me." Not once did his back-and-forth glide at her pulse hesitate. Though, at this point, she couldn't tell if the touch was to soothe her, or to keep his own rioting thoughts under control. Maybe a little of both.

Shaking more than she cared to show, she tugged her hands free of his grip and rested her arms at her sides.

His gaze warmed and gentled in an instant. "That's my girl."

A shudder moved through her, the simple, praising statement and the approval in his eyes eliciting warring responses she didn't have a clue how to process. No one talked to her that way. She couldn't let them. Couldn't risk ceding control to anyone. And yet the delicious, deep velvet of his voice whispered across her skin. Pushed her physical response higher and dared her to try.

"I don't know how to do this." It was barely more than a whisper, but the plea was plain even to her own ears.

"Do what, baby?" He slipped his hands beneath the hem of her sundress at her shins and languidly stroked her skin, inch by inch working his way up and over her knees and dragging the fabric higher with it. "Relax? Enjoy yourself? Take your time and just be for a little while?"

By the time he reached her thighs cocked and splayed on either side of his, she could barely think. Could barely hear over the incessant pounding of her heart. Let alone have the capacity to censor her words. "To not be in control."

His gaze snapped to hers and his fingers tightened near the apex of her thighs and hips. Her skirt pooled heavy over her sex, leaving only her legs and a hint of her panties open to his view, but in that second, she felt utterly defenseless. Laid bare at the most primal level.

Never taking his eyes off of hers, he cupped her hips over her dress. "Then it's time for you to learn, gorgeous." Up they went, dipping to her waist and along the sides of her breasts. "Because I can guaran-fucking-tee you aren't going to be in charge tonight." He hooked his fingers in the straps at her shoulders and tugged them down.

Her heart thrashed, fight-or-flight bunching every muscle tight even as goose bumps fanned in all directions. She fisted the soft chambray comforter in her fists and fought the need to squirm. To push away and run.

"Easy." He peeled the fabric lower, leaving only her bra in place. As daring selections went, it wasn't extreme, but the deep teal color had always been a favorite, its lacy edges and silk cups making her feel girly and sexy. With Beckett staring down at her though, she felt more like a sex goddess newly born.

"You're safe with me." Leaving the top half of her dress loose at her waist with her skirt, he bent and kissed her stomach. "Just breathe through it. Let me take you there."

Breathe? Her throat was too tight. Her lungs too constricted by tension and stark need. And the way he was looking at her—hungry and possessive—he wasn't *taking* her anywhere. More like slingshotting her through the stratosphere.

His tongue dipped for a quick taste just below her belly button and pleasure spiraled straight between her legs, the mere thought of feeling that same stroke much, much lower ramping the slow and steady ache to a demanding throb. "Beckett."

"I know, gorgeous." More kisses. Each one painting an indolent path higher and higher. He smoothed his hands up her sides and under her shoulder blades, lifting her so her back was bowed for his questing mouth. "Just give in. Give it all to me. I'll take it."

Easy for him to say. He wasn't the one being unwound from the inside out. Unlearning years of brutally exercised control. She squeezed her hands tighter, her grip on his comforter so fierce her fingertips ached. "Please, let me touch you."

His lips skimmed the swell of one breast, his hot breath as he spoke a tantalizing caress. "Almost." He licked just beneath the lace, a hit-and-run tease that speared fast and deep toward her sex.

She moaned and clenched her thighs against his, her back arching deeper, eager for more of his mouth.

"That's it." One shift and a muted snick, and the clasp on her bra came loose. "Just like that." Hands still behind her back, he shifted just enough to meet her eyes and guided the straps over her shoulders. "Want your eyes on me, Gia. Want you to see me drink you in for the first time the same way I watched you."

"You're killing me." As much as her heart had been through tonight and the amount of endorphins pumping through her system, she was sure of it.

A wolfish grin tilted his lips. "Hardly that." Slowly, he straightened, pulling her bra along with him and deliciously torturing her sensitized flesh in the processes. "Though, by the time I'm done, you'll come hard enough you think you've kicked it."

The lace slipped past her tightly beaded nipples and her lungs seized.

The room's cool air whispered against her breasts and shivers danced down her spine.

One heartbeat and the patient hunter was gone. Replaced with a voracious beast. One barely tethered and fighting against its restraints.

For her.

Warmth on par with the slow burn of a pricey Scotch blossomed in her belly and the fear that had battered and clawed along the edges of desire fizzled in its intoxicating wake. *She'd* created that response. Brought a man to the edge of control, not by driving things to completion, or performing at the top of her game, but with her surrender. Pausing long enough to really connect, to take a chance and set her own desires free, trusting someone else to lead the way. It was heady. A drugging power in its own way.

He tossed her bra to the floor and hooked his fingers in her dress gathered around her waist. "Wanted you right here—just like this—since the day I met you." He tugged the fabric over her hips, snagging her panties as he went, and threw the bundle well out of reach. "Just. Like. This." He snatched her ankles, guided them back so her thighs straddled his and prowled over her. "Put your hands on me."

The low and hungry command vibrated through her, every bit as thrilling as his intense focus. For once, she didn't hesitate, eagerly wrapping her arms around his waist and savoring the tight, hot skin along his back. His shoulders. Arms and chest.

Beckett did the same, skimming his big hands everywhere. Kissing her. Tasting her. Hips. Belly. Shoulders. Thighs. And thank freaking God, *finally* her breasts. He plumped them. Pushed them together and licked and sucked her aching nipples until her sex was drenched and swollen. There was no calculation to any of it. No expected destination. None of the Man 101 road map so many encounters seemed to follow. Just pure pleasure and exploration.

The muscles in his shoulders bunched as he shifted lower, the now warmed metal from his dog tags an odd but erotic glide along her stomach. Dazed from sensation overload, it took the rasp of his stubble just above her mound before her mind engaged and tracked his intent.

Forcing her eyelids open, her heart punched almost painfully at the site that greeted her. Countless times she'd imagined every scenario possible with this man, but nothing came close to the reality of Beckett's broad shoulders forcing her thighs wider or his devious mouth just inches from her sex. "Oh my God. Beckett."

He growled and slipped his hands beneath her ass. "Too early for you to say that yet, gorgeous." His gaze lifted to hers just as his breath wafted against her drenched sex. "But we're gettin' there. Fast."

And then his mouth was on her. Feasting from her with the same patient yet thorough approach he'd wielded all night. Licking through her folds. Circling and suckling her clit while his hungry groans resonated against her flesh.

She fisted her fingers in his hair and dug her heels into his back, hips flexing in time with his ministrations. She wasn't a prude. Had had other men give her the same pleasure, but never once had she responded like this. Never laid herself open and simply accepted the pleasure given. Never shut her mind off and turned a blind eye to what came next. But with Beckett, she couldn't help it. Didn't want to be anywhere except right here. Right now.

Lost in the feel of his mouth. In the sounds of his labored breaths. In the mingled scents they created.

He shifted and teased the mouth of her sex with his fingers. Circling. Pressing without fully breaching and giving her the fullness she wanted.

For a second, she was tempted to try to take over. To roll him to his back and scramble for control. But then he pushed inside her and the only thing that mattered was *more*. Reaching for the release that hovered just outside her reach. Diving over the emotional cliff he'd created and free-falling to whatever waited, no matter the cost.

"Give it to me." The dark demand wound through her. Notched her like an arrow on a taut bowstring aimed straight for the sun. "All of it. Everything." He thrust another finger deep and angled his wrist, dragging his blunt fingertips against that delicious sweet spot inside her. His lips encircled her clit, suckled deep—and she was gone. Her pussy clenching his fingers with a desperation that echoed clear to her soul and her startled cries mingling with his murmured words of encouragement. It was beautiful. A wild cocktail of liberation and exhilaration that scattered all the tidy dos and don'ts of her life so thoroughly she'd never get them back in the same humdrum order she'd known before.

Bit by bit, the world came back into focus. The easy glide of Beckett's lips just below her belly button. The slow but steady shuttle of his fingers inside her. Beckett's cedar-and-bergamot scent on her skin.

She opened her eyes and cradled either side of his head, urging him closer. Needing his weight and the comforting warmth of his skin to hold her steady.

He took his time, drawing out the aftershocks of her release with his fingers and skimming his lips and tongue up the center of her torso. No rush. No moving on to the main event. Just a slow and easy mood more fitting for a lazy Saturday morning. Only when he'd reached her sternum did he brace one forearm beside her and slide his fingers free. He cupped her sex, dipped his head and watched as he ran his thumb through her tightly trimmed curls and slicked his fingers through her sensitized folds. "You gave me that, Gia." A firmer grip, his big hand covering her completely. Possessive. "Not letting you take it back."

A shudder moved through her, the determination behind his words prodding her protective instincts to the surface even as a deeper part of herself purred and preened at the mysterious shift that had taken place. What it was, she couldn't pinpoint. Had no experience to assimilate what was going on. But it was huge, the air around them crackling with an inexplicable energy.

She covered his hand with hers, desperate for a connection. Needing his gaze and the emotion behind it to help her fill in the blanks. "Beckett?"

Up, up, up his hand went, the calluses on his palm strangely comforting on the slow and purposeful trek. His focus intent on his actions, he cupped her breast. A dominant yet reverent touch she felt like a claim.

Her heart thrummed and her near-whispered voice shook with uncertainty. "What just happened?"

He sucked in a slow breath and lifted his head. The rugged lines that defined his deeply masculine face were harsher, drawn tight with resolution, and his blue gaze burned hot and fearless. "That was the beginning of me and you."

Chapter Nine

Beckett braced. Whether Gia would try to fight her way out from under him and hightail it back home after his blunt statement, or just go for the upper hand via sex was a crapshoot, but she'd try something. It was right there in her eyes. Fear. Uncertainty and a whole lot of *what the fuck?* He knew the look staring up at him because the same messy trio was churning through him.

He might be scared and clueless about where he was taking them, but no way in hell was he fucking this up. Whatever she threw at him, he'd be ready. Whether she realized it or not, when she'd looked up at him and admitted she *wanted* him to take control, she'd all but handed him the keys to the kingdom. And, while it might make him the world's biggest dick, he was gonna use those keys to his advantage.

She swallowed huge and fidgeted beneath him, her sweet touch moving down his lats and in to brace low on his pecs. "I think you're getting ahead of yourself. We're having sex. That's it."

He grinned, even knowing he risked her throwing a right hook. If she thought he was getting ahead of himself now, she was gonna be shocked as shit in the next few minutes and the days to come. He'd known going into tonight that he wanted something more than casual between them, but somewhere between the gumbo and her throwing down in his foyer, then apologizing for not being like other girls, just how much he wanted had gotten a whole lot clearer.

As in the whole fucking enchilada.

He slid his hand up to her throat and stroked his thumb along her hammering pulse. "Gorgeous, if you can use a simple three-letter word to label what you just gave me, I'm gonna have to up my game."

Her eyelids grew heavy and he'd swear he could see the memories of all she'd felt moving behind her pretty brown eyes. "Your game's just fine." Her hands slipped higher, the fingertips of one hand idling, tracing the dragon inked on his shoulder. "I'm just ready to send in my offensive line."

So, sex was gonna be her play—along with a casual sidestep of the big fucking elephant stomping through the room. If his cock got a vote in the matter, he'd have lost his jeans about a split second after he'd tossed her dress to the floor, but after what Gia had just given him—letting go, moaning his name as she'd dug her heels in his back and come so pretty on his fingers— he'd go to hell if he gave in and took what his throbbing dick demanded.

It was what she expected, though. Which was exactly why he wasn't going to give it to her. He pressed a firm, lingering kiss to her lips and forced himself to push back to his knees, stroking her insanely soft belly and thighs along the way. "Sorry, sweetheart. Your team's gonna have to pack it in and do some thinking before we get back on the field."

"What?" Gia pushed upright as he backed off the

bed, her scowl and the sway of her full, outstanding breasts from the sudden movement nearly knocking him off his resolve. "Are you fucking kidding me?"

He forced a casualness he didn't feel and padded to the light switch by the entrance to his suite. "I'll kid you about a lot of things, but in this, I'm dead serious."

He hit the lights.

Darkness consumed the room, broken only by the distant glow of Dallas's downtown and streetlights through the wide window opposite his bed.

Rustling sounded on the bed a second before Gia's shadowed form came into focus and her footsteps sounded on the concrete floor. He caught her at her waist just before she rounded the king-size footboard and pulled her flush against him.

"Let me go." Her carefully modulated words didn't tie with the shaking hands pushing against his chest or the ragged breaths pushing past her lips.

"Shh." Spearing his fingers in her thick hair at the back of her head, he forced her cheek to his chest and tightened his arm around her waist. "Not shutting you down, Gia. Just slowin' our roll a little bit."

"No, you're not." She struggled for another second or two, then realized he wasn't budging and gave in with a huff. "You're playing games. I don't like it."

Damn, but he hated that. Hated how fast her shields came up and every fucking event in her life that had made the instinct necessary. He'd fix it, though. Show her she didn't have to assume the worst and guard herself every single second. Not with him. Not with his family.

"Relax." Needing the touch to ground himself as much as she needed the reassurance, he slid his fingertips along her scalp. Up and down from her crown to the base of her neck, he did what he could to ease her. To show her she was safe. "I need you to listen, sweetheart. And by that, I mean, I need you to *hear* me."

Silence.

No movement save the accelerated rise and fall of each breath.

Not exactly the warm and open response he'd wanted, but it beat the wrestling match he could have had on his hands, so he took it. He cupped the back of her neck. "I know what you think I am."

He hadn't thought she could get any stiller, but in the seconds that followed even her lungs seemed to stop.

He kept going. "You think I'm a player. You think all those women you've seen me with end up in my bed because that's what I wanted everyone to think."

Her hands moved just a fraction, more of a flinch followed by the slight rasp of her nails against his skin. "You're saying they don't?" So vulnerable. Soft and barely loud enough to reach his ears, but the words were raw and open.

"No." He took a chance at easing his hold and combed his fingers through her hair, the slick strands uncoiling his tension as they slipped across his knuckles. "Not going to pretend it never happens, but only with a few and they know going in it's nothing more than physical. I love women. Love everything about them. Love great sex. But the ones who can give me physical and not want more when it's all said and done are few and far between. Me being me and not wanting any strings, I'm not gonna take a chance and hurt someone just to get my own needs met."

She rested her forehead on his chest. "Why are you telling me this?"

The fear in her question tangled with his own. He slid the hand in her hair to her jaw and lifted her face to his, the soft glow through the windows painting her beautiful features and accenting her dark eyes. No matter the tough-as-nails image she showed the rest of the world, he'd always seen her as blatantly feminine. And now...now he knew he'd been right. She might not be like other women, but she was all woman. His woman.

He ran the back of his fingers along her jawline. "Because you're right. I'm playing a game. Just not the one you're thinking."

"What game?"

Whisper soft. Innocent and open.

"The one where I win you."

Her lips trembled and her eyes got wet a second before she ducked her head, hiding them from view.

He'd give her that. After the way she'd taken a chance on him tonight, she deserved a little privacy and a chance to process what he'd shared.

"What about you?" she murmured. "You didn't..." She shrugged and slid her hands to his sides, her grip telegraphing her uncertainty.

"No, and I'm not going to. Not until you get that this is more than casual and are ready to take me on."

She sniffed and dashed one hand across her cheek. "What if I'm never ready?"

"Oh, I'll get you there." In that he was certain. And he'd leverage every scrap of information she'd given him tonight to make that happen. He wrapped her up tight and kissed the top of her head, giving her a few more precious seconds to gather her emotional shit before he pushed his luck even further.

"You're a cocky son of a bitch."

"Baby, you just came so hard on my tongue I can still taste you."

He barely managed to brace before she jabbed him in the gut, but she was laughing when she did it so it lacked its usual wallop. It also gave him the opening he needed to sweep her up and treat her like the woman she was, whether she wanted him to acknowledge that side of her or not.

"Beckett!" She grappled and tried to counter him as he strode toward the bed, but finally gave up and wrapped her arms around his neck. "What are you doing?"

He yanked the comforter back, put a knee to the plush mattress and laid her out in the center. "I said I was givin' you time to think and prepare. I didn't say I'd let you do it somewhere else." He paused long enough to let the image of her stretched out on his bed and covered in moonlight burn into his brain, then tucked the covers around her. "Plus, there's the fact I'm a greedy bastard. I might give up feeling you come hard on my cock, but hell's gonna freeze over before I give up sleeping next to you again."

For a second, she just stared up at him, either dumbfounded by his blunt comment, or turned way the fuck on by it. He backed off the bed, yanked the button fly on his Levi's and made a mental note to explore how dirty talk worked on her the next time he got her naked.

She curled on her side and tucked one hand under her head, watching him as he stripped to all but his black boxer briefs. "Um, if I'm naked, doesn't it seem fair if you're naked, too?"

He chuckled and slid between the sheets. "Nice try, gorgeous." He pulled her into the crook of his arm and tangled his legs with hers. "Now, settle in and do whatever you need to do to fortify your defenses. Come morning, I'm coming at you with all guns loaded."

She smoothed her hands along his sternum and toyed with the chain of his dog tags.

That was another boon with Gia. She already knew about the brotherhood and how tight they were as a family. Knew how they guarded each other's backs and looked out for the women they loved. She'd just have to adjust to what it meant to be one of the ones being protected. No small feat given she spent her days looking out for other people. He'd have to talk with Sylvie and Ninette about that. Maybe see if they couldn't work her from a female perspective and help her see being cared for wasn't a bad thing.

Her hand inched lower, tickling the light hairs low on his stomach and reviving his cock's barely diminished interest.

He caught her wrist just as the heel of her hand touched his briefs and gave her a warning squeeze. "I know you like me holding you down. Wanna find out if you like me paddling your ass, too?"

Her body flinched like he'd actually swatted her behind and her breathing jumped to that of a runner early in their workout, but she held her silence.

Guiding her hand back so it rested against his heart, he let himself smile into the darkness. "Think I just added another thing to explore to my list." Just to make sure she got his point, he wrapped her up tight, slid his hand to her perfect ass and gave her a meaningful squeeze. "Sleep tight, gorgeous."

Chapter Ten

One more mile. One more and maybe—just maybe—
the edge Beckett had woken up with would take a hike
and he could get back to finessing Gia into giving them
a chance. He cut the corner at the next block and put
some extra steam into his strides up the street's minor
incline. At eight o'clock on a Saturday morning, the
warehouse yuppie/artist haven was almost void of activity save those like him who favored exercise over
sleeping in. In August in Texas, it was also the *only*
time worth exercising outside unless you were a sick
fuck who got off on insufferable heat. Today promised to be no exception, the sun already beating down
on the asphalt streets without a single cloud in sight to
offer relief.

Risking busting his ass for not looking where he
was going, he thumbed his phone to life and checked
the app that monitored the security in their apartment.

The bold red swatch that showed his system was still
activated beamed back at him and pushed his pace a
little faster. If Gia opened the door and bailed before he
got back, he'd get a notice all of a second later. So, why
he needed the visual confirmation stymied him almost
as much as the number of times he'd checked the app.

Because you're afraid she'll bolt.

The itch that had wormed beneath his skin this morning dug a little deeper, warning him to back the hell up and rethink the path he was on.

No. He wasn't backing up.

His brothers thought he was good enough. And Gia wasn't some shallow woman focused on money, education, or status. She was real. Honest. Nowhere near the cold woman who'd left him with a drunk for a father. Her own demons and insecurities might make her fight him tooth and nail on a personal level, but she wouldn't bolt on him. Not without a damned good reason.

He punched the home button and started to drop his hand just as the phone vibrated, Knox's name and phone number plastered across the front of it. Not missing a beat, he punched the answer button, let the call take over The Killers blasting in his Bluetooth earbuds and focused on the road. "You get that clip taken down?"

"Well, good morning to you, too, Hercules. Or, should I call you Blue Balls since you took the extra long run route today?"

Fucking Knox. Beckett might have a stick up his ass with security, but his brother took tracking people to insane levels. "You always check people's GPS before you call, or am I just special?"

"Well, I wasn't gonna call if you were stationary at the loft."

Good point. But he wasn't gonna stoke Knox's stalker tendencies by agreeing out loud. "You didn't answer my question. The clip down?"

"Yeah, it's down. No bead yet on who posted it. Whoever put it up took pains to cover their tracks, but we'll get there."

Beckett grunted and took the next street that would land him back at the loft. "I take it Sylvie and Ninette have glutted the two of you with food by now?"

"Me. Darya. Plus, the whole rest of the crew. Trevor and Nat brought Levi out about an hour after we got here, so Zeke and Gabe decided to round out the crowd and came out, too. The moms are in hog heaven."

A definite plus. Not to mention convenient. If he was lucky, he could get Knox to do a little of his dirty work in one swoop. "You think they'd be cool with adding Gia to their next girls' day out?"

Quiet drifted through the phone for a good three heartbeats before Knox answered. "I take it Gumbo à la Beckett went pretty damned good."

Good didn't even begin to cover it. The fact that he was anywhere near the emotional ballpark called Relationships was a fucking miracle. "It was a simple question. Forget I brought it up. Is there a reason you're calling this early on a Saturday? Or could you just not wait to bust my balls?"

The dastardly laugh Knox always used whenever he'd hacked his way into someplace he shouldn't be filtered down the line. "Relax, brother. Darya's already planted the seed with Sylvie and Ninette."

Beckett grunted, not daring to take that line of conversation any further. Although, he made a note to take Darya on another shopping trip to one of those high-end purse or shoe stores. "What else? You calling this early, there's a reason for it."

Another hesitation, this one loaded with a nasty vibe that promised Beckett wouldn't like what came next. "I got into the range's system."

"And?"

"Well, the good news is their security footage is all cloud storage and they've got a bird's eye on all the lockers."

Yep. There it was. The vibe was never wrong. "What's the bad news?"

"There are two missing chunks of history a week prior for the streams pointed at Gia's locker."

"System maintenance?"

"Doubtful. Both are mid-morning, about the same time one day after the other. Not good practice to do maintenance during the day. One day for an emergency update, I'd buy. But two days in a row at the same time? Sounds fishy to me."

Still a few blocks away from the loft, Beckett gave up his pace and slowed to a lazy walk. His heart beat strong and steady, but the hazy edge he'd been fighting all morning narrowed and sharpened. "You think someone's covering their tracks?"

"I think guns don't end up with a hair trigger without some kind of adjustment. Especially not a competition piece that's kept isolated in a locker. Even if it'd been a fluke malfunction, the clip ending up on YouTube smells an awful lot like a smear campaign."

It did to him, too. The real question was if Gia could get past her initial damage control reflex and focus on who and why someone would be inclined to fuck with her in the first place.

He stopped at the crossing opposite his loft, hands on hips, starring up at the wide window that ran the length of his suite. His lungs churned overtime from the incline he'd put behind him, but the sound still couldn't compete with the shit churning through his head.

Knox's voice cut through the silence. "How far are we going with this, brother?"

Digging in deeper with Gia was a risk. The biggest one he'd taken in a long damned time. Maybe ever. But man, if it worked like his gut told him it could—if he could nab a fraction of what Knox and some of his other brothers had—it'd be worth it.

"Beck?"

She wouldn't bolt. She might hide. Might fight the idea of the two of them for a while, but she wasn't a chicken and she wasn't heartless. She'd proved that last night in spades.

The words came out rough, thick with fear he couldn't have hidden if he'd wanted. "She's protected. Everything we've got."

To his credit, Knox didn't laugh. Didn't bust his ass or make any clever remarks, but a smile and maybe even a little relief filled his voice. "I take it we're coverin' this at rally on Monday?"

"Yeah." He crossed the street toward the loft's primary street entrance. "Keep on it until then. I wanna know who posted that clip."

"I'm on it."

"Anything else?"

One beat. Then another. "It's not gonna be that hard, you know."

"What's not?"

"Tellin' the rest of the guys. The only one of us who didn't see it comin' is you. Every one of 'em is gonna be tickled shitless." He chuckled. "Except maybe Axel. Think he considered makin' a move a time or two."

"I'd break his fuckin' arms."

Knox laughed full-on at that one. "Yeah, but it

would've got your ass off dead center a whole lot faster."
Movement sounded through the phone. "You sharin' all
of this with Gia, or are we keepin' things quiet?"

Oh, hell no. Secrets with Gia would be a lethal back-
fire. "I'll talk to her. My guess is she'll either ignore it,
fight it, or a little of both, but I'll get her there."

"Mmm. I bet you will." In the background, an exu-
berant voice that could only belong to Levi sounded.
"Gotta go. Sylvie's gone all out on breakfast. You need
something, give me a shout."

The line disconnected a second later.

Typical Knox. Nothing got him focused and moving
faster than a challenge, food, or sex—all three he had in
abundance these days. Considering how they'd grown
up and all they'd overcome, he was due for every bit of
it. Hell, they both were.

He yanked open one of the double glass doors to
the main lobby, bypassed the elevators and tripped the
security locks to the stairs with his phone. Five floors
later, he eased the industrial metal door to his loft shut
behind him.

Quiet.

No water running.

No noises from behind the closed door that segre-
gated his half of the floor from the common area in
the center.

Gia's purse was still on the kitchen island.

So far, so good.

Careful to keep his movements quiet, he slipped into
his suite. Like Knox's, it was mostly an open space, his
office/living area closest to the entrance separated from
his bedroom only by a high and wide bookshelf that
stopped just three feet from the twelve-foot ceilings.

The style had a whole different feel from his brother's, though. *Rugged,* Sylvie had called it when she'd taken him shopping and he'd pointed out what he'd liked. Lots of natural, weathered wood, exposed brick walls and colors that blended in rather than stand out. Most important, there wasn't a chair or scrap of material that didn't feel fucking fantastic.

He sat his phone on the coffee table, snatched the hand towel he'd dropped on the couch before he'd headed out and headed for the opposite side of the suite.

The second he cleared the bookcase, his heart leveled out and the buzz that had chased him all through his run unplugged.

Gia was still there. Curled on one side with her back to him and her dark hair spilling over his pillow. The sheet was tucked under her arm, but dipped just enough down her back to show a tempting amount of skin.

He fisted his hands in his towel and just stood there, soaking it in and fighting the need to wake her the way he wanted. To stroke every inch of her the way he had last night. So soft. Firm and yet all woman in just the right places. She hadn't freaked at his indulgence last night either. More, she seemed to like it. Seemed to float and glide on the sensations right along with him.

But giving in would go against the path he'd set and he wasn't going backward. Not with her.

He wiped the sweat off his face and neck and padded closer, sorely tempted to hop in the shower before he woke her. Then again, there was no way in hell he was going to take her when he was sweaty from a long run, so maybe the no-shower approach would help him keep his shit in check.

He sat on the side of the bed and her eyes snapped open, her startled gasp filling the otherwise quiet room.

"Beckett?" She frowned, blinked a few times and pushed up to an elbow, scanning the room as she moved. The second she got upright, the sheet slipped, barely covering one nipple. She grabbed it and her sleep-weighted brown eyes got huge, her memories of last night no doubt coming back online in a rush. "What time is it?"

God, she was cute when she was flustered. Not that he'd share that opinion just yet. He liked his balls where they were and he had a pretty good idea Gia could go from cute to she-devil in a second this early in the morning. "Not late. Only a little after eight." He smoothed her hair away from her face and cupped the side of her neck, stroking his thumb along her pulse. "You hungry? Want some coffee?"

She studied his clothes and gripped the sheet a little tighter. "You worked out already?"

He grinned, though given the way her eyes narrowed, maybe he shouldn't have. "Well, it was either go for a run and relieve some tension, or give in and wake you up with a different brand of cardio, so yeah."

Her lips softened and the keen focus in her eyes heated. When she spoke, her voice still had the same raspy morning sound to it, but it came out lower. Huskier. "That wouldn't have been so bad."

Hell, no it wouldn't have. Except then he'd have lost the upper hand and no way was he doing that until he got what he wanted. "Oh, it would have been stellar." He leaned in, teased her lips with his and ran his nose alongside hers. "But it's not gonna happen until you agree to more than casual."

The tiny hitch in her breath worked him as thoroughly as a velvet fist to his cock and the outline of her amazing tits pressed against his sheets made him halfway tempted to say to hell with his plans. He gently squeezed her neck, kissed her forehead and said the one thing that guaranteed to keep him on track. "Slide out of bed, gorgeous. I've got news on the thing that went down at the range and want you caffeinated before I share."

He'd barely managed to back away before she snapped to attention, pushing fully upright. "Knox got the clip down?"

"Knox had the clip down before I had you in my bed." He rounded the footboard and headed for the door.

"Beckett!"

He didn't look back. Didn't dare. Gia sweet and cuddly was a turn-on. Gia madder than hell was a goddamn sexual demand. "You wanna know more, you're gonna have to get dressed and come get some food and coffee."

A sound between a grunt and an indelicate snarl chased him out of the room, and if she'd had anything worth throwing in reaching distance, he'd have likely had it hit him square between the shoulder blades.

Fortunately, he made it out of the room and got the single-brew coffee wonder warmed up and ready for action before Gia stomped around the corner. Her cheeks were pink and her hair not nearly as messy as he'd like to see it first thing after crawling out of his bed.

And man, was she was on a mission.

She yanked a bar stool out from under the kitchen island. "Tell me."

He turned to the coffee machine and got to work. God knew, he wasn't stupid enough to let her see how hard he was fighting a smile. He ran it down, conveying every detail Knox had shared, then back-and-forthed a line of questions that almost identically matched the ones he'd traded with Knox.

The machine finished its gurgle and hiss just as she fired off, "So, what? You think someone's intentionally trying to make me look bad?"

He handed her the cup and braced his elbows on the polished concrete countertop. "You gotta admit. The pieces fit. The kind of business we're in, it's not uncommon to piss people off. The real question is *who* you pissed off."

She glared at the counter, eyes distant.

"Need you to be smart about this, G. I know you're pissed at yourself over what happened, but it happened. And my gut tells me it wasn't a freak deal. You gotta be smart. Look at every angle."

Her mouth pursed tight, but she still didn't look at him.

Well, what the fuck. In for a penny, in for a pound. "And just so we're clear, you're not the only one looking."

Her head snapped up, the contemplative look on her face replaced with sharp awareness. "What's that mean?"

"It means Knox is digging. It means Axel's probably already made a call to Maury and told him to get the lead out on checking your gun. Not sure how the rest of the guys are gonna dive in, but you can bet they're already chewin' on what they can do."

"Why would they do that? I can handle this just fine."

"Sure, you can. You're just not going to."

"Says who?"

"Me. And them."

Her eyes narrowed, the heat behind them practically licking against his skin. "That's not your call."

Right. If he was going to do this, he might as well do it with everything on the table from the get-go. He pushed away from his side of the counter and paced toward her.

Her grip on the coffee mug tightened, but otherwise she kept her place. "Do not think for a second you can intimidate me, Beckett Tate. I'm not like the rest of the women in your family. I can take care of myself. And if you think this is helping your *I want more than casual* argument, it's not."

"You're wrong." Careful not to burn her, he pried her mug from her fingers and sat it out of reaching distance. "Every woman in my family is strong as hell. Just like you." He crowded closer, purposefully working his hips between her thighs so she couldn't make good use of her knee against his nuts, then leaned in close. "I know you can take care of yourself. I know you can whip most men's asses and not break a sweat doing it, but if I can make it so you don't have to lift a finger in the first place, you can bet your sweet behind I'm going to do it. That's who I am. That's who my brothers are, and that's what you *deserve*. A man who'll look out for you whether you can handle it on your own or not. And if that's not making my case for me, then I don't know what the fuck would."

She swallowed huge and the fire in her gaze shifted to uncustomary wariness. Or maybe it was just flat-out confusion. The latter wouldn't be surprising. From the hints she'd given last night, she'd never had anyone throw down in her best interest before.

"Truth, gorgeous. Last night. How'd it feel letting go? Letting someone else steer the course?"

Her lips tightened. As if she couldn't quite form the words or find the strength to set them free.

So he did it for her. "I watched you, G. I *felt* you. You liked it." Risky as it was to push the gentle approach, he cupped the side of her face and swept his thumb along her cheek. "The deal at the range could've gone a lot different. That near miss could have been a hit. Worse, it could have been you that got hurt. You've helped me. You've helped my brothers and their women. You let go on this and let us return the favor, you'll find another kind of freedom." He kissed her forehead, stepped back and slid her coffee back in front of her. "You find the courage to face what I'm offering on both fronts, you'll never be safer."

Chapter Eleven

Gia paused the security footage Knox had emailed her, dropped back in her desk chair and sighed. Beckett was right. Two outages so tightly paralleled one day after the other was suspicious. Paired with the confirmation she'd gotten from Beckett's gunsmith and the video posted on YouTube, she'd be an epic fool if she didn't face reality.

Someone had set her up.

But why?

Outside her window, Klyde Warren Park was almost deserted, the late afternoon August heat too much for anyone save the most hard-core outdoor lovers. From her heavily air-conditioned home office, the view was pretty, though. Five acres of green stretched over Wood-all Rodgers Freeway for an odd mix of urban bustle and manicured beauty.

She rolled her head and stared up at the ceiling. Like her bedroom, the modest space was deeply feminine— pale dove-gray walls, matte white trim and matching furniture with ballet-pink accents. Nothing like where Beckett worked. But then, working only contract jobs instead of providing every aspect of security the way he and Knox did, she didn't need the corporate look.

Didn't want it. Her home and her office were her oasis. A place where the woman inside her didn't have to hide.

Shaking off her wandering thoughts, she straightened and pulled up the working list of possibilities she'd started. Not that she'd tallied many options. One corporate nut job who'd tried to off his boss right before she'd left Atlanta, the two gigs she'd helped Beckett and his brothers with in the last few years, and one over-the-top stalker who'd scared the bejesus out of one of her clients before she'd helped the cops put him away. Of the four, she was banking on the last one given he'd been released from jail on a technicality a little over three months ago.

Her phone rang and her heart jolted.

Beckett.

She grabbed the device, almost reflexively swiping the answer button until her brain registered her father's name on the display instead of the one she'd expected to find. Her thumb froze and her smile slipped. She should let it go to voicemail. At least then she'd get some clue on what her father was up to so she could prepare and have a decent counterattack. Of course, then she'd have to field a call from her mother within a half hour and, while Gia loved her mom, finding common topics to talk about was a strain on a good day.

She took the call. "A phone call from Atlanta's most esteemed criminal attorney on a weekend? I thought Sundays were reserved for brunch at the club and a leisurely eighteen holes with Judge Allen and his cronies."

"Don't be snide, Gia. It doesn't become a lady."

Gia barely bit back a derisive bark of laughter and managed a delicate chide instead. "I thought we'd agreed I don't fit the standard Southern belle mold."

"I have no doubt my daughter could accomplish whatever she sets her mind to. She just seems to be inordinately obstinate when it comes to occupational choices and taste in men."

His daughter.

No mention of his wife. Which was ironic given Reginald Sinclair had only participated in her upbringing at a financial or figurehead level for the first eighteen years of her life. After she'd lowered the boom and changed her major to criminal justice, even that support had all but dried up. "I prefer to think of myself as stalwart and self-aware."

"Indeed."

God, that word. She'd lost track of the number of times she'd heard it growing up. A minimalist approach to swiping whatever she had to share under the rug, always spoken in that deep, cultured and highly superior voice that made her feel as insignificant as rat dung.

Her dad cleared his throat. "Actually, it's your job I wanted to talk to you about."

The gentle *whoosh* of the air-conditioning through the ceiling vent seemed to whisper a retreat and her stomach clenched, braced for the worst. Not once had her father ever willingly brought up her chosen career. "What about it?"

"I hear you had an unpleasant altercation at the gun range. I'm sure I don't have to share how awkward it was to learn about such an event from a colleague, but I also thought it wise to see how you were faring."

He what? Gia sat ramrod-straight and snatched her pen off the desk, squeezing it for all she was worth. "Are you asking because you're concerned for my well-being, or because my time on social media made for unwelcome conversation on the golf course?"

"You're my daughter," he ground out, the rugged emotion of his voice a complete shock. "Just because I don't approve of the life you've set for yourself doesn't mean I don't care."

She waited, genuine surprise clogging her throat. When he didn't elaborate, she stood and forced a calm response while she paced the suddenly too small space. "It's fine." Okay, maybe that had been a little too sharp. "It was an accidental discharge. A weapon malfunction." One intentionally created, but she wasn't adding that tidbit into the mix. "No injuries, and a man I work with had the video down within hours, so any damage to my business should be limited."

Turning, she paused, a hunch that wouldn't quite materialize tickling at the back of her mind.

Reginald grunted, though it was a bit tough to tell if it was one that indicated he didn't believe her, or wasn't quite sure how to dig himself out of his show of concern without losing his edge. "I'm glad to hear it."

He was?

Gia spun and frowned out the window, scanning the late afternoon view like some environmental clue might help her figure out what was going on. "I appreciate the concern, but since when do you keep an eye out on my career or my competitions?"

Distant laughter sounded through the phone line just before the background noise shifted to deep silence. Her father's voice dropped, almost as if he were sharing some covert secret he was loath to utter. "Since I gave your name to a friend of mine. He's in charge of a political fund-raiser next month and the man he hired to oversee security hasn't followed through on the level of service promised. I told him he should consider you as a replacement and told him about the work you've done since leaving Atlanta."

"You vouched for me?"

A sound suspiciously close to a choking gurgle answered before her father did. "I mentioned you specialized in personal security, and he suggested I share his contact information in return. You'll have to submit your proposal like everyone else. Whether or not you obtain the assignment will be up to you."

Gia stopped by the window and focused hard on the park in the distance. Weird. She'd thought for sure she'd find ice covering the grass and surrounding streets, because hell was definitely freezing over. "Of course. I'm just...well, I'm shocked." Not to mention suspicious. Her dad had never even recommended her for a babysitting job in college. There had to be something else behind the gesture. Though, for the life of her, she couldn't imagine what.

"Don't read too much into it. I'm still against what you do. It's not fitting for a woman. You'd be happier and safer following your mother's example and building a family. It just seemed a good way for your mother to be able to see you in person."

There it was. Granted, it hadn't been quite the underhanded scheme she'd expected, but an underlying reason nonetheless.

"Now, seeing as it's Sunday and people are waiting on me," he said without giving her time to respond, "I need to go, but I'll email Peter's contact information to you tonight."

"Right. I'll keep an eye out for it."

"Excellent. If that's all—"

"Dad?"

A pause.

The words she wanted to speak sat odd and foreign on her tongue. "Thank you."

That garbled sound rumbled up his throat again before he said, "For God's sake, call your mother."

She couldn't remember the last time she'd felt a genuine smile while talking with her dad, but somehow, he drew one out of her. Even her voice was softer. Calmer. Less guarded. "I'll do that."

The background noise cut to nothing.

She pulled the phone away from her ear and stared at the screen, halfway tempted to check her recent calls and make sure it had really been her father who'd called. This was huge. If the Peter he'd mentioned was Peter Trannell—an extremely well-connected lobbyist throughout Georgia and surrounding states—landing the fund-raiser would be a superb addition to her resume. But even more than that, it was momentous on a personal level. A chance to show her parents that she was not only good at what she did, but she *excelled* in it, obstacles or no.

The ever-ready planner in her head kicked into gear, drawing on what she knew of resources in her hometown and assimilating the tasks she'd need to tackle in preparing a proposal. She rubbed her hands together and rounded her desk, a pleasant buzz skimming beneath her skin.

On her laptop, the list of possible sources she'd gathered beamed back at her.

The buzz dimmed and she dropped into her chair. That was a definite problem. Or two really. If her father

knew about the clip, that meant Peter would, too. She'd
have to have a damned good explanation before he'd
dismiss it. And, if Beckett was right and she did have
someone targeting her, she'd do good to find them and
deal with it well before the fund-raiser. A misfire and
short-lived YouTube clip was one thing where her professional reputation was concerned. Letting someone's
personal grudge wreck a political fund-raiser would
end her career.

She palmed her phone, her thumb scrolling through
her contacts almost on autopilot.

Beckett's name and number shone up at her, the soft
white backdrop like a pulsing beacon.

*You've helped me. You've helped my brothers and
their women. You let go on this and let us return the
favor, you'll find another kind of freedom.*

The same flutter she'd felt when he'd uttered those
words took wing in her belly once more. She traced
the edge of her phone. As if the action might somehow
coax a divine answer.

But she already knew it. Had caught multiple
glimpses of it in the time she'd known Beckett and his
brothers. Had experienced it for herself Friday night in
Beckett's touch and in the way he'd seen to her needs.
In his honesty about his need for touch and his fears
where relationships were concerned.

No, it wasn't answers she needed, but courage.

She rubbed her hand along her thigh, the yoga pants
she'd lounged in all day nowhere near as comforting as
Beckett's warm skin. Lifting her hand, she sucked in a
deep breath and braced.

Before she could push the button, the screen display

switched and Beckett's name flashed big and beautiful against the black backdrop.

Letting it ring at least once more probably would've been the smoother move, but at this point she didn't care. Just wanted to dive in before another wave of self-doubt could crowd in and take over. She punched the answer button. "I thought you were giving me time to think on things."

"I said I'd give you time. I didn't say I'd stop my campaign."

She grinned and dropped back in her desk chair, anchoring one bare foot up on the edge of her desk. Typical Beckett. When he wanted something, it would take a battering ram to his head before he stopped chasing it. Even then he'd likely find a way to keep crawling.

"You should know, I don't like flowers."

"Good thing I just bought you a replacement Glock instead."

Her toes curled and she had to bite her lip to keep from squealing like a teenage girl. "If we fight, I'll be more inclined to throw a punch than I will to reason things out."

"Already established that's been working for me since I was a kid." He paused, but she could practically picture the wicked grin on his face at his next words. "Plus, after we're done throwing punches, you'll be worked up and ready for quick and dirty make-up sex."

Mouth suddenly dry and fighting a rapid-fire pulse that left her light-headed, she hooked her heels on the edge of her chair and hugged her knees. "I don't cook," she nearly whispered.

The heat in his low response moved through her in a velvet stroke. "Know that, gorgeous, but I can. And when I'm too tired from fucking you silly and don't want to get out of bed, I've got lots of money to call out for provisions."

She could do this. Just a few words and the gravity that was Beckett Tate would take over. And oh, how sweet just the idea of it felt. "Do you like pizza?"

"Depends. Am I eating it before or after I reward you for telling me what I want to hear?"

Her arms shook and her palms were so sweaty it was a wonder she could keep ahold of the phone. "Before. I'm hungry."

"Then, odds are good I'd eat the cardboard box if you ask me to." One beat. "What time you want me there?"

The clock at the bottom of her screen showed nearly five o'clock. She could drag it out. Take one last stab at refusing what burned between them. But why? She'd known she'd wanted him from the second she'd laid eyes on him. "Is six too soon?"

Movement sounded through the phone. She hadn't thought his voice could drop any lower, but the near growl that answered her proved her wrong. "Better brace, gorgeous. I'm grabbin' a pie and headin' over. You've got one hour to batten down the hatches."

Chapter Twelve

She was scared to death. No one else would have noticed it, but Beckett had made studying Gia an art in the years he'd known her. While she hid her nerves supremely well, the signs were still there. A slight flush on her cheeks and collarbone. The hit-and-run way her eyes met his. Her sharp, yet still graceful movements. How he'd made it through half a pizza without hauling her across the couch cushion she'd intentionally left between them and kissing her until she couldn't do anything but moan was a goddamn miracle.

He snagged her discarded crust off her plate, using it as an excuse to work himself closer, and tried to stay on topic. "I don't get it. Your dad did you a solid with the lead. What's the problem?"

She shrugged. "My dad hates what I do for a living. The last thing he'd do is support it in the form of a lead."

"You think he's up to something?"

"He says it's just to get me back to Atlanta for a visit." Gia semi-stood, leaned and slid her plate onto the coffee table, giving him a prime view of her ass in those tight-as-fuck black pants she wore a lot when she worked out. Not that she'd worked out. Her hair was loose, her tasteful makeup in place and the Fort Knox–

style sports bra she always wore for exercise MIA, replaced with a light blue cotton tank and a matching bra
that peeked out every now and then to taunt him.

She slid back to the couch and tucked one leg underneath the other. "I don't know. Maybe I'm overly suspicious and that's all there is to it."

"Even if he is up to something, what's the down-
side?"

"If all goes well? Nothing."

There it was. The niggling agitation he'd picked up
on the minute she'd mentioned her dad's call. "You're
worried about what happened at the range."

She studied him for a beat, considering. "This is a
big deal for me. A chance to show my dad I'm really
good at what I do. Not to mention, having a connection
with Peter Trannell. One of his events on my resume
would be a huge score. You and I both know it's a risk
to even submit my proposal not knowing who's behind
what happened."

"When's the gig?"

"About a month out."

He popped the last bite of crust into his mouth to
fight his grin and stacked his plate on top of hers. If
he ever met her dad, he'd have to be sure to shake his
hand and buy him some top-dollar Scotch for the opening he'd created. "We'll figure it out before then. And
if we don't, we'll take precautions."

"We?" A little curiosity. A whole lot of a woman
ready to tussle.

Not about to wade into the waters lapping at his feet
without being in touching distance, he shifted closer and
faced her head-on. "Already covered this, G. My brothers love you. My sisters love you. My mothers love you."

"I've barely met your mothers."

Yeah, that was gonna change and soon. Thanks to Knox, he'd heard from Sylvie and Ninette all of twenty minutes after he'd driven Gia home yesterday and kissed her stupid outside her front door. "It doesn't take them long to get a bead on people. And even if they hadn't met you, they'd have your back for what you did with Nat and Darya. Family's family. Period."

God, that look. He could count on one hand the number of times he'd marked uncertainty on Gia's face and still have fingers left over, but in that second, she was raw. Totally on uncharted ground. "Your version of family and mine are two vastly different things."

Oh, he'd figured out that much. Not once when she'd shared about growing up had there been much warmth. No funny stories to tell outside of those where she'd out-maneuvered her parents to get into trouble, and no reminiscent memories that made her seem to miss Atlanta in the slightest. But something told him, now wasn't the time to clue her into just how close she was to learning the difference firsthand. He'd tackle that later. Preferably after he'd worked her body and she was utterly sated and pliant beneath him. "Already told you, my brothers are digging into this. So, how about we talk logistics and figure out how to make this thing happen."

For a second, he thought she'd argue, the spark behind her eyes saying she'd cottoned on to the fact that he was dodging something. Instead, she nodded and dug into the details her dad had sent her. How the previous security lead had overpromised and under-delivered right out of the chute. The date of the event and the people needing protection. Most important, the fact that the governor trying to retain his office had done significant damage to drug traffic in his state and had credible safety concerns with a drug cartel who'd lost their foothold since he took office.

She frowned and wrinkled her nose like she'd caught a whiff of something from a men's locker room. "Much as I hate to admit it, I'm not sure I can pull together the crew I need to pull this off on such short notice. Not without risking losing credibility like the first guy did."

"You need what? Five to ten on-site bodies and a handful running back-end surveillance?"

"Maybe. I won't know for sure until I get specifics from Peter."

"I've got that many easy. Me and however many other bodies you need. Problem solved." Three mini-malistic sentences that rolled off his tongue without so much as a breath of hesitation. But it was a huge offer and Gia knew it. Hell, everyone who worked in or around Texas knew it. Beckett and Knox hoarded their staff the way his little-old-lady neighbor growing up stockpiled restaurant Sweet'n Low packets. With the comfortable salaries and benefit packages they offered almost no one jumped ship.

Breaking eye contact, she stared down at her lap and swept nonexistent crumbs off one thigh. Her voice was quieter. More cautious. "Beckett, if I get this, I'd cover the primary."

"Yep."

A pause and a tight squeeze of one hand on her thigh. Then she lifted her head and met his eyes. "So, if I'm covering the primary, I'm calling the shots."

So that was the issue. Though after the shit she'd been through with Judd, he couldn't blame her for being careful. "Yep."

She dipped her chin and glared up at him with that disbelieving look reserved only for women dealing with thickheaded men. "I've never seen you *not* lead a crew. Do you even know how to take a back seat? On anything?"

Well, now. Wasn't that just the segue he needed. And a topic they'd do well to get well out into the open from the get-go. He covered her hand with his and stroked his thumb along the inside of her wrist. "You and me—if we're diving into what I want—then we're gonna have to figure some things out as we go, but I can tell you two things are carved in stone already."

One of her eyebrows cocked almost as fast as the hammer on a revolver. "Carved in stone?"

"Absolute."

On the surface, she seemed utterly calm, but her pulse beneath his thumb raced a little faster. She pursed her lips in a half smirk. "This I gotta hear."

God, he loved her spunk. Loved the ten-foot-tall sass that came out of such a petite package and the razor-sharp wit that backed it up. He slid his fingers up and manacled her wrist, the grip just tight enough to make sure he had her attention. "I don't play games at work. If you're on the primary and calling the shots, I'll have your back. That goes without question. Always."

This time it was both eyebrows that hopped high. "You mean that?"

"Absolutely."

She studied him, gaze roving his face as if looking for some hidden evidence to discount what he'd said. "And the other?"

His own pulse kicked into high gear, the anticipation he'd barely kept in check since she'd said the word *pizza* shoving all but right here and right now into the very deep background. Keeping his grip on her wrist, he stood, pulled her to her feet and wrapped her up tight, one arm banded low on her waist. He held her face steady at one side and got nose to nose. He should have gentled his voice, but what came out was all him. The unvarnished raw man under his barely civilized veneer. "When we fuck you absolutely will not have the lead. Ever."

Her gasp was slight, but sexy as hell. So potent she may as well have slid one of the hands pressed to his chest straight down to his dick and fisted it tight. Her eyelids got heavy and her lips parted just enough to make him want to trace the lower one with his tongue, but true to form, she didn't give in. Steel mingled with her husky voice. "Just because I let go last night doesn't mean that's all I want."

He risked the knee to the nuts she was in prime position to deliver and let his lips curve in a triumphant grin. "Sweetheart, that's *exactly* what you want and I'm willing to prove it."

Her gaze sharpened in an instant. "Prove it how?"

He inhaled deep and skimmed his nose alongside hers, her mouth close enough he nearly tossed his plans in the gutter. But that wouldn't prove the point he needed to make. That she needed to feel and understand at a fundamental level so she could actually enjoy and not fight him every step of the way. He squeezed her tighter for all of a second, then forced himself to step away. "You lead."

The loss of contact was staggering. An affront to every instinct in him and one she seemed to struggle with as well if the scowl she aimed up at him was any indication. "I what?"

"Tonight. You lead. Whatever you want. However you want me."

Cocking her head to one side, she sidled closer, gobbling up what distance he'd created and splaying her hand low on his stomach. "Anything?"

Fuck, he was going to regret this. At least he would until she figured out how much better things worked when he kept his hands on the wheel and let her soar. Then he'd launch them both as far as they could go and wallow in the aftershocks. "Anything."

"What's the catch?"

"No catch." He kept his hands at his sides, though it nearly killed him. "So long as you feel good and get what you need, we'll play your way."

The smile she shot him was dirty and deadly. "I like this plan." She moved in so her tits teased his chest, laced her fingers with his and craned her face toward his. "I'm an excellent leader."

It was a taunt and a promise all rolled up into one. His cock strained behind his jeans, more than ready to answer to both. "I'm six foot four and weigh twice what you do. You gonna lead this attack down here, or get me upstairs where I can stretch out and enjoy the ride?"

For a second, he thought she'd push him down on the couch just to prove a point, but she finally backed away, keeping one hand clasped in his as she scanned his body. Her gaze stopped pointedly on the blatantly hard bulge behind his fly and then shot back to his. "Well, you are big."

Yep. Definitely a long, hard stretch of patience and control ahead of him.

Before he could throw a quip about other things being long and hard, she led him toward the stairs, hips swaying with enough confidence to level a roomful of men. "Can't have you uncomfortable now can we?"

Uncomfortable? Was she fucking kidding him? He kept the thought to himself and focused on getting up the stairs without his jeans cutting off the blood supply to his cock.

Broaching the threshold to her refined, yet deeply feminine room, a weird sensation moved through him. Something foreign he couldn't quite put a label on. As if some deeply recessed territorial instinct had tripped, bound only by the vow he'd given to let her lead.

"You look a little uncertain." Gia pulled him deeper into the room then circled him until she had him positioned between her and the bed. Splaying her hand on his sternum, she urged him backward until his legs hit the mattress. "You sure you're up for this?"

"Don't doubt giving you control, gorgeous. Just makin' sure I can keep my shit on lockdown long enough for you to work your way to the truth."

Her hands slipped under his tee and pushed it up, up, up. "What if I don't want your shit on lockdown? What if my whole goal is to push you until you let go like I did last night?"

As tall as he was, she had zero chance of getting the shirt off him without an intervention, so he peeled it off, rolled his shoulders to try to ease the building tension and tossed his shirt to the floor. He rested his hands on her hips with far more control than he felt. "Oh, I'll let go. When you're under me and coming on my cock."

If he hadn't been touching her, he'd have missed the tremor that worked through her torso, but the rasp in her voice said plenty. "What makes you think I'm letting you on top?"

All too easily, the image of her straddling his hips, her tits bouncing as she rode him, blasted through his thoughts. "Baby, it doesn't matter what position we end up in. I'll always be on top in every way that counts. We're just playin' this out so you can process reality."

She pursed her mouth. "Mmm-hmm." With that, she shoved him backward.

He went with it, letting the king-size plushness absorb his fall before he scooted back and situated himself smack-dab in the middle. He tucked his hands behind his head. "Gotta admit. So far, your brand of foreplay's a huge turn-on. What else ya got?"

Her mouth twitched like it was all she could do to fight back a grin. "Shut up, Beckett." She tugged one of his Timberlands off and dropped it to the floor, the muted thunk as it hit the rug-covered hardwoods like an exclamation point to her command.

"I'd ask if you'd spank me if I'm bad, but we won't make it that far."

The second boot joined the other and she started on his socks, for all intents and purposes ignoring his taunt.

"Now spanking *you*," he said, intent on getting her eyes back on his, "*that* I have a feeling we'll get to."

She tossed his socks aside and lifted her head just enough to lock stares.

Perfect.

Eyes heavy. Full lips tipped in a sultry smile. Dark hair loose around her shoulders. Even in a tank and those stretchy workout pants she wore, she gave every screen goddess a run for their money. "Spanking you wouldn't turn me on in the least, but I'm considering possible gag options." She gripped the hem of her tank and casually peeled it up and over her head.

Not the move he'd expected. Not even close. But if she'd wanted a way to shut him the fuck up and keep him dumbfounded, displaying her amazing rack in a lacy sky-blue bra was the perfect play. Her pants came next. By the time she straightened, tossed her hair over one shoulder and crawled onto the foot of the bed, he was pretty damned sure the only thing his tongue was meant for was to sample every inch of flesh she'd bared.

Standing tall on her knees, she skimmed her fingertips from his toes along the top of his feet toward his ankles.

It was such a simple touch. Almost innocent. But paired with the way she looked at him and her outstanding curves on prime display, it was the most erotic thing he'd felt in his life. "You remember that talk we had about touch, right?"

Her fingers skimmed higher, trailing his shins as far as his jeans would allow before retracing back to his ankles. "I remember." Soft, but focused. A singled-minded determination to put everything she had into every second. "You don't like it?"

She knew damned well he did. The knowledge and the power that went with it practically crackled in the air around her. He forced himself to stay still as she made another pass. "I fucking love it."

This time her smile was playful. She leaned over him and stroked her hands along the outside of his jean-clad legs, her head cocked at a sassy angle. "So, you like me being in control."

A statement. Not a question. Though, with her hands working the top button on his fly, it took a five-second delay before the content fully registered. He fisted his hands behind his head and his biceps jumped from the sudden action. "Sweetheart, I never said I didn't like you being in control. I said you *needed* me in control. If it's between what gets me off and giving you what you need, you'll trump me every time."

The statement stopped her cold just as the last button popped free and her gaze snapped to his. Without the denim caging him in, his cock stretched long and thick against his belly, his über soft boxer briefs the only thing between him and heaven. But the only thing worth processing was the look on her face. The sheer surprise and vulnerability. The want and disbelief. He wanted to hold her. Needed to roll her underneath him, cover her skin to skin and impress what he'd shared in the most physical way possible.

But he'd made her a promise, and hell would freeze over before he broke it. Though, moving things a little closer to her revelation wouldn't hurt. He lifted his hips, drawing her out of her stupor and back to the task at hand. "Get these off me."

She bristled at the near growled command, the look on her face hinting at rebellion until her gaze dropped to his unbuttoned fly and curiosity seemed to get the better of her. Hooking her fingers in his clothes at his hips, she worked the fabric down, her focus so fixated on his dick he swore it stretched even farther. "Beckett."

Damn, but he liked the sound of his name when she said it like that. Husky and heated. "Not sure if that's praise for what you're staring at, or you queuing up a complaint."

"Not a complaint." She dragged his jeans and briefs the rest of the way off and tossed them to the floor, never once taking her attention off him. "Definitely not a complaint." She anchored one knee between his ankles and nudged his shin with the other. "Let me in."

He chuckled, but widened and cocked his legs, the space he'd created quickly gobbled up as she knelt between them. "Don't have to ask me twice."

The quip didn't faze her. Hell, he wasn't even sure she'd heard it the way she drank him in. She gripped his legs just above his knees and stroked upward, her palms teasing the fine hairs along his thighs. Her fingertips grazed the V at his hips and his cock jerked.

She smiled like a kid who'd just been gifted with a new and fascinating toy.

"All for you, gorgeous." And boy, was it. Never in any experience had he been so revved and ready to go as he was in this moment, and he hadn't even felt her body against his yet.

Continuing her exploration, her hands made a teasing detour on either side of his aching cock and back in to run her thumbs through the trail of hair low on his stomach. "Oh, I like that. Very much." She took her time. Learning him. Savoring every muscle. Tracing every line of ink. The head of the Celtic dragon roaring over one shoulder. The intricate knots lacing his rib cage. The tip of the dragon's tail near his hip.

Out of ink to follow, her fingertips drifted across his clenched abs and down to the juncture of his thighs, her touch barely skimming his supremely tight nuts. "I have to admit. This surprised me."

What surprised her? And why was she talking? Her hand was right there. All she had to do to unwind the gruesome tension was cup his sac in her tiny palm. He fought the need to lift his hips in encouragement. "What surprised you?"

Her touch whispered against his most sensitive flesh. "This. I didn't take you for the shaving type."

Fuck. More conversation. And what were they talking about?

Ah...right. "Feels better," he all but growled. Unwinding his arms from behind his head, he splayed his hands on either side of his hips, thankful for the slick comforter beneath him.

Rather than build the contact to something more tangible, she broke contact entirely, the shock at the loss a painful lash beneath his skin.

He opened his mouth, a command on his tongue and his breaking point teetering dangerously close—until his brain clocked her intent.

She guided one bra strap off her shoulder, then the other. "What do you mean it feels better?"

Okay, *this* he could totally hang on for. Hell, he'd level all of Dallas with his bare hands for her if it meant he got to watch her unveil the rest of her fantastic body. She dipped her chin just a fraction, bit her lower lip and reached behind her. The action pushed the swells of her breasts even higher and the ache in his cock ramped to a demanding throb.

Before he could answer, she undid the clasp and peeled the silky fabric away.

Beautiful. A hundred percent natural and just a little more than a handful, which was saying something considering the size of his hands.

She pressed her shoulders back and skimmed her fingers beneath them. "Beckett?"

Goddamn but she was good at this. Good, but not

the only one who could play the game. He grinned and gave himself what she hadn't, widening his legs even further and cupping himself in one hand. "I mean it feels better when I've spent time wrestling with a certain curvy brunette and can't stop thinking about the dirty things I want to do to her."

"Oh my God." It came out like a prayer, her hands splaying on the inside of his thighs and her gaze rapt on his actions. "That's insanely hot."

"Hotter if you'd get those panties off and do the same."

Her focus shot to his face, apprehension and intrigue both openly evident. Whatever sexual experiences she'd had, they clearly hadn't entailed anything so blatant, but she was considering it. Likely even trying to figure out how to one-up him.

He upped the ante and got his other hand in on the action, rubbing the length of his cock. "Stroked one off more times than I can count thinking about what you'd look like playing with your pussy. How you'd touch it. How you'd work your fingers inside. What sounds you'd make when you come."

Her hips flexed and her fingers tightened. "Beckett."

"Do it, gorgeous." Another pump. Then another. "Unless you're ready to let go of the wheel. I'd be more than happy to peel those panties off and fuck my fingers inside you instead."

Now, would you look at that.

Even hell couldn't claim a fire that burned hotter than the one behind her eyes. Another man would've put distance between them. Maybe donned steel briefs to keep his junk protected.

But he wasn't just any man. He was hers. And he'd

by God keep pushing her until she accepted it, or he'd die trying.

She slipped her fingers beneath the waistband of her panties, the matching blue lace perfectly accenting the flare of her hips. "I've got a better idea."

"Mmm." He shifted his grip and made a show of slicking his thumb through the pre-come at the head of his dick. "Lay it on me."

The lace pooled around her knees, revealing the tightly trimmed landing strip he'd appreciated to the fullest the first time he'd undressed her. She dropped to one hip, tugged the panties past her ankles and tossed them to the floor. "You say it feels better, huh?" Back on her knees she went, teasing her fingers through her curls. "Maybe I should try that."

He tightened his grip on his dick, about a hundred different ideas rushing his brain at once. "You'd probably need someone to help you. A steady hand." He squeezed his balls and flexed his hips. "A tongue to check and make sure you got it all after."

She dipped her fingers lower, circling her clit even as a devious smile tilted her lips. "You've got all the answers, don't you?"

"Got everything you need and then some."

"Hmmm." She closed her eyes and slid her fingers through her folds as though savoring her triumph. Relishing some secret victory.

Buddy, you are so screwed.

He knew it the way a man with a gun pointed at his temple knew he was a dead man. Although, in this instance, he couldn't fucking wait to have her pull the trigger.

Opening her eyes, she slowly slipped her hand from

between her thighs. "I think I've got what I need at the moment, but thanks for offering." She wrapped her fingers around his wrists, tugged his hands free of his busy work and pressed them to the comforter at his sides. "Now be good and keep those there."

Be good.

Right.

He could do that.

Maybe.

She stroked her hands from his hips to his chest, intentionally pressing her plump tits on either side of his straining cock.

He flexed into the soft valley, fixated on her mouth as she pressed a lingering kiss to his sternum. On her tongue as it sampled his skin. On her hot breath whispering over his chest.

Christ, but she was beautiful. Strong and delicate all at once. So determined to prove she could hold her own even though they both knew it wasn't what she wanted. Watching her almost killed him, powerlessness cutting him from the inside out even as her full lips and searching fingers painted a sweet path down his torso.

He groaned and speared his fingers in her hair, the silky weight of it against his hands and spilling down his forearms an instant comfort.

She licked his belly and lifted her gaze to his, her mouth still skimming against his skin. "Your hands aren't where I put them."

God, that was hot. A challenge thick with need. Forcing a gentle touch instead of fisting the slick strands the way he wanted, he rubbed his fingertips against her scalp. "You want to stay behind the wheel?"

She smiled and slipped a little lower, her cheek grazing one side of his shaft. "Absolutely."

"You remember what I said about needing touch?"

She shifted, her mouth poised just above the root of him. Her warm breath coiled around him as she answered low and husky. "I remember."

His fingers tightened, a subtle warning he couldn't have stopped if he'd tried. "Then you give me this, or all bets are off."

Her lips curved in a wicked smile. "I guess it's only fair to give you something to hang on to." With that, she licked along one prominent vein and firmly cupped his nuts, but the time for teasing was clearly over. Where every touch had been light and controlled before, now she seemed ravenous. Boldly exploring with her lips and tongue. Rolling his sac and stroking the base of his shaft. Engulfing him in her hot, wet mouth.

No mercy.

Not one shred.

He let out a ragged exhale and forced his hands to relax. He couldn't blow this. Figuratively or literally. Even though the latter was exactly what she was after. "I know what you're after, gorgeous, and it ain't happening. Not tonight."

She gave his nuts a gentle squeeze and moaned around his shaft, the vibrations from it alone enough to make him want to flood her mouth.

Focus, dumbass.

White ceiling. Dark skies outside. Detach. Detach. Detach. "You want me to come in your mouth, I will absolutely oblige. But not the first time."

She shifted and took him deeper, his cockhead grazing the back of her throat.

Fuck.

His lungs burned and his heart hammered out a war beat. "I'm giving you what you want, Gia, but you steal that gift from me, I'm gonna be pissed."

Another bob of her head, this one paired with a needy groan.

He fisted his hands, ready to force her away.

But she lifted her head, her breath coming fast and her lips slightly swollen. While she might have given him a reprieve from her mouth, her clever hand still worked the base of him. "You realize you're the pot calling the kettle black, right?"

In the real world, she had a point. But not here. Not now. "You want to debate this later, I'll do what I can to share the jacked-up male logic going on in my head. Right now, you're gonna have to accept it's a big fucking deal and make a concession."

For a second, he thought she'd argue. Or worse, storm away and leave them both miserable. Instead, she licked her lower lip. "I don't have condoms."

Thank you, Jesus. "In my pocket."

She scrambled off the bed and snatched his discarded jeans. "Which one?"

"Front."

As soon as he answered, her hand slipped free of the denim, at least four condoms filling her palm. "Not just a Boy Scout, but a confident one, too."

"Got more in the other pocket."

She cocked one eyebrow, tossed his jeans to the foot of the bed and straddled his hips. "Now that's just being cocky."

"Not bein' cocky if I can pull it off." He palmed the

outside of her knees and stroked up to her hips. "Now, you gonna glove me up, or are you gonna delegate?"

"Neither." She tossed the packets to the bed and leaned over him, her hands braced on his shoulders. "You did say you wanted to watch me get off." Centered perfectly above his dick, she widened her knees and brought her folds flush against the base of his shaft. She flexed her hips. "Far be it from me not to deliver."

And here he'd thought he'd bought a reprieve. God, she was wet. Drenched and coating him with each sultry grind. "That's it, baby." He dug his fingers into her hips, the need to shift and plunge inside her a white-hot demand. "Work that pretty pink pussy on my cock."

She sucked in a sharp gasp. "Beckett." A command and a plea. Her nails dug into his shoulders and her head dropped back, her hair spilling more than halfway down her back. Back and forth, she worked him with her sex, rolling her clit against his hard length with each downward stroke. But it wasn't enough. She knew it. He knew it. The trick was getting her to admit it. Assuming he lived that long.

"Inside," he all but grunted. "Glove me up and get me inside."

Lost, she rolled her hips again, but a tiny frown marked her features.

"Gia." He flexed against her on her next glide, dragging his glans against her clit. "Baby, you need to come. Glove me up, or let me take over."

With a tiny whimper, she eased back, swiped a packet and ripped it open, the tremors moving through her nearly making her fumble the condom.

"Goddamn it, Gia, give in."

"No." She slid the condom on and guided him into place. "I've got this."

No, she didn't. Not even close. But he was done trying to prove a point. All that mattered now was easing the frustration that gripped her body and giving her what she needed. He might not have full use of his hands, but she hadn't said shit about not using his mouth. "Know what I'm thinking of right now?"

She notched the tip of him inside and her sex vised around him. "You're thinking?" So breathless. Her nails dug into his wrists as she sunk a little lower, shattering his control bit by bit. "I must be doing this wrong."

"Not wrong." *No touching.* "You just don't have the view I do." *No driving. No taking over.* "Can't see my cock sinking inside your cunt. Stretching it."

A spasm racked her. Not the release he was after, but a powerful warning shot. "And all I can think about is how your bare pussy felt on my dick. How I've never hated a condom so bad in my life. How I want to drive deep inside you with nothing between us and fill you up. Mark you with my come."

"Oh my God." Her eyes slipped shut and she took him to the root, slowly finding a rhythm and chasing her release. Up and down, she rode him with a building wildness. A desperation that twisted his gut and made him grind his teeth.

He shouldn't push it. Shouldn't take advantage of the promise he'd given, but he needed more. Anything to ground him. He skimmed his hands from her hips down the outside of her thighs then up the inside, pausing just inches from her sex. "You're clit's so swollen, sweetheart. Your pussy tight around my cock. All you have to do is say the word and I'll take over."

"No."

A little closer with his thumbs, almost to the seam where her legs met her sex. "You, on your back, hands pinned above your head and my cock pounding inside you. That's what you want, isn't it?"

"No."

"Or maybe on your hands and knees with me driving into you from behind."

"No."

"No shame in it, Gia. You're a woman. *My* woman."

Her eyes snapped open, the raw fear and need behind them spearing to the heart of him. "Beckett."

"Give me the word."

Her lips parted.

"Now."

"Yes!"

One brutal kick from his heart and he was in motion. Her back to the bed. Her hands pinned to the mattress beneath one of his. He hitched one of her knees high with the other, dipped his hips and drove home.

Her eyes slid shut and her back arched, a moan of pleasure and relief ripped up the back of her throat.

He tightened his grip on her wrists to get her attention. "Eyes open, baby. Look at us."

Her eyes fluttered open and locked on him.

So beautiful. Splayed open. Held down. Tits bouncing with every advance and those gorgeous brown eyes staring up at him. Trusting him.

"You're safe," he growled between thrusts. He stroked his hand from her knee to her sex. "Feel it." He slicked his thumb along where they were joined. "Right here, all you need to be is a woman." Coated in her wetness, he dragged his thumb up and around her clit, the sweet nub painfully hard beneath his touch.

"Beckett." A throaty plea paired with a flutter in her sex.

"No control. No expectation." He strummed harder, his hips slapping against hers. "Just *my* woman. Taking *my* cock the way she needs it."

Her pussy tightened around him.

"Fuck, yes. Own it, baby. Let go. Swear to Christ, I'll catch you."

Her heels dug into his back and her back bowed, her cunt fisting and releasing in the sweetest vise on earth. So strong. As potent and powerful as the woman beneath him, her sweet cry as she came undone flaying him wide.

His cock jerked inside her, the slick, hot grasp of her sex forcing his own release. Stealing his come. Milking him in a greedy, demanding grasp. Releasing her wrists, he gripped her hips and ground himself against her. Willed his body to make a mark. To burn an impression so deep inside her, she couldn't forget him. Could never walk away.

In and out, he pumped inside her. Watched his dark, hard shaft disappearing into her pretty pink heat. Wished he could see his release mingled with hers. That he could feel her scalding flesh with nothing between them.

Mine.

He didn't dare say it out loud. Couldn't risk giving her reason to run or doubt where they were headed, but the claim was there. A brand he'd never thought he'd want, let alone bend over backward to take.

But she was his. And he'd level any and every obstacle to make sure she stayed that way.

He slowed his hips, the demanding throb of release easing to a languid pulse.

Gia's touch registered on the tops of his hands, her featherlight fingertips dancing over his brutal grip at her hips. "Beckett?"

A rumble in the room registered right behind her soft voice. Fuck, was he growling?

He unclenched his hands, white spots where his fingers had dug into her flesh flashing before they blended in with the rest of her flushed skin. "Shit." Lungs chugging like he'd sprinted ten miles uphill, he smoothed his hands over where he'd manhandled her. "Gia, I'm sorry."

She stilled his hands with her own. "I'm not." She stared up at him, what was left of the walls she'd kept between them eradicated. This was Gia. The unvarnished woman, bared in so much more than just flesh. Her touch skimmed higher. Up his forearms. Over his triceps and shoulders. Cupping his neck. Fingers trembling and eyes wide with fragile trust, she urged him closer. "I liked it."

So sweet. Honest and open. Braced on his knees, he leaned into her, dipped his head to kiss her sternum and gave his hands free rein. Petting her glorious body and grounding himself in the process. Her thighs. Her belly. Hips, breasts and neck. But this was more than just feeding his sensory needs. This was gratitude. Deep, abiding gratitude.

She speared her hands in his hair, not fighting him. Just taking what he offered. Feeling it. Riding what she seemed to understand he needed. "You were right."

Years now, he'd known her. Watched her hold her own in a world that insisted she could never be an equal to her peers. He'd be damned if he let her feel anything less than equal here. He pressed a kiss to her shoulder and lifted his head. "It wasn't about me being right."

Her lips trembled and her eyes got wet, just enough sheen to let him know she was perilously close to showing a side to herself few other people had ever seen. "What was it then?"

He smoothed her hair away from her face and swept one thumb along her cheek. "You knowing that, with me, you can just be you. A business owner. A friend. A badass."

She smiled huge, the sudden shift nearly knocking a tear free. "I like that last one."

"You *are* the last one." He cupped the side of her face and held her steady. "What you don't seem to get, gorgeous, is that you might not be like other women, but you are *all woman*. The fact that you get off having someone else be in control with sex doesn't mean you're weak. It means you know what you want and you're not afraid to make it happen."

"Well, I kind of was afraid to make it happen."

He grinned and rolled his hips, wishing like hell he didn't have a fucking condom between them. He'd have to work on that. Pronto. Though, how he was gonna broach that subject this fast without freaking her out escaped him.

"I think we're over that hurdle." He nipped her lower lip, his cock stirring at the highly promising ideas floating through his head. "But if you want to practice for good measure, I'm stocked up and absolutely on board to volunteer."

Chapter Thirteen

"That's quite a strut you're sportin' for a Monday afternoon." Axel's smooth voice hit Beckett the second he stepped across the threshold to Crossroads' dark conference room. Situated on the third floor of Jace and Axel's club, Crossroads, their offices flanked the wide room on either end and gave a bird's-eye view of the main dance floor below. "Thought the girls in the office were gonna break their necks watchin' you stroll through the lobby."

Per usual, Axel looked like something out of a men's fashion magazine—tailored black pants, a gray button-down, and leather shoes that probably cost a mint. Braced with both hands on the oblong table, he looked up from a blueprint rolled out in front of him and grinned, that long red hair of his as wild as ever.

Beckett glanced at the big flat screens mounted on one end of the conference room wall. As big as Crossroads was, there was no way the four monitors could cover everything going down in Dallas's premier hot spot, but the one aimed at the lobby seemed to have gotten the job done this time. He ambled to the industrial stainless fridge built into the long wet bar lining one wall. Given his primary agenda item for today's rally, a beer was definitely in order and the options Jace and Axel kept on hand were cream of the crop. "Remind me next time I do an install for you to work in some kind of override."

"He's just jealous," Jace said from his place in a plush black leather chair at the far end of the table. He glanced up from the swath of manila folders thick with documents stacked in front of him, a dirty smirk quirking one side of his mouth. "Only one thing that puts that much swagger in a man's step and I know damned good and well our Don Juan's on a dry spell."

"Dry spell my ass," Axel grumbled. "More like self-preservation."

Jace's smile deepened. Where Axel was an odd mix of suave and Scottish warlord, Jace was more the old-school biker type complete with longish dark hair, goatee and a white Led Zeppelin tee with lettering so faded it could have been from their debut tour. He was also perceptive as a hungry wolf. So much that almost nothing got past him, and the way he was staring at Axel, Beckett had a good hunch there was more to Axel's dry spell than either of them were letting on.

Tempted as he was to do a little digging and see if he could get Jace to offer up a few clues, Beckett snagged a Bell's Ale, popped the top and left well enough alone. "Anyone need a refill?"

Axel grunted, snatched his nearly empty tumbler off the table and meandered toward the bar. "Don't let that bloody bastard have one. Not until he's done with my paperwork."

Jace chuckled and went back to studying the doc in his hand. "Pretty sure every other legal document I've filed for you the last thirteen years was founded on Scotch. You sure you wanna break that streak with your pet project?"

That was the other thing about Haven's founding brothers. Axel's high-end clothes aside, most people wrote them off as hard men who'd lucked into their fortune solely on street smarts. The truth was, they were wickedly intelligent, both with degrees that made them a formidable pair in business—Axel in operations and Jace in corporate law.

Beckett snatched the Macallan off the shelf behind him and topped Axel's glass off. "This the new concert venue? Thought that was all nailed down."

"Nailed down, yes. Bulletproof, no. Got a few uptight assholes grumbling about an outdoor stage drawin' a bad crowd to downtown." Axel grabbed the bottle, turned and reloaded Jace's glass. "I need bulletproof."

Jace shook his head, a good-natured air of exasperation coloring the act, but Beckett saw it for what it was. He and Axel had grown up together the same way Beckett and Knox had, and Jace would move heaven and earth if it meant keeping Axel happy.

The security door at the bottom of the stairs slammed shut and at least two sets of footsteps pounded their direction.

The two proved to be three, Zeke finding the doorway first with Knox and Danny only a beat behind him. Zeke scanned the room, claimed a chair and dropped into it like he'd just tackled a double marathon. Given the blue trauma scrubs he had on and his tired eyes, he probably had. "Where's Trevor?"

"Runnin' down a loose end on Ivan. He's five out at most." Knox halted in front of the wet bar, planted both hands on his hips and scowled at Beckett. "Either hand me a cold one, or stop blockin' the supplies."

Damn. Knox seldom went for alcohol before quitting time on a workday. Maybe Beckett should've hauled his ass into the office this morning instead of annoying Gia in hers.

Nah. He spun for the door and shrugged the guilt off almost as fast as it had hit him. For all Gia's fussing about him being an overbearing oaf and hogging her space, she'd liked having him there. A fact confirmed when she'd curled up next to him with her laptop on that tiny excuse for a couch in her office, tucked her feet under her legs and shown him the details of the suspects she'd narrowed down.

"Breakfast Stout or Zombie Dust?" Beckett said, scanning the insane number of options available inside.

"Too late for the stout. Shoot me the Dust."

"Who the fuck drinks a beer called Zombie Dust?" This from Danny, who'd given in to his nosy nature and was crowding Axel and his blueprints.

"Enough to make it a top ten beer pick for this year." Jace flipped to the last page on his document, huffed and tossed it back to the pile. "Brings in a premium price, too, so I ain't bitchin'."

"No shit?" Danny eyeballed the bottle in Knox's hand. "Lager?"

The stairway door clanged shut, heralding Trevor's arrival.

Knox knocked back a healthy swig and let out a satisfied hiss before he answered. "Pale ale. Out of Indiana."

Trevor moseyed through the conference room door, a little on the haggard side appearancewise and clutching a folder in one hand. He clocked everyone in one fell swoop, then locked in on Knox's beer. "Cool. Zombie Dust." His gaze cut to Beckett still manning the bar. "Hook me up."

Danny shrugged and dropped into the chair closest to him. "What the fuck. Give me one, too then."

Beers doled out and everyone with their asses situated around the table, Knox zeroed in on Trevor. "So? How was Chicago?"

A handful of words at most, but eerily effective for derailing the fifteen different approaches he'd planned for telling his brothers about Gia. Beckett volleyed a stare between Knox and Trevor. "What's in Chicago?"

Apparently, he wasn't the only one lost on the topic, because all the other brothers looked just as stymied.

Knox grinned. "You know how Ivan's first background check showed nada prior to 2009? Well, we got a lead on him."

Trevor huffed out an ironic chuckle over the rim of his beer and murmured, "More like a lead handed to you."

"Handed by who?" Jace said.

Shrugging, Knox snatched the folder out from in front of Trevor. "Ivan."

"You mean he slipped and shared something we could use?" Axel said.

"He made it look that way." Trevor set his beer on the table, one of those satisfied smirks on his face. "You ask me, it was a test. No man in his right mind is gonna lay out the kind of things I confirmed today without being damned sure about the skills of the men he's trusting."

Beckett chin-lifted toward the folder. "What's the news?"

Knox dragged a small stack of papers from inside,

a mix of photos and articles printed out on plain copy paper. He slid the biggest photo across the table to Beckett. "Meet Bowen Sanders, aka Ivan Moody. Born 1981, age 36. No father listed on his birth certificate. One sister, both of whom lived with their single mother. Disappeared in late 2008 in Chicago."

Appearancewise, there wasn't much difference in the man they worked with today. Way shorter hair, no dreds and much younger, but still a built man with rock-solid determination in his eyes. Most of the shots were candid with Ivan mostly in the background. "You get these off social media?"

"Yeah, and this is about all that's out there. Which makes sense because Bowen Sanders didn't have much time for a social life. Dropped out of high school one semester into his sophomore year. That ties to about six months after his mom suffered a back injury and lost both of her jobs."

"He went to work to pay the bills," Danny said, stating the obvious.

Knox nodded. "Looks like it, and never went back. Though I did find that Ivan Moody has a GED."

Jace propped an elbow on the arm of his chair and twirled his toothpick. "No incentive there for a man to disappear."

"No, but his sister has records at a Chicago hospital that show her in intensive care about a month before he went MIA."

"Think I got an idea where this is headed." Zeke scratched the back of his head. "Let me guess—domestic abuse."

"She never claimed as much, but the doctor made comments about suspected abuse."

"She married?" Danny asked.

"No, but she had a man," Trevor answered before Knox could. He shifted enough to meet Danny's gaze. "That man disappeared a week before Bowen followed suit."

Silence lasted all of a few heartbeats.

"Where's the sister now?" Beckett said.

Trevor hung his head, the weight of the things he'd learned seeming to press down on his shoulders. "Dead. Drug overdose roughly six years ago."

"Hold up." Danny leaned into the table and eyeballed Knox. "His little girl, Mary, is six."

"She's not his kid," Jace said, filling in the blanks everyone else was closing in on.

"Nope." Knox kicked back in his chair, the pose of a man wrapping up the end of a wicked story. "From what I can tell, the woman he claims is Mary's mom is a connection he made after Ivan disappeared. He set it up so she's the momma on paper, but that's it."

"Smart move." Axel ran his thumb through his beard along his jaw. "Get someone pliable. Someone who needs money and won't talk. He ends up with Mary legally in the system with him as the dad and undeniable rights."

The room got quiet, every man looking from one to the other.

Jace homed in on Trevor. "You brought him to us. This change anything for you?"

Trevor stared at the table, thoughtful. "If someone fucked with Natalie or Levi, no question in my mind how I'd react." He lifted his head and met Jace's stare. "He took care of his own. Maybe not the way the law says he should, but to my mind, he's more solid now than before."

"Not gonna argue with that logic," Zeke added.

Jace looked to Beckett.

Like he was gonna naysay a man who'd looked after family. Ten days ago, if someone had so much as bruised Gia, he'd have been hard-pressed not to arrange the need for a body cast. Now he wasn't sure he'd even be able to stop until he was painted in someone's blood. "He's got my vote."

"Mine, too." Knox craned his head to Trevor. "Though for the record, I think the tip was less of a test and more his way of saying he wanted in."

"Maybe." Axel stared at Jace from his end of the table for a few beats, then dipped his head. "I'm in."

"Right. Looks like we're moving from seven to eight." Jace straightened, snatched his Scotch and raised it to the men around him. "We're gonna need a bigger table."

Just that fast, the weight of the room lightened, plans as to when and how Trevor planned to broach the topic with Ivan flying back and forth with the same levity as the beer conversation had gone. Not that Beckett was tracking a word of it. His brain was still stuck on Gia and the primal protective urge the day's topic had surfaced. She'd all but convinced him the primary suspect was the stalker she'd helped put away, but what if it wasn't?

"We gotta talk about something else." The statement wasn't pitched to carry, but the fact that he'd cut through his brothers' banter to make it silenced the room as effectively as a gavel.

Knox smiled big enough to show teeth.

Danny and Zeke raised their eyebrows almost in perfect sync, where Axel and Trevor just chuckled.

Jace leaned a forearm on the table and swirled his Scotch. "Do we, now?"

Fuckers. Though, he guessed he'd earned getting his chops busted over the last few years. Especially with Jace. He hadn't exactly been warm and fuzzy when he'd brought Viv into the fold. Not at first anyway. "I'm claiming Gia."

Trevor, Danny and Axel all spoke at once, irony the common element between them.

"Now there's a shocker."

"No…"

"Ya don't bloody say."

For the first time since he'd walked in, Zeke looked like he wasn't five seconds from hitting the sack. "Not nearly as hard as you think it'll be, is it?"

Knox tipped the mouth of his ale Beckett's direction and cocked an eyebrow. "Told ya."

Jace cocked his head and studied Beckett. "Knox shared about the YouTube thing over the weekend. How's she doin'?"

"Still beatin' her own ass for not catching her trigger was off before she started and plotting ways to cut the nuts off whoever posted the clip, but other than that, she's dealin'."

"Maury call you back?" Axel asked.

Beckett nodded. "Someone definitely altered it, but whoever did it knew what they were doing."

"I don't get it," Zeke said. "Why would anyone set her up like that?"

Danny scoffed and crossed his arms on the table. "Not all that hard to piss someone off in the security business. Figured that out in the first few gigs I worked for Beckett."

That was absolutely true. Nothing pissed people off more than the person who stood between them and causing pain or trouble for their intended target. "Yeah, well, whoever it is, I need to find 'em and shut 'em down. G's got a chance at a big detail in Atlanta in about a month. Political fund-raiser and a lobbyist she'd do good to get on her resume. If she lands it, having an unknown like this hanging over her head could back-fire in a way she wouldn't easily bounce back from."

"She got any suspects?" Jace asked.

"Four. Possible fallout from the two deals she helped us with on Natalie and Darya, a pissed-off corporate termination she had to intercede with in Atlanta and a stalker she helped put away on one of her first jobs here. The stalker got released on a technicality about three months ago."

"Darya's thing we can trace down easy enough," Knox said. "I'll put in a call to Sergei and ask him to dig."

Trevor shook his head. "I don't think it's Wyatt. He's got incentive for sure, but between the Feds keepin' him on a tight leash and our come-to-Jesus intervention, he's kept a healthy distance."

Come-to-Jesus indeed. He bet Natalie's ex never walked into a dark parking lot again so long as he lived.

"Still smart to check it," Jace said. "Could be he's keepin' quiet and covering his tracks."

Trevor shrugged and scooted back enough to stretch his legs out and cross one boot over the other. "Not a problem."

"You got the name of the guy from Atlanta?" Knox said.

Beckett nodded. "And the stalker."

If Knox's laptop had been in reaching distance he'd have likely settled in and started searching ASAP. Instead, he whipped his phone out and typed in a note. "I'll check 'em out, but my money's on the guy who just got out of jail."

"Mine, too." Axel shifted his focus to Beckett. "Might not be a bad idea to put a man on him until Knox is done runnin' traps."

The primal urge kicked up a notch. As if it had locked onto a slice of sunshine at the edge of its dark cage and was primed to escape. "Oh, he'll have someone on him 24/7 as soon as we find him, but the first window we get, I'm combing his place. I'm not dickin' around with this one. Not with Gia involved."

"I'll run it with you," Danny said, openly perking up at the prospect of tapping into some of his shadier skill sets. "Two sets of eyes, we'll be in and out in no time."

Jace cleared his throat, lips twitching with the smile he was doing a piss-poor job of hiding. "I see you've adjusted to havin' Gia be a part of Haven, but how prepped is she to be wrapped up in our overbearing arms?"

Overbearing? What the fuck? "What's to prepare? She knows us. Gets the gist of what we are even without me running things down. And I've lost count of the places we've broken into for info in the last decade. It's standard operating procedure."

"For us, yeah," Zeke cut in, "but don't forget how Gabe took to our little B&E stint a few years ago."

Beckett shook his head. "Nah, Gia's good. The only pushback she'd give me is if she wasn't in on the job."

"You gonna let her in on it?" Trevor asked.

"Hell, no." As soon as he said it, a warning buzz fired

across his neck. Kind of like he had a shock collar on and Gia had punched the remote without even knowing it. He gripped the armrests on his chair. "She's got too much exposure already. I'll tell her after the fact."

Axel grinned. "Not always easier to get forgiveness, brother. Plus, you'd be smart to give her some kind of warning shot about what she's gotten herself into being a part of our family. I heard the moms planning something this morning. Gia might get the gist of how we operate, but you might want to help her gird her loins before all our women descend en masse."

All too easily, the image of Gia surrounded by the women in his family drew his focus from the room at large. Knowing her, she'd employ the same no-bullshit approach on them that she used with the herd of men she worked with every day, but he also had a feeling she needed what they could give her. An acceptance from equally strong women she'd never found growing up.

"I'll talk to her." He'd also hit Sylvie up for details and see if he couldn't figure out a way to be a fly on the wall when the descent actually happened. In the meantime, he was gonna do what he could to get Gia stockpiled with goodness on the professional side of her life. "Got another favor I need to ask."

"Not a favor if it's family." This from Trevor who was still watching him with far too knowing eyes.

Beckett shrugged it off and scanned the rest of the crew. "Anyone know a guy out of Atlanta named Peter Trannell?"

"I don't know anybody out of Atlanta," Zeke said. "Who is he?"

"The guy runnin' the event Gia's trying to land. A lobbyist."

Axel stood and paced toward the wet bar. "Name doesn't ring a bell, but I know a few people there. Wouldn't mind askin' around."

"If Axel doesn't, I'd bet Sergei does," Knox said. "He might be based out of New Orleans, but the man's made more connections since he moved to the States than half the politicians in the senate."

"There a reason you're asking?" Jace asked.

Beckett hesitated, the same cautionary pause he'd felt when he and Knox had first met the rest of the guys and they'd offered their help bubbling back up like it was yesterday. Back then, having family besides Knox to back him up had been a hard concept to wrap his head around. Now he knew better, and thinking even for a second they wouldn't be there this time was wasted energy. "Because I want her to get this detail."

Danny chuckled and thunked his now empty beer bottle on the table. "Stacking the deck, huh?"

"Fuck yeah. It's what we'd do if we wanted a contract. Why not do the same for her?"

Axel tipped his head and stared down at the empty dance floor and the crew readying the place for opening later on. "Can't argue with that logic."

"There's also the fact she's been undercut way too many times," Beckett said barely pausing. "Way more than I ever knew, and it's bullshit. She wants this job and I want her to have it."

Knox's gaze got wicked sharp. "Undercut by who?"

"Only one I know personally is that pompous fuck, Judd."

"Judd Rainier?"

"That's the one."

Zeke perked up and leaned into the table, eyes on Knox. "Who's that?"

"Works the same biz as us. Moved here from Atlanta a little after Gia did. Total douche. Thinks he's MacGyver, but comes off more like Malibu Ken with a stick up his ass."

"Turns out they grew up together," Beckett added. "As in right next door to each other—if you can call five-million-dollar homes and five-acre lots neighbors."

"What'd he do to her?" Trevor asked.

"She called him in on a corporate gig right before the thing at the range went down. The principal was traveling with extended family and she needed someone to cover the mom and kids. Turns out Judd arranged an earlier flight, played the man card with the exec and pushed Gia out to cover the mom and kids."

"That's whacked," Danny said.

Knox tipped his beer toward Danny. "It's also an industry insult. You book the deal, you cover the primary."

Axel turned from the window. "You say this happens a lot?"

"Judd's the only one she named, but yeah. Everything she gains in our business takes three times the effort, and she's had no one at her back. Not her peers or her family."

"Well, then." Jace lifted his Scotch and scanned the room, that crafty smile of his slipping into place. "I'd say her days of flying solo are over."

Chapter Fourteen

On her belly, naked with Beckett's weight pinning her to her bed and his cock languidly shuttling in and out of her still quivering sex—*now* Gia knew what all the fuss was about morning sex. She'd thought she'd hate it. Thought she'd never be able to get past bed head and morning breath to enjoy it, but in the last few days Beckett had taken great pains to demonstrate just how easy those hurdles were to clear.

At least with him they were. And the more she was with him—the more she got to know the man beyond the limitations of work—the more she realized how deep she could fall with him. How easy it would be to just let go and let all those hard lines she'd established soften and mingle with his. But then what? How would she ever be able to erase or rewind how it felt to linger in her kitchen with him? Having him send her this way and that to get what he needed while he cooked, and how he often trapped her in between tasks to sneak a kiss or a subtle touch? How at home he looked on the couch in her office, even if it was too small for his big frame?

She sighed and rolled her head, resting her cheek on the cool sheets and pushing her worries to the side. For now. She'd figure things out later. Preferably when

Beckett wasn't petting every inch of her and her brain was capable of something besides oohing and aahing about his sexual prowess.

With one forearm braced by her shoulder, he swept her hair to one side and nuzzled her neck, his deep, raspy morning voice stirring a whole new wave of flutters low in her stomach. "Not sure if that's a contented sound, or one I need to head off at the pass."

"Oh, I'm content." She smiled and stretched like a cat beneath him, the act seating him flush inside her. "Veeery content."

He chuckled and swept his hand down her side and lingered on the curve of her hip. Another trait she could easy grow addicted to. When they were alone, his hands were always on her. Sometimes still. Sometimes tracing patterns on her skin. But after sex, his hands were everywhere. Reverent. Comforting. As if he were thanking her for what she'd shared and checking to make sure she was real at the same time.

"Gotta deal with this condom." He nipped her earlobe then licked the sting he'd left behind. "You gonna be where I left you when I get back, or am I gonna have to work the hustle right back out of you again?"

Beyond her window, the early August morning skies were still a hazy blue, the sun not yet up enough to cast its heat or vibrancy on the waking city, but enough to blanket the room in an intimate glow. Even if she wanted to crawl out of bed and face the day, she wasn't sure her legs were ready to function yet. "I'm not going anywhere."

The sound that rumbled from his chest was somewhere between a growl and a hum and sent delicious ripples along her skin. "Holdin' you to that." With that, he kissed her cheek and slipped free of her still quivering flesh.

She sucked in a sharp breath at the loss, the emptiness and the rush of cool air against her skin a startling slap against her senses. She tugged the rumpled bedcovers up to her shoulders and snuggled on her side. It was nowhere near the warmth Beckett generated. Nice, but not as pleasant.

Kind of what life would be like if you lost Beckett.

God, what had it been? Ten days since they'd started their odd dance? Half of that since their first date, but she was already sliding dangerously deep. She smoothed her hand over Beckett's pillow and savored the lingering scent of him. Was that why her mother never stood up to her dad? Never called him on the string of affairs he'd done nothing to hide over the years? No matter how hard she'd tried, she'd never once been able to conjure a memory of her parents showing the kind of affection for each other that Beckett showed her. Couldn't remember a time when she'd seen either of their eyes light up when the other walked into a room, or heard an easy laugh shared between them. But maybe they'd had that once. Maybe it'd been good enough that her mom had clung to some desperate hope that she'd get it back.

Or maybe her mom was just too weak or unwilling to stand on her own. Maybe she'd lost so much of herself in her marriage she could no longer imagine herself as an independent unit. Whatever the case, Gia refused to fall into the same traps. She was strong. Smart. A whole person who didn't need someone else to define her. But, having been with Beckett, she was starting to see how easy it would be to get lost.

The water in the bathroom shut off and Beckett strolled back into sight, every gloriously muscled and tattooed inch of him on prime display. "You keep lookin' at me like that and we're not gonna be able to get any talking done."

She rolled to her back, enjoying the primal way he moved through her space. How he dominated simply by being. "Who said anything about talking?"

"I did." Rather than slip beneath the covers with her, he stretched out beside her, tucked her close to him and anchored one leg over hers, effectively caging her in. "You on the pill?"

Whoa. As conversation starters went, that one was about as subtle as his right hook. She propped herself up on one elbow. "Why? Did something happen?"

He grinned and cupped the side of her neck. "Condom didn't break if that's what you're asking." His gaze softened and he stroked the line of her pulse with his thumb. "But I wanna ditch 'em."

A whole host of flutters took flight in her stomach, just the idea of feeling him slide inside her unprotected sending goose bumps out in all directions. "Beckett, we've only been at this for five days."

"Been at this for almost three years. We just took too damned long getting to the good parts."

Her throat got tight and her palms got as sweaty as they had on her first protection detail, doubt and uncertainty clouding her thoughts. "I don't know. I've never…" Well, shit. What was she supposed to say without looking like an idiot? "This isn't exactly subject matter I'm familiar with."

God, she loved his smiles. Especially the one aimed at her right now. Full of teeth and so light she thought she'd float ten feet off the ground. "Me either."

She dropped back to her pillow and huffed up at him. "Would you be serious?"

In an instant, he was over her, his weight blanketing her and his intense blue eyes locked on her. "I am serious." He studied her, his gaze soaking in every feature of her face. "I'm not going to be with anyone else. You can try to be with someone else, I guess, but then they'll end up with broken arms, legs, or both."

"Possessive much?"

He cupped the back of her head and his gaze heated. "You have no idea."

And there were those ripples again, her breasts growing tight and heavy even as her sex threw out a *hallelujah*. "I don't want to be with anyone else."

Admitting it was a risk. A huge one. Especially with thoughts of her mother and how she'd all but become a doormat for her father still fresh in her mind. But seeing the look on Beckett's face as they registered—watching the shock and disbelief flash behind his eyes—the risk was worth it. "I'm also on the pill."

Hope.

Triumph.

Hunger.

All three tangled in his expression at once. She hadn't thought his voice could drop any deeper, but the words that came out rumbled a deep bass. "My woman's a regular Girl Scout."

"Always pays to be prepared."

"I'm inclined to agree at the moment."

"And for the record, I was a Camp Fire Girl, too."

"Mmm." He skimmed his lips against hers, the tightness when he spoke a stark contrast to the gentle touch. "So, we're gonna do this?"

"By do this, do you mean you're gonna work the hustle out of me like you promised?"

He lifted his head, all traces of humor wiped away. "No. I mean you're gonna give me you?"

Holy hell. Looking at her like that, open and completely vulnerable, she'd try to walk on water if he wanted. She swallowed huge, all her fears and whacked-out family history forming a painful knot that made the process almost impossible. "I'm going to try."

He cupped her face, his fingertips tangling in her hair. "You get I'm probably gonna be overbearing as hell?"

"You get there's a high probability I'll slug you when you are."

His quick smile rained down on her like sunshine. "I kind of like that side of you."

"I kind of like your overbearing side."

Something sparked behind his eyes. An ornery twinkle on par with a little boy who was two steps away from getting away with something. "That mean you won't get pissed if I tell you I tracked down Brantley Davis?"

"My stalker?" She bit her lip, enjoying the banter and where this was headed too much to spoil it too fast. "Yeah, so did I."

He frowned. "You did?"

"Um yeah. I've been doin' this a while, too, Beckett."

He cocked his head a little, the deep furrow between his brows still in place. "You find the guy in Atlanta, too?"

"Mmm-hmm."

The frown shifted to open suspicion. "What else aren't you telling me?"

This time she couldn't hold back the giggle. "That I also know you put a man on the guy here in Dallas."

"Bullshit."

She rolled her lips inward, trying to hold in a full belly laugh. God, but he was funny when he was flummoxed.

"How?" he said.

"How, what?"

"How'd you know?"

"Because I was already following him. I saw your guy move in."

"And you didn't tell me?"

She smoothed her hands up his arms and over his shoulders, hopefully imitating the calming touch he never hesitated in giving her. "Well, I'm a smart businesswoman. It didn't seem prudent to waste my time *and* theirs."

"Good point." Even though his words agreed with her, his voice sounded like he was waiting for a kick in the pants.

"Then there's the fact I hate tailing people."

He grunted, still obviously waiting for the surprise attack.

Well, it was coming. And it was going to be interesting to see how things played out. "But I was also waiting to see how long it would take you to share."

His eyes narrowed. "You were testing me?"

The belly laugh ripped free. "Testing you? Beckett, I've known you for three years and seen the lengths you and your brothers go to for people you care about. I knew what you'd do the minute I picked up the phone and said the word *pizza*." She paused long enough to get her laughter back in check and traced the line of his hard jaw, enjoying the prickly sensation beneath her fingertips. "I guess I just wanted to learn how you'd handle it. If you'd treat me like a peer, or treat me like a woman."

"They don't have to be exclusive."

"Not always, no. But Beckett, this time you treated me like a woman."

He studied her the way a man would when handed instructions in a foreign language. "I don't think I can help that, gorgeous."

"I know," she nearly whispered. As honest as he'd been he deserved the rest. "And to tell you the truth, even though I was a little pissed at first, another part of me liked it. I've never really had someone look out for me like that before. It was nice."

"Yeah?"

"Yeah." She ran her fingertips through the short hairs above his ears. "But if you treat me like anything other than a peer at work, I'm gonna have to kick your ass."

The taunt worked, nudging his smile back into place. "You can try."

"Oh, I will." She toyed with the chain that held his dog tags and let the moment settle around them. "Anything else you want to tell me?"

He hesitated. Nothing huge. Just a tiny pause paired with an almost imperceptible squint. "Not yet."

Not yet. As in, *Yes, but I'm not ready to spill.* She let it sink in a beat. Wrestled every knee-jerk response that fired into submission. He was a smart man. Good at what he did and loyal to a fault.

But so was she. "Don't forget this is my deal, Beckett. I have a right to know what's going on, and I'm experienced enough to deal with it."

"I know you are." And he meant it, too. It was right there for her to see, respect and appreciation filling his steady stare. "Just give me this. Trust me."

Trust. That fragile thing her dad had shredded over and over with her mother. But Beckett wasn't her dad and she damned sure wasn't her mother. She nodded. "Okay."

"Okay." He kissed her, a lingering one that did a superb job of soothing her more stubborn side's feathers. Just when she'd thought he might've changed his mind and get to soothing her far more primitive needs, he lifted his head and frowned. "There is one other thing I should mention."

"Now?"

"Now." He leaned for the nightstand and snatched his phone, checking the display for the time and groaning at what he saw. "Actually, probably should have told you about thirty minutes ago."

"Tell me what?"

"Remember how I told you to block off today?"

"Yeah? I thought you had work you wanted to do." Or that he'd just wanted to stay home and roll between the sheets. With Beckett, either option was something to look forward to.

He shrugged. "I fibbed a little."

This time it was her turn to frown. "Fibbed how?"

"You've got about thirty minutes before my moms and all my brothers' wives show up."

"Show up for what?"

"I dunno. Whatever it is women do when they've got the day off."

A slow burn tangled up in sheer panic blossomed beneath her skin. She squeezed his shoulders, not the least bit bothered by the fact her nails were digging in a little deep. "You're telling me I've got thirty minutes to get ready to spend the day *with your mothers*?"

"Pretty much." He rolled off her and planted both feet on the edge of the bed, well out of kicking distance. If he hadn't beamed such a killer grin at her when he leaned in for a quick peck on the cheek, she'd have tried anyway. "Welcome to the family."

Chapter Fifteen

Gia's feet hurt, her mad money fund was shot to hell and she was pretty sure wherever her kidnappers were headed next was going to be an exercise in patience, but she honestly couldn't remember a better day in her life.

Sandwiched between Natalie and Gabe in the middle row of the black Escalade, Vivienne propped both feet on the center console between Sylvie and Ninette. "You realize once Axel finds someone to tolerate his ass, we're gonna need a bigger vehicle."

Ninette glanced over her shoulder, checked for cars in the far lane and shifted like she was driving an Indy car instead of one of Beckett's bulletproof security SUVs. The woman might have been old enough to be Jace's mother, but she was striking in both appearance and attitude—long gray hair well past her shoulders, a model's physique and a strut to back it up. "Already got a plan for that."

"We're gonna rent a Hummer," Sylvie said with an almost scary level of glee. Unlike her son, Axel, who always seemed to have an underlying, barely restrained edge even when he was outwardly relaxed, Sylvie was pure joy in human form. She twisted to Vivienne, her dark cherry hair twice as bold with the sunlight bouncing off of it. "One of those big stretch ones."

Natalie dug another dark chocolate almond from the stash she'd bought at the candy store on the way out of the mall and popped it in her mouth. "The way we go out, it'd be more cost-efficient to buy one and hire a full-time chauffeur."

"God," Gabe said, "don't give the guys any ideas. Ninette driving I can tolerate. Some dude named Charles would make me bonkers."

"It wouldn't be a Charles." Seated next to Gia in the back row, Darya's Russian accent was just a tiny bit thicker after the glasses of wine she'd paired with lunch. "Knox and Beckett would hire a Rex. Or an Ace. A sharpshooter and a badass who'd rat us out at a moment's notice."

Vivienne nodded in agreement. "Right, because shopping is dangerous business."

The comment drew an easy round of laughter, the same laid-back camaraderie they'd surrounded her with since they'd shown up on her doorstep.

Outside her window, the Knox/Henderson exit sign whipped past and the Escalade's big engine eased. She opened her mouth to see if she'd have any luck digging their big surprise destination out of one of them, but something Vivienne had said finally clicked in her brain and an entirely different question sprang free instead. "What do you mean, *Once Axel finds someone to tolerate his ass?*"

Vivienne craned her head enough to beam a big smile back at Gia. "I mean the official Haven women count will leave us too damned crowded to keep taking the Escalades. We gotta have someplace left to haul all our loot home."

"Official Haven women?"

The drone of the tires on the road softened as Ninette drew the vehicle to a stop, but otherwise the cab got quiet. Ninette's eyes locked on Gia's in the rearview mirror. "Beckett hasn't talked to you?"

"Talked to me about what?"

Darya chuckled and shared a knowing look with the three women seated in the row in front of her.

Sylvie twisted in her chair. "Ye mean ta tell me the bloody arse haesna told ye?"

Ninette turned off the access road and cleared her throat. "Well, then. Guess we'll cover that for him before we take her back."

Per usual this time of day, the upscale stretch of businesses and restaurants along Knox Street was swamped with those running late afternoon errands and others escaping their office jobs in favor of one of the many trendy bars. Usually Gia loved this part of town. If not for the food available, then for the excellent people-watching. Today, it didn't so much as draw a spark. "Cover what?"

Natalie's smile was a mix of soft understanding and pure chagrin. "It means you're one of us. Family."

"Jace calls it a claim," Vivienne said with a low chuckle. "Which, on the surface, probably sounds like one step up from a guy hiking his leg and marking his territory." She paused a minute, thoughtful, and the smile on her face softened. "But it's really pretty sweet." She met Gia's gaze. "It means Haven's as much yours as it is ours and no secrets."

She'd heard about Haven from Knox and Beckett—

a sizable property north of Dallas owned by Jace and Axel that was only open to those inside their circle. A circle she now appeared to be a part of whether she wanted to be or not.

Typical Beckett. Once he set about doing something, he wouldn't rest until he made it happen on a spectacular level.

"They don't tell us all their secrets," Gabe said dryly. "Only the ones that don't kick their macho protective instincts into overdrive. Otherwise, you're on a need-to-know basis."

"Oh, I've already experienced the joy of the need-to-know status," Gia said. "Beckett put a tail on one of the suspects for the incident at the range last week and didn't tell me until after the fact."

"Hey, at least he told you," Gabe said. "If they get it in their head things could backfire and land on you, they'll never breathe a word of it."

Sylvie leveled a pointed and very motherly look at Gabe. "Nothing wrong with a man protecting the woman he loves. You ask me, that's putting your needs first. That's what a good man does."

The woman he loves.

She'd said it to Gabe, but the words moved through Gia with all the subtlety of an electric current. Which was silly, really. They'd officially been a thing for less than a week. Love couldn't be a factor yet.

"What did you say when he told you?" Darya asked.

"I already knew."

Ninette turned onto one of the less crowded blocks with more of a shopping focus than nightlife. Her words were spoken casually, but had a prodding edge. "How'd it feel when you found out?"

"Him telling me? Or the fact that he did it?"

Ninette pulled into a parking space and pinned Gia with a stare in the rearview mirror that was every bit as sharp as the no-bullshit looks she'd seen Jace employ a time or two. *Like mother, like son.* "The latter."

A good question. One she still wasn't sure how to answer. At first, she'd considered telling the guy watching Brantley's place to take a hike. But the longer she'd sat there and worked through the logistics, the more her irritation had shifted to something far more foreign. Kind of how she'd always imagined it would feel to have someone wrap her up in a soft blanket if she'd fallen asleep on the couch. Not that she had any experience with that scenario either.

Gia leaned and stared out the window at the stylish Sur la Table marquee over the building. Better that than to give Ninette any more clues to work with. "The jury's still out."

"Hmmm." She put the Escalade in park and swiveled in her seat. "You know we normally have family night out at Haven on Wednesdays."

"Everyone takes a turn picking the food," Sylvie said.

"And the games." Darya shifted so one leg lay cocked on the open bench seat between them and anchored her elbow on the seat back. "I don't know why we even bother asking Knox what he wants to play anymore. He lives to trounce everyone in Call of Duty."

Gabe giggled. "He lives to trounce everyone no matter what game we play."

"Unless it's Levi's pick," Natalie said. "There seems to be a phenomenon that happens when it's Levi's turn to pick the game. Suddenly, not one of the brothers can manage to beat my nine-year-old."

Gia frowned, bits and pieces clicking together. Her gaze shot to Ninette who, not surprisingly, had eyes on Gia as if she was simply waiting for two and two to equal four. "Today's Wednesday. Why are you with me?"

If there was any doubt Ninette Kennedy was Jace's mother, the devious smile that split her face would have eradicated it. "Well, we always do girls' day out before family night, but normally by now we'd be out at Haven."

Sylvie's eyes hopped high and her voice dropped to a barely audible whisper. "Ninnie, what are you doin'?"

"Uh-oh," Vivienne said.

Natalie scooted so she faced the front of the car and Gabe slunk lower in her seat like she was braced to avoid any flying debris.

Ninette held Gia's stare. "Beckett asked us to move family night to Saturday this week. Said something about having a window of opportunity and needing to make sure his woman was nowhere near that window while he took it."

A window?

As soon as her brain tossed up the question the answer swung right in behind it. *Brantley Davis.* "He's breaking into Brantley's apartment, isn't he?"

"Jesus, Mary and Joseph." Sylvie popped her seat belt. "The lad just landed the woman he's always wanted and here ye are stirrin' the pot." She twisted and faced Gia. "Don't get too mad at him, lass. It's just their way."

"He would have told you afterward," Darya said low beside her.

Gia wasn't sure what shocked her more. The fact that she'd been referenced as Beckett's woman, that Beckett had orchestrated the whole day to make sure he got what he needed, or that Jace's mother had tipped the whole plan on its head. She focused on Darya. "You knew?" She scanned the rest of them. "You all knew?"

"Well, we knew family night was rescheduled," Gabe said.

Natalie glanced at Vivienne. "And that something was up."

"So," Ninette added in a verbal equivalent of dusting her hands after a hard day's work. "Now we're here. Let's get inside and introduce Gia to the wonderful world of cooking."

Obviously eager to escape the building emotions in the SUV's interior, Gabe and Sylvie both popped the passenger doors in perfect synchronization.

Vivienne dared a glance at Gia and grinned as she scooted out behind Gabe. "Sylvie, I think we might have miscalculated this idea. You sure it's a good idea to let Gia play with knives right now?"

So tangled up with what she'd learned and wrestling with what action she most wanted to take, she was two steps into Sur la Table's entrance before the words *cooking* and *knives* took root. She stopped so hard Natalie nearly plowed into her back. "What are we doing here?"

Ninette moved in next to her, wrapped an arm around her waist and guided her to a wide room off to one side. "Well, if you ask Sylvie, she'll tell you she wants to share her love of cooking with you. Truth is, she's got the hots for one of their instructors."

Sticking close to her other side, Darya leaned in and muttered, "Don't tell Knox I said so, but he is pretty cute."

Sylvie paused right before crossing the room's threshold and hissed. "Hands off. You've got one." Her gaze cut to Ninette. "You—haud yer wheesht."

"I will *not* be quiet." Keeping Gia close, Ninette steered her to the front of the room. "What's the fun in having a new daughter if I can't teach her a thing or two along the way?"

Before she knew it, Gia was standing behind a stainless-steel cooking table big enough for two. All kinds of bowls, spoons, knives and gadgets she didn't recognize were neatly arranged on top and on shelves beneath.

Family.

Daughter.

The woman he's always wanted.

Beckett's woman.

She splayed her hands on the cold table, needing something—anything—to hold her steady through the storm wrecking her insides. "I don't know how to cook."

Ninette snagged the crisp ivory and sage apron folded in front of her and shook it out. "Beckett might have mentioned that little tidbit, too." She lifted the top loop over her head and leaned in for a conspiratorial whisper as she tied the string around her waist. "Personally, I'd keep it that way. Kind of sexy seeing a man in the kitchen. Especially if it's breakfast they're cooking and they're all rumpled from a good tussle the night before."

Gia stared down at her own apron. She knew she should put it on. Knew she should just let go and roll with the moment, but her body wouldn't move. Was too weighted down and distracted by foreign emotions grappling for control. Hell, even breathing was a challenge.

Ninette sidled closer, her posture such that, to everyone else, she probably just looked like a woman getting the lay of the land and striking up a casual conversation with the woman beside her. But her voice was that of a wise and comforting mother. "Which part got you? The fact that he went all out for you, or the number of people that fell in with him to do it?"

God, she was good. Freakishly adept at lasering straight to the heart of the matter. Nowhere near the head-in-the-clouds, detached perspective her mother seemed to have had for the last decade. "I've always taken care of myself."

Ninette nodded, hummed as though she understood and unfolded the apron still waiting in front of Gia. "You're a strong woman. Beckett loves that about you."

For some reason the comment struck deep, jarring her head up the way her foot would respond to a reflex test. "Then why not let me take care of this, too?"

The smile Ninette beamed on her was as bold and bright as the late afternoon sunshine slanting through the room's wide windows. She hooked the apron's loop around Gia's neck and spun her to tie the strings in back. "Maybe it's his way of showing you you aren't alone anymore. Of showing you you don't have to shoulder everything solo the way you've always done. My boy's got lots of muscle on the outside, but his heart's just as strong." She patted Gia's shoulder and squeezed. "Let him show you."

Easy chatter from the other women and other class attendees filled the space around her. Gabe's quiet but husky voice. Natalie's honey one. Vivienne's snark and Darya's accent. Sylvie's Scottish lilt was mingled with them all while she peppered the instructor who'd made it all of two steps into the room before she'd moved in for a highly flirtatious welcome.

Ninette slid onto the bar stool, quiet for the first time all day. As if she knew there was more just waiting on the tip of Gia's tongue and was content to wait however long was needed.

"Why did you tell me?"

For several heartbeats, Ninette stared at the brushed steel tabletop, her gaze unfocused. Only when she seemed to find the right words did she look up. "I was a lot like you, once upon a time." She waggled her eyebrows. "Still am." She studied Gia's face. "The difference between now and then is I'm not alone anymore. I have family. I have strong sons with solid moral compasses who know what it means to protect and provide for the women they care about. I have strong daughters who can hold their ground when they need to and can give their men safe haven when it's needed." Her gaze drifted to Sylvie and her smile softened. "And I have a best friend who's stood with me for longer than I probably deserve."

She looked back to Gia. "I told you when you were with us because I remember how hard it was to be strong and to try and come to grips with the fact that I didn't have to be anymore. But I also told you when you were with us so you'd have absolutely no doubt." She covered Gia's hand and squeezed. "You're not alone anymore either."

Chapter Sixteen

The only thing that tanked Beckett's mood faster than
a bad answer when he went digging for one was coming up with no answer at all. Considering he and Danny
had canvassed every inch of Brantley Davis's place and
walked out with a big fat zero, his mood was seriously
in the shitter. The fact that Gia hadn't called or texted
him back after a string of attempts to make contact
cranked his mood to downright dangerous.

Rounding the front of his 'Vette, he scanned the
parking lot fronting Gia's town house—partly out of
habit, but more so to combat the constant itch beneath
his skin. The eastern sky was already slipping into the
deeper blues of evening, but the sunset on the far side
of the town houses was still strong enough to cast a
few glints off the high-rises along the edge of downtown Dallas.

Something wasn't right. Not with the lack of answers
he was finding and not with Gia being silent either. He
knocked on her front door, putting enough juice behind
the contact she'd hear him even if she was camped out
on the roof. Hands braced on his hips, he strained for
any hint of sound and waited. And waited. He dug his
phone out of his back pocket and checked the useless

piece of shit for the fiftieth time since rolling out of Brantley's parking lot.

Nothing.

He knocked again then punched in Gia's number. Like it had the last ten times, it went straight to voice-mail. He ended the call without leaving a message, flipped to Knox's number and stalked back to his car. One thing was for damned sure. First thing when he found Gia, they were trading keys to each other's places and he was putting a tracker on every purse she owned.

"Yo." No nonsense and straight to the point. Thank God for Knox.

Beckett slid into the driver's seat and slammed his car door. "I can't find Gia."

Apparently, Knox was distracted enough he didn't pick up on the anxiety riding his voice, because what came back to him was a quip he hadn't expected. "Yeah, they're tricky that way. Kind of like cats. But if you feed 'em enough cream and make sure you pet 'em the right way, they usually come back."

"Brother, you're missin' what I'm saying. My woman isn't where she's supposed to be, she's not answering my calls and someone's got a beef with her. Where's Darya?"

This time the alertness he needed was fully online. "With me. Got home a few hours ago."

"*Fuck*." He floored the gas and pulled out onto the main road. "This doesn't feel right. Need you to see if you can track her."

"I'm on it. Where are you headed?"

"I'm gonna run by her gym. See if she's there. Maybe swing back by Brantley's place in case she got any ideas to tail him on her own."

"Right. Give me five and I'll call you back."

Beckett tossed his phone to the front seat and all but begged Dallas's finest to pull him over with the speeds he was pulling. Gia would be fine. No matter what happened, she could absolutely hold her own. He knew that on the same level he knew he'd find her—one way or another.

Unless she doesn't want to be found.

His mother sure hadn't. Not that he thought his dad had bothered to look, at the time, but he and Knox had years later. Out of all the people they'd tried to track, Evie Tate—or whatever she went by now—was the only one who'd ever ended up a complete dead end.

He pulled into the offbeat gym Gia used a few miles away from her place and killed the engine just as his phone lit up with Knox's name on the display. "What'd you find?"

"Her phone's off. I've got nothin' to track."

Beckett peeled himself out of the front seat, shut the door with enough force to rattle the whole car and all but jogged toward the gym's front door. "Call the guys in. Find out where the women went today, what time they broke up and where they last saw Gia."

Knox cleared his throat and a whole lot of discomfort coated his voice. "Don't think we need to."

"Why the fuck not?"

"Because the whole time I was on my computer my hot little Russian was staring me down with a smug look on her face."

"She knows where Gia is?"

"If she does, she ain't talking."

"Did you ask?"

Knox shifted so his voice registered away from the

phone. "Baby, you gonna chime in and keep Beckett from forming a search party, or make him stew a little longer?"

Darya may not have been right next to him, but her sassy Russian accent traveled the distance just fine. "You men handled everything else on your own today. Surely you can figure this out, too."

Knox chuckled and shifted back to Beckett. "You hear that?"

"I heard it. Don't know what the fuck she means, but I heard it."

"You ever tell Gia what you were doing today?"

Fuck.

Knox chuckled. "I'll take the silence as a no."

"I told her I'd tell her more when we were done. Hell, I called her almost as soon as I cleared Davis's apartment."

"My guess, the girls got a jump on you."

"Well, I can't fix that situation *if I don't know where she is*." He paced outside Gia's gym and fisted his hand in his hair. "Put Darya on the phone."

"He wants to talk to you," Knox said to Darya.

Beckett could easily visualize the pout that went with her answer. "I don't want to talk to him."

Knox paused a second. "Okay, tell me this much. Is she safe?"

"Very."

Knox's voice got clearer. "You hear that?"

"I heard it and it's not good enough."

"Brother, that's the best you're gonna get tonight. My suggestion? Suck it up and start figuring out how you're gonna grovel and get back in her good graces."

"Suck it up? Are you kidding me?" Earning a suspicious look from a guy ducking out the front door and heading to his car, Beckett forced his voice down a notch, but the heat was still there. "I don't know where the fuck she is!"

Silence echoed back at him.

When Knox spoke again, his tone was that of a man all too familiar with the panic beating through Beckett's veins. The verbal equivalent of one man helping another back away from a fatal ledge. "Beck, she's pissed. She's taking a breather. Probably so she doesn't cut your nuts off the second she sees you. But that's all this is. Nothing else. Whatever your past is hittin' you with, *let it go.*"

Axel had tried to tell him. Hell, they all had one way or another. "It's not that I don't trust her, I just—"

"Wanna protect her. Yeah, I get it. She will, too, if you give her time."

The phone beeped in his ear indicating an incoming call.

He checked the screen and barely managed not to toss the damned device across the lot when he saw Axel's name instead of Gia's. "Axel's calling."

"Good. Talk to him so I can get on with smoothing my Russian's feathers."

"If she tells you anything, you call me."

"Yeah, she's not gonna tell me shit. You think we men are tight, those women are cutthroat mercenaries when it comes to loyalty."

The phone beeped again.

"Talk to Axel. I'll call you if I hear anything."

Too pissed to do anything else and out of options anyway, he stalked to his 'Vette and punched the answer button. "What?"

Axel was apparently not only in a much better mood than him, but found a shitload of humor in Beckett's abrupt greeting. "Who shoved the monster cactus up your arse?"

"I'm not sure. One of the women. I'm banking on Ninette at this point, but someone told Gia what we were doin' today, now she's MIA."

For a few seconds, Axel held his tongue, but movement sounded in the background and a whole different vibe drifted through the line. When he spoke again his voice was hushed. "The lass isn't MIA. She has a bottle of wine in with the moms and Vivienne in the kitchen."

"She's at Haven?"

A door clicked shut in the background and Axel's big voice went back to normal volume. "Safe as a babe and laughin' loud enough you'd think they'd known each other their whole life."

The 'Vette's engine revved to match the beast roaring in his head. "I'm on my way."

"You sure you want to do that?"

"Why wouldn't I?"

"I might ought to reiterate—they're in the kitchen."

"So?"

"They're cooking."

Okay, that *was* weird. He turned the corner onto the feeder road that would put him on Highway 75. "Gia hates cooking."

"Well, from the looks of the boxes scattered on the counters, Gia's now the owner of a lot of cookware, one of them a particularly nice set of knives."

"I'll handle it."

Axel grunted. "Think I'll go pry Jace outta the garage before you get here. Maybe see if Zeke's on call.

You and Gia goin' at it with booze and sharp objects involved, not sure if Haven's about to get a hell of a good show, or its first bloodbath."

"I'll be there in twenty." He started to hit the end button, but Axel's next question cut him off.

"Don't you want to know why I was calling?"

Beckett punched the button to send the call to Bluetooth and dropped his phone in the center console. "Does it include how to keep women from being a pain in your ass, or how to keep 'em tied up and out of trouble?"

"Well, the first option doesn't exist. A simple Yuki knot here and there would do the trick on the second one if you'd ever slow the hell down long enough for me to teach you one."

"Get to the point."

"That man in Atlanta—Peter Trannell."

"Yeah?"

"I got an in. You want Gia to get the deal, we can make it happen."

"Do it."

Axel hesitated for all of a heartbeat but the smile in his voice was evident when he finally spoke. "You sure you wanna do that without talkin' to the lass first?"

"It's good business. You know that as well as I do. When you find an in, you take it. Gia knows good business. She'll get it."

"Christ, it's gonna be a bloodbath," Axel muttered almost under his breath.

"What?"

"Nothing. You want to dig a hole, far be it from me to pry the shovel out of your hand."

Beckett shifted to the far left lane and opened up the

engine, his lungs drawing the first solid breath since he'd left Brantley's apartment. "Anything else?"

"Yeah, what was the name of the clawbaw who cut Gia off at her last gig?"

"Clawbaw?" That was a new one.

"Wanker. Ball fondler. General prick. The Ken doll she grew up next to. What was his name?"

"Judd Rainier."

"Yeah, that one."

"Why? What about him?"

"A handy FYI. This whole thing is split into teams. The one Gia wants is the lead detail and if she gets it, she'd have full authority over all teams, but there are four other teams for other big names on the invite list and Trannell's done the initial hiring. Judd's already got an assigned team and is angling for the lead."

"Well, he can't have it. He's screwed Gia enough times."

"Way I understand it he's got good connections, too."

"Good enough he can top ours?"

A smile moved into Axel's voice. "Hell, no. But he's already in, so he's likely to be a pain in Gia's ass regardless."

Figured. But if she had full authority over all the teams she could handle him. Plus, Beckett would be there this time to make sure Judd couldn't screw her again. He'd deal with that just as soon as he dug himself out of the hole he'd created today. "Just make it happen. I'm on my way."

Chapter Seventeen

Chili probably wasn't the most impressive or season-appropriate meal to launch her culinary exploration, but Gia figured starting somewhere was better than not starting at all. And, given how the kitchen smelled right now, Sylvie hadn't steered her wrong when she'd said her recipe was foolproof.

The sliding glass door that led to the impressive backyard and the walkway to the eight-car garage beyond it hissed open. "How much longer till it's done?"

It wasn't the first time Jace had posed the question. He and Axel had both made their fair share of trips through the kitchen to check on progress, but it was the first time his deep, gravelly voice had held a thread of concern.

Gia peeked over her shoulder and, sure enough, Jace's laid-back demeanor had been replaced with shrewd eyes aimed on the long driveway and a possessive hand on his wife's shoulder. Axel was right behind him. "I take it Beckett found me?"

Jace pegged his mom with a warning look that would have made most men take a healthy step back. "One of these days, you're gonna pull your shit and it's gonna backfire."

As she'd learned today, Ninette Kennedy wasn't easily cowed. Not even by her son. "I bet today's not that day."

Beside Ninette, Sylvie raised her wineglass toward Vivienne opposite her at the table. "Och, but I'll bet we donae get ta drive his car for at least a year."

"You'd be bloody well right on that one," Axel murmured.

As soon as the words left his mouth, headlights cut across the lawn and the angry roar of a very big engine swelled outside the house.

Jace patted Vivienne's shoulder. "Come on. Beckett doesn't need an audience." As Vivienne stood, he locked stares with Gia at the stove. "You gonna be alright?"

Gia couldn't help but smile. Even knowing Beckett had to be fuming mad, the protective streak that seemed to run through all of them couldn't help but rear its head. "Beckett won't hurt me. And if he tried, I can hold my own."

Axel chuckled and ushered Sylvie and Ninette out in front of him. "Might be better to ask if she's gonna hurt Beckett."

Ninette was already out of sight, but she bellowed back, "Give him hell, sweetheart!"

Bringing up the tail end of the exodus, Jace paused and lowered his voice. "For what it's worth, he didn't do what he did without reason."

"I know that." Just like she hadn't taken Sylvie and Ninette up on their invitation to explore Haven without her own reasons. Reasons that were crucial she follow through with if she had a prayer of holding her own in this relationship.

As if he'd heard her thoughts, Jace grinned and dipped his head. "Then go get him, tiger."

The door to Beckett's 'Vette slammed shut as if to punctuate Jace's encouragement, and then she was alone. Waiting. Just her and the imminent arrival of one very pissed-off alpha male.

She covered the big stock pot full of enough chili to feed an army and checked the burner. Low where it was supposed to be. Sylvie had said something about simmering for at least thirty minutes, which should give her enough time to weather the worst of the storm, or at least get the storm relocated somewhere else so Sylvie could take over.

The sliding glass door whisked open with far less softness than when Jace and Axel had entered.

She sucked in a deep breath, braced and faced him.

The air she'd stockpiled whooshed out faster than she'd gathered it, and her body practically sang at the image that greeted her. She'd known he'd be angry. Known he'd be wrestling to keep his control. But holy hell, the man filling the doorway was pure primal rawness, eyes ablaze as they surveyed his surroundings and muscles straining. Had it not been for the T-shirt, jeans and boots marking him as somewhat civilized, a stranger would have called him savage. "I didn't know where you were."

Of all the ways she'd expected this confrontation to start, his growled admission wasn't one of them. So raw. More powerlessness and unchecked fear coating his words than anger.

She forced herself to relax and leaned one hip on the thick granite counter. "I wanted some time to think and get to know your family."

"I didn't know where you were." Every word low, distinctly punctuated and rumbling with the power of thunder.

My mom left me when I was two.

The memory stabbed deep, the pain she'd sensed that day now magnified tenfold on his face. She closed the distance between them in short order, instinct more than wisdom driving her actions. Before she could extend her arms and smooth her hands along his sternum as she'd intended, he yanked her flush against him. Speared his hands in her hair and crushed her cheek against his chest even as his other hand anchored her hips to his. His body shook against hers, his hold possessive and unrelenting. His lungs heaved as though he'd run the distance to Haven, but the kiss he pressed to the top of her head was so reverent and fragile it unwound the bulk of her resolve and anger.

God, she was an idiot. She'd sensed his mother's abandonment ran deep. Knew firsthand how childhood scars could mark a person, but she'd ripped those wounds wide, whether she'd meant to or not. Smoothing her hands along his back as much as his tightly banded arms would allow, she gave him the touch he seemed to need. "I'm sorry, Beckett. I was angry. I had my reasons, but I didn't think about how not telling you where I was would impact you."

He cupped both sides of her face and kissed her temple, breathing her in. "Ninette told you what we were doing today." Not a question, but a statement. And didn't that say loads about how involved this family ran in terms of being in each other's business?

"*You* should have told me. Should have trusted me with what you planned to do."

Still not meeting her eyes, he skimmed his nose alongside hers, and his fingers tightened as if he was afraid she'd try to slip away. "I do trust you."

"Then why not tell me?"

He rested his forehead on hers and drew in a steadying breath before finally lifting his head. "Because I don't give a shit if I get busted. My brothers would post my bail and I'd roll with the fallout no matter what it looked like. But your reputation means everything to you. You worked your ass off to build it. Why the hell would I let you risk that if I can risk it for you?"

Not chocolate.

Not wine or long-stemmed roses.

But the effect just as potent. Maybe more so, flooding her bloodstream with enough giddiness it was a wonder her heart didn't punch right out of her chest. She rolled up her toes, letting him straighten to his full height as she skimmed her fingertips through the soft scruff along his jawline. She murmured against his lips, "You could have just said that to begin with."

His head snapped back. "Would you have listened?"

No. Probably not. At least not without a healthy amount of debate and undoubtedly demanding she be involved in some capacity. But she was smart. She'd made it a point to learn from her mistakes thus far. With Beckett, her incentive was tenfold. She hooked her hands around his neck and urged him to her. "I will next time."

He fought the pull, his still-wild eyes scanning her features. "This mean you'll forgive me?"

She tugged harder, the need to taste him and still the restlessness she'd fought all afternoon with his kiss nearly overriding the need to press her argument. "Will you do it again?"

"If it was for you, or to keep you safe, hell yeah, I would." He fisted his hand in her hair at the back of her head and lowered his lips closer to hers, his deep voice rolling through her. "What I won't do is lie to you and promise something I can't guarantee."

Truth.

Not flowers and fluff. Not some bullshit line crafted to move them out of the danger zone and into safer waters, but the real deal laid bare at her feet. "I can work with that."

Who kissed who, she couldn't say. Didn't care. Only knew that the taste of him on her tongue seemed richer. Bolder than every other kiss. And there was nothing soft about it. More a sensual sparring match with tongues, teeth and touch as their weapons of choice. Only when her back met wall did the reality of where they were and the undoubted number of people with ears straining not far away yank her focus long enough to drag her lips away from his. "Beckett."

He growled and used his grip in her hair to yank her head to one side, leaving her throat open to his demanding mouth.

"Beckett, the back door's still open."

He slid one hand from the small of her back, up over her hip and higher to her breast. "I was supposed to show you Haven." He lifted his head and plumped the aching mound, an animalistic claim that only fueled the raging fire he'd started. "I wanted to give you that."

"I haven't seen your room yet."

One heartbeat and her feet were off the floor, her legs around his hips and his mouth consuming her gasp in a breath-stealing kiss. The door slid shut with enough punch it was a wonder the glass didn't shatter, and then he was on the move. The background noise of a TV grew closer along with the rapid-fire back-and-forth of a somewhat heated discussion. How Beckett made it up the stairs without dropping her she couldn't say and frankly didn't care. Or didn't until Axel's deep baritone voice stopped mid-sentence and a chorus of feminine laughter filled in behind it.

Gia ripped her mouth from Beckett's, her heart slamming overtime even as her mind scrambled to process the five smiling faces locked on her and Beckett moving fast past the game room's wide entrance. With any other audience, she'd have been mortified, or at least felt the need to demand Beckett put her down. With this crew, all she felt was free and giddy. She grinned over Beckett's shoulder and locked eyes with Sylvie. "Don't let my chili burn!"

Sylvie giggled and covered her mouth with one hand, but it was Jace's voice that answered as Beckett hauled her out of sight. "Not thinkin' it's her chili she should be worried about."

"He's got that right." Beckett peeled right where the hallway branched toward a separate wing and squeezed both hands palming her ass. "You've been after quick and dirty and you're about to get it."

The words whipped through her, landing square between her legs and making her sex clench. She tightened her arms and legs around him and nipped the taut muscle where his neck and shoulder met. Licked the same spot and moaned at the taste of his skin. "Beckett."

"I know, baby. Just hang on." Shadows wrapped around them. A door opened and slammed shut and his heavy footfalls sounded on thick carpet. A second later, her back met plush mattress, her body laid sideways in the middle of a king-size bed and Beckett at its side yanking off her heels. "Shirt off."

As if he'd have to ask her twice. With nothing but the moon slanting through a far window and their heavy breaths filling the room, they shucked everything. Her shirt. His tee. His boots. Her bra. When she didn't move fast enough on her jeans, he batted her hands out of the way and dragged them and her panties free in one swoop.

Taking advantage of the opening, she scrambled to her knees and fumbled with the button at his waist.

Just as fast, the shadows spun around her and she was on her back again, her legs braced wide by Beckett's shoulders and her breath whooshing out into the darkened room as his mouth locked onto her sex. No buildup. No teasing words or touches. Just blatant consumption. A ravenous predator bent on taking and claiming what it wanted.

And dear God, it felt great. The sheer force of his hunger bending her will to his. Demanding she submit. That she surrender herself at the most intimate level and slake his carnal thirst.

The wet heat of his mouth surrounded her clit and he suckled hard, plunging two fingers into her slick and ready sex.

Her back bowed off the bed, a release that promised to utterly consume her barreling closer. She fisted both hands in his hair and let her legs fall open wider. No way would she fight him. Not him or what his thrusting fingers and wicked mouth offered. In this, he was all-powerful. A master to be obeyed.

The sensation grew tighter, the muscles around his fingers drawing tighter. Close. So close.

And then he was gone. His mouth. His touch. His heat. All of it snatched away and taking oblivion with it. "Beckett!"

"Not yet."

His grated words launched her into motion, sheer

impulse and a wildness born of denied fulfillment fueling her muscles as she all but vaulted toward him.

Before she could gain her feet, he caught her at her hips, flipped her to her belly and yanked her backwards so her tiptoes reached the floor, his knees bracing her legs wide.

She pressed with all she had against the sinfully soft black comforter and tried to wriggle out from under him, but his massive hand was an iron shackle at the back of her neck, pinning her in place, the other a hot brand at her hip where he kept her bent at the waist. "Damn it, Beckett. What are you doing? I was right there."

"And I'll get you there again, but you're not goin' without me." His hot, labored breaths against her cheek matched her own and his weight blanketed her back, the dog tags he never took off an icy brand against her spine. He uncoiled the fingers digging into her hips and shifted so the back of his hand teased the globes of her ass.

No, not teasing. Working the buttons on his jeans.

She lifted her hips higher and pressed backward, a needy mewl slipping past her lips.

The hold at the back of her neck tightened and his jeans rasped harsh against the back of her thighs, but then he was there. Velvet steel pressed against the cleft of her ass.

A condom packet landed on the bed beside her.

Leaning back over her, Beckett slipped his hands between her legs and slicked his fingers through her drenched folds. "You get two choices. I glove up and fuck you hard like this, or I roll you over, sink my bare dick in your hot, wet pussy and mark you as mine for the first time. Either way, you're gonna come hard enough the whole damned house is gonna hear it happen and I'll have to carry you down to dinner."

She whimpered, the impending release he'd stolen from her surging back to life.

His fingers slipped from between her legs and he covered the packet beside her.

She stilled his hand with her own before he could pull it away, her heart kicking a ragged yet powerful rhythm. "I trust you."

His teeth grazed over her shoulder then rubbed the stubble on his chin along the same spot. "No pressure, sweetheart. You wanna wait—want me to prove I'm clear of anything—I got no issue with that."

It wasn't that. In the time since they'd been intimate, he'd made it abundantly clear any entanglements before her had been far more discretionary than she'd ever dreamed. No, what moved her—what speared so deep it pierced her very soul—was what it meant. She got it now. This wasn't a game. Not for him, or his family. A family that was hers now, too, if she accepted it. "I want this." She pulled in a deeper breath and shifted her focus to him, her hips lifting in invitation. "I want it all."

The hand at her neck clamped harder and even in the moonlight his eyes sparked with a possessive glint. "Then that's what you'll get." He rolled his hips against her, the weight of his shaft wedged against her cheeks a blatant reminder of what she'd just agreed to. "You gonna be a good girl?"

Oh, hell. She fisted her hands in the comforter and groaned, the mix of his grated voice and the dirty implications his words painted making her sex weep. Years of control and common sense tried to clamp a restraining hand over her mouth. Tried to silence the woman writhing inside her with ideas of what was wrong and what was right.

It didn't work. She tossed her head to one side and met his steely gaze. "No. I'm gonna be phenomenal."

He snarled, straightened and smacked one side of her ass. "On your back. Legs spread."

Oh. My. God.

Nothing could have put her into motion any faster, every muscle working in concert to heed his command. Before she'd even finished moving, his hands were at her hips. He yanked her to the edge of the bed, her hips flush with his where he stood and his cock a ready weapon straining toward his belly. He palmed her knees and squeezed. Pushed them up and wide.

And stared at her. Drank her in. Not just her exposed sex, but everything. Every detail. An out-of-control beast leashed for a surreal moment before it feasted. His eyes locked on her. "Guide me in."

Her choice. Even with what he wanted so close, he gave her one last out. A chance to run and hide behind the walls that had kept her safe for so very long. She stroked his thick length instead. Teased her fingertips along the underside of his tight sac and traced the vein that ran root to tip with her thumb. Swirling the pre-come she found there around the flared head, she held his blazing stare and slicked him through the wetness he'd created, mingling his essence with hers.

His fingers tightened on her knees and a low, delicious rumble resonated from his chest, vibrating from his skin to hers. Hip to hip. Sex to sex.

She notched him inside.

His nostrils flared and his face hardened, a prominent tic jumping at the back of his jaw. Standing eerily still, every delicious muscle was tensed and on prime display. Power waiting to be unleashed.

On her.

On binding them together.

"Do it." She flexed her hips, nudging him deeper inside her.

His gaze dropped to their connection and his hands slid inward. "Beautiful." He pinned her hips and sunk an inch deeper. "So goddamned beautiful." Another inch. "Taking my cock." Another. "Taking *me*."

He thrust forward and buried himself to the hilt. Filling her. Claiming her with the sweetest stretch. He pounded into her. Rolled and bucked in a demanding rhythm to match her heart. Rode her as only an untamed animal could, driving her release higher and higher.

Sounds, scents and sensation were all that mattered. The slap of his hips against hers. The plundering stretch of his thick shaft, nothing between them but the heat and slick wetness they'd created. The heady musk of sweat, sex and man.

"Beckett…" It was the most she could manage, her mind too tangled and dazed from the sensual onslaught. Her muscles coiled and poised to take flight and her heart struggling to keep up. She gripped his forearms and held on for all she was worth.

"Take it." He lifted her hips and angled his thrusts so his glans grazed just right, rolling his hips with each advance. "You wanna come, *now* you take it. Take it all."

A cry ripped up her throat, the force of her release too wild to contain the ragged sound and shoving her from reality's ledge into a soaring free fall. No boundaries. No fears. Just pure bliss crashing through her in a carnal wave so powerful her body bowed to meet it. Welcomed it with the greedy clasp of her sex around

Beckett's pistoning shaft and her legs pinioned around his waist.

And then she was up, her torso plastered against his, his arms banded at her back and shoulders and his growl rolling into her as he took her mouth. Claimed it as his cock jerked inside her, his hips grinding against hers as he filled her.

Amazing.

Two people, utterly free and yet bound. Separate parts connected by so much more than flesh. It was terrifying. Exhilarating even as it left the very heart of her exposed and vulnerable.

The rhythm of his hips eased. The hand manacled at the back of her neck loosened and swept down her spine. Soothing her. Grounding him.

She smiled and sighed into his neck, running her fingers through his hair with one hand and returning the calming contact along his back with the other. Funny, how fast she'd come to accept that part of him. That need for a tactile anchor. And it wasn't a burden. Wasn't something he expected or demanded. More a gift that fed her own soul and strengthened the bond they'd forged as friends for years. "I'm sorry I didn't wait to let you show me Haven."

He nuzzled the spot just below her ear. "I'm sorry I didn't tell you about what we were doin' at Brantley's place."

"Did you find anything?"

"Nothing."

Hmmm. Still floating on the wild ride he'd given her, the singular thought was all her brain offered up. As if it couldn't be bothered with details, plans or plots beyond the man who held her.

Holding her close, he put a knee to the edge of the bed, lifted them both and laid her out in the center, keeping their connection. In only moonlight, the black down comforter was more of a midnight cloud welcoming them into a secret place. For who knew how long, they simply lingered. His hips cradled between her thighs. Her fingertips dancing along his skin. His mouth and hands paying homage to every place he could reach.

His warm breath whispered across her shoulder where his lips lingered. "I think protocol dictates I get you cleaned up."

"I think we get to set our own protocol." She skimmed her fingers along his jawline and rolled her hips against his, savoring the feel of them together. "I'm not in any hurry."

His gaze cut to hers and he grinned.

"Okay, I'm not in a hurry *now*."

He braced one forearm beside her head and smoothed her hair away from her face, the levity in his expression giving way to one far more serious. "I need to tell you something else."

So solemn. Open and yet pensive.

She smiled despite the tone he'd led with and tightened her legs around him. "I'm listening."

He studied her, fingers stilling as he seemed to gather the right words. "When I want a job, I make it happen. Connections, outmaneuvering the competition, or outright undercutting them if I have to, but I make it happen."

"Isn't that what we all do?"

His lips twitched. "When I say undercut, I mean I've been known to do it dirty. Fair means or foul, so long as no one innocent gets hurt."

She traced the thick chain that held his dog tags. "I think I figured out you're comfortable with shades of gray the day you asked me to help set a dirty doctor up with the Feds. I didn't have a problem with how you ran your business then any more than I do now."

"What if I used that approach on *your* business?"

Her brain tried to connect what were probably obvious dots, but after the day she'd had and the lingering aftereffects of her tussle with Beckett, nothing lined up. "What'd you do?"

"Nothing yet."

While he hadn't emphasized it as such, there was no doubt in her mind *yet* was the key word. "But?"

He shrugged. "Axel found a thread to pull with Peter Trannell."

"And you told him to pull it."

"It's business. Nothing I wouldn't have done to gain the job myself."

Part of her wanted to scold him simply on principle. To remind him she'd held her own just fine for years and wanted to land her jobs on merit. The other, far more competitive half perked up, ready to take notes and high-five his tactics. She shot for somewhere in the middle. "So, maybe next time you clue me in and ask me what I think before you cast your net and see what threads are out there. Or better yet, introduce me to your net so I can do my own casting."

"You've met my net. Five of them are out there right now rating how well I got you off based on how loud you screamed."

In the darkness, he might not be able to see her flush, but she sure felt its burn. "I'm not used to family being in hearing range."

His smile was instant and full of teeth. "Well, you'd better get used to it. Haven's yours now as much as it is mine. That includes the family that goes with it."

Odd. She had her own family, albeit a small one, but up until today the word meant something else. More a strict representation of marriages, bloodlines and emergency contacts. But with Beckett and his brood it brought on a different meaning entirely. A cohesive unit brought together by blood *and* choice that was stronger together than any of them would be apart. She pressed her hand above his heart and the H tattooed on his chest. "I like that."

"I like that, too." He kissed her nose. "You're not pissed?"

Spoken like the cautious little boy who wanted to make sure the coast was clear before he headed out to find more trouble. "Well, I did say I'd listen the next time." She wrapped her arms around his neck. "So, I'm listening."

Smiling, he pressed a lingering kiss to her lips. "You hungry?"

"Starving. And I cooked!"

He chuckled and nipped her lower lip. "Well then, I guess I'd better get you cleaned up and haul your ass downstairs for chow."

He started to pull away, but she tightened her legs around his waist.

Raising both eyebrows, he waited, a light playfulness she wasn't sure she'd ever seen before moving behind his blue gaze.

She traced his lips and savored the moment. Just the two of them, painted in shadows and wrapped in each other. "For the record, I liked your tour of Haven better."

Chapter Eighteen

Loud voices, a whole lot of laughter and an underlying current of unfaltering acceptance. From Beckett's place on the catwalk that fronted the massive upstairs game room, he couldn't see much of what was going on in the kitchen below, but he could feel it. Could take the easily followed commentary and bustling sounds and paint the picture in his head. He leaned his forearms onto the iron and woodwork rail that overlooked the big living room below, closed his eyes, and soaked it all in. The Haven crew was up, kicking off a Sunday morning—or in this case, picking up where last night's family night had left off—and welcoming Ivan, his daughter, Mary, and Gia into the fold. It might have only been four days since Gia had visited Haven for the first time, but from the sounds of things downstairs, she'd settled in like she'd been here for years.

"It's pancake batter, lass," Sylvie admonished from somewhere near the prep area. "Ye can't mess it up."

"Give me time," Gia said. "If there's a way, I'll figure it out."

Vivienne's voice came from somewhere near the kitchen table, a little dry humor coating her response. "This from the woman who made chili and came downstairs an hour later to find out there weren't any left-overs."

Footsteps muted by the hallway's thick rugs sounded behind him a second before Axel's smooth voice drowned out whatever else was said in the kitchen. "Never thought I'd say this, but I like havin' 'em here."

"Odd coming from you. You love women."

"I do." Axel leaned into the rail beside him. Like Beckett, he only wore jeans and an old T-shirt, his feet bare and his wild red hair loose to his shoulders. "But there was a time I worried they'd tear Haven apart. Ends up they've made it stronger."

He could see that. Lots of friends he'd had over the years hooked up with women and ended up all but dis-appearing shortly after. Like they got sucked into some relationship black hole that zeroed in on couples only. Maybe the difference for them was Haven's gravita-tional pull—a mass that just kept on building and get-ting stronger with every new addition.

They stood beside each other, silent. In the kitchen, Knox handed off a Breakfast Stout to Danny, extolling the virtues of a beer not just made from oats, but cof-fee and chocolate, too.

The topic and the familiar banter struck a memory. Namely the way Jace had stared Axel down at their last rally. Beckett straightened and eyeballed Axel. "You got someone you're not tellin' us about?"

The question knocked Axel out of whatever thoughts had gripped him. "Me?" He pushed away from the rail and shook his head, but didn't quite meet Beckett's gaze. He rounded behind Beckett and clapped him on the shoulder as he headed for the stairs. "Happy for what you found, brother, but not sure there's a lass out there willin' to put up with my shite." He paused at the top of the stairs, his unruffled mask back in place. "You gonna moon over your woman up here all alone, or get your ass down there and enjoy some hands-on?"

Son of a bitch. Axel McKey was fixated on someone. Who remained to be seen, but Beckett had never once seen or heard his brother dodge a topic the way he'd just done. He'd have to give Jace a nudge and see if he knew who it was.

"Nothin' wrong with enjoying the view," Beckett said as he headed down the stairs behind him. "Although, hands-on is a no-brainer with Gia."

Axel's sharp laughter preceded them into the kitchen, bringing all the conversation to a halt and drawing every eye at once. Sure enough, the images he'd created in his head had been almost spot-on. Everyone was up, the table overflowing with people nursing their morning coffee and the prep area bustling with the moms and a few of the women. Even the dogs were in on the action, Lacy and Ruger tight on Levi and Mary roving from one family member to another.

Gia spoke first, her eyes dancing and a sweet smile on her lips. "I'm making pancakes."

"I see that." Despite Sylvie being in full coaching mode parked on one side of Gia at the island and Darya on the other cutting strawberries, he moved in behind Gia, planted his hands on her hips and kissed her cheek. "Morning."

She paused stirring the batter long enough to crane her head for another lip-to-lip kiss. "Morning."

"Enough of that." Sylvie shooed him away and dumped baking powder and sugar into the bowl. "Get yer coffee and settle in like everyone else. The lass is on a roll."

She was indeed. Dressed in loose gray cotton sleep pants she'd brought from home and one of his tees, she looked like she'd spent countless nights at Haven instead of just one. He plunked a coffee pod in the brewer, punched the button to start the fancy thing up and leaned a hip to the counter to enjoy the show. He wasn't sure what he liked more—the fact that Gia had almost as much flour on her as what ended up in the bowl, how she seemed determined to mark every ingredient to memory, or the marksmanship-level concentration she put into pouring the batter on the griddle.

"Hey, Beck," Zeke said from the far side of the kitchen table, "what happened to you being first one up in the morning?"

"No kidding." Viv looked up from cleaning blueberries at the sink and jerked her head toward the dogs. "You not going for a run means they're stuck under our feet."

Jace grinned at Beckett and snagged his coffee. "Not thinkin' he needed any more exercise after last night, sugar."

"Oh, yeah," Knox said, not looking up from the laptop in front of him, though his smirk was still there. "A hard night, for sure."

"Emphasis on hard," Trevor snickered.

"What are you guys? Thirteen?" Nat nudged Trevor with her shoulder and dipped her head in Levi and Mary's direction. "Tone it down, already."

Despite Nat's worry, Levi was too engrossed in whatever Danny was showing him on his phone to latch onto the direction their conversation had taken, and Mary was in a whole different world playing with a doll on Ivan's lap. Like Ivan, her hair was long, but full of braids instead of dreds. She also had a killer set of warm amber eyes. Blended with her sharp features, it gave her an exotic look that would no doubt drag trouble to Ivan's doorstep in another eight or nine years.

"Now, ye just loosen the edges and give it a flip." Like it was the easiest thing in the world, Sylvie flipped the pancake in her wide skillet.

"I can't do that."

For a second, Sylvie looked at Gia like she'd proclaimed she couldn't walk or breathe. Then comprehension settled in. "No, no, lass. Ye don't have ta do it like that. Not for starters anyway. Just use the spatula."

"She can flip it." Even as the words left his mouth, Beckett acknowledged the shit wading in was going to earn him with the rest of the guys, but he couldn't help it. He'd already had one round of playing with Gia in the kitchen and he wasn't about to pass up a second, no matter how many spectators they had. He set his coffee aside and moved in behind her, one hand on her hip and the other covering her hand on the small griddle. "She just needs a little help."

"Beckett, I'm cooking!"

He leaned in close enough only she could hear and murmured, "So am I, now move the cake around and make sure it's unstuck."

She snickered under her breath, but did as he asked. "Like that?"

Fuck, he didn't have a clue. His mind had all but glazed over the second she'd pressed her ass flush against him. He gave the pan a flip, only halfway focused on making sure the pancake ended up back where it was supposed to be instead of directly on the stove. The rest of him was considering how fast he could get her out of the kitchen and back up to his suite.

Apparently, he'd done a decent enough job, because Gia let out a delighted squeak and twisted enough to beam him a huge smile. "That's way more fun than with a spatula."

Gabe snorted and shut the refrigerator door with her hip, her arms loaded with three syrup bottles and a huge tub of butter. "Why is it my brain processed that statement in a whole different scenario outside the kitchen?"

"Because you spend a lot of time in the kitchen and have a man who's shown creativity while you're in there," Zeke fired back.

Jace shook his head, pushed from his seat and snagged his coffee cup from the tabletop. "Brother, while seeing you at a stove is novel as hell, and I'm sure Gia appreciates the hands-on coaching, you've got eight men, seven women and two kids chompin' at the bit for breakfast. You wanna get a move on?"

Levi didn't seem to agree with Jace's approach. "Uncle Beck, I wanna flip pancakes!"

"Me, too!" Mary said.

At the kitchen table next to Trevor, Natalie cut the kids off at the pass before Beckett could wave them over to take turns. "How about you two take Ruger and Lady out back first and if we have batter left over you can practice after we eat?"

"Cool!" Levi slid out from the crook of Danny's arm, the messy blond hair he was determined to grow as long as Trevor's still wild from sleep.

Trevor's border collie, Lady, was on Levi's heels before he was two steps in. Ruger, on the other hand, stayed sprawled out on the floor next to Jace's chair, his chin on his paws and eyes locked on the food prep.

Levi latched onto his collar as he circled the table, not the least bit intimidated by the oversized and deadly-looking Doberman, then glanced back over his shoulder to make sure Mary was following suit. "Come on, Mary, I'll show you Uncle Jace's fixer-upper while we're out."

Mary slid off her dad's lap. "What's a fixer-upper?"

"A black 1969 Camaro," Jace answered.

Danny looked up from his phone, his face pinched in an incredulous scowl. "You're still workin' on that thing?"

"He's been workin' on that thing for five years," Ninette said from the stove where bacon sizzled in the skillet in front of her. "My guess is if he ever finishes it, he'll just take it apart again."

Still snuggled with her back to his front, Gia's body shook with silent laughter.

"What?" he murmured close to her ear.

She shook her head like the lot of them were crazy then flipped the griddle for all she was worth, sending the cake about twice as high as it needed to go. "You guys are nuts."

The cake landed on its side first, then settled on the non-stick surface. Beckett helped her slide it off on the platter and moved the batter closer so she could pour another one. "You keep forgetting, gorgeous. It's a *we* now, not a *you.*"

She hesitated with the batter over the griddle just long enough to know what he'd said struck home, then nodded and got back in the groove. "We're all nuts. Every damned one of us."

Beckett splayed his hand low on her belly, kissed the top of her head and filled his lungs with her paradise scent. "Feels good, doesn't it?"

Before she could answer, Axel's voice cut from the kitchen table. "Hey, Gia. What's the word on the thing in Atlanta?"

"The word?" Axel might not have learned the subtleties of Gia's teasing, but Beckett clocked the smile in her voice even without a direct visual.

"Did you get it or not?"

She set the batter aside and craned her head to peer around Beckett's torso, her wry tone strong enough to match Jace or Ninette's humor. "You know I got it. Why bother asking?"

Beckett grabbed his coffee and moved out from behind Gia in time to see Axel grin, kick back in his chair and drape one elbow over the back of it. "Well, a man might hope he'd get a sweet kiss on the cheek and a solid hug for helpin' a lass out."

Leaning back against the counter, Beckett crossed his feet at the ankles, sipped his coffee and studied Axel over the rim. "You know, for a guy who likes his arms and legs working like they're supposed to, you sure hit on my woman a lot."

"Now, boys," Sylvie said from her place next to Gia at the stove. "No fighting or bloodshed in the kitchen."

Either Trevor wasn't the least bit clued into the good-natured ribbing or his coffee hadn't kicked in and he was operating on a time delay. "Yo, Beck. Where are we with the tampering deal? Anything come out of your visit to Brantley's place?"

"Nothing," Knox said before Beckett could answer. "The guys we've kept on him haven't reported anything suspicious either."

Zeke looked to Beckett. "How's that play into Gia's thing?"

"It's a risk." For the first time all morning, Gia frowned and gave up all pretense of becoming a pancake profession. "Gives me an extra complication to plan for and introduces an unknown element I'd rather not have."

"We'll cover it," Beckett said. "We'll keep someone on Brantley and the guy in Atlanta and keep digging for answers."

Refilled on coffee, Jace settled back into his chair. "What about Nat's ex? Any possibility he's the one behind this?"

Trevor shook his head. "Me and Ivan have been diggin', but he's got alibis for the gaps in the range's footage."

With a knowing grin on her face, Natalie stood and headed toward the stove. "Plus, Wyatt's an idiot with guns." She waved Gia away and snatched the spatula out of Gia's hand. "You're gonna burn 'em. Go. Sit. Plan and plot."

"But—"

"Not gonna be your last breakfast at Haven, G." Beckett handed her the coffee she'd kept parked next to the stove and guided her to the massive table. "Not gonna be your last chance to flip flapjacks either."

"Anything from Sergei?" Danny asked Knox.

"Wasn't any blowback from Darya's deal so far as he can tell."

Darya laid bowls loaded to the rim with blueberries, strawberries and chopped pecans on the table. "No, but he did warn us he's coming for Christmas and bringing a few of his men with him."

"Good Lord," Ninette said turning from the stove, an almost frightening amount of bacon piled on a huge plate. "We're gonna have to expand."

Zeke chuckled and hugged Gabe who'd snagged the

chair next to him close. "Like you've got a problem with that."

"Ye'll not hear me complaining." Sylvie hustled toward them with a stack of pancakes, eyes locked on Vivienne. "They had to force me back on the plane in St. Petersburg. Russian men are easy on the eyes."

Vivienne snickered and took her place next to Jace. "I don't think they're used to brash Scottish women. I swear you made at least two of them blush."

Axel grunted, snagged the stack of pancakes before anyone else could and dropped two on Gia's plate next to him. "You know, my guy mentioned your buddy Judd's got one of the teams lined out for himself already."

If Gia was disconcerted by his actions or the rapid shift in topic she didn't show it. Just rolled with it like she'd lived with them forever. "He's not my buddy."

Ivan planted both forearms on the table, curiosity drawing him out of his shell a little. "What is he?"

She hesitated in buttering up her cakes for a second, thoughtful, then shrugged and kicked back into gear. "Somewhere between a neighborhood kid I grew up with and an annoying cousin your parents adore but you can't decide whether to hug or punch."

Ninette shook out a napkin and dropped it in her lap. "Your parents like him?"

"My parents adore him. Between my senior year in high school and halfway through college they tried every trick in the book to get us together. He's a good guy, but he's not for me." She bit into her bacon and scrunched her nose the way someone would if an unwanted guest had just shown up. "It's funny. We had a ton in common growing up, but somehow always end up butting heads."

Natalie opened the sliding glass door. "Mary! Levi! Breakfast!"

"Damn." Gabe snagged two more slices of bacon. "You know Levi hogs the bacon."

Zeke chuckled and added another two strips to her plate before sliding the platter over to Natalie.

"When's your event?" Ivan said to Gia.

"September 30th."

"Still four weeks away," Axel said. "A lot can happen in that kind of time."

"Probably not as much as I'd like," Gia said. "I've got a full team to put together, the event to research and travel to figure out."

Trevor took the plate Natalie handed him and pulled her into the chair next to him. "Think you're forgetting something on that last one."

Gia paused mid-forkful of pancake. "Forgetting what?"

"Family comes with a built-in travel service. Not thinkin' logistics on getting your team to Atlanta's gonna be a hardship."

For a second she frowned like she didn't understand what he meant, then her eyes widened when the pieces came together. "Trevor, I can't do that."

Jace set the syrup bottle on the table and shoved the slowly disappearing stack of pancakes closer to Gia. "Shut up and eat, woman. Family flies. Get over it."

Yep. They were loud, funny as hell and sometimes hard to keep up with, but as a whole they were unbreakable. Beckett wrapped an arm around her shoulders, pulled her in close and kissed the top of her head. "Tough love, gorgeous. This family's got it in spades."

Chapter Nineteen

So many trees. Tall maples and fat magnolias with flow-
ering dogwoods dotted here and there, all of them with
an unmarred stretch of deepening blue evening skies
overhead. The familiar beauty blurred past Gia from the
passenger side window, the foliage lining the winding
streets of Atlanta's most elite neighborhood still stub-
bornly hanging on to summer's rich green colors even
at the end of September. Logic or at least common decency said drawing this close to where she'd grown up
should build all kinds of warm and fuzzy feelings, but
with every mile Beckett drove the knot in her stomach
grew bigger.

"You wanna talk about it?" Beckett covered her
fisted hand on her lap with one of his, easily navigating the secluded neighborhood with the other.

"Not much to talk about." She uncoiled her hand and
laced her fingers with his. The heat from the simple contact was a godsend. A welcome respite from the ice that
seemed to have penetrated her bones. "Visits with my
parents are a crapshoot. Either we'll go, make mostly
meaningless conversation and escape before our cheeks
end up frozen in a fake smile, or we'll find ourselves in
land-mine-rich terrain inside of ten minutes and start

plotting our escape before dinner starts. There's not much hope for anything in between."

The playful smile she'd grown to crave beamed down on her and he squeezed his hand in hers. "Maybe next time we'll bring Sylvie and Ninette. They'd loosen up a convent inside of five minutes if they put their mind to it."

"God, there's an image." She huffed out an ironic laugh. "I can't fathom one good reason we'd ever get them in the same room together, but seeing Dad have to hold his own with Ninette would be a hoot. Not to mention, it might teach my mom a thing or two."

Beckett's smile shifted, softening a little as an emotion she couldn't quite tag moved behind his eyes. "I could think of a few reasons they might have to share close quarters."

For a second, she just stared at him, torn between simply appreciating the warmth in his expression and scrambling to figure out what the heck he was talking about.

And then it clicked.

She swallowed hard and shifted her attention back to the carefully manicured wonderland around them. The last four weeks had been perfect. A leisurely exploration into each other's daily quirks, pet peeves and outright annoying habits. Some nights they'd spend at Beckett's loft with Darya and Knox, or with the whole family at Haven, but most ended at her place. A fact evidenced by Beckett's growing presence in her bedroom and bathroom. It wasn't anything major. Not like he'd taken over drawer or closet space, and he was insanely minimalist on toiletries, but the feel of her place had changed by his being there. As if the air had taken on a protective, masculine energy.

"Too soon to talk about it?" he said.

Too soon? God, she wished that's what she thought. As it was, she'd caught herself drifting off into happily-ever-after scenarios more times than she cared to admit. "We haven't even let anyone outside your family know we're seeing each other yet."

"Gorgeous, that was your demand. Not mine. Remember?"

Oh, she remembered. Since the head-to-head and consequent make-up sex at Haven they hadn't had too many heated discussions, but her asking to keep things quiet on a professional level had been one of them. "It wasn't a demand."

He glanced away from the road long enough to cock an eyebrow.

"Okay, maybe it was. But I wanted us to have time to ease into things without people we work with giving us shit."

"That mean you're ready now?" He kept the question light and his gaze never strayed from the road, but she'd be a fool not to recognize the underlying edge to his words. He wanted this. Had made it crystal clear he wanted everyone and anyone to know she was his and vice versa. And while the idea of letting the universe know that she'd scored the man of her dreams appealed on a variety of levels, the risk of possibly losing him on a very public scale terrified the hell out of her.

But it was time. He'd been patient. Given her everything she'd wanted and then some. "Maybe after this weekend we could do something." She chanced a look at him. "The guys are always arranging happy hours. We could go to one?"

His gaze slid to hers and his thumb skated back and forth along the back of her hand, calming them both. "We could do that."

She nodded, her heart jogging just a tad faster than it had before.

"'Course if you think I'm gonna wait for one of those morons we work with to get a social burr up their butt, you're out of your mind. I'll set up my own damned happy hour."

"Beckett."

"What?" He grinned and turned onto the long drive that led to her parents' house. "You know what happens when you give me the green light."

She scoffed and straightened in her chair as if her mom could already see her lousy posture. "Oh, don't blow that smoke at me. You don't even need a green light once you decide what you want."

He winked. "You got that right." He turned the corner that brought the gate and the main house into view and his smile slipped. "Jesus, Gia."

Yeah, that pretty much summed it up. Propertywise her parents' estate stretched over three acres, but one of the three served as the front yard. A wide ivory fountain stretched between the incoming and outgoing driveways just beyond the gate and the Mediterranean masterpiece that was her father's pride and joy sprawled at the far end. "It does what Dad intended it to do."

"Shock the hell out of people?"

Gia snickered. "Reginald Sinclair does *not* shock people. He impresses them."

Beckett scoffed. "Gorgeous, that's the structural

equivalent of a go-fuck-yourself if I've ever seen one. Either that or he's got serious issues with the size of his dick."

Her sharp laughter filled the Escalade's interior, unwinding a huge chunk of the knot that had built on the drive over.

"Seriously, how many rooms does it have?"

Still chuckling, she cocked her head and tried to see it from Beckett's perspective. Red slate roof, butter stucco walls and stone terraces. With the sweeping drive and the trimmed hedges around it, one would think they'd either reappeared in Italy or relocated to Hollywood. "Nine bedrooms."

"Only nine? Hell, we have ten at Haven and it doesn't look like that."

"Wait till you see the bedrooms." She shook her head. "The funny part? There are twelve and a half bathrooms."

"Why?"

"Because one can't be troubled to walk all the way to a bedroom when you're in the cigar room, the theater room, the salon, or any of the other more traditional rooms. Oh!" She raised her hand for added emphasis. "Let's not forget there are three kitchens. Because... well, I don't know why."

Beckett stared straight ahead, his jaw slack and his eyebrows high. "That's whacked." His eyes narrowed as though a whole new scheme had popped into his head. "Though, Sylvie might dig extra kitchens."

She giggled and waved Beckett to the intercom poised outside his window. "Just punch the button already and let's get this over with."

Needless to say, there was no back-and-forth through

the speaker. Ever since her dad had cameras installed, no one bothered to actually greet the people who came to meet them. At least not at the gate. Once guests had parked and ambled up the big stairs fronting the main porch with their mouths hanging open in awe, *then* it was all hugs, air kisses on either cheek and manly handshakes.

Beckett parked dead center of the front door, but before Gia could hop out, he snatched her hand and gave it a reassuring squeeze. "No matter what happens, I've got your back. Just be you and we'll get through it."

God, he was good at warm and fuzzy. In the last month, he'd spun her up in so much of it she barely felt like her feet touched the ground anymore. And as gifts went, having someone beside her while she waded into one-on-one time with her parents was about as good as they got. She opened her mouth, the words she'd almost spilled more times than she could count nearly leaping out. "Thank you," she said instead.

He smiled and nodded. "Now keep your ass in that seat and let me help you out. I have a feeling your dad's the old-fashioned type."

The front door opened just as Beckett opened her car door, the timing so perfect Gia halfway suspected her mother had watched through a window for the most ideal moment.

"Gia!" How her mother could offer such a greeting and still come off on the dry side, Gia couldn't figure out. It'd been years since she remembered a genuine laugh or emotion coming from her mother. Even her bouts of worry seemed strained through a polite filter specially designed to muffle any undesirable uncouthness. "I thought you'd never get here."

Translation: *You're beyond the acceptable limits of fashionably late.*

Gia shared a look with Beckett she hoped conveyed something on par with an eye roll and cleared her throat to fight back a scoff. "Sorry, Mom. Beckett and I had to finish running through some things with hotel security before we could leave."

Her father strolled through the open front door, bringing with him a rigid restraint she'd swear made the setting sun dim a little. He didn't say a word. Just stood there tall and proper in a deep charcoal suit that had to have cost a grand while her mother hurried down the steps.

"You and your father—both cut from the same cloth. Work, work, work." She grasped Gia's shoulders and did the air-kissy thing to each cheek before standing back for a thorough once-over. "My goodness, look at you."

Gia braced. Either she'd get two thumbs-up for the jaunty tweed jacket with its fringed three-quarter-length sleeves and black pants she'd paired it with, or a subtle nudge toward laying off the sweets. Given that her mother was the picture-perfect modern Southern woman in a crisp white linen suit and not so much as an ounce over one-twenty-five, the assessment could go either way.

"Colette, at least get her in the house before you start swapping designer labels." This from her father who still hadn't deigned to leave his post by the front door.

"Oh, yes. Of course."

The second she released Gia's shoulders, Beckett moved in behind her and splayed his hand low on her back.

Her mother tracked the movement and her eyes widened.

Years of well-drilled manners kicked in even as a wave of dread on par with a slow-motion head-on collision bowled her over. "Mom, I want you to meet Beckett Tate."

Beckett held out his hand. His attire might not have run up the same tab as her father's, but the way he wore his black slacks and gray Oxford with the sleeves rolled up to his forearms, it didn't matter. Beckett was pure power. Not the kind that came from money, but that came from the very core of him. "Nice to meet you, Mrs. Sinclair."

Not once in her lifetime could Gia remember her mother dumbfounded, but the tiny pause as she stared at Beckett's outstretched hand marked the first. She recovered quickly, gently placing her hand in Beckett's. "Gia mentioned she was bringing someone." She glanced back at Reginald whose face had grown even sterner. "I'd thought she meant one of her girlfriends."

So…what? She'd thought Beckett was her driver or something? She managed to keep the thought to herself, but only barely. Gia moved in tight to Beckett's side and curled her hand around the inside of his bicep. "Beckett's my someone. My *date*. Is there a problem?"

Another glance from Colette to Reginald. Almost a silent plea for guidance.

Her dad lifted his chin almost imperceptibly. "Not a problem at all. You just hadn't mentioned you were seeing anyone. We're delighted, of course." He stepped to the side and motioned to the door. "Why don't the two of you come in so we can hear about your flight?"

Colette hurried up the stairs as fast as her Pradas and common decency would allow.

Beckett took advantage of the wide berth she'd created and leaned close enough only for Gia to hear. "If they're this opposed to me on good behavior, I'm afraid to see how they'd respond to the unvarnished version."

"I don't give a shit what they think."

Her father pinned her with a look that made her think he'd heard her quip, even if logic and the limits of human hearing insisted he couldn't have.

She lowered her voice further just in case and locked eyes with Beckett. "Whatever they say tonight, can I offer a blanket apology in advance?"

He chuckled at that, slid his hand to her hip and squeezed. "Your opinion's the only one I care about. Worry about navigating tonight, not my tender male ego."

Her father's gaze dropped to Beckett's possessive grip at her hip a second before Gia and Beckett moved across the threshold.

To Beckett's credit, he masked the initial impact of the foyer better than most. Just strolled right into the cavernous opening with its Italian marble tiles and scarlet carpet-covered grand staircase as if he dealt with such excess every day. He even managed not to crane his head and gawk at the soaring ceiling with its crystal chandeliers and gold filigree woodwork. Where the exterior was all Mediterranean extravagance, the inside was closer to the Palace of Versailles.

Heavy quick footsteps clipped against the tiles from the far side of the stairway, still out of sight. "Is she here?"

Gia stopped dead in her tracks, the voice still echoing through the big room unmistakable.

Sure enough Judd strode into sight, a smug almost superior look locked on her and Beckett.

Beckett moved in tight behind her and cupped her

shoulders. "Judd." Not a friendly welcome. More of
a warning statement masquerading as an ambivalent
hello.

"What is Judd doing here?" She paired the question
with a demanding glare at her father.

"Gia!" Despite the scolding tone to her mother's
voice, she kept the volume at a respectable level and
moved closer to Judd as if he needed to be shielded
from Gia's lapse in decency. "Judd's been welcome in
our home since the day his family moved next door. We
knew he'd be in town for the event, too, so we invited
him to join us."

And just like that, the pieces clicked together. Her
father hadn't wanted to support her career. He'd wanted
to dip his toes back in the matchmaking waters and see
if he couldn't navigate his daughter back to the man
he'd picked for her. Given the subtle glide of Beckett's
thumbs where he gripped her even tighter, she wasn't
the only one adding two and two together.

Gia cleared her throat and straightened as much as
her five-foot-four frame would allow. "Sorry, Judd. I
didn't expect to see you here. It surprised me."

"I can see that." Judd's attention shifted to Beckett's hands at her shoulders and his face hardened. "I'd
heard rumors you two had started something, but wasn't
aware things had moved quite this far."

Beckett waded in, his deep voice just as lethal and
uncompromising as the man. "You weren't on the list
of people who needed to know."

Talk about your lines in the sand. In one phrase,
Beckett had not only shut Judd down and staked his
claim, but had thrown up an unmistakable boundary.
Gia covered one of his hands with hers, praying he'd

look past her sweaty palm and see the contact as a *thank you* instead of a silent plea to haul her out the front door. "Well," she managed with a fake smile to match her mother's. "Now that we're all here, what's for dinner?"

An hour and a half and a whole lot of uncomfortable conversation later, she wished she'd opted for Beckett hauling her out the front door. Never in her life had she been so aware of her father's dogged ability to grill someone and make it look like a simple conversation about the weather. Which was stupid considering he was Atlanta's premier criminal attorney. She'd just never had a circumstance where his skills were targeted on someone she cared for so deeply.

Not surprisingly, Beckett gave as good as he got. When he wanted to answer something, he did. When he didn't—which was usually when someone edged too closely to his childhood—he simply dodged and redirected. The only clues that tipped her off to his growing irritation were the brief yet affectionate caresses he gave her—a touch to her cheek or a soft stroke along her forearm—and the occasional times he'd casually slide his hand in his front pocket.

That was where his hand was now. Reclined against his dining room chair with his fingers loosely coiled around a delicate china coffee cup he could crush on a whim, no one else in the room seemed to notice he'd slipped his hand inside. Gia certainly never had noticed the trick before she'd learned of his need for touch, and she'd watched him plenty.

But she knew now. Knew how he almost always kept something incredibly soft tucked inside to help level him out when he couldn't get a more tangible form of contact and was close to losing his shit. Knew that the *something soft* between his fingers was something of hers. Or more to the point, a scrap of what was left of a black silk nightie she'd had on when things had gotten delightfully rough.

"That's an impressive business you've made for yourself," Reginald said after all but asking for an itemized P&L on Beckett's company. "I'd wager your partner's technical services turn a more lucrative profit considering more limited overhead."

"It's not about which service turns more profit. It's about leveraging different skill sets so we maximize income on every outlet across the board." Beckett lifted his coffee cup and held Reginald's stare. "Kind of like family."

Apparently, tired of grilling Beckett and getting nowhere, her father shifted his steely focus to Gia. "So, if the bulk of your team is being provided by Beckett, I guess it's fair to say it's his company providing the core leadership for the event tomorrow?"

"My company's got nothing to do with tomorrow," Beckett said before she could answer. "Gia built her own team. The fact that she interviewed and cherry-picked from the best sources proves she's smart and efficient."

Dear God, could this night get any worse? Her temples throbbed and her stomach was so tight she wouldn't have to do sit-ups for a month. And the worst part of it all was a part of her had secretly hoped her parents would see the good in Beckett she did. Instead, all he'd gotten was the third degree and glares from both Judd and her father.

Per usual, her mother seemed to float in a whole different dimension. A fact proven when she chose that moment to interject. "Gia, why don't you and Judd go and grab dessert for us? Marisela made us a lovely key lime pie before she left."

Judd smiled like he'd just been handed the perfect Christmas present and scooted his chair away from the table. "My favorite!"

"I know!" her mother chirped. "She was so happy to hear you'd be by tonight she insisted on making one for you." Her gaze slid to Gia. "Do you mind, darling? It would give your father and I time to get to know your friend, Beckett, a little better."

"No." A single word that drew every eye to her and seemed to pause the Earth's rotation all at once. She didn't care. Not anymore. Treating her like shit for years was one thing. Rubbing their superior attitudes in Beckett's face and disrespecting them both with their match-making schemes was something else entirely. "I'm not going to go get dessert with Judd. I'm not going to bond with him in the kitchen over key lime pie and suddenly change my stance on what I've told you a million times before. But just in case I wasn't clear enough on all the other occasions, let me state it unequivocally now. I am not interested in a romantic relationship with Judd. We're friends who work together on occasion and even that is something I'm reconsidering repeating in the future."

"Gia—" her mother started, but it was Reginald who finished.

"Are you done?"

"No, I'm not." In that second, she understood Beckett's need for touch on a level she'd never thought she'd experience, but it took everything she had to keep from reaching out for his hand. To feel his strength and support. "I brought Beckett here to introduce him to my family. I stupidly thought you'd be interested in getting to know him and maybe—just maybe—appreciate him the way I do, but it seems the only agenda that matters to you is *yours*."

Colette set her napkin aside and leaned in, the picture of concern and remorse. "Of course, we're interested in your business associates, Gia, we just wanted—"

She slammed her hands down on the gleaming dining room table and surged to her feet. "He's not my *business associate*, he's the man I love!"

Nothing.

Not a single movement or sound in the whole damned house for the space of two heartbeats.

Had she really said that?

Or in this case, roared it?

Out loud?

From the far end of the table, her mother stared wide-eyed and slack-jawed. Her father's glare from the opposite end was nothing short of glacial where Judd's face fiamed hot enough it was a wonder his starched collar wasn't already drenched.

But it wasn't them she gave a damn about. It was Beckett and the utter lack of response or movement beside her that kept her locked in place, too terrified to turn and witness his response. She swallowed hard. Her lungs strained to drag in a decent breath and her heart hammered loud enough her pulse echoed in her ears.

Forcing herself into motion, she faced him.

Oh, holy hell.

He hadn't moved. Not one inch. But his eyes were locked on hers, raw, unmasked pride and possessiveness etched on every line of his face and searing straight to her soul. He stood, slow as if he had all the time in the world and zero concern for the people watching. He smoothed the backs of his fingers along her jawline, then cupped her neck and drew her next to him.

So warm. Utterly safe. Accepted.

Protected.

Her father cleared his throat. "I think that's enough theatrics, Gia. Have a seat."

"That wasn't theatrics," Beckett said with more than a little warning in his voice. "That was your daughter trying to get you to hear her." He tossed his napkin on the table, guided Gia away from the table with a hand low on her back and focused on her mother, effectively dismissing her father and Judd. "Sounds like my woman's not interested in dessert. We'll let ourselves out."

Chapter Twenty

He should say something. For thirty minutes on the drive back to the hotel, Beckett's conscience had read him the riot act for keeping his silence and not doing something—*anything*—to ease Gia's obvious tension, but he didn't trust himself to speak. Could barely function well enough to safely navigate the winding highway interchanges of downtown with the wildness burning through him. He'd pushed the envelope on his control before. Had known the second Gia's dad had started in with his pompous bullshit the night would end with him on the edge.

But he hadn't counted on Gia.

Hadn't suspected she was anywhere near feeling about him the way he felt about her and had been totally blindsided by what she'd said. Had felt the passion behind her words clear to his bones. Hell, the only reason he was still halfway sane was the steadying contact of his hand manacled around her wrist. The heavy thud of her pulse beneath his thumb and her tender skin beneath his fingertips.

He's the man I love!

Two seconds at most, but they were burned into him. The conviction in her voice. The certainty and confidence in the way she'd stared her family and Judd down. While she might have been the tiniest person in the whole damned room, when she'd surged to her feet she'd been a giant. Bulletproof. And she'd thrown down *for him*.

He whipped the Escalade into the parking garage, the need for caution and slowness in the tight confines scraping like barbed wire beneath his skin. Even the harsh fluorescent lights overhead hurt. Like a thousand tiny, razor-sharp rakes dragging beneath his skull.

Gia covered the hand he kept locked around her wrist with her free hand, slowly stroking his knuckles then up to his forearms. Giving what she could to help despite the fact he hadn't done the same.

Were her fingers shaking? Or was it his imagination?

Of course, they're shaking, you fucking moron. You haven't said so much as "thank you" since you got her into the car.

He gripped the steering wheel so tight he nearly bungled swinging into the nearest parking spot. He squeezed her wrist and ground out, "Stay put," before he punched the gearshift into Park, killed the engine and unfolded out of the driver's seat.

The simple act of walking was a challenge, his muscles too tight from his self-imposed lockdown. Not to mention, his dick had been hard as a concrete pillar from the time she'd started reading her parents the riot act. Professional Gia was a turn-on. Sweet Gia was a treat. But badass Gia? The second her attitude flared and she got down to business, the end of the world could be ten minutes away and he'd ignore the whole damned thing in favor of watching her do her thing.

He jerked her car door open and held his hand out.

She took it, but stayed in her seat. "Are we going to talk about this?"

"Talk about what?" He tugged her hand enough to get her in motion, but the questions kept coming.

Her feet touched down on the concrete and she craned her head back and kept her gaze locked on him. "About what I said."

So beautiful. Hitting him head-on with what she needed to know despite the dangerous waters she had to sense she was wading into. "Did you mean it?"

"Yes."

No hesitation. Not even a beat. And damned if the confirmation didn't battering-ram his determination right up into the stratosphere. "Then no."

"No?"

Beckett slammed the car door shut, backed her up against the Escalade and crowded close, dragging in much-needed air before his answer practically growled out. "I didn't lay you out on your parents' dining room table and do what I wanted to. I've made it the long-ass drive from that stick-up-the-ass house to downtown Atlanta without pulling over and giving my instincts free rein. So, no. We're not going to talk." He fisted her hair at the back of her head and got so close her ragged exhalations danced across his face. "We're gonna make it through this garage and all the way upstairs to our room and then we're *still* not gonna talk, because I'm gonna be too busy *showing* you what I thought about what you said."

By the time he was done, both of them were breathing heavy, her hands trembling against his chest and her big brown eyes so wide anyone passing by would've thought she was staring up at the big bad wolf. "Okay."

Okay.

A simple word, but shockingly effective in how it pacified the animal inside him. A soft yielding on par with a willingly bared throat that forced his beast to take a step back and practice patience. He uncoiled his fist and cupped the side of her face, her full lips slightly parted and so close he could almost taste them. He skimmed his thumb across them, the simple, soft contact and the promise of more a much-needed sedative to his raging tension. "Upstairs."

He'd meant to convey more. To let her know she deserved more than an ill-timed kiss in a parking garage or the selfish gluttony his need for touch demanded he take.

But she didn't need it. Just smiled that sweet smile of hers and stroked her hands from his sternum to each side of his neck and whispered, "Upstairs."

An overcrowded elevator. The understated ding as it landed on each floor. Hunter-green carpet as they finally stepped out into their hallway. Gold trim on the ivory painted walls. Last door on the left.

The details kept him focused. Kept him grounded in the present and detached from the painfully physical manifestation of his need for touch. The scorching burn from muscles held too tight for too long, and the impulse to feed his weakness no matter the cost.

He punched the key card in the room's lock, his fingers shamefully unsteady and his arms trembling from fatigue as he pushed the door open and guided Gia inside ahead of him. The door latched behind him and his lungs expanded fully for the first time in hours.

Touch.

Take.

Now.

As if she'd heard his thoughts, Gia paused beside the bed, shrugged off the prim jacket she'd worn for dinner and locked eyes with him. Waiting. Willing. She *knew* him. Accepted all that he was. His high-handed bullshit. His need to dominate and protect her. His fucked-up disorder.

And she loved him anyway.

The knowledge soothed him. Settled him as sure as a caress along his spine even as it made him ache for more. He forced himself to move slow, crossing the room in a gait that he hoped demonstrated confidence and calm, rather than the greedy desperation gnawing on his bones. When she lifted her hands to the tiny buttons on her white shirt, he caught them with one of his own. "No."

"Beckett, you need to give in. You're hurting." She splayed her hands above his sternum and stroked up to the top button on his own shirt. "Let me help you."

Before her fingers could latch on and start working, he nudged her backward until she sat on the foot of the bed and crouched at her feet. She had no idea. No clue that she'd gone so far beyond helping him it was laughable. She'd saved him. Reforged the bridge that had been burned to his heart when he was far too young and then boldly stormed across it and claimed it for her own.

"I'll get what I need." He slid one shiny black patent leather heel off. A peek-a-boo pump, she'd called it when she'd put them on earlier. All he knew then was that they were sexy as fuck and he had serious plans for them in the future. The second heel thudded to the floor and he pulled her to her feet. "Tonight, you come first."

She started to argue, but he cut her off by trading her

places, sitting on the edge of the bed and pulling her between his knees. He tugged her silk shirt free of her tailored black pants and slid the first button free. Then the next, not stopping until both sides hung loose, exposing a long, tempting line of her creamy skin.

"Take it." She moved in closer, her voice as soft and encouraging as her hands stroking over his shoulders toward his neck. "Touch me, Beckett. Take what you need."

God, he wanted to. Wanted to savagely strip every stitch of clothing off them both and blanket her body with his. To drown in all that was her and not come up for air for days.

"Beckett, look at me."

He gripped her hips and forced his eyes away from the sweet stretch of flesh up to hers.

"I didn't mean for how I felt about you to come out the way it did, but I meant it. Every word." Slowly, she peeled her shirt free of her shoulders and let it whisper to the floor. "Part of loving someone means when they hurt, you hurt, too. If you won't touch me for you. Touch me for me. Ease my ache."

So much skin. Petal-soft skin he could easily bruise in his current frame of mind. That flushed when he did something that shocked the hell out of her and right before she came. That bore the marks from his beard when he had a mind to leave one. "You deserve slow."

She slowly unfastened her pants and wriggled them past her hips, dislodging his hands in the process. "Slow or fast doesn't matter. What does is feeling the man I love touch me exactly the way he needs to."

A silk ivory bra that lifted her perfect, full breasts up for him and a matching lacy thong that accented her curvy hips. That was all that stood between him and the feast he wanted. He leaned in and her clean ocean scent surrounded him. Warmth beneath his palms. Her skin. Soft. Giving. His tongue flicked out for a taste and his fingers dug into her hips. A sound that scared even him rumbled up his throat. "Gia."

It was the best warning he could give, his tone conveying more than his mind could offer with words.

She wrapped her arms around him, one hand sliding firmly along his spine and the other spearing into his hair and encouraging him to take more. "I want *you*, Beckett. I need it. Just like you want to give it to me." She fisted the hand in his hair. "Please."

A plea. A stark need that matched his own and snapped the leash on his control. One second she was in front of him. Barely three heartbeats later, the bra and panties were gone and she was under him, his mouth consuming hers, her legs splayed wide over his thighs and his hands taking full advantage of her bared body.

Muted pops and pings registered in the back of his mind and Gia groaned into his mouth. She arched her back and neck, breaking his unforgiving kiss even as the soft *skreetch* of fabric tearing mingled with their frantic breathing. "Beckett…" Her hands skimmed his bare abs, his pecs, his shoulders and biceps, the touch as hungry and demanding as his own. "Fuck, you're burning up."

More tearing and then the room's chilled air settled on his skin. He groaned, palmed both of her tits and squeezed as he sank his teeth into the soft skin where her neck and shoulder met.

Her body bucked beneath him and her nails dug into his back, but the ragged cry that went with it spurred him harder. Lashed the beast into a deeper frenzy and encouraged him to take more. She fumbled with the button at his waist, the action putting too much distance between the two of them to tolerate. With a frustrated growl, he rolled to the side of the bed and shucked his shoes and socks. "Don't move."

She did anyway, nudging him just a little farther beyond reason when she shifted to her knees and crawled toward him, her voice low and husky. "I'm not feeling obedient at the moment."

He surged upright before she could reach him, shoved his pants and briefs free and caught her with a fistful of hair just as she lunged forward, her kiss-swollen mouth just inches from his straining cock. "You don't know what you're dealing with..." He tightened his grip and tried to pull her away, but she fought the tension. "Don't push me."

Her gaze shot to his, every hot exhalation from her mouth whipping across his shaft. "I know exactly *who* I'm dealing with." She leaned a little closer, the sting it earned her along her scalp showing in her wild eyes. "And I want all of him."

An odd stillness moved over him. The eerie calm before the storm. A predator in the frozen seconds before it struck.

She must have sensed it because when he cupped the back of her head and massaged his fingertips along her scalp, she stayed frozen in place, her wary gaze locked on him.

He moved in closer, guiding his cockhead along her lips.

She parted her mouth, ready to welcome him, and her tongue flicked out for a taste. "You think you can scare me." Another lick. "But I'm not afraid of you, Beckett Tate." She pressed her mouth against the root of him and beamed a wicked smile up at him. "Not even a little bit."

A toss to her back that landed her in the center of the bed. A flip to her belly. Her cheek to the mattress and her ass in the air. His hands on her hips and his dick poised and ready at the mouth of her.

And then he was *there*. Buried to the hilt in the hot clasp of his woman.

Home.

Whole.

Loved.

She widened her knees farther, tipped her hips higher and pushed back into every thrust, not just accepting his wildness, but demanding more.

He gave it. Pounded into her welcoming heat. Stroked her sweat-dampened skin. The backs of her legs. Her ass. The flare of her hips. The long line of her spine. He blanketed her back, one hand braced by her shoulder while the other skimmed up her inner thigh to her drenched sex. All for him.

He circled her swollen clit, not quite giving her the pressure she needed to get off.

She bucked beneath him, tossing her head and baring her neck in the process. "More. Harder."

Fuck no, he wasn't giving her more. Not yet. Every detail was too vivid and he was too greedy. Too lost in the slick fist of her pussy. In the sweet give of her body. In the slap of his hips against her ass and the drugging scent of Gia and sex.

He sunk his teeth into the tender junction at her neck

and shoulders and she cried out, her hard nub jumping under his fingers.

"Beckett, goddamn it!" She wrapped one hand around his wrist anchored against the mattress, ground back harder and growled to rival something that would have come from him. Her nails dug deep and her cunt tightened around his cock.

"Oh, no you don't." He jerked her upright, banded one hand around the front of her throat and cupped her mound with the other, holding her steady for each thrust. Their eyes locked in the mirror mounted over the dresser across the room, both wild and weighted with lust. Her dark hair spilled untamed to her shoulders, a priceless silk against his sensitized skin. And her tits. Fucking full and beautiful. Bouncing with every unmerciful stab of his hips.

He tightened his arms and crushed her to him, the fingers at her throat squeezing, not tight enough to mark or hurt her, but enough to make his point. His voice came out strained. Grated and thick between ragged breaths. "Say it again."

She lifted one hand from the death grip on his thigh, reached back and cupped the back of his head. The other covered his hand at her sex, her fingers encouraging his to move faster. "I love you."

His nuts drew tighter.

She fisted his hair and rolled her hips. "I love you." Erotic-as-hell flutters rippled through her sex. Her eyes slid closed and her muscles vised around his cock. "I love you."

"Fuck!"

He surged to the root, his own release powering into hers. Filling her and freeing him all at once. No more

pain. No wanting. No more stench of lacking taint-
ing his insides. Just him and the woman he loved. The
woman who loved him.

In and out, he savored the slick glide of his cock inside her hot sheath. Held her close and buried his face
in the crook of her neck. Breathed all that was her into
him as the last of his tension floated away.

Hips undulating lazily in sync with his, Gia stroked
him—one hand dragging tender fingertips through his
hair and the other petting the stretch from his wrist to
elbow. Her legs trembled and her head lolled heavy
on his shoulder. She rolled it toward him and nuzzled
him with her cheek. "Remind me to push your buttons
more often."

So sweet. Already absolving him of the rough treat-
ment he'd dealt her with her playfulness.

He smoothed his fingers around her throat and
pressed a soft kiss to her neck, the pulse beneath his
lips still finding its way back to normal. He skimmed
his mouth along her jawline and guided her face to his.
"No talking, gorgeous." He nipped her lower lip and
palmed the back of her head. Threaded his fingers in
her thick hair and held her steady. "Not yet."

He kissed her with everything he had in him. Every
hope. Every need and fear he'd kept hidden for as long
as he could remember. It all went into that moment.
With her body flush against his and his cock still rooted
inside her. Only when she tried to twist her body for
more of his kiss did he pull away.

The lust-filled daze that had weighted her eyes before was gone. Replaced with a languid awareness and
tenderness that moved across him like a warm spring
breeze. She knew. Had to know how deeply her accep-

tance moved him. How tightly it bound him to her. If she didn't, she would soon. In word and deed.

He tucked her close and leaned forward, gently laying her on her belly. Red marks marred her hips and sweat beaded along her spine. He traced each spot. Gave her the gentle care and attention he'd wanted to in the first place and caressed her arms, shoulders, back and thighs.

A shiver worked through her and goose bumps lifted across her skin. Much as it killed him to lose the connection, he pulled free of her welcoming heat and rolled her to her back.

"Beckett, let me—"

He cut her off with another kiss. This one gentler than its predecessors, but no less effective. Satisfied he'd settled her for the time being, he pulled away. "Stay put and let me take care of you."

"But Beckett—"

He cocked an eyebrow and she snapped her mouth shut, a lopsided smile playing on her lips.

In the bathroom, he took care of himself and got what he needed for her, his heart ramping right back up to the double bass drum rhythm it'd churned out minutes before. He'd done a lot of shit in his life. Dangerous and sometimes flat-out stupid shit. But he'd never been as aware and focused as he was when he walked back in the bedroom.

Gia waited, propped up on her side with an elbow underneath her and one knee cocked a little higher than the other. One hand moved a little uncertain across her belly, as though she couldn't quite figure out what to do with it.

Not once in the time since they'd gone without condoms had she let him see to her afterward, skittering off to the bathroom with one excuse or the other. He understood the hesitation. It was a whole different level of intimacy. Maybe not as sexy on the surface, but as honest as things got in the way of caring and he wanted that for her. Wanted her to know she could count on him no matter what the situation.

Kneeling on the bed near her feet, he urged her to her back, but she kept her knees bent and tucked to one side and her cheeks flamed a pretty pink.

He gently cupped one knee.

She bit her lip, the flush on her cheeks and collarbone deepening.

"Baby, it's me. Let me do this." He skimmed his thumb along the inside of her knee, all too aware of the goose bumps beneath it. "Let me take care of you."

Maybe it was the phrasing. Maybe it was the tone behind the words. Whatever it was that got through, she hesitantly parted her legs and bared herself to him.

He understood. More than she probably realized. Hell, if she had any clue how nervous he was about getting the next few minutes right she'd lose all self-consciousness and laugh herself silly.

He tended to her, mindful of how rough he'd been with her and her sensitive skin. When he was done, he killed the lights, scooped her up and tucked her under the sheets. She curled toward him the second his arms slid out from under her, her brown eyes wide and studying him in the mix of Atlanta's downtown glow and moonlight.

He cupped her face and soaked every second of it up. Her skin was so much lighter than his. So soft compared to his rough hands. Her lips were always full, but now they were puffy from his kisses. Beautiful.

She loves you.

It still rattled him. Probably always would. But he'd protect and shelter that love with everything he had in him. Wouldn't let it go. Not ever. And he'd give her all of him. Even the words that he'd never uttered to another soul in his life.

Sliding in beside her, he propped himself up on one elbow and pulled her close, giving her a little of his weight and his warmth. He smoothed her hair away from her face and cupped the back of her head. Made sure she could see his face and every emotion that moved through him. "You okay?"

She dipped her head. A single, cautious motion that echoed the heightened gravity coiled around them. "Are you?"

He smiled, the lightness she'd created inside him surging forward and punching a hole through his nervousness. "A beautiful woman I've watched and admired for years told me she loved me tonight and then met the basest side of me pound for pound in bed. I'm way past okay."

Her cheeky grin rivaled the full moon outside their window. "You were pretty intense."

Intense was putting it mildly. He had no doubt the red marks at her hips would turn to bruises before morning. But she'd been all in. Completely into every second of it. His match. In everything. He tightened his hold and sucked in a deep breath, his heart kicking so hard it hurt. "I know it yanked your chain about Judd being there tonight. I know you were pissed at your parents and their digs toward me. But what you said tonight—

the fact that you not only said it to them, but threw it in their face—gorgeous, you need to know, I've never felt more awed. More grateful and proud than in that second." He swallowed hard and his throat constricted to the point his voice cracked on the rest. "And you need to know—I love you, too. Have for weeks."

Her eyes widened, glittering with wonder in the bright moonlight. She trailed her fingers through the scruff at his jawline and studied his face as though searching for some hint she'd misheard his words. "You do?"

"Knew it the day I couldn't find you. Took me another handful of days after that to admit it, but I knew. My mother's the only other woman I remember loving this deep. Or maybe I just loved the idea of her. I lost her." He tried to swallow, for all the good it did him, and his voice dropped to a low rumble. "I don't want to lose you."

"You won't lose me." Absolute conviction. Not even a shred of doubt.

"I can be an asshole."

She grinned, undaunted, snuggled up against him so he had no choice but to settle in and hold her tight, then sighed, repeating the words she'd given him earlier. Only this time they were thick with love and contentedness. "I'm not afraid of you, Beckett Tate. Not even a little bit."

Chapter Twenty-One

So far, so good. Aside from some protesters waiting outside the hotel when Gia's primary, Governor Lansing
from the great state of Florida, arrived yesterday along
with his entourage, Beckett hadn't seen any threats to
warrant the level of detail that had been demanded.
Granted, the guy was an incumbent and had done more
than his share to choke out drug suppliers in and out of
the US, but not once had Beckett tweaked to suspicious
activity. Certainly nothing on par with the attacks al-
legedly threatened by several cartels.

Now, Judd on the other hand… Judd had tweaked
Beckett plenty in the last thirty-six hours. From the second the varied teams had met up early yesterday morning, to this afternoon's pre-event glad-handing with
elite donors, Judd had undermined Gia at every turn.
Questioning her decisions in front of everyone. Subtle
digs about her ability to handle such a large-scale en-
deavor. Even purposefully ignoring the more detailed
checks and balances she'd laid out. It all seemed to be
fair game to Judd, and Beckett was chomping at the bit
to clock the bastard.

Muted masculine chuckles rumbled from the far end
of the vast penthouse living room, the cluster of donors

huddled around Florida's current governor each vying
for favors for one cause or another. While the room was
as big as some ballrooms, it was decorated with light
colors that made it easy to see every detail and wasn't
overcrowded in a way that made protection difficult.
The number of guests was a challenge, though, each of
them roving from group to group and waiting for their
turn to schmooze with the man of the hour.

There weren't supposed to be that many people. Gia
had insisted on a limit before they'd ever left Dallas, but
they'd found out ten minutes prior to moving in *someone* had countered the restriction only yesterday—that
someone being Judd.

And Gia was pissed.

She'd covered it with everyone else, but the tight
concentration on her face and hard line of her lips said
she'd drawn up at least fifty gruesome ways to free
him of his nuts.

Beckett couldn't fucking wait to watch it happen.

As it had far more often than it should have with
him in charge of protecting the governor's wife, Beckett found his gaze straying to Gia on the far side of the
room. In a sea of business suits, she should have blended
in with her tailored black pants and jacket. Even her
hair pulled back in a slick ponytail was designed to
avoid notice.

She still stood out. Whether it was the fact that she
was a curvaceous woman amid mostly men, or that she
was a good head shorter than the rest of them was hard
to say, but every single person in the room noted her.
Men *and* women. Though, those from the latter group
tended to deliver their consideration with an edge of
competitiveness or envy.

The governor's wife hugged the woman next to her in an airy way that lacked any warmth at all and discreetly scanned the people gathered outside her circle for her next move. Sure enough, she departed the cluster that had held her attention for a solid ten minutes and moved toward another group closer to the door.

Beckett stayed in lockstep. Not quite in arm's reach, but close enough he could get there with little effort.

She gave Beckett a coy head-to-toe, grinned and murmured, "And to think I was jealous my husband had a woman looking out for him this weekend. If I'd realized I'd get you rather than the standard fare, I wouldn't have even blinked. Any chance you'll have time to spare after the gala tonight?"

While her comments hadn't been loud enough for the people around them, they were clearly audible for the rest of the team through his headset. Beckett gave the usual response he got under such circumstances—a bland smile that was more warning than it was welcoming.

Her grin turned into more of a wry mew. "Well, you can't blame a woman for trying, now can you?" With one last glance from under her eyelashes, she faced the next group of women and started in with the faux hugs.

Beckett zeroed in on Gia still locked in place on the other side of the room.

Blank. Eyes rooted on Governor Lansing and hands clasped loosely in front of her. Not a single hint she'd heard, much less responded to the blatant invitation.

But she'd heard it. Had to have considering the barely suppressed smirk Danny aimed at him across the room.

Tempted as he was to call Danny over and have him take over with the governor's wife, Beckett stayed where he was. Such propositions weren't at all unusual. Hell, more men than he cared to count actually welcomed them. Surely Gia knew he wasn't one of them. Never had been and had no respect for the ones who did.

He watched her for a few more seconds, the sudden realization she'd likely had similar offers lighting an uncomfortable burn in his gut when he scanned the room out of habit and caught Judd's gaze on Gia.

And it wasn't a friendly look. Far from it. More something fitted to a self-righteous man pre-killing spree.

The burn in Beckett's gut sharpened and every warning instinct he'd honed from his earliest days fending for himself in a run-down apartment complex fired at once.

A competition.

That was how Gia had described her relationship with Judd. Said it had lasted for as long as she could remember. And the way he'd undercut her at the gig not too long ago supported that behavior. Come to think of it, he'd bragged about his gun knowledge at one of their happy hours about a year back. Beckett had chalked it up to empty bluster at the time, but if it was accurate, Judd would have had the skills to mess with Gia's piece.

Forcing his shoulders to relax, Beckett looked away just as Judd turned Beckett's direction.

Danny strolled along the far wall. Unassigned to any specific person, his primary job was to stay mobile and keep an eye on the general guests and check for anomalies.

Beckett waited, most of his focus on the governor's wife, but his peripheral attention narrowed on Danny. It took a good ten minutes, but Danny finally ambled close enough for Beckett to motion him over with a subtle lift of his chin. He muted his headset, an action Danny noted and repeated.

Moving in shoulder to shoulder with Beckett, Danny clasped his hands in front of him. "What's up?"

Indifferent expression back in place, Judd mirrored everyone else's professional stance about fifteen feet away from Gia, his attention back on the man he was supposed to be watching.

"Need you to call Knox when we're done here," Beckett said. "Have him run some checks on Rainier. See if he's got an alibi for those gaps in the range's security footage. If I do it, Gia might overhear and now's not the time to make her jumpy."

The statement knocked the blank mask off Danny's face and made him whip his head toward Beckett way too fast, drawing more than one eye their direction. Almost as fast, he shrugged the shock free and played it off with a grin that made it look like they were shooting the shit. "You shitting me?"

He wished he was. Gia wouldn't just be pissed if his guess was right, she'd be gutted. Judd might not be her best bud, but they'd clearly been close at one point, and nothing hurt worse than a knife in the back from a trusted source. "Just a hunch."

"That's a wild-ass hunch."

"Is it?" Beckett paused long enough to check a man strolling past as he slipped a hand in his pocket. When all he lifted out was a cell phone, Beckett kept going. "We've found nothing. No more suspects. No more actions toward Gia." He paused a beat, letting the possibility settle in his belly. "What if we've been looking in the wrong direction?"

Danny shrugged.

Gia's low voice cut through their headsets before he could answer. "Beckett, is there a reason I can see your lips moving and not hear you in my headset?"

Meeting her gaze across the room, he flipped on his mic. "Danny wanted to know if I really made you gumbo."

Danny snickered then turned his own mic back on.

"Gossip on your culinary prowess can wait," Gia said. "Get back to work." Quiet moved through their headsets for all of a second. When she spoke again there was a smile in her voice. "But for the record, he did and it was great."

Every one of the men positioned around the room kept their hard stares, but there was a lightness behind their eyes that hadn't been there before. Not just shared humor, but appreciation for the way she'd handled it.

Except for Judd. His expression was too hard. Anger barely contained.

Beckett shared a look with Danny.

Danny nodded and sauntered off to finish his sweep of the perimeter.

And that was it. Not another word spoken over the course of the next hour save what was necessary to convey one party or another taking their leave. The stragglers—mostly those who hadn't managed to score time with the governor or one of his aides during the prime crush—hung on until the bitter end, then practically bolted in the governor's wake.

He'd walked side-by-side with Gia, tailing the governor and his wife to their high-security suite. Where the governor had been quick to give Gia his assurances he'd stay behind closed doors and not venture out without contacting her first, his wife had saddled Beckett with a request for assistance with luggage—a less than subtle ploy to get him to reconsider her previous offer.

Finally able to escape, he exited the suite and found Gia braced between the two guards stationed outside, her attention sharp and her voice sharper as she ran down her expectations for them both.

Beckett waited, not crowding them too much, but painfully aware that Jamey and David—two of the men he'd volunteered from his own staff to save her hiring time—were struggling not to crack a smile. When Gia circled back for another run from the top of her expectations, Beckett took mercy on them and stepped in. "G, we've got two hours tops before we gotta be back here."

She stopped mid-sentence, frowned up at him for all of two seconds, then seemed to realize she'd waded neck-deep into overkill. "Right." She refocused on Jamey and David. "Let me know if you run into any problems."

This time they both nodded and smiled, one of those *yeah, boss* good-natured gestures they'd cast at Beckett more times than he could count.

Before Gia could remember any last bits of wisdom, Beckett cupped her elbow, guided her toward the elevator and lowered his voice. "Jamey's got it."

"I know."

He punched the up button. "So does Dave."

"I know that, too." She punched the button again like that might make the thing come faster and she glanced at the suite's front door. "I just don't want to screw up."

"The only way you're gonna screw up is if you don't let the men you hired do their job, or you're too tired to function when you need to. You need the downtime and so do I."

The elevator dinged and the doors whooshed open. He'd thought she'd settled into the quiet she usually preferred after a job, but all of three seconds after the doors closed and the car started downward she craned her head up at him and spoke, her voice distracted and more than a little fatigued. "What were you and Danny really talking about?"

There it was. Proof his woman was a tough one to dodge. Though, he'd thought he'd at least make it until after tonight before she dug in.

For a second, he considered laying it out. But considering how much she was putting into this gig already and the night still ahead of them, he scratched that approach and took a different direction. "Just running down a hunch. Rather you let me check it out instead of distracting you."

Her gaze narrowed. "Not something about the event?"

"No, an idea I had on the stuff back home."

"Nothing that'll blow back here?"

It better not. If it did and he could prove Judd was behind it, Beckett couldn't guarantee the fucker would live to see another sunrise. Still, Judd wasn't stupid. If he pulled a stunt here, he'd risk implicating himself on proximity alone. "Can't imagine how it could."

Guilt jabbed like a knife at the back of his neck, but when she simply nodded and faced the door again with an audible sigh of relief, his conscience took a hike and eased up on the pressure.

The rest of the trip to their own suite settled into the quiet he'd expected. That quiet was knocked on its ass, though, the second Beckett opened the door and Axel's booming laughter filtered out into the hallway.

Gia aimed a *what the hell?* frown up at Beckett then hustled past him and into the big living room.

Knox he'd expected. After all, he'd been the one to insist on setting up their central communications in the general area between the two bedrooms on each end. And Knox was right where they'd left him this morning—camped out behind a big table with five huge computer screens.

All the other people in the room were a complete shock.

Apparently, it was for Gia, too, because she planted her hands on her hips and cut into whatever humorous conversation was under way. "What's going on?"

As one, Axel, Ninette, Sylvie, Jace, Vivienne and Darya all turned eyes on them from the sitting area. Personally, Beckett found the formal red sofa with its gold trim and the even stuffier gold club chairs at either end uncomfortable as hell, but the way the women were settled in them made the space look downright cozy. Jace and Axel stood between them and Knox, each nursing what was undoubtedly Scotch out of crystal tumblers.

Dark hair loose around his shoulders and dressed in his usual jeans and T-shirt, Jace had probably given the hotel's staff a coronary prowling through the lobby. He grinned and lifted his chin in greeting. "You didn't think we were gonna let you have all the fun, did ya?"

"I can't wait!" Sylvie clasped her hands in front of her and stopped just short of bouncing like a six-year-old girl who'd just been given a lifetime supply of tiaras. "A woman can never have enough chances to dress up. You should see the dresses Ninette and I found last week."

Ninette anchored her elbow on the arm of the sofa

and propped her chin on her hand, a devious smile on her face. "Don't let her fool you. She's really hoping she gets to see Gia kick somebody's ass. Dressing up is just a bonus."

"Ha!" Viv chortled. "I've seen that dress. She's got a man hunt on her mind."

"Oh, that should be fun." Darya shifted in the club chair and craned her head for a better view of Knox. "Please tell me you've got good angles in the ballroom."

Knox snickered and gave his woman a sidelong look. "Sweetheart, I've got all the angles that count."

Axel volleyed his gaze between Darya and Knox. "You mean to tell me we flew all the way up here and I don't get to see your leggy Russian all dolled up again?"

From Axel's angle, he wouldn't have seen Knox's smirk, but Beckett could. "I'm puttin' her to work. Need someone I can trust tracking network activity."

More than a little dazed and obviously clueless on how to handle the curveball his family had thrown, Gia slowly pivoted her head and gazed up at him. "They flew all the way here?"

"Appears so."

"Why?" She shifted her attention back to the general audience now aiming pleasantly smug smiles her way and repeated, "Why?"

Jace finished off his drink, set it on the end table and ambled over to Viv. "Well, the good governor has a decent reputation. Far be it from us not to be good contributing citizens."

"Contributing citizens, my arse," Axel grumbled. "The bawbag's getting twelve large a plate. For that, I'd better see top shelf everything and no cash bars."

"Yeah, don't hold your breath on that," Knox said.

Chuckling along with everyone else, Ninette stood, motioned for Sylvie and Viv to do the same and grabbed the two designer shopping bags near her feet. "Come on, you guys. These two only have a little time before they're back at it and Gia looks like we short-circuited her brain."

She wasn't wrong. In the time he'd known Gia, he wasn't sure he'd ever seen her so dumbfounded. He slid behind her and wrapped one arm around her waist, his other hand bracing her at her shoulder for the well wishes he was certain were headed her way.

Sure enough, everyone but Knox and Darya filed their direction, Ninette leading the pack. "You're gonna do great tonight, beautiful girl." She cupped one side of Gia's face in that strong but motherly way she used with everyone and smiled. "And the answer to your question is, we're here for you. Simple as that."

"Yeah," Viv said, stopping just short of shouldering Ninette out of the way. "Gabe, Nat and the boys would've been here, too, but Levi's got football games all weekend, and Gabe said the only place she's wearing a dress to is your wedding."

Sylvie moved in beside her and mock-whispered, "On the off chance ye do get to flex yer bonny muscles, be a good lass and try ta do it where I can see. I'll try ta get a picture."

"Bloody hell, Ma." Axel shooed them both toward the exit, aimed a wry smile at Gia that said he wasn't nearly as put-out as he sounded and winked. "Though, I wouldn't mind gettin' a look at that either."

Jace chuckled, swung the door open for the lot of them and jerked his chin at Gia. "Go get 'em, tiger."

Her hand covered Beckett's at her shoulder, the subtle tremor in it echoing the emotion in her voice. "Thank you."

Without another word, they shuffled out.

The door clicked shut and Gia still didn't move. Just stared at the now empty space where they'd been, mindless of Knox and Darya across the room pretending not to be aware of her response. "I can't believe they flew all the way here."

It was quiet. Spoken more to herself than to anyone else. But Beckett remembered the feelings that went with it all too well. How an impenetrable warmth and foreign awe had shifted beneath his sternum the first time they'd shown en masse to give their support. How they reinforced that feeling every single day just by being who they were. A little over-the-top sometimes, but always steady in showing their love.

He kissed the top of her head and hugged her close. "Get used to it, gorgeous. That's what family does."

Chapter Twenty-Two

A sea of sparkle and refinement on a classic backdrop of pale peach walls and ivory accents. Crystal chandeliers hung from the ballroom's soaring ceilings overhead, their lights strategically dimmed to create what the event planner had called an intimate setting.

Sure, it made things more cozy. More elegant. But Gia knew the strategy for what it really was. Atlanta's elite might want for nothing in the financial sense, but even the best couture, workout regimens or plastic surgeons couldn't make them as picture-perfect as they strove to be. The subtle lighting helped that. Let those all too aware of their physical flaws mingle with more self-confidence in their finest evening wear.

It also made security far more challenging. More shadows to contend with among the thick crowds. Fortunately, the formally attired waitstaff had just moved into their assigned places along the side walls, indicating the time for the plated dinner was near.

Keeping to his promised schedule like the pro he was, Peter Trannell strode to the podium on the raised stage at the front of the hall with the confidence of a man riding the peak of yet another successful event. His slicked-back dark hair and sharp features were a little

too much for Gia's taste, but as a successful business-
man and a recent divorcé he'd had more than his fair
share of women dancing attendance on him throughout
the night. He cleared his throat and leaned toward the
microphone, his voice as well-practiced as his movements. "Ladies and gentlemen. My name is Peter Trannell. As the coordinator for this fine event, I'd like to
thank each and every one of you for your attendance
this evening. I know Governor Lansing, his wife and
children are also equally appreciative for you joining
us tonight and for your generous support toward his
campaign."

He paused long enough to let the polite swell of ap-
plause accent his words and scanned the room with a
charming smile. "If each of you will take your seats, our
waitstaff will begin our service and our first speaker
for the night can take the stage."

Smooth and efficient, the attendees did as instructed
and the waiters moved in.

Gia followed the governor to his table and clocked
Beckett trailing the governor's wife from across the
room. Beside her was South Carolina's Governor, Ron
Tandy. The two of them chatted as they meandered toward the head table with a comfortable familiarity that
went far beyond political affiliations. Beckett on the
other hand was nowhere near as relaxed. Understand-
able since Governor Tandy's point man was Judd.

Judd had been an absolute thorn in everyone's side
and a general pain in the ass since go-time on Friday. If
she hadn't been so tight on staff already and painfully
aware that what she'd blurted Thursday night had to
have been the source of his irritation, she'd have taken
advantage of the full authority Trannell had granted

her as head of security, sacked him straight off and backfilled with someone local. Though why he was so pissed was beyond her. It wasn't like she'd ever led him on. Quite the contrary. She'd been brutally honest with him about how she felt—or rather, how she didn't feel—from the first time he'd asked her out in high school.

Satisfied Governor Lansing was comfortably situated at his table, Gia eased a polite distance away, never taking her eyes off her target.

Judd's dry voice cut through the headset. "Boss lady's sure lost the stick up her ass, Beckett. Did you let her tie you up and whip your ass into submission over downtime?"

Beckett's head whipped Judd's direction for all of a beat before he locked his fury down and shifted his attention back to the governor's wife. His tone, however, was nowhere near controlled. "Got no problem rippin' your tongue out of your mouth and shovin' it up your ass, Rainier. You want that to happen, keep talkin' smack about my woman."

Judd shrugged and kept trailing Governor Tandy like they were talking sports instead of throwing down gauntlets. "Just sayin' what everyone else is thinking. All the rest of us like to be the one in control and she's turned us down cold, so we figure that's gotta be the missing link."

Beckett met Gia's stare across the room, cold fury burning in his startling blue eyes.

"You like someone to hand control over with a pretty pink bow and bat their lashes," Gia said before Beckett could answer him. "Beckett doesn't ask for it. He takes it and makes me come so hard I scream every time. There's your missing link."

Silence filled the headset for all of a heartbeat, followed by a muted snicker and more than one man clearing their throat.

Beckett's lips twitched right before he gave Gia his back and pulled a chair out for the governor's wife.

Judd, on the other hand, was livid, his whole face a mottled red.

Gia didn't care. She'd tried to ignore his petulant bullshit all weekend, but that little stunt was beyond the line. "Now, if you're done trying to convince everyone your dick's bigger than everyone else's, keep your focus on your job and the headset clear for what matters."

No one said a word. Not even Judd. But a few of the men lined up along the far wall dipped their head for a split second to get their expressions back under control.

The rest of the gala's attendees made their way to their assigned tables. A few tables away from the governor, Jace pulled a chair out for Vivienne. The only other time she'd seen him in a tux had been at Darya's wedding, but he wore one well. Even dressed to blend in he still looked like a predator among sheep, his charisma and dangerous air the same as all the rest of the brothers. Vivienne looked amazing as always, her evergreen gown with its low back clinging to every perfect curve and her curly brown hair twisted up in a neat updo.

Just fifteen feet away, Axel guided Sylvie and Ninette toward them. Unlike Jace's understated ponytail, Axel had snubbed conformity entirely, leaving his wild russet hair loose and pairing his tuxedo jacket with his clan's navy blue and green kilt. Given the smug grin on his face and the proud lift of his chin, he knew damned well the vast majority of the women in attendance were not only intrigued by his getup, but him as well.

Ninette was gorgeous. Pure elegance in a soft sil-
ver gown that made her matching hair that much more
glorious. And Sylvie? Well, Vivienne hadn't called it
wrong about the man hunt. Axel's mother might be well
into her sixties, but she had a body to rival women half
her age and the black sheath dress she'd picked out accented every inch of it.

They settled in beside Jace and Vivienne. Sylvie
twisted in her chair, scanned the security personnel
along each wall and locked stares with Gia, offering a
proud smile and one of those waves a parent gave their
kiddo from the front row at the school play.

Gia's cheeks warmed and the space behind her
breastbone tightened as though a giant fist had squeezed
around her heart. She could've sworn she heard Beckett's chuckle through the headset. Or maybe it was
someone else's.

She didn't care. For all the experiences in her life,
that goofy wave was the first like it she'd ever received
and there was no way in hell she'd dishonor it with embarrassment.

From there, everything was quiet. No suspicious activity. Just the muted clicks of knives and forks on fine
china as the attendees ate and hushed side conversations as the first speaker droned longer than they were
supposed to.

Eventually, it was Governor Tandy's turn at the podium. Serving the tail end of his final term in office,
he'd made the rounds in recent months at events just like
this one supporting new candidates for his party and
those like Governor Lansing looking for a second term.

The transition of speakers went off without a hitch.
Tandy took the podium and Judd stood off to one side

of the stage, well out of the spotlight, while Gia and Governor Lansing slipped from the main ballroom to the backstage area where he could appear like a rock star from the center.

For the next fifteen minutes, the governor from South Carolina extolled Lansing's virtues, paying special attention to his tough stance on narcotics and his unflappable support of law enforcement over the past four years. When he rounded out his speech, the crowd applauded, slowly rising to their feet in a haphazard wave.

The curtains opened.

Governor Lansing stepped out into the spotlight and offered his hand to his counterpart while Gia and her support team moved into place.

Everyone was on their feet, clapping. Some wore genuine smiles while others were pasted in place. Some didn't even bother.

Everything exactly as it should be. Not a thing out of place.

Governor Tandy strolled toward the stairs down from the stage, all smiles and waves to those in the crowd. Governor Lansing watched him, a benevolent host patiently waiting for his turn in the limelight.

Except Judd wasn't following his man. At least not as close as he should be. His gaze wasn't trained on his target either, but rather out at someone in the crowd.

Gia followed his line of sight.

One man standing motionless. No smile. Not even boredom. More of a concentrated stare.

The two women in front of him took their seats—and all hell broke loose.

It couldn't have been more than three seconds, but for Gia they passed in a blur.

Seeing the gun.

Surging toward the governor.

The flash from the gun in her peripheral and the report behind it.

Knowing even as the vibration rippled through the air, she was too far away to do any good.

The next thing she knew, Judd was covering the governor.

Not her. But Judd.

In the audience, Beckett and two of his men had the shooter on the ground and well in hand.

Her whole body shaking with the flood of adrenaline, she shoved Judd off the governor and hauled Lansing to his feet, the rapid-fire flashes from cameras and cellphones in the audience like shocks against her skin. "Let's go."

Before she could put herself between Lansing and the audience, Judd took over and crowded close, teaming with one of her men to get the governor backstage.

Gia followed, but on much slower footsteps, the reality of the last few seconds sinking poisonous, humiliating claws deep. She'd been too slow. Had missed the danger and left her man unprotected. Had been the most ineffectual person on the entire team at a time when she'd been most needed.

She glanced back at the crowd just as they moved out of sight and spied Jace and Axel carting Viv, Ninette and Sylvie away from the panic.

They'd come to see her shine. Flown all this way to show their support.

And she'd failed.

Miserably.

Chapter Twenty-Three

Life was seriously bad when even ice cream didn't appeal as a viable tool to soften a girl's ugly reality. Tucked into the crook of Beckett's arm, Gia dug her spoon into the pint of Ben & Jerry's Vivienne had dropped off thirty minutes ago and forced a bite into her mouth.

Urban Bourbon.

One of her favorites.

But tonight, it tasted awful.

She stuck the spoon back in the still firm ice cream, reached across Beckett's wide torso and slid the pint onto the room service cart by his side of the bed.

His big hand splayed between her shoulder blades over the top of her cotton tee pajama top then coasted up to the back of her neck, guiding her head so her cheek rested against his chest. "Don't think I've ever seen you leave Urban Bourbon unfinished."

"Don't think you've ever seen me with my head stuck up my ass like you did tonight either, but there's a first time for everything."

He didn't argue. Not this time. The other fifty or so times she'd verbally lashed herself, he'd tried to placate her with everything from *You're the only one who thinks that* to *No one can do this job perfectly.*

On the bright side, Lansing was on a chartered jet headed to Orlando and all the other protected guests had headed back to wherever they were from, so she was finally in a place where she could privately lick her wounds. The fact that it was nearing two in the morning only added to her maudlin mood.

Beckett's heartbeat drummed a peaceful rhythm against her ear and the steady rise and fall of his chest on each breath lured her own to follow. At least she had him. Had his family—every one of whom had either come by in person the second she and Beckett had come back from the airport, or called to support her in their own unique way. One thing she wouldn't have in large supply for a very long time was business. Not until this disaster blew over.

She huffed and sat upright, snagging her phone off the bed beside her hip as she went. The worst of the four news stories was still conveniently pulled up on her browser, the horrid snapshot of her standing there, worthless while Judd covered the governor, taking up most of the screen. "He saw it before I did. Moved faster. I should have caught it."

Beckett snatched her phone out of her hand and tossed it next to the ice cream. Unlike her, he'd yet to do more to get ready for bed than ditch his Timberlands, leaving him barefoot in jeans and an insanely soft black T-shirt that molded every muscle. "Cut the shit, Gia. It happens."

"Right. Like you wouldn't be saying the exact same thing if the roles were reversed." The fury she'd barely kept in check all night bubbled up, ready for a fight. "Oh, wait. It wouldn't happen to you. Hell, you were three times the distance to the shooter that I was to my primary and you *still* got there quicker than I got to Lansing."

Beckett didn't bite. Just ran his thumb along the side of the television remote near his hip and studied her like he was trying to figure something out. "What if there's a reason Judd was on Lansing faster than you?"

Of all the counterarguments he could have come back with, that was the last one she'd expected. "What's that supposed to mean?"

Another slide of his thumb, this one paired with caution in both his expression and his tone. "I mean, Judd's good, but he's not telepathic. No one else clued into the shooter. What if Judd knew the guy was gonna be there?"

"Are you kidding me? Like he set something up?"

"You said once that things between you and him have always been competitive. He undercut you at your last deal. He questioned every move you made this weekend."

"He's just jealous I got the lead detail."

A sharpness she'd learned to not only appreciate, but to rely on intensified his steady gaze. "Maybe he was pissed enough he wanted to do something about it."

Surely not.

Yeah, she and Judd had been trying to beat each other past the finish line for as long as she could remember, but what Beckett was proposing defied logic. "What kind of idiot would risk another man's life just to make himself look better than someone else?"

"Gorgeous, you've worked in this business almost as long as I have. How many times did the bad guys actually have reasonable motives? Judd wanted the lead spot on this gig and you got it instead of him. That's got to sting for a man like him. And let's face it—that crash and burn at dinner with your parents trying to set you two up wasn't the first one. How many were there before that?"

For the first time since the pre-event this afternoon, the brief and all too distracted conversation they'd had in the elevator came back to her. "Is that what your hunch was?"

Beckett shrugged as though he was trying to play it off, but something about the action was off. Like there was more emotion locked inside his big body, but he was hell-bent on containing it. "My gut's good about shit like this."

A statement, but one chock-full of regret. She cocked her head, pushed past the self-pity she'd nursed all night and really studied him. She'd thought his quiet and the restrained restlessness was from having to deal with her piss-poor mood, but now that she looked his features were strained. Almost unforgiving. "Don't tell me you think you could have stopped this."

"I saw the same thing you did, G. Judd wasn't close enough to his man. Wasn't even watching him." The muscle at the back of his jaw ticked as though the words still to come had to fight their way free. "I could have stopped him."

"And then the shooter could've got off another round. You did the right thing. I was the one who was slow."

"You were the one who didn't have a chance and *that's* what makes me wonder if Judd's not behind all of this. It's too convenient."

It wouldn't compute. No matter how many times she tried to fit the concept together in her head the pieces pushed apart like magnets repelling against each other.

On the nightstand, Beckett's phone lit up and vibrated against the gleaming mahogany surface. He glanced away only long enough to grab it and check the screen, then met her eyes. "Just think about it." He swiped the screen and sat upright, planting his feet on the floor. "You find anything?"

Knox.

Beckett never used that tone with anyone but his brothers, and Knox was the brotherhood's resident bloodhound. Given how fast Beckett had moved to take the call, she'd bet good money the trail Knox was on tonight was Judd's.

Slowly, Beckett straightened from his relaxed stance, a predator waking from its slumber. The air around him snapped with unspent, furious energy. "Are you fucking kidding me?"

Gia scrambled to his side of the bed for a look at his face. For some clue as to what was going on.

"When?" Beckett asked, glaring at the floor.

One word that amplified every subtle background noise to the point it grated against her ears. The low drone of an old *Bourne* movie she'd seen a thousand times. The chilled air whirring from the vents overhead. The muted *beep, beep, beep* of a truck backing up somewhere out on the street. Even the soft glow of the lamp on the nightstand seemed harsh. A spotlight minus an incriminating voice demanding an alibi.

A knock sounded on the door, three quick but heavy raps loaded with either insistence or impatience.

Gia got all of two steps toward the living room portion of their suite before Beckett hauled her back to the bed with a fistful of T-shirt and aimed a pointed glance at her cute red sleep shorts. "Start digging," he said to

Knox without breaking stride toward the door. "And get Jace on point. If this shit's true, we'll need him ready to lawyer up." He checked the peephole and muttered something she couldn't quite make out. "Fuck, I gotta go. Gia's dad's here with some jackass I don't know."

Her dad?

Gia shot off the bed, shimmied off the shorts and snatched the jeans she'd thrown haphazardly on the chair next to the desk.

"No, I got it," Beckett said, monitoring her progress. "You work with the rest of the guys. I need my focus on Gia until we can get him gone. We'll be over when it's clear." He punched the end button just as Gia fastened the waistband on her jeans.

The knock came again, her father's voice stern but loud enough to carry. "Gia, open up."

"What's going on? Why's my dad here?"

Beckett held her stare, that muscle at the back of his jaw doing double time. The way he held his body, he looked like he was seconds away from ripping the first person who crossed him into tiny shreds. When he spoke, his voice was low enough her father wouldn't hear it, but there was no mistaking the cold fury behind his words. "I'm gonna open this door and your dad's probably gonna drop a shit bomb on you, but we're gonna deal with it. You and me. Together. You got it?"

Not good.

Not good at all.

She swallowed hard and jerked a terse nod.

"Play dumb," he said. "Don't let on you know what's going on."

"I *don't* know," she all but hissed back at him, just barely stopping herself from stomping her foot.

The snippy retort earned her a tight grin, but did little to dim the burn behind his eyes. "Well, *I* do and that means my brothers will too in about five minutes. No point in your dad knowing we've got an inside track. We'll deal with it. You remember that."

Too frustrated to stand still any longer she stomped closer and motioned toward the door. "Just get on with it."

He nodded, gripped the knob and gave her a last once-over as though trying to assure himself she was solid before yanking the door wide.

The hallway's fluorescent lights spilled down on her father in slacks and a button-down, and a haggard, half-asleep man dressed in jeans and a wrinkled Oxford she assumed was one of his interns. There were only two circumstances that warranted her father openly displaying the level of indignation on his face in that moment—to convince a jury, or his daughter straying outside the lines of what he deemed appropriate. Since there wasn't a panel of twelve people lined up off to one side, she could only assume it was her turn up at bat. "It's two o'clock in the morning. What are you doing here?"

Her father's lips tightened as though it was only his superior dignity that kept a slew of vile words in check. "I think a better question is what the hell have you gotten yourself into?"

"Excuse me?"

Reginald jerked his gaze away from Gia, raked Beckett with a disdainful glower, then jerked his head toward the suite, motioning the man next to him to move inside. "Inside, Steve. We're not doing this in the hallway."

Beckett moved in, not blocking him altogether, but stilling the stranger with a hand at his shoulder. "You'll do what you're here to do and you'll do it with a mind to Gia's comfort, or you'll find yourself on your ass on the floor." His stare shifted to Reginald. "That includes you."

Her father hesitated for less than a heartbeat, then pushed through, forcing the man he'd dragged along on his errand through ahead of him. "I see Judd was right."

Fucking Judd.

As if she hadn't had enough to deal with already without hearing his name one more time. Gia shifted, stood beside Beckett, and crossed her arms. "Right about what?"

Her father walked the length of the suite, studying every detail. Whether he was surprised at the size of it, or still found it lacking his standards was hard to tell. "He said you've changed since moving to Dallas. Said your values weren't what they used to be." He glanced at Beckett. "That the people you deal with aren't exactly trustworthy."

Beckett didn't move. Didn't give a single indication her father's barb hit a nerve, much less heard it.

But Gia felt the sting the second it connected. Felt the energy around them pulse and a subtle tingle flare along her skin. "If you came to insult me or Beckett, it was a wasted trip. You've done about as much damage as I'm going to let you do to me."

"But it's not an insult, is it?" Reginald said. "Given what I learned tonight, I'd say it's fact." Still standing by the sofa, he mirrored her stance and crossed his arms. "The authorities called me tonight as a courtesy. It seems the shooter at tonight's event received the information they needed to get through security from an inside source." He paused and grimaced as though just looking at her hurt. "From you."

"What?"

Beckett's hand splayed low on her back. A gesture meant to calm her. To keep her steady through the un-expected storm.

But she didn't need it. Didn't want a buffer or any-one holding back the rage exploding through every inch of her. She stalked toward her father. "Are you out of your mind? You think I'd leak information and risk my principal getting hurt?"

Her father didn't budge. "It came from your IP ad-dress. Traced back to your email account."

"Bullshit. That makes no sense. What's my motive?"

"Apparently, money." He looked at Steve and jerked his head toward Gia. "Show her."

Looking like he'd rather shove his hand down a live garbage disposal, Steve glanced at Beckett then took the few hesitant steps to hand over a plain manila folder. "The Feds found an offshore account in your name. Money was wired into it the same day the email was sent. The money trail ties to a cartel out of Mexico and the shooter was a known player in their organization."

Gia yanked the file from his shaking grasp and jerked open the pages so hard she nearly sent the pages inside it flying. "I don't have an offshore account."

"You expect me to believe that, Gia?"

"Why the hell wouldn't you? Tell me one thing I've ever done that even hints at criminal activity."

"The Gia who left here three years ago was one thing, but who you are now—I don't have a clue. You all but disappeared. Random calls or visits at best. Then you show up with some stranger—one with a record and an unsavory past—claiming to love him when your mother and I don't even know him. Now the job I rec-

ommended you for has turned into a federal investiga-
tion and all the evidence points to my daughter selling
out the man she was supposed to protect."

Gia snapped the folder shut. "Get out." The words
were nowhere near as loud or heated as her father's had
been, but they came from the deepest part of her, an
iron resoluteness that shocked the entire room into utter
stillness. "Get out and don't come back. Don't call me.
Don't even think of me."

"Sir," Steve said under his breath. "We have to make
the call soon."

Reginald huffed out a disgusted sound, not taking
his eyes off her even as he answered. "I come to help
her and that's the response I get." He pulled in a deep
breath, squared his shoulders and clasped his hands in
front of him, as if he were pulling his moral cape more
tightly around him. "You clearly have no idea how dire
your situation is, Gia. Homeland Security has issued
a warrant for your arrest. However, given my connections, they've agreed to let us bring you in voluntarily
to avoid unwelcome press. While I'd be content to let
you drown in the consequences of your actions after the
way you've repaid my trust and support, your mother
would be devastated to see you suffer. Therefore, my
office will represent you."

"My *mother* would be devastated?" Her whole body
trembled, adrenaline rushing all directions in a burning wave of fury. "Maybe she would be, but what you
really mean is *you* want to avoid embarrassment. Want
to throw your weight around and do what you can to
keep things tucked away from the press." She crossed
her arms and jerked her head toward the door. "Go. I
don't need your help. Didn't need it when I was growing

up, or when you ridiculed what I decided to do with my life. And I damned sure don't need a man—any man— trying my case who doesn't even believe I'm innocent."

The soft chunk of Beckett opening the door sounded behind her. "I think we're done."

If the moment wasn't so abysmally pathetic, the open shock on her father's face would've been funny. A picture worth capturing and passing around to the bevy of people who knew him. He quickly blanked it and lifted his chin in that arrogant slant that usually ended in him getting what he wanted. "You don't mean that. Despite your anger and what you've done, you're family. I'm willing to see this through and make sure you're taken care of. We'll get you through this and help you get back on the right track."

One second.

One tiny click in her head where a detached understanding overrode all the years she'd waited, struggled and wondered what it would take to earn his approval. She could talk until she was blue in the face. Could try to explain her wants and desires—who she was and what she enjoyed—but he'd never listen. *Never.* What Reginald Sinclair wanted to see was all that mattered in his world. So why keep trying to show him who she was? Why keep trying to gain ground when the attempt was nothing more than a never-ending treadmill?

With more calm than she'd ever felt in her father's presence, she turned, met Beckett's steady stare and padded toward him.

Still holding the door open, he pulled her into the shelter of his free arm and squeezed her hip reassuringly.

Steve's stupefied gaze volleyed between Gia and her

father, the sheer novelty of anyone standing up to Reginald Sinclair clearly not something he'd ever expected to witness.

Her father noted it, too, and his voice took a cutting edge. "You'll regret this, Gia. If you take this step, you're on your own. Support. Money. You'll get none of it."

Once upon a time, the threat might have worked. Not because of the money, but because she couldn't imagine a life without them. But in that second, she felt nothing for the man glaring at her. Not hate. Not fondness. Not even respect.

A quite calm filled her. Grounded and bolstered her courage. "You came here tonight with your mind made up. Tried and convicted me without so much as asking for my feedback. A shooter aimed toward the man I was hired to protect and you didn't even call to see if I was okay. To my mind, it was you who took the first step. Years ago."

Beckett's arm tightened around her.

She dragged a deep breath and took the plunge. "I didn't really know what it meant to have family when I left Georgia, but I do now. Mine's in Texas. With Beckett." She jerked her head toward the door. "You can go."

Her father's face flamed an enraged red and, for a second, she half expected for him to lose his much-vaunted control. He glared at Beckett for all of a heartbeat, then pulled himself together and prowled toward the door, Steve hurrying in his wake.

They cleared the threshold and Beckett released the knob.

Gia shot forward and caught the door before it could close. "Dad."

He paused in the hallway and only halfway turned to hear what she had to say.

A sharp ache pierced through her sternum and her ribs seemed to clamp down like a skeletal fist around her lungs. Even in this he couldn't give her a modicum of respect. Couldn't spare the decency of meeting his own daughter's eyes.

Her eyes burned with the threat of tears, but she fought them back and straightened her spine. She'd be fine. It might take a while, but she'd make it. Somehow.

She forced as much confidence as possible past the tight knot in her throat and locked her trembling legs to keep them from buckling. "You screwed up not trusting your daughter and I'm going to prove it."

Chapter Twenty-Four

The sharp, sweet jolt of pain up his forearm. The sting of the heavy bag's rough leather abrading his knuckles. The burn deep in his delts, pecs and biceps.

Beckett reared back and put his hips into the next punch.

It still wasn't enough. He needed more. Needed a fist aimed at his jaw or a forearm pressed at his throat.

He swung again, growling at the swinging bag and Haven's otherwise empty gym. Fuck, but he wished his brothers would hurry up and get here. Wished they'd line up and each take a swing at him so he could find his fucking center again. Better yet, he wished *Gia* would take a swing at him. Wished she'd slap him, kick him or drag those nails of hers down his back. *Anything* but look at him with the emptiness that had filled her eyes in the three days since the door had slammed shut on her father.

Cock-sucking, no-good son of a bitch.

Over and over, Beckett rained fury on the innocent bag, imagining Reginald's face with each impact.

But not Judd. No, that motherfucker wouldn't get the benefit of anything so quick and easy. He needed something worse. A slow drawn-out pain that made his mind fragment into bits and pieces until there was nothing left but an empty husk.

Three days since she'd turned herself in. Aside from the crying jag that'd hit all of five minutes after her dad left, she'd kept her chin up and her back straight through the whole ordeal. Ignored the reporters scrambling for the best snapshot or sound bite like she was raw meat in a shark tank. Sat through twelve hours of Homeland Security's finest grilling her up one side and down the other. Every second, Jace said she'd been tough as nails.

But those brown eyes of hers were dead. Like someone had unplugged the vitality and emotion inside her and left only skin and bones behind. The only hint his woman was still there was when she curled herself up tight against him at night or when they were alone. When her fingers laced with his and she squeezed as though a damned army of demons tortured her insides.

Heavy footsteps sounded on the stairs leading up from the garage below. Unlike his gym at work, this one was like the places he'd clung to growing up. Unfinished. Nothing shiny. Every weight, bag and mat as haggard and scarred as the life he'd been born into.

"Zeke's got on scrubs with enough bloodstains to cover a transfusion in a pinch," Trevor said with his dry Southern drawl, "but I'm thinkin' he'd rather not have to deal with the hassle. So, maybe you can beat the shit out of that thing with gloves on like you're supposed to."

Blood.

The word flipped a switch in his head and brought what had been a tan leather bag into focus, deep red marking the rough surface. His knuckles connected with one of the bigger spots and a wet slap echoed through the room.

"Jesus, Beck." Trevor jerked him away before he could land another, his arm banded around the front of his shoulders like he would if he were breaking up a fight.

Beckett fought the grip. Tried to twist and unleash his fury on Trevor.

But Trevor had his own skills. Street smarts earned early in life that made him lock Beckett down in a choke hold before Beckett could escape. "Brother, you gotta get a grip on your shit or you're not gonna be worth a damn to Gia."

The arm at his throat was a damper, but her name was far more potent. An instant leash, muzzle and cage rolled up into one. He held his arms up in surrender and lifted his chin for a better breath, the burn in his lungs making it clear just how long he'd been unloading his frustrations.

Trevor loosened his hold just enough to let him inhale. "You gonna get a grip?"

Beckett jerked a short nod and gripped Trevor's forearm. The starched button-down grated against his palms, but there was heat behind it. A tiny tether to humanity. "What time is it?"

"Just past one. Everyone's inside and finishing up lunch."

Past one? Christ, he'd come up here before noon. No wonder the bag was so damned bloody.

Trevor unwound his hold, but stayed close, either prepped to catch his ass if his legs boycotted the idea of staying upright, or to put him back on lockdown. "Gia's hanging in the kitchen with everyone else."

When Beckett spoke, his throat burned as bad as his

knuckles, but the first bit of hope he'd felt in days poked its head out from under the covers. "She is?"

A wry grin crooked one corner of Trevor's mouth. "Sucks watchin' a woman you love hurt, doesn't it?" Apparently satisfied Beckett was back in reality, he took another step back. "She's not tradin' verbal jabs with Axel or givin' Knox shit like she usually does, but she's present. Listening. Jace even got her to smile once."

Thank God.

He exhaled hard on the thought and the knotted muscles in his neck and shoulders unleashed their death grip. "Thought she'd never get out of that bed."

"Brother, she's been through hell. Even if all she'd had to juggle was the arrest, the press and the questioning, she'd have needed some time to bounce back. Adding in that bullshit with her dad, you might as well have thrown a funeral on top of it. She's strong, but she's still human."

The sound of her sobs after her dad had left were still in his head. Like a bad song you couldn't shake loose and grated on every nerve. Every time she curled up close to him or squeezed his hand the volume got louder. "I should have tossed that fucker out into the hall. Should have dislocated his jaw before he could say the shit he did."

Trevor scanned the room and locked eyes on the hand towel Beckett had tossed on the scarred, unfinished floor. He ambled toward it. "Looking back and second-guessing yourself isn't gonna help. You did what you did and it's over. You ask me, you stood by her while she faced down a demon. Anything else would've just delayed the inevitable. Now's the time to build her back up and make sure she's vindicated. You wanna pulverize

someone, let's make it the motherfucker who set her up."
He snatched the towel and tossed it at Beckett. "Now get
your ass cleaned up so you don't jolt Gia out of her stupor the wrong way when she gets a look at your hands."

As incentives went, both were bull's-eyes and got
him back on track with unerring efficiency. Especially
knowing Gia was up and reengaging for the first time
in days.

He washed up, making a bloody mess in the mud
room just off the kitchen that Ninette would no doubt
raise hell about, then pacified Zeke who showed up halfway through the process—no doubt thanks to Trevor
ratting him out—while his brother bandaged up the
worst of the damage. Fifteen minutes later, he prowled
into the kitchen behind Zeke.

And there she was.

Quiet just like Trevor had said and still sporting pajamas and no makeup, but watchful. Both of her elbows
were braced on the kitchen table while she nursed the
cup of coffee between her hands and took in the chaos
around her.

All of two heartbeats was all he got to soak it in. To
see for himself the alertness behind her beautiful brown
eyes. Then the whole damned room registered his arrival and the chatter stopped.

Gia's gaze shifted to him then down to his bandaged
hands. She was on her feet a second later, the coffee
abandoned in favor of seeing up close what he'd done
and a whole lot of pissed-off in her tone. "What the hell
did you do?" She gripped the wrist with the most ban-
dages, lifted his hand up for a better look, then scowled
back at Jace. "I thought you said he was working out.
Not maiming a razor-lined fence."

Oh, yeah. His woman was back. Maybe not at full strength yet, but over the hump and at least ready to kick his ass. "I'm fine." He twisted his wrist out of her hold, cupped the side of her neck and pulled her in close, hugging her tight with his other arm low on her waist.

Finally.

He kissed the top of her head and filled his lungs with her scent. Let the press of her lush body flush against his wipe away the last of his tension.

"He might be fine," Trevor said, pulling the majority of the attention away from him and Gia, "but the heavy bag looks like Freddy Krueger started a work-out routine."

Just like that, the chaos was back in motion. Ninette, Sylvie and Viv vying with all of his brothers for space at the island where an insane amount of sandwich meats and toppings were splayed out, or for a seat at the table.

Taking advantage of everyone minding their own business for the moment, he dipped his head to murmur in her ear. "You hungry?"

She glanced back at the island and wrinkled her nose, then seemed to reconsider. "Not really, but I should probably eat."

"Skip the sandwich then and go right to dessert," Sylvie said without turning around. She layered a slice of roast beef on the bottom half of a hoagie roll then waggled her finger toward one side of the sink. "Pumpkin bars with cream cheese frosting are in the white plastic tub."

Gia perked up and eyed the container over one shoulder.

"So much for thinking we had a private moment." Beckett kissed Gia's temple, turned her in the direction

Sylvie had pointed and smacked her butt. "If you're gonna get one, get me one, too."

In the end, she only ate half of the seriously sweet treat, but she took a few bites of Beckett's second sandwich and snacked on a handful of chips, too, so he called it a win. Everyone was mostly done and shuttling back and forth to the dishwasher with empty plates and glasses when Jace reclined against his seat next to Viv, wrapped one arm around the back of her chair and proceeded to shock the shit out of Beckett.

"You know the eight of us meet pretty often," he said to Gia. "Brainstorm business deals, go over P&Ls and investments, see what shaky areas need bolstered."

Beckett shoved his plate a few inches back and shifted in his chair, braced to either intervene or haul Gia out of the kitchen. Wherever his brother was headed was anyone's guess, but he wasn't about to let anyone shove her back into the mental cave she'd lingered in since Georgia.

Gia's mouth quirked in a softer version of her usual sassy smile. "I have a feeling *shaky areas* doesn't always mean shoring up financial weak spots."

At the sink, Sylvie shook her head and Ninette outright snickered. The rest of the guys got a chuckle out of it, too, but Jace just aimed that evil shit-eating grin at her, his after-lunch toothpick anchored at the corner. "There might have been an occasion or two where we've talked about things we wouldn't want repeated outside of family, yeah."

Whether Gia consciously homed in on his mounting tension, or it was just a byproduct of their deepening relationship he couldn't say, but she leaned into his torso a little and smoothed her hand over his thigh. "I take it that's why you're all here on a Tuesday when normal people are at work?"

Axel kicked back in his chair and braced one booted foot on the rung of Danny's empty chair next to him. "No fun in being normal, lass. Thought we'd got that through your beautiful stubborn head." He lifted his **Dark Island Reserve**—a Scottish ale he'd had a hell of a time getting his hands on in Texas but had finally talked Trevor into hauling back on one of his overseas gigs—and met Jace's stare across the table. "Get on with it, already. You know our stance. It's her ass on the line and she's one of us."

Son of a bitch.

No way was Jace about to do what Beckett's gut insisted was about to happen, but the calm steady stares of his brothers around the table said otherwise. Said they'd not only had their own rally without him and had stacked hands in advance, but were ready to get down to business. Serious business given the hard edge in their eyes.

Jace studied Gia for another beat, nodded as though some internal thought had echoed Axel's admonishment to get on with things, then leaned into Viv and gave her a kiss on the cheek. "Gotta get to work."

Viv rolled her eyes and playfully shoved him away with a hand at his chest. "Yeah, yeah. Innocent spouse and plausible deniability. Blah, blah, blah." She stood and shared one of those beleaguered spousal looks with Gia. "You know, for all his rebellious exterior, his hidden legal persona can sure ruin my fun sometimes."

"How do you think I feel?" Ninette draped her kitchen towel on the dishwasher handle and scowled at Jace as she headed toward the arched kitchen exit. "Killjoy."

Sylvie was right behind her, but had her focus on Gia. "We'll keep the telly down low. See if ye can't get 'em riled up enough to talk loud enough we can hear."

Vivienne scoffed and trailed them out the door. "Screw that. Darya and I are tag-teaming her afterward for the full scoop." She smiled huge over her shoulder and wiggled her fingers at the lot of them. "You've got your ways, we've got ours. Have fun, boys!"

With the women gone and the men all watching Gia, a weird silence settled on the kitchen.

One by one, she scrutinized them, her mouth slightly parted. "You want to talk about what happened."

Knox huffed out a chuckle, but there was steel behind it. Sharp, deadly steel. "Someone fucked with one of our own. If you think for a second we've waited until now to start talking, you haven't learned how deep this family runs."

Gia glanced at Beckett, then back at the opening where the women had disappeared through. "And you're trusting me, but not them?"

Surprisingly it was Ivan who answered, his long dreds falling over his big shoulders as he leaned into the table and covered one fisted hand with the other. "Jace is your attorney. You don't have to say shit about what you say or hear from him and neither does he."

She scanned the table. "What about the rest of you?"

Danny chuckled. "We'll lie through our teeth and swear you don't know a thing."

"For God's sake, you guys." Zeke jerked his chin toward Gia and pushed back on the hind legs of his chair. "Stop draggin' it out and yank the Band-Aid off."

Axel's low laugh was a mix of genuine mirth and pure danger. The kind of sound that left you wondering if you were about to get a hug or a knife in the gut. "What we're sayin' is, we're gonna take care of things whether you want it or not."

Gia's back got ruler-straight. "You don't—"

Axel raised his hand and cut her off. "Yes, we fucking *do* get to." He paused and lowered his voice. "But we also know who you are and get it's your career we're messing with. So, we're breakin' our rules and givin' you the choice. Are you plannin' things with us, or bein' that stubborn lass we first met and tryin' to do things on your own while we do ours?"

In that second, Beckett wasn't sure what he loved seeing more—his brothers circled up and showing their consolidated support, or the dawning comprehension in Gia's face. He squeezed her shoulder and fought the need to pick her up and settle her in his lap where he could hold her while the truth took up roots.

She glanced at him, let her gaze linger on each man, then cleared her throat. It took a few times of her opening and closing her mouth before she finally opted for a quip in lieu of what was probably a whole lot of sappy she couldn't find the right words for. "I'm stubborn, not stupid. Nine minds are better than one."

Trevor beamed one of those smiles generally reserved for when Levi did something that made his chest puff out and his stride lengthen. "Atta girl."

Jace's expression wasn't too far off from Trevor's, but his gaze sobered a little as it slid to Beckett. "I'm assuming you're good with this?"

Good with it? Hell, he couldn't have orchestrated a better approach. In one action, they'd not only taken him out of what could've been a serious tight spot in his relationship, but shown Gia how much she mattered to all of them. "Golden."

Axel nodded and zeroed in on Knox. "Alright then. Tell us what you've got."

Knox locked eyes with Beckett for all of a second as if verifying for himself he was good with moving forward, then dove in. "I spent the last few days combing router logs from the time we hit the hotel to the time we left. I've narrowed down the device ID that sent the email. It's a smartphone. A knockoff brand and probably a burner, sold in Dallas about a month ago."

"Any chance you tracked the purchase back to Brantley Davis?" The confidence in Gia's voice was more choked back than normal. Hesitant in a way that spoke volumes about what she was really asking.

Knox knew what she was hoping, too, cushioned the blow the best he could. "No."

"I was on Brantley the whole time your event was going down," Ivan added, though he was far more matter-of-fact with the info. "From the time the wheels went up on Trevor's G6, to the time you landed, he was either working, passed out cold, or gaming his brains out."

"When Danny and Beckett swept his place, we set up a direct line to his network and loaded a remote access Trojan that let us infiltrate his mobile devices," Knox said. "Outside of cash transactions, there's not a single thing Brantley's done in the last month we didn't have an electronic eye on."

"And the cash transactions, we covered with manpower," Beckett added.

Knox leaned into the table and crossed his forearms in front of him, his gaze rooted solidly on Gia. "Whoever sent the email had to have close proximity to the hotel and access to the private IP I set up for our team. Brantley had none of those things."

Everyone waited, patiently letting her work her way to the real question. She splayed her hand on Beckett's thigh, the unsteady contact slicking against the loose track pants he'd worked out in. "Could you trace the device ID to Judd?"

"Via the purchase, no. Whoever bought it paid cash."

"But you think it was him?" A little bit of a question from Gia, but a whole lot more of a demand to hurry up and get to the point.

Knox straightened and cleared his throat. If the discomfort in his posture didn't warn Beckett he was about to hear something that would piss him off, the way his brother suspiciously avoided eye contact would have cinched it. "Beckett told me he was worried Judd might be up to something, so when we got home, I hacked back into the shooting range's networks and ran their access logs. I crossed member entries to the days when the camera footage blanked out to see if Judd happened to have been there."

Beckett's gut got tight and that creepy crawling sensation that promised a shitload of trouble was right around the corner scampered across his shoulders.

"Both days tie out," Knox said. "He had access."

"How long have you known?" Beckett asked before Gia could get a word in edgewise.

Regret was stamped all over Knox's face when he slid his attention to Beckett. "You gotta know I wanted to make sure of things before I told you."

"When?"

"Yesterday morning."

Dead silence.

Over a full day his brother had known and hadn't ponied up the intel. And while he understood the action on a logical level, the side of him that could have been plotting Judd's murder for the last twenty-four hours was pissed as hell.

Gia sat motionless beside him, a little of the numbness she'd kept wrapped around her like a shield since climbing on board the plane to fly home circling all over again.

"What else?" Beckett demanded. If Knox wanted to be sure of something that meant there had been a whole lot of digging in places other people wouldn't dare to go, and he didn't quit until he dredged up the good stuff.

Per usual, he didn't disappoint. "I started tracing the money trail on the wire transaction Homeland Security found and the creation of the overseas account before we left Georgia. The guy I traced it to is a hacker for hire. Works out of Baton Rouge. Interestingly enough, your dad defended him on a charge based out of Atlanta about three years ago. If your dad had him as a past client and Judd's as tight with Reggie as he lets on, it wouldn't be too much of a stretch to assume that's where Judd made the contact. There were also two fifty-thousand-dollar withdrawals from Judd's trust account—one about three days after you got the gig in Atlanta and another last Monday."

Axel hooked an elbow around one corner of his chair back, lifted his ale and muttered, "Bloody well got an idea where this is headed."

"I didn't want anything getting back to us," Knox said, "and Sergei's been yankin' my chain for a chance to repay Gia for helping Darya with her thing with Ruslan, so I called the favor in and had his boys pay the guy a visit."

"Is that guy still breathin'?" Jace asked.

Knox chuckled. "Sergei only gets bloodthirsty when people don't see things his way." He refocused on Gia and gave it to her straight. "The hacker couldn't give a name because he never had one to work with, but the number he used to communicate from ties to the burner phone's device ID."

"So, all we've got to do is get in Judd's place and see if we can find the phone," Zeke said.

"We don't even have to get inside," Knox said. "We can use a pineapple to search for the device ID. If he uses it within range of our device, we'll confirm it's him without him even knowing."

"A pineapple?" Trevor said.

"A wireless portable router," Beckett said. "Knox can narrow it to look for specific IDs and use it like a homing device."

"But we're talking about a burner phone," Gia said. "The whole damned point behind them is that they're disposable. If he's smart he ditched it before he left Atlanta."

"I've seen the wanker and I'm not convinced he's all that smart." Axel narrowed his gaze on Gia. "You're giving up the ghost before it's time to say grace, lass. If it's a stone left unturned, then we'll by God give it a kick."

"How the hell are you going to do that?" she said with a little of her usual kick. "Even if he's still got it, he'd be an idiot to leave it on."

"Easy. We just give him an incentive to turn it on," Knox said with far too much excitement lighting his face. "And I've got some bait I don't think Judd will be able to pass up."

Chapter Twenty-Five

"This is a shit plan," Beckett grumbled to the wind-shield. Cramped spaces made him itchy on a good day, but with Gia gearing up to put Knox's fucked-up idea in motion and no space in the service van to do more than fidget in the driver's seat, he was ready to claw off his own skin. "We've got no guarantee Judd's gonna keep his head when she shows and his condo's only got one access point. I'm not liking that setup."

"Relax, Beckett." Stationed at the back of the van, Gia handed her purse over to Knox so he could attach the audio device that would allow them to listen to her conversation with Judd. In the parking garage's shadows, it was harder to see the strain the last five days had left on her face, but there was worry in her eyes none-theless. Or maybe it was fear. She'd already been tried and convicted by her father without so much as a chance to tell her side of the story. Processing the highly prob-able fact that a man she'd considered a close friend her whole life had set her up and nearly committed murder to do it couldn't be comfortable.

"Your guys have been tracking Judd for two days and he's been as steady as a rock," she said. "Even if Judd's behind all this, what's his incentive to bite? He's already accomplished what he set out to do. My license is suspended until the trial is over and my career is screwed no matter what happens."

True, but he still doesn't have you.

He could try and point it out again, but she wouldn't buy it. No matter how many times he'd tried to explain that Judd's actions were likely grounded more in his inability to land an intimate relationship with her than bruises to his career-based ego, Gia wouldn't listen. Couldn't fathom how much deeper a blow it would be to a man—especially one like Judd—with repeated failed overtures the likes of which he'd made. Even with their parents' blessings and an inordinate amount of matchmaking he couldn't get a first date on the board.

So, yeah. She didn't get it at all.

"I'm not gonna argue about it being a shit plan, though," Gia said. "It's bad enough we're counting on Judd keeping the burner, but this ploy to bring Haven into the mix rubs me wrong."

Knox pulled up a screen on one of the two monitors affixed to the van's side wall and checked the audio readings. As mobile command stations went, the van wasn't glamorous, but was loaded for bear with every possible gadget needed, including the portable router to lock in on the device ID they were after. "It's just a story, Gia. He's not gonna have time to act on anything you say anyway." He glanced at his buddy from the Department of Justice next to him. "Ain't that right, Ted?"

For a government employee, Ted Maxwell defied the norm. No suits, no uptight attitude, and a whole lot of gray space when it came to red tape. He also knocked his job in the Computer Crime and Intellectual Property division out of the park. Or he did most of the time. When he couldn't he called Knox. "Man, I don't care how many times you've bailed my ass out of a bind. After this one, we're even. You've got no idea how many strings I had to pull to get the Homeland crew to bite on this idea."

Freddie Tanner—aka the jackass who'd interrogated Gia for hours on end the morning she'd turned herself in—cocked an eyebrow from his place in the passenger's seat. One of those *I like breakin' the rules even less than I like bein' here* looks.

Cocksucker.

Beckett wasn't stupid. Ted might have had some pull, but if the soft evidence Knox had already gathered hadn't been so substantial, Freddie and the rest of his team parked right next to them wouldn't be here. The only reason they'd taken the risk was they stood a chance at wrapping things up in a neat and tidy bow, which made Freddie a *lazy* cocksucker to boot.

Danny's voice came through the speakers mounted on either side of the equipment rack. "Yo, Knox. Judd just exited the tollway onto Lemmon. You guys ready?"

Ted got to work on his own keyboard and the hallway they'd been monitoring on Judd's floor switched to a map with a marker that reflected the GPS they'd put on Judd's Audi. "This guy's routine has less flavor than vanilla."

"Hey, I like vanilla," Gia said.

Knox snickered. "Not what I heard."

In the rearview mirror, Beckett got a straight view of her mouth dropping open for all of a second, then enjoyed the flash of irritation in her eyes. "Don't let him goad you, gorgeous. He's diggin' for clues, not workin' on actual knowledge."

"She already said enough with that look." Knox handed her purse back to her. "But if Beck gets boring, just let me know and I'll pull him aside for a few pointers."

Humor lightened her features, which was undoubtedly what Knox had set out to do in the first place, and the clenched muscles in Beckett's gut gave just a fraction.

"Your team always pull a slapstick routine when you're out on an op?" This from uptight Freddie, who kept scanning the garage like special forces might march around the corner with automatic weapons loaded any second.

"You'd rather we hash out all the worst-case scenarios and get her stress level high enough Judd'll sniff her out in under thirty seconds?" Beckett hit Freddie with a potent glare, then twisted in his seat for a direct view of Gia in the back. "I don't want you in there longer than you have to be. Get in, drop the info and get out."

She quirked one brow and flipped the overlapping flap on her purse closed. "Afraid he'll seduce me? Or you just don't want me breathing the same air as him?"

"If he tries the first one, we'll never finish this drill 'cause I'll break him in half before he can fire up that phone." He paused a beat. "I know you, G. You're thorough and you're gonna wanna nose around while you're in there. Do me and everyone else in this van a favor and don't."

Her lips curved in a soft, knowing smile. "Got it. In and out. No fun stuff that might make you use Freddie for a stress ball."

"Heads up," Ted said. "He's pulling in."

From there, the chatter was nonexistent. Parked on

a back row well away from Judd's reserved spot, they waited for Judd to park his shiny black A7, unfold himself from the front seat and stroll to the elevator.

Surprisingly, it was Freddie who broke the silence. "Does he actually work out at that gym? Or does he just go to get his ego stroked?"

The quiet that followed seemed even more stark than what had filled the van before. Beckett dragged his gaze away from Judd still waiting for the elevator. "Why, Freddie. Did you just take a stab at humor in the middle of an op?"

"Well," Knox said with his usual dry humor, "he does look like a walking Nike ad and doesn't have a single hair out of place, so you can't fault Fred for noticing."

Danny chuckled in the speakers. "He was there for an hour and a half, and I clocked at least half of it with him pseudo-posing in the mirrors and rearranging weights, or making busy work around a blonde with a sweet ass on the elliptical."

The elevator opened and Judd disappeared inside.

Beckett twisted back to Gia. "You ready? I'd rather you show up right behind him and see if catching him off guard works in our favor."

She nodded and anchored her purse strap on one shoulder. "Yeah, let's do this."

He wanted to get out with her. Maybe steal some much-needed touch from her and stretch his legs while he was at it, but she quelled the idea with a pointed look and yanked the sliding door open.

"You remember the plan," Beckett said.

"Yep. Stick close to the door. Divert him from locking it behind me if I can swing it. Give the cue if things get dicey." She hopped to the cement and hesitated before shutting the door long enough to add, "I got this."

Then she was gone, striding between two parked cars with her hips swinging. If she was still hurting inside, she didn't show it. Wouldn't unless she was alone with him or the rest of his family.

Their family.

The thought moved through him with a strength that rattled him. Yeah, she'd gotten along good with everyone before the gig in Atlanta, but now that he thought about it, there'd been something different in the last few days. Like in processing the loss of one part of her life, she'd opened up more fully to her new world. She hadn't balked when his brothers had bullied their way into solving her problems. At least not like she would have a month ago. The boundaries were looser now. The edges blended to allow one cohesive unit.

He grinned at the windshield, thankful Knox didn't have a straight view of his face. Gia loved him and she was owning her place in their family. Man, if that wasn't the universe's thumbs-up for finagling a ring on her finger, he didn't know what it was. And as soon as they got this shit behind them he was making that priority number one.

The van's door slid open and Danny hopped inside just as the elevator chimed through the speakers. Gia's voice came low right behind it. "I'm engaging."

"Sweet." Danny maneuvered his big body back to the seat Gia had vacated. "Thought I was gonna miss the good part."

Gia's knock sounded.

Beckett slipped his headset in place, then checked and holstered his Glock.

"What are you doing?" Freddie said.

"My woman's about ten more seconds from getting face-to-face with a man I think set her up to take the fall for murder. If she gives the cue, I'm gonna be a hell of a lot closer than an elevator ride when she gives it."

"That wasn't part of the plan."

"It's part of *my* plan. Don't worry, though. I'm not gonna screw this up unless she needs backup." Beckett glanced back at Danny and Knox. "You two got this?"

"Yup," Knox said not breaking a beat with whatever he was typing out on his keyboard. "Though if I was smart I would've brought Darya. Fucking Ninette and Sylvie are driving me nuts with texts wanting an update."

Beckett chuckled, exited the van and beat feet to the stairwell. If all Knox was getting were text messages from the moms then he was lucky. Both Ninette and Sylvie had lost their damned minds when they'd heard how Reginald had treated his daughter. Or, more to the point, how Colette hadn't interceded and castrated her husband when she'd learned what he'd done. Then they'd done what they did best and set out to make up for all the mothering they'd decided she'd missed out on growing up—whether Gia wanted it or not.

The muted chunk of a door opening sounded through his headset just as the stairwell entrance clunked shut behind him.

"Gia." Genuine surprise coated Judd's voice. In the space that followed, Beckett visualized Judd scanning the hallway outside his place for cameras or some clue he was being punked. "What are you doing here?"

When it came to a setup like this, Gia was totally in her element, but today she upped her game, her tone full of desperation. "Can we talk? Just for a minute?"

Her voice cracked as though she was seconds from a full meltdown. "I know I should have called, but I really need someone to talk to. Someone I can trust and I…" She sniffed and shuffled. "I don't know who that is anymore."

Another pause, heavily weighted.

Beckett took the next flight faster, his heart drowning out his echoing footsteps against the bland concrete walls. Gia might have been confident Judd would buckle and at least listen, but he couldn't shake that unguarded look Judd had cast at Gia during the pre-event meet and greet. The loathing and contempt. Whatever the source of Judd's emotions—jealousy, rejection or flat-out insanity—they ran deep. The kind that didn't recognize or condone reason.

One more flight.

"I thought you had Beckett. He's the love of your life, right?"

There it was. The ugly burn of a man scorned, and it didn't sound like time had done much to ease the sting. Not if the edge in his voice were any indication.

"I thought…" The quaver as her words died off was so clear it was like she was right next to him. "I don't know what to think anymore. Some of the things I've seen since Georgia. The things I've heard…" More movement. "Could we just talk for a minute? I know I hurt you, but I trust you, Judd. I need you."

Fuck, but that cut. Didn't matter that logic was right there to remind him it was bullshit.

"Man, she's good," Danny muttered through the headset.

"No shit," Ted said. "I'd have already given her my right nut and my firstborn."

Knox scoffed. "She hasn't even started yet."

"She's not in yet, either," Freddie added, but there was an equal amount of appreciation in his statement, too.

A muted shuffle sounded and Judd's voice shifted through the audio feed as though he'd added distance between them. "Only reason I'm doing this is for your parents."

The door closed and Beckett strained for the follow-up sound of a bolt sliding home. Instead, what he got was the muted, muffled sound of fabric on fabric. Gia's voice was muted, too, and nearly a whisper. "I'm sorry."

"Is she hugging him or smothering him?" Ted asked through the headset.

"You ever had a hug from Gia, you'd know it's more effective," Danny said. "No man in his right mind would pass up a chance for one."

Knox chimed in right behind it, but his words weren't nearly so playful. "Beckett, stay the fuck in the stairwell."

Yeah, Knox knew him. Knew Beckett's brain had already figured out she'd used the hug as a tactic to keep him from bolting the door and was tallying up twenty different ways to sever Judd's arms from his torso. "I'm not goin' anywhere."

As soon as he said it he reconsidered because Judd sucked in one of those audibly long, drawn-out inhalations a man used when he was appreciating the feel of a lush woman pressed next to him. His voice was low and way too intimate. "What happened?"

Something between a choked-back sob and a contemptuous chuckle came from Gia. "You were there. You saw what happened." Her voice got stronger. Shifted. "It wasn't me, Judd. I swear it wasn't. But I'm starting to think..." That little tease hung for a heartbeat and she moved. "Can we sit down? I need someone to talk things through with. Someone to tell me if I'm crazy."

Muted footsteps whispered on carpet and Gia must have laid her purse on a table nearby because the mic affixed to her purse rattled through the feed. The *whoosh* of weight on thick cushions registered right after.

"Your parents are worried about you," Judd said, still closer than Beckett would've liked. "Your mom said she tried to call."

She had. One of which Gia had finally answered and gently but firmly shared with Colette that while she had no intent of completely breaking ties with her, she was done with Reginald. Colette hadn't come right out and said she understood, but Gia had said there'd been a profound understanding in her lack of acknowledgment. Like in the silence she'd pointed at her own life and said she wasn't one to judge.

"We talked," Gia said, "but you know how Mom is. I couldn't go into details with her. Not without worrying her."

"You could've talked to your dad," Judd said. "He'd have listened."

"He'd have lectured. You know that."

"How do you know I won't?" Someone shifted. Probably Judd since the proximity of his voice drew closer to Gia. "I don't trust Beckett, Gia. Don't trust him or the people he runs around with. That *family* of his. You haven't been the same since you started working with them. I don't want to believe you're the one behind what happened in Atlanta, but the evidence shows otherwise."

"It wasn't me. I wouldn't do that."

"The you I *used* to know wouldn't do that."

"But Beckett would." The way she said it was more her completing his unspoken thoughts than an accusation, but it opened the door on where she needed to go perfectly.

Quiet filled the room. One of those long, drawn-out moments designed to make a point or emphasize the weight of a choice being made.

"You said you needed to talk something through," Judd said. "If it wasn't you that sold the info, then who do you think it was?"

"Oh, yeah," Knox said. "Just keep headin' down that trail."

The banter was normal for them on a deal like this. A way to keep the tension evened out. But for once, Beckett didn't want it. Didn't want anything impeding any audible clue Gia might need him.

"I didn't have a clue," Gia said. "Not at first. Then I was with Beckett and his family after we got home from Atlanta and...well, I heard something. Something that made me wonder if maybe..." Her voiced cracked and a tiny whimper trailed it. "God, I still can't even bear to think it. It hurts."

Rustling sounded and when Judd spoke again he was much closer to the mic. "I can't help you if you don't tell me, Gia. And while it probably makes me an idiot, I want to help you. I always have. After all these years, you have to know that. Tell me. What did you hear?"

Gia sniffled. "I overheard the guys talking. They thought I was with the rest of the girls and were supposed to be handling some business stuff, but one of them asked if the thing in Atlanta was going to work out like they'd hoped." She hesitated for all of a second and added a fragile desperation to the rest of her words. "It could just be a coincidence, right? They couldn't have set me up. Wouldn't have. Would they?"

Judd sighed. "I was afraid of this."

Another sniffle, the familiarity in her voice probably sinking deep claws in Judd's ego. "Afraid of what?"

"Surely you know they've got ties to narcotics."

The feed got silent.

Scary silent.

That was one topic he and Gia hadn't covered. While the brotherhood didn't deal drugs, they'd earned plenty of attention over the years for it because of their clubs. They'd even worked an exclusive territory agreement with a local dealer in exchange for muscle and keeping more dangerous product out of their venues.

"No. I didn't know." Way too authentic and more than a little shaken. "You're sure?"

"No question. Paul Renner almost took them down a few years ago. When he got too close, they set him up with some old stuff from his background and ruined his career."

"That wasn't over drugs."

"Sure it was. You just didn't see that part. Beckett and his so-called brothers put a spin on the situation and worked Renner out of the equation. It's what they do, Gia. It's what they're good at."

Knox chuckled through the headset. "Jesus, this guy's a piece of work. It's like he lives in his own alternate reality."

"Brother, I've followed him for the better part of forty-eight hours," Danny said. "Trust me when I tell you, he's so full of his own bullshit his feet never touch the ground."

For an uncomfortable stretch Gia said nothing.

Beckett had half a mind to stomp out of the stairwell, kick down the door and haul her out before any of Judd's nonsense could penetrate.

"You really think they'd do that? Set me up?"

"Governor Lansing's done more to clean out drug runners in Florida than the last three men in office combined. I don't know how far their reach goes, but if Beckett and his crew have operations in Florida, then yeah, they'd have seen some benefit from it. Or could also be they used your situation to barter for favors closer to home."

More quiet, the impact of it so powerful it rattled Beckett's bones.

"What do I do?" Gia said, the quality of it broken and almost a whisper. "I can't confront them. Beckett maybe, but not all of them."

Judd's answer was a little too sharp. Like a cheating man all of seconds away from watching his wife open the bedroom closet door when his mistress was hidden behind it. "No. Don't do that." His voice evened out. "There's too much risk."

"Well, I can't do nothing. I'm out on bail and have a conspiracy charge against a government official hanging over my head. On top of that, I can't work. How am I supposed to take care of myself? Pay my attorneys?"

One of those reproving sighs reserved for exasperated husbands and fathers around the world streamed through the feed. "What are you prepared to do?"

"What do you mean? To clear my name?"

"No, I mean about Beckett."

"What can I do? He's the one that posted my bail. His brother's the one coordinating my defense attorneys. If I leave him, who knows what will happen to me."

He waited only a few beats—just enough to make sure his answer carried the right impact. "You could let me take care of you."

"Wow," Ted said through the headset. "Nothin' says *love* like some good old-fashioned coercion."

"No shit," Knox said. "And he's such a classy asswipe, too."

"You'd do that?" Gia's voice was so soft it was hard to hear. "After what I said? After all the times I told you no?"

"I told you, Gia. I'm not giving up. Never will. We're right for each other."

"That's creepy," Danny muttered.

"Leave him," Judd said before Beckett could tell the crew in the van to shut their yaps. "Pack your things and come stay here with me. I've got more than enough money to take care of everything."

"More like your daddy does," Knox added.

Judd kept going. "I'll talk to your dad. He'd be better at your defense anyway and I'll call in some favors to get to the bottom of who set you up."

"But—"

"Let go, Gia." Movement sounded, the unmistakable rustle of someone moving on a well-cushioned surface. "Let me take care of you. It's what I've always wanted. What you've needed. All you need to do is let it happen."

Beckett strained his head from side to side, stretching the taut muscles along the side of his neck. Not that it did much good with his hands balled into tight fists and the burn searing beneath his skin.

It wasn't real. None of it. Just a hoax they'd concocted to lure Judd into taking action. But the banter felt too real. A custom-made nightmare from his deepest fears.

The silence stretched for too damned long, the white noise in his headset eating at his control.

Gia's quiet sob nearly broke him. "Okay."

Chapter Twenty-Six

Gia stood beside her car outside the high-rise that housed Judd's condo and stared down at the key in her palm. With Judd wedging her between the open door and the driver's seat, there was little room to move. A fact that went against everything in her. Made her want to shove him out of reaching distance and fill her lungs with something other than Judd's expensive yet overpowering cologne. At this point, though, it'd take a good thirty minutes in a scorching shower to escape the scent.

"The code's seven-one-five-two-zero-five." Judd coiled his hand around hers, forcing her fingers to close around it. "Don't worry. I'll take care of everything. You pack up some things from your place and bring them back here. I'll set things in motion on my end and meet you back here. You'll be safe."

Set things in motion. Another phrase that rang every warning bell and instinct to flee. If she'd had any doubt about Judd's involvement in the suspicious things that had happened to her lately, they were gone now. Eradicated by almost an hour's worth of his probing questions about Beckett and his brothers' professional lives and their comings and goings. Particularly anything that might be drug-related. As if he were looking for a particular spin.

She'd sat through it all. Forced a meek and defeated response and allowed Judd to hold her in the crook of his arm when what she really wanted was to cram Judd's nuts down his throat and get back to Beckett. If she'd had to sit through Beckett sucking up to another woman for as long as Gia had been with Judd, she'd have gone mental or beat the hell out of God only knew how many innocent bystanders.

And there was no doubt Beckett was close. With every word that had been spoken—every silence—she'd been painfully aware of him listening, but the second Judd had insisted on walking her to her car, she'd felt him. Known down to her soul he was watching over her.

Thank God, they'd had the foresight to park her car in the visitor lot before they'd put things into motion. Gia nodded her head and gently tugged her hand free. "Where are you headed?"

"Nothing you need to worry about." Judd cupped the side of her face and eradicated what space was left between them. "But I promise you—when I'm done, Beckett and his family will be too busy with their own problems to mess with you."

His fingers tightened, holding her head immobile as he lowered his head.

Her heart tumbled and kicked in a painful, irregular rhythm and her throat constricted to the point barely any air slipped through.

Too close.

Move.

Move.

Move.

She stopped him with a hand to his chest. "Not yet."
As in never.

Judd frowned down at her, his face still uncomfortably close. "I won't let you play me, Gia."

"It's not a play." She dropped her gaze and cuddled closer. Job or not, she didn't think her body would make it through the farce of his lips on her. No matter what it meant for her future. "This is just too important to rush." She petted the line of his sternum. Imagined the powerful thrum of Beckett's heart beneath her palm. She lifted her gaze to Judd. "Definitely not something that should happen for the first time in a parking lot."

His thumb skated along her jawline and the stern line of his mouth curved into a sly smile. "Fair enough." He studied her a second more then stepped back and opened the car door wider. "Get your things and I'll meet you back here."

She fought the nearly uncontainable urge to jump in the front seat, slam the door shut and peel out of the lot, and gave him a shy smile instead. Forced herself to settle in and buckle her seat belt with the hesitancy of a woman who didn't want to walk away from a new and blossoming relationship.

Judd watched her from the wide walk that fronted the building, his hands anchored in the pockets of the track pants he'd worn to the gym and the gentle autumn evening air tousling his blond hair.

She slipped her phone from her purse along with her keys and tucked it face up beside her thigh.

Circle one block west and park. The van will be right behind you.

No name. Just an unknown number, but there was no question it was Knox. Beckett wouldn't have taken his eyes off her long enough to bother with a keyboard, but he'd sure boss his brother into doing it.

She started the car and backed out of her spot, making sure to cast one last longing look and a wave at Judd. Only when she was on the street and taking the first turn to the direction she'd been given did she open the center console and dig out her headset. She'd barely settled the earpiece in place when her phone vibrated against her leg.

"We've got eyes on him," Knox said without waiting for a hello. "Just got in the elevator heading back to his floor. We're pullin' out of the garage now."

"Where's Beckett?"

"On foot, rounding the block opposite you." She'd known Beckett a long time, but she'd never heard his voice so grated and ripe with tension. Like a man who'd clawed his way up from the bowels of hell driven only by the slim hope of saving his soul.

"You pick up anything on the router?"

"Not yet," Knox answered, "but I wouldn't expect he'd have it on him. I'm hopin' that's what he had to go back for. Not thinking tonight's turn of events was what he'd planned for."

"No shit," Danny said. "And now we've got a key and a code if the burner approach doesn't pan out." Quiet registered just long enough for Danny to remember he had a Fed in the van and another two following in an unmarked car of their own. He cleared his throat. "Not that anyone here would access a property without proper authorization in advance."

Knox and Ted snickered.

On Gia's right was a parallel slot about two thirds down the block. She whipped her convertible into it and shoved the gearshift into park.

"Coming up behind you," Danny said.

She killed the engine and reached for the door handle, but before her fingers could close around it, the door whipped open.

Beckett's hand closed around her forearm and he all but yanked her from the driver's seat just as the van pulled up beside them. Three seconds tops and she was inside, her feet never touching the ground before she found herself on Beckett's lap in the shadowed rear of the van and tucked tight to Beckett's chest.

She splayed her hand against his sternum and tried to gain enough distance to see his face, but his arms had zero give. Beneath her palms, his heart galloped like he'd sprinted twenty flights of stairs. "Beckett," she whispered. Forgoing the rigid muscles in his torso, she smoothed one hand from his elbow toward his shoulder, her fingers dipping beneath the arm of his tee to maintain skin-to-skin contact. "I'm right here. I'm fine."

His biceps flexed and his fingers dug into her shoulder and hip. The warmth of his heavy exhalations feathered against her temple. "Where is he?" he all but growled at Knox.

"Went into his apartment about the time we turned onto Cedar Springs." The answer registered in real time only, the feed to her headset dead, which meant Knox had given them an extra layer of privacy.

Knox glanced at the two of them. The glow of the monitors wasn't strong enough to break the shadows that kept her and Beckett cocooned from everyone else, but was sufficient to spotlight Knox's worry for his brother. His gaze locked on her hand for all of a beat before it slid to her.

"I've got him." Gia quietly answered the unspoken question in his eyes, slipped her other hand beneath the hem of Beckett's tee at his back and stroked the length of his spine. "He'll be fine. We both will be."

Danny backed the van into a parking spot but left the engine running, the low rumble filling the awkward silence.

Much as she hated anyone outside of family even getting a hint at Beckett's vulnerability, she couldn't find the will to fight the closeness. Needed his strength and scent to wipe away the remnants of Judd's presence as much as he needed her touch to guide him back from the edge.

Time ticked past in a warped push and pull, part of her grateful for the cushion it provided Beckett to recalibrate and the other all too aware of the Feds' watchful eyes and the lack of activity from Judd. Bit by bit, Beckett's unrelenting grip shifted from one of frantic desperation to the protective strength she'd come to appreciate and crave. He speared his fingers through her hair and sucked in a long, stabilizing breath. "What he said about Renner—he wasn't wrong. We dredged his past back out into the open, but not for the reasons he told you."

So, that was it. Of all the bullshit and questions she'd sat through with Judd, she'd thought it would be Beckett's possessive alpha side that would've triggered him. Not the fear he'd lose her to Judd's inane chatter. She leaned back, letting him brace her head and back with his strength and met his worried gaze. "You can't seriously think I'd believe a thing that came out of his mouth."

He studied her, taking in every feature as though looking for any sign of insincerity. "Other people have."

Silly man. So strong and fearless in the face of everything. Hell, he'd all but raised himself with only Knox and friendly neighbors to cushion his time alone and made an amazing life for himself in the end. And yet, where she was concerned, all his shields were laid low.

She traced the hard line of his jaw and savored the soft tickle of his whiskers beneath her fingertips. Her voice was gentle, but her words cut straight to the point. "I'm not leaving you, Beckett. I know you. Enough to know you've got honor and a solid reason behind every action you take. What Judd said bounced off me before he even finished his sentence."

His fingers tightened against her scalp and the relief behind his blue eyes poured over her like sunshine after a damp and drizzly winter morning. His lips crooked with the promise of some witty response brewing on his tongue.

"He's on the move," Ted said before Beckett could speak.

Everyone perked to attention and the van's speakers hissed backed to life. "Who's taking point?" a man from the Fed car asked.

Gia slid off Beckett's lap, but only managed to get as far as a thigh-to-thigh before his arm banded around her back and his hand clamped onto her hip.

"We're up front," Knox said. "The router's only got so much range and I can't risk a blank spot."

"Check your app, McGillis." Ted typed out something on his keyboard at a speed that rivaled Knox's. "The GPS on Rainier's car is active and transmitting."

"Roger that," the man said. "We'll run parallel."

"How much leeway have I got?" Danny asked.

"A block. Block and a half at most," Knox said, his focus trained on his screen. "I'm not as worried if he's in motion. Not like he's gonna be able to do much with web connectivity while he's driving and I can trace his calls via carrier when he's in motion. It's when he stops that matters."

Ted twisted enough to meet Danny's gaze in the rear-view mirror. "He's pulling out."

Aside from Ted's periodic directional updates, the next twenty minutes ran eerily quiet. While they used the GPS to stay out of Judd's immediate line of sight, every now and then Gia caught glimpses of his Audi as he passed cars moving too slow for his liking. The black A7 might have been one of many in Dallas's upscale Turtle Creek, but the further he drove down Lemmon Avenue toward Love Field, the more out of place the gleaming luxury car was.

"Heading west on Northwest Highway," Ted said.

Freddie twisted in his seat and zigzagged a look between Beckett and Knox. "Don't you two have an office on Northwest Highway?"

Knox glanced at Beckett then refocused on his screen. "About a mile and a half west of here, just past Webb Chapel."

Freddie nodded and faced forward again, but for once he didn't have the smug attitude he'd nursed since taking Gia into custody.

Five minutes later, Judd turned off Northwest Highway onto a side street and pulled into a run-down self-storage lot.

Danny turned into the parking lot right beside it.

"How much authority have you got on this, Fred?" Knox asked, his fingers flying over the keyboard.

"Why?"

"Because Storage King doesn't exactly have the most secure network and I'm curious if browsing through customer lists falls under your list of no-nos."

Freddie twisted enough to share a look with Ted.

Ted started up with his own typing. "You don't have jurisdiction, but I do."

"We've got a visual," the man from the Fed car said just as they pulled into a parallel spot on the street in front of them. "He just went through the gate, but it's already closing. Any chance you can trigger it through their network?"

"Hold up and see if we get a lock on the ID," Freddie said before Ted could answer. "No point in tipping our hand yet."

The flashing dot stopped near the back of the storage lot.

Tipping their hand. Gia huffed out an ironic chuckle, planted her elbows on her knees and dug the heels of her hands into her eye sockets. They'd bypassed tipping their hand and darted right into long-shot territory the second she'd agreed to this plan.

Beckett's hand at her hip slid up and stroked the line of her spine.

"Uh…" Ted typed a few more words then froze. "Hey, Beck. Any chance you've got a long-lost account at this place?"

"Do I look like the kind of guy who'd keep anything at some offsite place with shit for security?"

Knox shifted for a better look at Ted's screen. "Holy shit." He dragged Ted's keyboard out from in front of him and entered in a few lightning-fast keystrokes. "It was opened a few weeks ago."

Gia sat upright. "What was opened?"

"A ten-by-twenty space. Y-10." Ted yanked his keyboard back and motioned Knox to his own. "See if you can find a facility map. McGillis, see if you can get authorization to search."

"They're not gonna buy it," Freddie muttered with something close to disgust. "Gia's too wrapped up tight on this one. It's gonna take something definitive to push them off dead center."

"I got it!" Knox jerked ramrod-straight in his chair, his voice still careening through the van. "Device ID is a match. Got a call going through now."

Gia froze, her heart squeezing to match the death grip on Beckett's thigh.

Freddie spun in his seat. "Knox, get a trace on that call. Ted, I want that gate up. McGillis, move in. Hold your approach until we've got access to the storage unit."

"Gate's going up. Call just connected with the same guy he used before in Baton Rouge." Knox twisted enough to shoot a grin at Beckett and Gia. "Sweetheart, your long shot just paid off big-time."

The next five minutes went by in a blur. Freddie sharing rapid-fire intel with his higher-ups on the phone. McGillis and his partner moving in. The shouts and pounding feet against concrete as Judd tried to escape. The surreal visual as Danny steered the van to the back of the storage lot and Gia got her first look at Judd face-down on the hood of his Audi, one Fed cuffing him while the other kept their gun trained in place.

It had been Judd the whole time.

Logically, the evidence had pointed to it. She'd even thought she'd accepted the probability of it. But seeing the truth play out—watching her childhood friend's cool veneer fall away as two more unmarked cars screeched to a halt on either side of his Audi and other men stormed the storage unit—it was all painfully real. The difference between imagining the sting of a knife and actually feeling the point pierce your flesh.

A cool October breeze drifted through the van's open side door, bringing with it the whine of multiple sirens. Off to one side of the storage unit, Beckett huddled with Danny, Knox and Freddie.

Beckett frowned, scanned the boxes inside the unit then snapped his gaze to her. Whatever it was he said to the men, it couldn't have been pretty. Not if the scowl on his face was any indication. He was on the move a second later, headed to the van with Freddie tight on his heels.

She'd meant to stay in the van. Had promised Beckett she would. But instinct and the need to ground herself in him while her past fell apart had her rushing across the concrete in a light jog.

"You fucking bitch!" Judd's words hit her just as Beckett's arms coiled around her. "I trusted you!"

Beckett turned her, buffeting Judd's ongoing tirade with his broad back and holding her cheek flush against his chest. He kissed the top of her head. "It wasn't you he wanted to set up. Not really."

Of all the things she'd expected to hear, that development wasn't even on the list. She pulled back enough to study his face. "What do you mean it wasn't me? All the evidence pointed to me."

Freddie moved tighter to Beckett's side. "The unit's in Beckett's name. It's full of every kind of street narcotic and controlled pharmaceutical you can imagine. McGillis pulled up right when Judd was about to lock the unit up. Judd left the phone inside."

All the questions about Beckett and his brothers... how Judd had insisted they were involved in dealing drugs...it all came together at once. "His endgame was Beckett. Not me." Her gaze shot to Beckett. "But why? I don't get it. Why go through me to get you?"

Beckett shook his head, fond exasperation mingling with that crooked smile he always gave her when she dug in her heels in on one of their frequent debates. "His endgame wasn't me, gorgeous. Getting me locked away for dealing dope and framing you to further my narcotics business was just a key step in getting what he really wanted."

She studied Beckett, then Freddie. "Which was?"

This time it was Freddie who grinned, a twinkle she wouldn't have thought possible sparking in his dark eyes. "You."

"He'd have killed your career and been your saving grace all at once," Beckett added.

She turned for a better view of the unit. Uniformed officers had teamed up with the Feds and were carefully combing the contents. It was genius really. Fucked up in so many different ways she couldn't catalog them all, but effective as a means to maneuver a lot of women into a tight spot.

Except she wasn't just any woman. She was stubborn. Smart. Downright ornery when the situation called for it. But most of all, she followed her gut and something inside her had always known Judd wasn't the one for her. The same way she'd known Beckett was.

Beckett moved in behind her, cupped her shoulders and kissed her temple. "It's over."

On many levels, yes. Digging her career out of the gutter would take some time, but she'd manage it the same way she'd tackled every other hurdle life had thrown her. And this time she wouldn't be doing it alone.

But there was one unfinished task left semi-flagging out on what felt like a post-war breeze. A chapter written with an incomplete and unsatisfying ending that needed correction. She covered Beckett's hands with her own and squeezed. "It's not over. Not yet. There's still one more thing I need to take care of."

Beckett turned her so he could get a straight-on view of her face, an unspoken question in his eyes.

Gia shifted her attention to Freddie, hoping like hell he'd play along and give her the leg up she needed to start her future with a clean slate. "How long can you keep news of Judd's arrest on lockdown?"

Both of Freddie's eyebrows hopped nearly to his receding hairline, and his gaze shifted between her and Beckett. "How long do you need?"

"It depends." She looked at Beckett. "How fast do you think Trevor can get me to Atlanta?"

Chapter Twenty-Seven

A discreet ding sounded in the posh elevator and the doors whooshed open, unveiling Gia's final battleground in a war she'd fought her whole life. Dressed in skinny jeans, a cobalt-blue tunic, her favorite knee-high black motorcycle boots and her hair pulled back in a low ponytail, she looked like she was ready for a trip to the mall rather than a face-off in a professional setting, but she was done with striving for just the right image. For being the chameleon that would let her blend into any situation and rise to the top of it. It was time to be *her*. Gia Sinclair. Whatever that looked like.

Pushing through the wide glass double doors to her father's office, she paused a moment to soak in the elegant yet alert and uncomfortable energy stretched out in front of her. It was barely after eight on a Friday morning, but the way people hustled from desk to desk or sat up ruler-straight behind their desks, you'd have thought it was Monday and the end of the world only minutes away. Either that or a taskmaster with a Taser gun and a nightstick was due for another sweep of the area any second.

That's how she'd lived her whole life. Always alert. Body and mind poised to jump on the next opportunity that might gain her father's attention. His approval. To be good enough to be his daughter and live up to the name he'd made for himself. The only thing she'd ever done to buck that convention was her career.

That had been the start. The launch in the war to free herself. Though, she hadn't figured that out until she'd spent the much-needed time at Haven licking her emotional wounds and taking a good hard look at her life.

Beckett splayed his hand low on her back. "You don't have to do this."

A part of her wanted to take him up on the out his comment offered. To race back down to the car they'd left waiting outside and get on with the rest of her life. But another far more instinctive voice insisted she follow through. Encouraged her to cut the cords that had kept her bound inside the rigid lifestyle she'd been born into and give the needy little girl inside her solid closure. "Yeah, I do. If I don't, I'll always look back and wonder if I should've done something different. At least this way I'll know I finally stood up for myself."

Sucking in a deep breath, she stepped out of the somewhat private entrance and into view of the receptionist behind her opulent mahogany desk.

The woman glanced up at the two of them, a polite but empty smile tilting the corners of her well-glossed red lips. With her perfectly styled shoulder-length blond hair and couture dress, she seemed more suited for a runway or a pageant than manning a busy law office. "I'll be with you in just a moment."

Gia kept moving, Beckett a solid presence at her side. "No need. We know where we're headed."

Surprises weren't something her father appreciated, a fact evidenced by how quickly Blondie shot to her feet and scurried after them in her four-inch heels. "I'm sorry, but clients need to wait for their attorney in the lobby."

"I'm not a client." Gia turned the corner that led to the massive office lining the entire west side of the building and the exceptional view of downtown.

Apparently, the direction was enough to clue the woman into where Gia was headed and she called in reinforcements. "Andie, we've got a problem."

Now *that* name Gia knew all too well. Although, the last time Gia had seen her father's assistant, she'd been skulking out of Reginald's office well after business hours with mussed hair and her clothes askew.

Andie stood and assessed the situation in under a second. "Gia! What a pleasant surprise!" She rounded her desk and placed herself squarely between Gia and Beckett and the door to her father's conference room. "Your dad's in the middle of his morning staff meeting."

Beckett slowed his strides just enough to let Gia take the lead.

Gia took advantage and kept on walking. "I'm well aware of when his staff meeting is. That's why I got here when I did." She glanced back at Andie, channeled the same superior bullshit she'd learned from her father and waved Andie back to her desk. "That'll be all."

Beckett chuckled low enough only Gia could have heard it.

She paused and met Beckett's steady gaze. "You don't have to go in. I can do this on my own."

"I know you can, but the point is you don't have to go it alone anymore." He palmed her shoulder and squeezed. "Plus, Sylvie and Ninette both threatened to kick my ass if I didn't bring back a firsthand play-by-play."

It was just the tension-breaker Gia needed. That tiny reminder that where she was severing ties to the family she'd been born into, she wouldn't be adrift going forward. She had people who loved her. Who believed in her no matter what happened.

She nodded and pushed the door open.

An older partner she recognized from past events hosted at her parents' home stuttered to a stop midsentence and eyeballed Gia like she'd just walked in with a severed head hanging from her fist. The reactions from the other men and women varied anywhere from fear to outrage.

Surprise registered with her father for all of a second before irritation pinched his stately features. "Gia, I'm in the middle of a staff meeting."

"Sir, I'm sorry," Andie said from beside Beckett who stood with arms crossed at the door. Like Gia, he'd bypassed any pretense of formal attire and stuck to his boots, jeans, and T-shirt. Between the muscles apparent for anyone to see and his formidable pose, Gia was a little shocked Andie had dared to get as close as she had.

"My daughter's known for her drama, though I'd thought Judd had a handle on it." Much as Gia had on the way in, Reginald waved her off. "I'll handle this." He stood and strode Gia's direction, that stern glare that used to put the fear of God in her firmly in place. "As for you, you'll wait and we'll talk about your case later."

"I don't have a case anymore." She stepped out of his trajectory and tossed the folder she'd kept a death grip on the whole drive from the airport onto the gleaming conference table. "But Judd does."

Damn, but that felt good. For days after her father had marched into her hotel suite and convicted her without a single second to defend herself, that folder full of trumped-up evidence had been like a brand on her memories. A tangible metaphor for the repeated disappointments she'd foisted on her family.

Today she was shoving that tome of disappointments back where it belonged, along with all the guilt and expectations that went with it.

Reginald wedged his way between the two attorneys blocking him from the file and snatched it off the table. "What the hell is this?"

"It's proof. I told you I was innocent, but you took Judd's word over mine."

He flipped one page. Then another. By the time he got to the end of the packet his brows formed a deep V and his face was a mottled red.

Gia couldn't help it. Had sworn she wouldn't fall back on the pop culture Knox had insisted was perfect for the moment, but it was too appropriate. A poke her father wouldn't get, but that she and Beckett would have a fine time retelling later. She crossed her arms, waited until her father raised his head and met her eyes then said, "You chose *poorly.*"

A snicker sounded from a seat at the far end of the table.

Lo and behold it was the poor intern, Steve, who'd had the misfortune of bearing the last folder full of information shared between father and daughter.

Reginald flipped back to the front of the folder and rescanned the information. "This can't be right."

Seriously? He'd take a second look for Judd, but not even listen to her side of the story? "It's not only ironclad evidence, but he was so pissed off when the Homeland agents took him in he confessed to everything. Putting the governor at risk. Using your former clients to plant the evidence. Setting me up to take the fall. All of it just so he could ruin my career and pin the endgame on the man I love to get him out of the picture." Gia uncoiled her arms and paced closer. "All so we could live happily ever after." She stopped close enough he couldn't avoid her eyes. "If it's all the same to you, I think I'll take the man and the family who took my back over the people who tried to force me to be someone I wasn't."

With that she turned and took her sweet time making her way back to Beckett, her hips swaying with every bit of the freedom and confidence billowing up inside her.

Given the pride and the heat in Beckett's eyes as he watched her approach, it was a hell of a spectacle guaranteed to make the recap for Sylvie and Ninette when they got back home, but she didn't care. She felt great. Free on a level she'd never felt before in her life. Like all the strings and worries that had tied her down before had finally slipped their knots and opened up a whole new world of possibilities.

It wasn't until she was five feet from the door that she remembered the conversation she'd had with her mother this morning. She stopped, dug the folded piece of paper from her pocket, and retraced her steps back to her dad. "I almost forgot. I called Mom on the flight to Atlanta this morning and told her about Judd, too."

She paused in front of her dad and cocked her head. "I also told her I'm moving in with Beckett and that my town house was available if she was tired of philandering assholes who get off banging their secretary and interns more than spending time at home."

More than one gasp and a few barely contained chuckles fanned out behind her.

Gia ignored them and handed over the name and phone number on the piece of paper. "She asked me to give you this."

"What's this?" her dad said as she headed back to Beckett, his arm already outstretched and waiting to pull her close to his side.

Gia didn't hesitate, just moved in tight and spared her dad one last glance. "Her divorce attorney." With that they were out the door, leaving a mighty wake of shock and God only knew how many weeks' worth of gossip behind them.

Beckett chuckled and punched the elevator button. "Any chance I can fire up some of that sass when we get home? That walk of yours when you're feelin' feisty's a killer."

The elevator dinged and the door swept open.

Gia grinned up at him, tugged him inside and rose up on her tiptoes, wrapping her arms around his neck. "Who said we had to wait until we get home?"

Bars on the windows, stark white walls and a whole lot of silence. At ten o'clock on a Friday night, the federal detention center just south of Dallas wasn't exactly a beehive of activity—a convenient development Beckett planned to take full advantage of before the Feds flew Judd back to Georgia on Monday.

If Judd's keepers happened to find him with a few cracked ribs and a whole lot of bruises in the morning, well…that was the reality of life on the inside, wasn't it?

With Danny next to him, Beckett paused at the door beside the desk with the bulletproof glass and jerked his chin at the guard behind it. No words were needed. Everything he'd needed to say and every string he'd had to pull to make tonight happen were all tidily tucked away. What had surprised the fuck out of him, though, was how much Freddie had been a factor in the groundwork.

A grating buzz shot through the lobby and the bolt disengaged with an ominous thud.

Danny pulled the door wide and held it open for Beckett. "Which room is he in?"

"Last one on the left." The door slammed shut behind them and the lock reengaged. With nothing but hard surfaces lining the long hallways there was nothing to muffle their clipped footsteps against the industrial gray tiles. "Freddie texted when we pulled into the parking lot and said we've got thirty minutes with the cameras off."

"Not thinkin' Judd's gonna make it ten given the look on your face." He glanced at Beckett. "You sure G's not gonna be pissed she missed out on this?"

Minutes from doling out the much-deserved punishment Judd had earned for his actions, Danny had hit on the one thing guaranteed to make Beckett smile. "She knows where I am."

Danny stopped dead in his tracks. "And she didn't want to come? I thought she'd be the first one in line to take a swing at him."

Beckett slowed his steps, chuckled and turned back to his brother. "She said she was done proving she was better than dickless wonders, but was kind enough to point out he was a complete pussy when he took a hit to the chin."

Danny smiled big enough to show teeth. "That's our girl."

Indeed, it was. She'd also added on that she had a hard time beating up on a guy who'd never known a hard day in his life and who'd probably be someone's bitch inside a month.

Truth be told, that last bit was the only incentive Beckett had to make sure the bastard was still breathing when tonight was over. He strolled the last few doors to the holding cell on the left.

"You sure you don't want an extra hand?" Danny said.

Oh, hell no, he wasn't sharing this moment. Not with anyone but Gia and she'd forked over her share of the pie. "Need you out here givin' me a heads-up if anyone decides to interrupt my conversation." He looked up at the camera mounted in the corner and nodded.

The same buzz that had deactivated the locks to the main door ricocheted down the hall.

The knob was frigid against his palm. As cold as the fury he'd nursed since the night he'd held Gia while she'd sobbed in his arms. He twisted it and found Judd standing against the far corner. Dressed in drab detention khakis instead of his usual trendy wardrobe, he looked more like the thug he'd proven himself to be. As Freddie had promised, his hands and feet were free. It took him all of two seconds to figure out the reason for Beckett's visit. "You won't get away with this. Not by a long shot."

So, maybe ol' Judd wasn't as stupid as he'd thought. Which was good, because Beckett wasn't in the mood to fuck around. He jerked his head toward the camera in the corner. "If you're talkin' about that thing saving you, you can let that idea go. I've got you all to myself for a solid thirty minutes."

He let the door swing shut behind him and the lock shot home like a gavel.

Judd shifted to the opposite corner, keeping as much distance between him and Beckett as he could and lifting his hands, ready to engage. "I'm not exactly some slacker you can take easy."

"God, I hope not," Beckett said. "You'd take all the fun out of it for me." He cracked his knuckles and stretched his neck from side to side. "But the fact is, you cut my woman deep. That means I'm not walkin' out of this room until you bleed in equal measure."

Epilogue

"Admit it," Gia said with that triumphant grin she always got when she'd mastered something new. "I kick flipping pancake ass!"

Beckett kept his mouth shut, folded his arms across his chest and leaned into Haven's kitchen counter, appreciating the sweet image of his woman in flannel sleep pants, a goofy Christmas graphic tee, and her hair still mussed from sleep. The bulk of the Christmas morning feast was already over and most of his family back in the big living room playing with Levi and Mary, but Gia had been adamant about making Beckett's food and he wasn't about to quash her fun.

As if to prove her newfound expertise, she gave the flat griddle a toss and sent the plate-size flapjack soaring well over her head.

Manning cleanup detail at the kitchen sink, Sylvie glanced over her shoulder at Gia and said, "Lass, ye could bungle boiling water and still make it look amazing with that rock on yer finger."

As she had countless times since he'd given her the early gift last night, Gia paused and studied her left hand, giving her ring finger a wiggle. "It *is* pretty, isn't it?"

Ninette took the pan Sylvie handed her and started

drying, a whole lot of good-natured ribbing in her voice. "It's a self-defense weapon."

Gabe paused in her trek from the table to the sink, her hands loaded with dirty plates, and ogled the ring over Gia's shoulder. "I don't know how you're not knocking it on everything. How big is it?"

"Three carats," Darya answered before Gia could. She poked her fork already loaded with a big bite of pancake toward Beckett for emphasis. "You wouldn't believe how many stores Beckett dragged us to before he settled on that one."

"And she loved every minute of it." Knox pushed his empty plate out of the way, leaned over and stabbed a bite off Darya's plate. "She also scored three pairs of shoes and four purses. Who the hell needs that many shoes or purses?"

Darya shoved his hand out of her way then shifted her body so it semi-guarded her plate. "Your wife, that's who. You play with your firewalls. I'll play with my accessories."

"Oh, I like playing with your accessories, too. Never doubt it."

"Uncle Beckett!" Levi's voice cut through the arched kitchen entry all of a second before he pounded into sight, his face flush from his syrup and Christmas morning high. Only the bottom half of his Iron Man pajamas were still visible, the top that went with it covered up by the one-size-too-large black Led Zeppelin concert tee Jace had got him. "You gotta come see what Uncle Axel got me!"

"Jesus, Mary and Joseph," Sylvie muttered under her breath. "What are the odds it's something Nat won't want to string my boy up for?"

"A hundred to one if you're lucky," Ninette drawled almost as quiet.

Gia chuckled, slid the last of Beckett's pancakes onto his plate and handed them over. "I'm thinking you'll need to eat these in the living room. You can't make him wait to show you after that kind of intro."

Beckett took the plate with one hand and pulled her close to his side with the other. "Well, then lead the way, buddy. I'm armed and ready to ogle your loot."

Fortunately for Nat—and Sylvie—the gift wasn't anything bad at all. Shocking? Well, yeah. Everyone knew Axel was a music lover, but very few people knew how deep that love went. How skilled Axel was at making it in his own right. But Levi was about to find out— just as soon as Axel was done tuning the new guitar he'd bought him.

Beckett settled into the corner of one leather couch opposite the fireplace and Gia curled up next to him. "Axel plays guitar?" she nearly whispered.

"Oh, yeah. Sings like you wouldn't believe, too, but it takes an act of God or a whole lot of Scotch to make it happen."

Across the room, Ivan was kicked back in an over-sized club chair, more relaxed than Beckett had ever seen him, nursing a cup of coffee and watching his daughter crawl all over Sergei as he read yet another Christmas story.

It was weird. The vast majority of people who met Sergei kept a healthy distance between themselves and the outwardly smooth Russian. As if some innate instinct pegged him for the predator he was and insisted on staying outside of killing distance. Even Darya who'd known him for years and considered him her brother was careful to offer respect and only approached him when she was sure he was open to it.

But not Mary. To her, he was her own dark knight and she had no compunction whatsoever in demanding he dote on her every spare second.

And Sergei? He did everything she asked, his mouth usually crooked in a wry smile that said he not only appreciated her spunk, but couldn't quite comprehend how he'd ended up so smitten.

One thing was for sure. Any man that came knocking when she hit dating age better have balls the size of Texas. Getting through Beckett and his brothers would be bad enough. Getting past Sergei would be murder.

Pancakes demolished and another cup of coffee down, Beckett shifted on the couch, pulled Gia between his legs and guided her so her back rested on his chest.

She dropped her head back on his shoulder and beamed a sweet smile up at him. "This is really nice."

"Not like Christmas at the Sinclair house?"

"God, no!" For all of a month, Gia's mom had stayed in Gia's town house while her attorney made Reginald's life a living hell. Then she'd decided she'd missed Atlanta and moved back home, but had built enough courage in her time away to get her own place well outside of Reginald's influence. The divorce wasn't final yet and would probably take another twelve months, given the assets at stake, but Colette was getting stronger every day, due in no small part to Gia, Ninette and Sylvie's influence. "I'm not sure anybody but me and my dad have ever seen my mom in her jammies."

"Well, we could fix that. Invite her out next year." Beckett toyed with the ring on her finger. "You given any thought to what kind of wedding you want?"

She laced her fingers with his and shifted enough to meet his gaze. "Something simple. Something that fits us."

"Does that mean fast is an option?"

She lifted their joined hands and pressed them against his chest. "You're just rushing to make sure I don't change my mind."

"Which proves I'm a smart man. So? When and where?"

Cocking her head to one side, her eyes got distant. "I don't know. Maybe someplace new. Ireland? Scotland? Someplace we could explore together?"

"We can do that." He tucked her hair behind her ear, more peaceful in that moment than he'd been his whole damned life. Like his SPD didn't even exist. He wasn't stupid. Knew it would rear its ugly head again, but for now he just went with it. Took it for the peaceful respite it was. "I'm still a fan of fast, though."

She giggled, but when her gaze dropped to the ring on her finger the smile on her face slipped a little, shifting to something wistful. "My Christmas present was lame compared to yours."

He shouldn't have laughed. Regretted it as soon as the hardy sound rumbled up the back of his throat and drew a whole lot of attention their way. He still had a hard time reining it in, but he lowered his voice and smoothed his hand up her spine. "Woman, you're out of your mind. I got *exactly* what I wanted."

"You wanted a new Glock? I mean, I'll grant you it's a sweet piece, but it can't stand up next to a honking diamond."

It was pretty big. One of those rings that not only

said, *This one's taken,* but added a big fat *Get the fuck back* on the end of the message.

"I gave you sweaters," she said. "And technically that was just me making sure you had lots of soft stuff around when I wasn't there to take the edge off."

Soft was a huge understatement. Wherever it was in Scotland Sylvie had found them, those sweaters nearly outdid the sweet stretch along Gia's inner thighs. And that had fast become one of his favorite spots in the whole damned world, so the comparison was truly saying something.

But Gia was still missing the point. He cupped the side of her face. "Gorgeous, you're forgetting the big gift. The one you gave me last night."

She frowned and cocked her head. "I didn't give you anything last night."

Nutty woman. Totally missing the point and so damned stubborn she was gonna make him spell it out. He dipped his head, teased her lips with his own then rested his forehead against hers. "Yeah, you did. You gave me you."

* * * * *

Visit www.RhennaMorgan.com *to find out more about her books!*

Read on for an excerpt from Rhenna's first book in a hot new series.

Author's Note

I first learned about Sensory Processing Disorder from a friend of mine who traveled abroad with me and had more than one uncomfortable run-in with odors that barely registered on my radar at all. Shortly after that adventure, another friend shared with me of her child's reliance on touch to soothe him when anxious.

This sent me diving into the world of SPD. What I found was that there are many manifestations for the disorder with the strength of each manifestation varying from person to person. So, while I've portrayed Beckett as craving an array of sensory stimulation to cope and maintain balance, that's only one of many possible presentations. For some, it's a simple aversion to certain fabrics, itchy tags, or overpowering scents. For others, it's discomfort with too much noise or crushing crowds. Like our personalities, each situation is different. Sadly, as of this writing, SPD is not recognized as a medical diagnosis and getting help is difficult. My hope in incorporating this broad-spectrum disorder into Beckett's story is to raise awareness and understanding.

Acknowledgments

Gia and Beckett's story was a heck of a ride that went down smack-dab in the middle of a whole lot of personal upheaval. Honestly, their story kept me sane, so the first high five for this book goes to them.

There were also several people who helped me fill in the blanks and made the whole Haven crew be their badass selves—Gary Glanz, Eric Fusion, Clark Brewster, Kevin Judice, and tech dude extraordinaire, Jay Donovan.

I also want to thank the growing ranks of Rhenna's Romantics. You ladies are a freaking HOOT! (And you post some damn fine eye candy, too.)

For Cori Deyoe, Juliette Cross, Kyra Jacobs, Audrey Carlan, Dena Garson, Lucy Beshara, Jennifer Mathews, and most important, my *amazing* daughters—you ladies are the bestest of the best. Honest to God, I'm not sure how I'd navigate these books (or life, for that matter) without you.

And hell's gonna freeze over before I miss giving Angela James a great big fat virtual squeeze. I wouldn't be living in such an alpha-rich alternate reality if it weren't for her. When it comes to champions, she gives the brothers a run for their money.

Chapter One

Safe with the Keeper. Guarded from the dark.

Over and over, Priest repeated the protective words in his head, merging his magic with the ancient symbols he inked at the base of Jade's nape and down her spine. Black and red swirling links with shades of gray joined each sacred talisman. No one would hurt her. Not her or Tate so long as he drew breath.

His forearm ached from his constant grip on the tattoo iron, but the steady drone and vibrations from the coils as he worked deepened his trance. Beneath his free hand, Jade's body trembled from the rush of pain-induced endorphins she'd endured for nearly four hours.

Safe with the Keeper. Guarded from the dark.

He swiped the excess ink away from the intricate design. The same intertwining scroll and symbolism that marked his shoulders, back and collarbone—and likely the only thing that had saved his life and sanity in the early days. Had Jade's and Tate's parents not guarded him after his brother's betrayal and marked him with the sacred symbols, the darkness would have consumed him entirely.

"Priest?" Jade pushed to her elbows on the padded table and peered over one shoulder. "Are you done?"

The art was perfect. A sufficient start in hiding her from the threat he sensed closing in. A malevolence he'd first felt with an unexplained summons to the Otherworld. Never since he'd been named high priest had he ever been called there so abruptly. Without warning or purpose.

Priest set his equipment aside and peeled off his latex gloves. As eerie as the memory had been, even if he covered Jade in ink, it wouldn't feel like enough protection. "For now."

Jade grinned, swiveled on the padded table, and snagged her blue tank top off the counter next to them. "How does it look?"

The tiny chimes above the front door jingled before he could answer, and Tate stalked through, his hands laden with yet another haul of the fast-food breakfasts Priest detested. The coffee, though—that he could use in abundance.

Through the open door, morning sunshine glinted off the storefronts on Eureka Springs's Main Street, only a few cars and Harleys motoring down the main drag. Not surprising for a Thursday, but by late tonight or early tomorrow they'd be flooded with tourists and bikers soaking up the spring weather.

Tate kicked the door shut and threw the bolt. The fifties throwback neon clock showed straight-up eleven o'clock, only one more hour until the shop opened.

"Tate, check it out." Jade shifted in front of the full-length mirror behind her and held the blue hand mirror higher for a better angle on Priest's work. "Mine's as badass as yours and Priest's."

Ignoring Jade, Tate set the orange and white paper bags and cardboard drink holder aside and stalked to the window overlooking the street. "Hey, Priest. Have you got an early gig today?"

A prickling awareness danced across his skin. Not danger or evil. Either of those would have stirred the darkness trapped inside him. Instead, it lay still and dormant like midnight fog. He turned from cleaning up his tools. "First client's at noon. Finishing up that biker from Fayetteville I started last weekend. Why?"

Tate twisted enough to meet his gaze. "'Cause there's a little old lady and two people about my age outside in the parking lot. They keep staring up here."

Jade sidled up beside Priest. "You sure you didn't schedule an early one?"

Hell yes, he was sure. Appointments before or after hours were only for customers needing more than art. Those needing protection, peace or comfort woven into his coveted designs. "Get away from the window."

Tate stayed put and studied the parking lot. "Looks like the old lady's coming in."

"Get away from the window. Now." Two weeks he'd waited, petitioning the Keeper as much as he dared for guidance. For some insight into the danger he sensed or Jade's subsequent terrifying vision. The Keeper's only answer was a promise that messengers would be sent to guide him, but his instincts screamed to brace and prepare. "Stay behind me. Say nothing until I know who they are."

"But I locked the door. We're fine."

The bolt flipped before Tate finished his argument, the remnants of air Priest used to unlock the mechanism fluttering the paper want ads on the corkboard beside the door.

"I want to know who they are, but I want you out of the line of fire," Priest said.

Footsteps sounded on the wooden stairs to the shop's raised patio, a light tread that would have gone unnoticed to someone without the benefit of a predator's keen hearing.

The door latch clicked and the chimes overhead tinkled as an older woman eased through the door. Her attire seemed more on par with something from Jade's closet—comfortable cotton pants the color of a robin's egg and a fitted white T-shirt. Around her neck hung three charms, each dangling from simple black leather cords.

Charms fashioned in the symbols he'd honored since birth.

His gaze snapped to hers. Deep blue-gray eyes he remembered from his youth stared back at him, the woman's shoulder-length gray hair framing her delicate face. "Naomi."

"Eerikki," she whispered, the emotion behind the sound so deep and fraught with bittersweet memories his knees nearly buckled. Countless nights he'd wondered if she was safe. If she and her children had survived the night his brother murdered so many—Naomi's mate included.

Before he could shake the surprise that held him rooted in place, she closed the distance between them and wrapped her arms around him. "I'd hoped you were alive. I tried to track you through my visions for years, but couldn't find you until a few weeks ago."

The messenger he'd been promised.

Finally.

His arms tightened around her, and the solitary weight he'd shouldered since Tate's and Jade's parents had died eased a fraction. As if the presence of someone from his own youth altered the gravitational pull around him and soothed his beleaguered soul.

Jade's and Tate's quiet footsteps sounded on the tiles behind him, their curious stares a tangible press against his back.

Begrudgingly, Priest released his old friend and stepped aside, bringing his two companions into view.

Naomi studied them. "These are your children?"

By now, he should be used to it. Everyone asked the same question, and yet it still knifed through him. He loved his wards. Would do anything to protect and guide them and never regretted their place in his life, but he craved his own mate. His own children.

A dangerous proposition with the tainted magic trapped inside him.

"No," he said. "These are Lisana's and Rani's children. Lisana and Rani healed me after my brother's attack."

Naomi blanched, but tried to mask her response with a weak smile. He couldn't blame her for her fear. The mere thought of his brother, Draven, still flayed his insides.

He motioned to his wards. "Naomi Falsen, meet Jade Mitchell and Tate Allen. They've lived with me since their mothers passed."

Hand outstretched, Tate stepped forward first. "Not too many people know Priest's real name."

This time her smile was genuine, and her eyes lit with joy the likes of which Priest had long forgotten. She cupped Tate's hand with both of hers. "I've known Eerikki since before the Keeper named him high priest. My mate, Farron, mentored him before his soul quest and afterward served him as warrior primo."

Tate released her hand and puffed his chest up a little broader than before. "I'm warrior house."

As soon as the words were out, Tate's excitement deflated, the reality of Naoml's information belatedly connecting with Priest's history lessons. How Priest's failure to ferret out Draven's plans before it was too late had cost every house primo their life and countless clan members as well.

Naomi patted Tate's shoulder, her petite stature compared to Tate's towering height making the gesture almost comical. "It's okay, Tate. Let it go. My mate faced his destiny the same way Eerikki and all the rest of us will."

"You mean Priest," Tate said.

Naomi swiveled toward Priest and frowned.

"The world's different now," Priest said. "Eerikki's not exactly a name that blends in. Rani started calling me Priest in the seventies." He shrugged. "It stuck."

"Ah." She scanned him head to toe, obviously connecting how the name tied with his image. He might have been an innocent when he'd stepped into his position fifty years ago, but now he reflected the hardened years in between. "It stuck because it fits. In more ways than one. Though for your mother's sake, I'll use the name she gave you unless we're outside our clan."

Decision made, she turned her gaze on Jade and studied her aura. "You're a seer. Who's the primo for your house?"

Jade hung her head, and it was all Priest could do to stifle his flinch. "We have no primos," Priest answered for her. "Our numbers are down. Most from the last generation refused their quests."

Naomi frowned and opened her mouth as if to share something, then closed it just as fast and dug in her purse. "Give me a minute. There's someone I want you to meet."

She pulled out her phone and typed out a message fast enough to rival Jade and Tate on a texting frenzy.

The same warning buzz he'd wrestled for weeks surged between his shoulders, both beast and man sensing a shift on the horizon. As though the answers he sought crouched nearby in thick shadow, poised to launch into the light. Whether the change he sensed was good or bad remained to be seen, but the sensation was too big to ignore. An emotional stirring that warned whatever lay ahead would pack a serious punch.

My mate faced his destiny the same way Eerikki and all the rest of us will.

If he remembered right, Naomi and Farron's son had been eight or nine at the time of Draven's betrayal. And yet Priest had never been summoned to join his soul quest. "Your family has always led the warrior house. Where's your son?"

She averted her face and dropped her phone back in her purse. Her aura dimmed, the vibrant gold of the seer house paling as though a cloud had moved across it. "My son and his wife couldn't come."

His wife. Not his mate. More evidence her son had shunned his gifts like so many others.

Before he could question her further, the shop door opened and sent the chimes overhead jingling. A tall and oddly familiar-looking man with short dirty-blond hair and a beard in the making stepped just inside the entrance, one hand braced on the knob. He scanned the room, his muscled torso locked tight until his gaze snagged on Naomi. "Everything's safe?"

"It will be now." Naomi shot the man a relieved smile and waved him in. "Get your sister and come inside."

Priest tweaked at her choice of words. "Why wouldn't it be safe?"

The man ducked outside, leaving the door open, and soft voices murmured from the raised porch beyond.

Naomi subtly inclined her head toward Jade and Tate. "I'll explain later. After you meet my grandchildren."

Well, that explained the familiarity.

Her grandson strode back through the door and stepped to one side, holding it open for the woman behind him. The second she came into full view, Priest froze.

"Eerikki, this is my grandson, Aleksander, and my beautiful granddaughter, Kateri. Kateri, Alek, this is our clan's high priest, Eerikki Rahandras. Though, now, he just goes by Priest."

Granddaughter.

Beautiful.

Kateri.

Some dim corner of his mind registered Naomi had shared more with her light-hearted words, but those were the only three that mattered. Except the woman in front of him wasn't just beautiful. She was perfect. Dressed in a flowing tan skirt and fine white linen shirt tied at the waist, her willowy body gave the illusion of fragility, but strength beamed from her intelligent blue-gray eyes. Her hair fell well beyond her shoulders, a soft blond the color of endless wheat fields.

But it was her aura that gripped him most. No colors to represent a house, but powerful nonetheless. Shimmering as though the moon shone directly behind her.

My mate.

His beast stirred and scented the air.

"Eerikki?" Naomi's touch pressed just above his

elbow, her fingers light against his skin, but trembling. "Is something wrong?"

Nothing was wrong. Not anymore.

Seventy-seven years he'd been alone, but now she was here. His to win. To protect. To provide for and pleasure.

The darkness rose, and crude, devastatingly vivid images blasted across his mind. Him above her. His cock powering deep and her breasts bouncing with each thrust. Her soft cries filling his ears.

Kateri crept forward and held out her hand. A lifeline and a temptation. "My nanna's told me a lot about you."

He should step away. The evil was too close, waking with a devastating hunger and licking the edges of his control. To hurt this woman would be the end of him. The annihilation of his soul. He clasped her hand in his anyway, the contact zinging through him as profound as his connection with the Otherworld. He needed more. Wanted her hands pressed against his chest. Her nails scoring his back and her palm working his shaft.

Tugging gently, he pulled her to him.

She stumbled slightly, but didn't resist, splaying her free hand above his thrashing heart. She lifted her face to his, her beautiful eyes wide and mouth slightly parted, her soft pink lips ready for his kiss.

His panther chuffed and purred, the uncontainable response rumbling up the back of his throat and filling the room.

Two seconds. No more than that and his mate was ripped from his arms and thrust behind the unknown male, her startled gasp still lingering in the air around him.

"What the hell?" The stranger's terse voice slashed through the otherwise quiet room.

Priest's cat screamed and clawed for release. The tingle and burn that came scant seconds before each shift raced beneath his skin, and his breath crept up the back of his throat in a hot hiss. He stalked forward, his prey mirroring each advance with a step backward.

Logic tried to surface, a flicker of knowledge as to the man's name and who he was clawing at the back of Priest's mind.

It doesn't matter who he is, the darkness whispered. *He took her from us. Kill him.*

Through his beast's lethal focus a movement registered. A woman blocking him from his target. "Don't move, Alek. Not so much as a step."

Priest stopped. He knew that voice. Trusted it. He fought the thickening black haze around the edges of his vision and focused on the woman in front of him.

Naomi.

An innocent.

An elder and a friend.

Her words pierced through the murderous fog, a pinprick at most, and echoing as though she whispered from the depths of a cave. "He's her sister, Eerikki. Their parents were killed two weeks ago. He wants only to protect her."

Her brother.

One of his clan.

Safe.

He touched her, the darkness countered.

His cat growled in agreement.

Eliminate him. Take what's rightfully ours.

Naomi inched closer. "Alek, take your sister to the car. Wait for me there."

The two shifted for the door, but froze at the warning growl that rumbled up Priest's throat. "No."

"He'll bring her back." Lowering her voice, Naomi crept within killing distance. "Your companion is angry. Insulted and raw. He doesn't care that he's her brother. Only that he's a stranger he doesn't know. But *you* know, Eerikki. Take the time to find your balance. Tate and Jade can go with them. Tate's a warrior. You can trust him to keep her safe."

As though she'd summoned him with her words, Tate stole closer to Priest, the wary nature of his coyote obviously sensing Priest barely held his panther in check. He kept his silence, but his watchful amber eyes burned with curiosity and confusion.

Never in all the years they'd been with him had Priest ever lost control. Hadn't sunk this deep into the darkness in years.

Still braced protectively in front of Kateri, Alek stared Priest down. Such innocent bravery. Clueless of the torture Priest could wield with little more than a thought.

End him. The dark encouragement danced all too enticingly inside his head and sent fire licking down his spine.

Behind Alek, Kateri watched him with wide eyes. Not afraid. Surprised, yes, and curious given the tilt to her head, but not afraid. She swallowed and flexed the hand clutching her brother's shoulder.

His panther bristled at the sight, jaws aching to sink its teeth into the usurper who enjoyed her touch.

"Go," he ordered Tate, not daring to break eye contact with his mate for fear he'd lose what little control he had left. His muscles flexed and strained, blood pulsing with a ferocity that left an aching throb in its wake. Naomi was right. If he didn't find his balance, he'd slaughter Alek where he stood. "Stay close, but don't let her out of your sight. No one touches her." The darkness and his beast coalesced with his own voice and unleashed a feral claim. "She's mine."

Pick up your copy of Guardian's Bond
by Rhenna Morgan

Available now in eBook, print and audio

About the Author

Rhenna Morgan is a happily-ever-after addict—hot men, smart women, and scorching chemistry required. A triple-A personality with a thing for lists, Rhenna's a mom to two beautiful daughters who constantly keep her dancing, laughing and simply happy to be alive.

When she's not neck-deep in writing, she's probably driving with the windows down and the music up loud, plotting her next hero and heroine's adventure. (Though trolling online for man-candy inspiration on Pinterest comes in a close second.)

She'd love to share her antics and bizarre sense of humor with you and get to know you a little better in the process. You can sign up for her newsletter and gain access to exclusive snippets, upcoming releases, fun giveaways, and social media outlets at www.rhennamorgan.com.

If you enjoyed *Stand & Deliver*, she hopes you'll share the love with a review on your favorite online bookstore.